dancing
on
broken
glass

dancing
on
broken
glass

a novel

KA HANCOCK

G

Gallery Books

NEW YORK LONDON TORONTO
SYDNEY NEW DELHI

G

Gallery Books

A Division of Simon & Schuster, Inc.

1230 Avenue of the Americas

New York, NY 10020

First Gallery Books trade paperback edition March 2012

GALLERY BOOKS and colophon are registered trademarks of Simon & Schuster, Inc.

For information about special discounts for bulk purchases, please contact Simon & Schuster Special Sales at 1-866-506-1949 or business@simonand schuster.com.

The Simon & Schuster Speakers Bureau can bring authors to your live event. For more information or to book an event contact the Simon & Schuster Speakers Bureau at 1-866-248-3049 or visit our website at www.simonspeakers.com.

Designed by Meredith Ray

Manufactured in the United States of America

10   9   8   7   6   5   4

Library of Congress Cataloging-in-Publication Data is available.

ISBN 978-1-4516-3737-3
ISBN 978-1-4516-3738-0 (ebook)

For Mark, who kindled a fire in me with his 1-in-64,000,000 odds. I love you madly!

Acknowledgments

Oh my, how does one really go about thanking all those who have contributed to this feat? I will start with a husband who kept me in Pepsi and paper, and always gave me and my imaginary friends plenty of space and freedom. I love you Mark Dee! To my daughters who read each word and gushed indulgently, Hilary, Abby, and my comma queen, Whitney—fine and generous critics each, not to mention extraordinary women. And to Shawn, a great little son who is equal parts sarcasm and charm, always inspiring, always encouraging. Special thanks to Bear, Ryan, Weston, and Cesiley—the awesome kids I got the easy way. To Joyce and Lavell Lloyd, tireless cheerleaders, nurturers of all dreams, and the finest parents a girl could have. Huge thanks to my small but utterly priceless writers group; Dorothy Keddington, Carol Warburton, LuAnn Anderson, and Nancy Hopkins—friends, sisters, and believers all—and to Ed, whose voice I still hear in my head. Gratitude is too small an expression.

   I am indebted to Mollie Glick, my agent extraordinaire who sent me the nicest rejection letter but threw me a lifeline—if you ever revise this, I'd like to see it again—and meant it. You made all the difference! And kudos to Kate Hamblin for taking care of all the details. Thanks to the awesome Stephanie Abou for her expert navigation of DANCING through the foreign market; what an incredible adventure! And to Jerry Gross for his generous praise and wise suggestions early on.

Deep and humble gratitude to my brilliant editor, Lauren McKenna, for being so good at what she does! (You were absolutely right about Priscilla . . . and pretty much everything else.) Thanks to Megan McKeever and Alexandra Lewis for keeping me on track. Massive appreciation to Kristin Dwyer for patiently guiding me through the uncharted territory of publicity—what would I do without you! Thanks to John Paul Jones and Meredith Ray for making everything look so good! And to all the wonderful people at Gallery who have taken such great care of this story and of me, I couldn't have wished for a more fabulous experience.

dancing
on
broken
glass

prologue

I met Death at a party. It was my sister Priscilla's twelfth birthday and I was five. She wasn't particularly frightening, Death, but then I had been told all about her, so seeing her made no adverse impression on me. Until I realized she was there for my dad.

When I was a little girl, I shared a morning ritual with my father. It started with the sound of gushing water through rebellious pipes, a moaning screech when Dad first turned on the tap. I still live in the house where I grew up and it's the same today. But back then the sound meant my dad was awake.

I remember I would trundle up the stairs, rubbing sleep from my eyes, feeling my way in the dark hall to the closed bathroom door. Of course I would knock, and my dad would sing out, "Is that my Princess Lulu?"

I loved that because it gave Lucy, my given name, a fairy-tale flair, and such things are hugely impressive to a five-year-old. He would open the door wide and the light would sting my eyes as he ushered me into the bathroom, our inner sanctum—just me and my dad. It was a small bathroom; the tub took up one whole wall, and the sink had this minuscule counter that could barely accommodate his shaving things and a bar of soap. Mickey whines about that same thing, even today. I would climb my little self up onto the toilet and open my book. That was my ostensive purpose for being there after all: to practice my phonics.

Meanwhile my father, standing over the sink, would start to

shave, and every day when he was fully foamed, he would swoop in for a kiss and a giggle. I'm thirty-three now and can still smell his shaving cream, still hear my own laughter.

My father was a big man. His belly practically hung in the soapy sink, and sometimes when he leaned close to the mirror to inspect this or that, he would straighten to find a froth of suds clinging to his bare stomach and he'd say, "Well, looky there, Lu, got me a creamy middle just like an Oreo." Another kiss and giggle.

When he was all finished cleaning and combing and gargling and spitting, he would splash Old Spice over his face and fill the bathroom with that unforgettable scent. I'm still a sucker for Old Spice, but I won't let Mickey wear it.

I remember everything about those mornings. From the yellow towels on the floor to the sink full of soapy water, to Paul Harvey down low in the background, and the freshly pressed uniform hanging on the back of the door.

The town where we live, Brinley Township, knew my father as Sergeant James Houston—Jim to the world and Jimmy to my mom and his partner, Deloy Rosenberg. I loved watching the transformation from sleepy, hair-everywhere, shirtless dad, to Sergeant James Houston. When he walked out of that bathroom in the blues my mom ironed for him every night, I thought he was invincible. It was utterly inconceivable to me that anything could ever hurt him, least of all two tiny bullets. I thought that's what it meant to be Sergeant James Houston of Brinley Township—indestructible.

But then Mrs. Delacruz, my kindergarten teacher, told us all things die. "Everything, no exceptions," she'd said, and it got me worried. I'm sure I must have asked Dad about it, though I don't really recall. I just remember him kneeling by my bedside one night to discuss it. Lily, who was four years older than me, was pretending to be asleep in the next bed, so he was whispering when he made this terrible declaration: Mrs. Delacruz was correct, all things did die. I suppose it was in response to my horror that he took my hand and kissed it and ran it over his bristly chin. He said to me, "Lulu, you don't need to be afraid of death. In fact, there are secrets about death that not everyone knows." I remember he came even closer and said, "Do you want to know what they are?"

"Secrets?" I said. It sounded far-fetched, but my father never lied to me so I kept listening.

"Lulu, there are three things about death that I promise you. I promise you it's not the end. Feels like the end—that's why people cry—but it's not the end. And it doesn't hurt. That's another very important part of death that people get afraid of if they don't understand. It doesn't hurt. And finally, if you're not afraid of death, Lu, you can watch for it and be ready. Do you believe me?"

His face was so earnest, so reliable, that I simply nodded. "What does it look like?"

"I'm not sure, but I bet it's pretty."

"Is it nice?"

"Very nice, and very gentle." At this point he explained to my little, spongelike brain that death was not the same as dying. That sometimes dying did in fact hurt, but with it came a little bit of magic because you got to forget the hurt as if it never happened. This opened up a huge discussion about all the gory ways a person might die, and how lovely it was that you got to forget. I must have seemed skeptical, which is strange because I didn't doubt what he was telling me. Still my dad said, "Lulu, do you remember being born?"

I recall soberly considering this and answering, "No."

He nodded. "See, death's the same. You get to forget."

I was amazed. My dad was right. He was always right. I don't remember everything my father said, but I do remember the way the mystery of death utterly dissolved that night in his honest eyes. I trusted him completely, and his words have stayed with me and petrified in my grown-up soul. Of course I realize they were merely a gift bestowed on my innocence; reassurance to a little girl who couldn't sleep. But who knew the calm he gave me would see me safely through so much loss and cradle me when I almost lost myself.

Of course he was right: death happens to everyone. But if it's not the end, and it doesn't hurt . . . well, then what was there to fear?

Certainly this was the logic of my five-year-old self. So, when Death showed up at Priscilla's birthday party, I was intrigued, but not alarmed.

The party was in our backyard. The barbecue was sizzling with hamburgers, the coolers overflowing with beer and Hawaiian Punch, and Mom was arranging candles on Priss's cake. Besides half the junior high, a lot of my parents' friends were there. Jan and Harry Bates, from next door, were trying to get their goofy son to stop chasing my sister Lily around with his ferret. (They were nine years old, but I knew even back then that Lily would marry Ron Bates. Everyone did.) Dr. Barbee was there and the Witherses from the funeral home down the street, my dad's police friends—even the mayor was there.

I was setting paper plates on the picnic table when I noticed her. I knew immediately who she was, and she didn't seem all that threatening or wrong. In fact, she looked as if she'd be kind, though I've come to wonder about that. If I had to describe her, I don't think I could, because how do you really describe the feeling attached to an apparition? It seems to me now that it was more like a raw knowing that took on a shape and dimension that something in me recognized. I've seen her since and have personally assigned her as female, mostly by instinct and impression rather than anything resembling proof. All the same, I'd know her anywhere.

I wasn't scared by her presence at all. In fact, I remember being quite intoxicated by the sound of her whisper above the noise, though I never heard what she said. I watched her kind of float among our guests, her whole bearing no more substantial than the inside of a cloud. At one point she even looked at me, right in my eyes. If my father had never told me about her, I think I would still have known who she was. It was an irrepressible connection, completely undeniable. She knew me, too. She smiled at me—at my little-girl self—but she saw my grown soul and my grown soul understood. She would come for me, too. But not then.

No, she was there for my father. And my dad must have felt it, too, because he found my gaze from across the yard. I can still see his face, the knowing in his eyes. They told me not to be afraid—he wasn't.

I still thought him too big to die and much too solid to ever spring a leak that would kill him. But two tiny bullets did just that. He died the day after Priscilla turned twelve, when he tried to stop a drifter from robbing Arnie's Gas N' Go.

Death came for my mother twelve years later. And then it was just we three girls, Lily, Priscilla, and me.

one

D r. Barbee. Lunch with Lily. Pick up dry cleaning. Hospital to hug Mickey. I was lying on the exam table, freezing, planning my day out on my fingers while I waited. Charlotte Barbee said she'd be right back to finish up with me, but that had been several minutes ago. I counted my fingers again. Lunch. Dry cleaning. Mickey. There was something else but I couldn't remember. Actually I just couldn't think past Mickey. He'd been there six days so far—but of course not really Mickey for days before that. But this morning he sounded good, he sounded nearly back.

Charlotte hurried back in apologizing. "Darn insurance company! Think I have nothing better to do than . . . ," she huffed, then breathed. "Now, where were we, Lucy?"

In just a moment, I was back in position, my bare feet firmly resting in the metal stirrups, freezing just like the rest of me. "Why do you keep it so cold in here, Charlotte? That's just mean."

When she didn't answer, I lifted my head off the pillow and watched her face float between my bent knees. She was down there adjusting a pair of duckbills to get a better look at what should never, in my opinion, be looked at in the first place.

"So how's Mickey this week?" she asked, still probing, ignoring my concerns about the temperature.

"Better than last week," I said, gasping at her touch.

"Is he still in the hospital?"

"Yes. But he can come home Friday, if he's good. And I so hope he's being good."

Charlotte Barbee smiled her knowing smile. "How long have you two been married now?"

"Almost eleven years."

"It hasn't been that long, has it? Where does the time go?" she said. "Now give me some deep breaths."

The deep breaths made me cough and then I remembered: pick up cough drops.

It was my annual physical and Charlotte Barbee was nothing if not thorough. She knew what she was looking for, and if she found it, I would see it in her face where I'd seen it before. To the casual observer, this might have seemed like an ordinary physical exam, but the truth was more complicated. I was being scrutinized for recurring cancer. I'd had my first bout seven years ago, when I was twenty-six. That pathology used to place me not in the healthy-adult-female column, but in the more tentative cancer-survivor column—that is, until I'd been clean for five years. I breathe a little easier now that I'm in the healthy column with my two sisters. The same cancer that claimed our mother and grandmother threatens Lily, Priscilla, and me as well. With these fickle genetics skulking through our blood, we're all very vigilant, especially Dr. Barbee, in whom we put our trust.

Lily offered to come with me today for moral support, but in all honesty, these checkups are almost harder on my sister than they are on me, so I declined her generosity. Lily is the real worrier among us, and me getting sick again is the absolute sum of all her fears. These days, where physicals are concerned, she prepares for the worst possible outcome, the whole time praying to hear Charlotte's magic words of reprieve: Everything is fine. That pronouncement is like winning the lottery every time, and until Lily hears it, she is convinced dedicated worry will produce a good outcome.

As for me, I just expect more time. For five years I was happy to be granted life in half-year rations, which I relished and celebrated as if I'd outsmarted fate. Now, if I'm healthy at my checkups, I'm entitled to bigger chunks of time. Today marks my second *annual* physical, and I have to say, twelve months beats the pants off six. Even so, my routine is the same—I get the good news, praise the Lord, and dance on through my life. But only until it's time to gear up for my next appointment and again ponder the statistical possibilities, which are bleak. If cancer returns, it usually returns with a vengeance. When fear creeps up on me, which it does occasionally, I repel it with my father's words from so long ago.

I wonder sometimes if he had any idea that I would take his wisdom so fully to heart. But because of it, at the end of the day, death doesn't really scare me. The dying part, however, does give me pause. I've done that before and I was not good at it. To watch the people I love, the terror in Mickey's eyes . . . I thank God every day we're through that because I've figured out that I'm much better at letting go than I am at being let go of.

"I need a urine sample, and then I'm done with you," Charlotte said, jolting me back to the business at hand.

"So, am I good?"

She placed strong, capable hands on my shoulders and looked me in the eye. "I think we'll send all your juices to the lab and they'll call me and tell me you're fine."

"I knew it. So I shouldn't worry that I'm tired?"

"Lucy, I'm tired. You don't have the corner on tired," she scolded.

"What about this little tickle in my throat?"

"Open up." She probed my mouth with a tongue depressor. "I don't see anything here that concerns me. Tell me again how long you've been coughing?"

"I don't know, a few days maybe."

"I'll swab you for strep, just to be safe."

"You're such a good doctor." I gagged as she reached back for her sample.

"I try." When she was done, she placed her swab in a small plastic vial and smiled at me. "Alrighty then, wrap this gown around you and go across the hall for your mammogram."

"Yippee," I said sarcastically. Having my small breasts crushed between two sheets of Plexiglas and examined for microscopic changes was, for me, the hardest part of this ordeal. Cancer starts in a single cell that recruits the surrounding cells in its rebellion, and then proceeds to destroy the neighborhood. Once dots appear on a mammogram, damage has a toehold. Charlotte lifted my chin with her finger and looked at me as if she'd read my thoughts. "Lucy, I'll call you if we need to talk. But I don't have any concerns, so don't be surprised if I call just to chat."

I nodded. "Okay. Good. Let's go to dinner next week."

Across the hall, I forced small talk while Aretha manhandled my boobs like they were so much bread dough. She was Brinley's only mammogram technician, so she knew the breasts in our small community probably better than their owners. She was a tall, horsey woman—all-business—and I found myself wondering what came to mind when she saw us outside the office living our regular lives. Did she recognize the chest before the face registered?

I liked Aretha. Her son, Bennion, was a student in my history class over at Midlothian, and I knew she checked his homework. I thought of thanking her for that, but as I said, she was busy. In all the times I'd been coming here, Aretha never really said anything to me until she was finished, and this time was no exception.

"There ya go, Lucy. Always nice to see you. Benny sure liked your class."

"He's one of the good ones. You should be proud."

"I am."

I got dressed and brushed my hair. It's long, so I kind of lost track of the brushing as I stared into the mirror looking for *her*. I have to do this every time I have a physical—it's part of the ritual. I look for any sign that Death might be lurking in the corner, or in the mirror standing behind me, or floating just outside my periphery. But there was nothing, which was profoundly comforting—right up there with Dr. Barbee's magic words.

After I got dressed, I walked to Damian's, where I was meeting Lily for lunch. The stroll through the sunshine and warm breeze was delicious on my face. I love living here. Brinley, Connecticut, is a small town where you can walk just about anywhere in less than fifteen minutes. From the boat harbor to the Loop—Brinley's answer to a town square—it's nearly two miles, and the side streets that make up our neighborhoods stretch only about another mile on either side. Connecticut is rife with history and charm, but to me, Brinley is just about the best of everything: dignified, old neighborhoods, tree-lined streets, the grizzly kind of politics unique to small towns, like emergency meetings in the Loop to discuss the problem of dog poop or the need for a hose-winding ordinance.

A lot of people were out and about this afternoon, and none seemed in a big hurry to be anywhere. But maybe that was just because I didn't have to be anywhere now that school was out for the summer, and I'd finished grading 170 finals.

I saw my neighbor Diana Dunleavy, walking her granddaughter, Millicent, to ballet class. The little jelly-bean-shaped girl was pirouetting her way past Mosely's Market in a hot-pink tutu. Diana waved at me. "She gets all that talent from me, you know," she shouted from across the road.

I laughed watching as Millie glissaded right into Deloy Rosenberg, who was coming out of the Sandwich Shoppe with a takeout order. He dropped his cardboard tray and a bag tumbled, but apparently no damage was done. Still, Millie hid her red face in the folds of Diana's skirt until Brinley's police chief gave up trying to soothe her and walked away with his lunch. Every time I see Deloy in his uniform, I think of my dad.

I spotted Lily and Jan across the street, so I jaywalked toward them. Jan Bates, our next-door neighbor, did eventually become Lily's mother-in-law, just as I'd predicted when we were kids. What I didn't know then was that she would become every inch a mother to me as well.

Oscar Levine was pounding a sign onto the gate of our tiny park when he saw me. The bony little man dropped his hammer and shouted, "Lucy, you're coming to the Shad Bake on Saturday, right?"

"Of course she is, Oscar," Lily answered for me.

Jan gave me a quick hug. "Just say yes," she whispered in my ear.

"I wouldn't miss it," I said. "And Mickey will be home by then so he'll be there, too."

"Atta girl."

The Shad Bake was a spring ritual all along the Connecticut River Valley, but we Brinlians did it up right. We pay homage to the supposedly endangered fish by nailing it to oak planks around a pit fire, then gorging ourselves on it until we can't move. It's just one of the many things I love about living in Brinley.

"Well, I'm off to teach little boys how to paint pine trees," Jan said, laughing. "You girls stay out of trouble." Jan pecked us both and we watched her walk away.

My sister then turned to me with an overly broad smile that failed to hide her anxiety. "So how did it go?" she said, linking her arm through mine.

"I'm good. Charlotte had no concerns. And Aretha said my boobs look fantastic."

"Yeah, I can just hear her say that."

"Actually, she said they're nicer than yours."

Lily laughed. "Well, now I know you're lying." My sister was beautiful, with short blond hair, fair skin like Mom's, and in the sunlight, she looked almost translucent. "So you're good?" she asked, turning serious.

"I'm good," I promised on a little cough.

She leaned her head into mine and I felt the shudder of relief pass through her. "Liar."

"What?"

"I know it's too soon to know that for sure."

"Maybe, but Charlotte was not one bit concerned, so neither am I."

Lily bored her eyes into mine as if searching for a hidden truth. She'd done it our whole lives.

"I'm fine, Lil. I feel it."

She nodded, but did not move her eyes from me. "Okay. Because . . . you know, I refuse to bury you, Lucy."

"I know," I said, squeezing her hand.

At the corner George Thompson, the only florist in town, was loading flats of spring flowers into the trunk of a Cadillac. He grunted an indeterminate greeting at us as he arranged the blooms with a scowl on his grizzled face.

"How's Trilby, George?" Lily asked as we approached. "Is she feeling any better?"

"No, and she's grumpy as a wet hen. Somehow it's my fault she broke her foot. Wasn't me who was jazzercising, for hell's sake. Stop your laughing, Lucy!" he scolded. "It's not one bit funny!"

Lily elbowed me and said to George, "Well, tell her the antique mirror she ordered came in. She can pick it up when she feels better."

George stopped what he was doing and straightened. He didn't seem aware of any antique mirror and the moment was just about to turn awkward when Muriel Piper saved us. "Hello, my angels!" she cackled. "Isn't it a glorious day! Look, I'm going crazy with flowers." She laughed, deep and throaty. Muriel was a Brinley matriarch, pushing ninety but not about to admit it. She was wearing pleated blue jeans, a cashmere hoodie, and diamond studs so heavy they made her earlobes droop—a casual gardening ensemble, for sure.

Muriel pulled me close in a firm embrace that belied her age. "Lucy, you're too thin. I want you to come over so I can cook for you. You never take care of yourself when Mickey is doing poorly."

"He's coming home on Friday. And I'm eating just fine."

"Not till Friday? He'll miss Celia's memorial service tomorrow." I nodded.

"Well, bring him by this weekend so I can give him a hug. I just love that boy." She turned to Lily. "And yours! Do they come any better looking? Oh, my goodness."

"I'll tell him you said so, Muriel."

"Don't you dare! I'd be so embarrassed! Well, I better skedaddle.

These flowers aren't going to plant themselves." Muriel waved at us as she drove away with a trunk full of petunias and gerbera daisies.

My phone buzzed in my pocket, and I flipped it open. "Hey, Priss."

"Is all well?" my oldest sister said with no preamble.

"Charlotte said I looked fine. But she'll call if my labs are off."

"Good. I'm headed into a meeting, so call me later. I want the details." Then she was gone.

I snapped my phone shut and looked at Lily. "No wonder she's a great lawyer."

"She just wants to know you're okay." Lily shrugged. "So," she started as we walked into the diner, "Mickey's coming home on Friday. Did he know about your appointment today?"

I shook my head. "He's just barely getting back on top, so I didn't want to tell him until I had all the good news to go with it."

"You're a good wife, Lu. Mic's lucky to have you."

I shrugged off her compliment thinking it was really the other way around. After all we'd been through, I knew I loved Mickey Chandler more today than the day I married him.

two

*It's taken a week to lift myself out of the hole this time. But
at least I didn't let go of the edge and drown in its depths. I
knew I was in trouble as I balanced on the rim and once more
imagined I could lift my feet and be airborne—swoop and glide
over and around the chasm that I knew could swallow me. It
has before, thankfully this time it didn't.*

*That's my life: continually stepping up to and away
from the edge of a hole that is by turns fascinating and
terrifying—filled with whatever my faulty imagination
dictates at any given time. It is absolutely imperative that
I keep my distance, but the closer I get, the better I feel.
Or the worse. And that's the ridiculous irony because I
am compulsively drawn to this danger, and the closer I
get, the closer I want to be. Those depths hold unimaginable escape—at times utter exhilaration, at others, pain
so intense I can't begin to describe it. Either way the edge
calls to me with its lies that sound like promises. Soft,
seductive lies that I can't always resist.*

*Medication helps. That, and regular therapy. My own
willpower helps when I can find it. So does my intellect,*

which astoundingly is not tied to the other rogue functions of my disabled brain. I have the highest education personal experience can offer. In the midst of it, I almost always know what's happening to me, even if sometimes I know it at a distance, like a spectator. Still, I try to implement one of the many strategies designed to keep me from being swallowed up. It doesn't always work.

My strongest influence is my wife. And thanks to her, I am determined to stay a good distance from the edge, even if I'm not always successful. Sometimes, like when she got sick, the edge comes to me. Sometimes that happens for no reason. The chasm widens inexplicably even as I run from it—run for my life—until the ground beneath me evaporates and I am again lost despite my best, but futile, efforts.

For most people this hole does not exist, but it's a real threat for those who have bipolar disorder. I know I sound like a drug addict, but no drug feels the way mania feels right before it blows up in your face, or despair just after you give in to it.

JUNE 7—LATER

As I reread the journal entry, I checked it for any telltale bullshit that would prompt my psychiatrist, Gleason Webb, to toss it and make me do it again. But I didn't see any place I'd overdone it too horribly. It was pretty much me, and I thought I'd articulated the situation pretty well for a nut job.

I was waiting for Lucy on the front steps of this old asylum that sometimes felt like my home away from home. I was having a good day, inside and out. I could feel my stable self emerging slowly but surely, and I had *to admit I'd missed that guy. I was content with him. He wasn't too exciting, but he was comfortable and safe and I could count on him to be a clear thinker.*

I checked my watch and wondered where Lucy was—she said she would be here by now. I got up and started to pace but quickly sat back down. She'd be here when she got here, nothing to get worked up about. I chuckled because, just like that, I realized my meds had kicked in. I was able to reason with myself and it made me smile . . . the miracle of psychotropics. This would make Lucy happy—she liked Stable Guy better than she liked me, which isn't exactly true. Lucy loved me—the me made up of loose parts and extra parts and screwed-up parts. She loved the whole package—she said she had to or there was no point in loving me at all. She'd sworn it was true a lifetime ago, and she's been true to her word. Who would have believed it? I'm still in awe of that woman. Especially at times like this, when the first thing I can clearly make out as I climb foggy-brained out of the hole is her love. Every faultily wired nut job of a human being should be so lucky.

Mickey was waiting for me on the steps of Edgemont Hospital looking not one bit like a patient in his jeans and gray T-shirt. As soon as I walked across the street and he saw me, he lit up and I wanted to giggle, he looked so good, so healthy. His broad shoulders and long legs were signature Mickey. But his smile was the barometer for his sanity, and from this distance it looked just about right. He stood up and pushed his sunglasses into his dark hair that was still thick, the silver thatch of bangs, still as prominent as the day I met him. Mickey walked toward me with a slow grin, and when he got close enough, he wrapped me in his arms and just held me tight. Tight, but not death-grip tight; that was a good sign. I even thought I could see my

Mickey in there, in his dark eyes that just days ago had been wild and unfocused.

"How you doing?"

Mickey pulled back and ran his hand over my hair. "I'm better, Lu. And I saw Gleason this morning. He said he'd definitely okay me going home Friday."

I kissed him. "Good for you. Good for me."

"Yeah." He pulled me close again. There he was. There was my Mickey.

"What are you doing out here?"

"Waiting for you. Peony said she's watching me." He looked up and I followed his gaze. Sure enough, Mickey's nurse, Peony Litman, was standing at the third-floor window wagging her finger. She was seventy if she was a day and, true to her early training, was outfitted completely in white, including a cap. "She said we can go for a walk if you'll be responsible for me."

I looked up and waved. The old nurse smiled, then wagged her finger at me, too.

Edgemont is an old colonial hospital that's been restored a couple of times. It still looks quaint and antiquated on the outside, but this full-service facility accommodates Brinley and New Brinley. The hospital sits in the midst of impeccably tended grounds, and several patients were roaming around on this warm afternoon. I pulled Mickey's arm over my shoulder and sucked in the soft fragrance of lilac and lavender.

"I've missed you, baby," he said.

"Me, too."

"At least I didn't get on a plane or steal anything. I didn't dig up the yard."

"Small blessings."

Last week, Mickey's mood and energy had been sky-high, which had come on gradually as he'd tweaked his medication. That's the rub with Mickey; keeping his depressive symptoms at bay with, say, Prozac, can sometimes push him into hypomania—which he rather enjoys and is not eager to amend. He always thinks he can contain the energy. But this time, despite his doctor's attempt to manage him outpatient, he'd stopped sleeping. Psychosis would have followed without intervention. Thanks to an adjustment of his medication and a little time here at Edgemont, he was now hovering around what is considered normal for the rest of the world, but feels a lot lower than that to my Mickey. Still, mania was easier to recover from than his depressive episodes.

"What have you been up to?" I asked.

"Not much. Just a whole lot of stabilizing. And when that gets boring, I count Peony's chins."

"Don't pick on her; she's got a hard job taking care of you. Has Jared been by?"

"Twice. He heard back from the architect and wanted to show me some plans. They're good. I think we're going to knock down that far wall, open it up for more tables."

Mickey and his business partner had been talking about this expansion of their club for the past year. It would be nice to see something finally happen.

Mickey looked at me. "I need to tell you something, Lu."

I stopped. Those words were usually a prelude to disaster, so I steeled myself. Had he bought another bus on eBay, hired more migrant workers to paint our house, borrowed a goat to eat our weeds? "I'm listening," I ventured.

"It's not that bad. It's just that about four months ago, Lucy, I . . . I was good then and I booked us on a cruise."

I looked hard at him. "A cruise?"

"I wanted to surprise you."

"Okay, I'm surprised. When do we leave?"

"Well, we were supposed to leave last Thursday. You know, your last day of school."

"Oh," I sighed. "That would have been fun. Why didn't you tell me?"

"I was going to, but I wanted it to be a surprise."

"That's sweet."

"I'm working on getting the money back. I might be able to get half back because it was an emergency hospitalization. I'm sorry, babe."

"Me, too! Can you imagine? Beach sex at midnight. Skinny-dipping in the ocean. I almost wish you hadn't told me."

"Beach sex?"

"Beach sex, Michael. A lot of it."

Mickey grinned down at me, my perfectly gorgeous, astoundingly normal-looking husband. "How about this—how about Hawaii for your birthday, in September?"

"Hmmmmm."

"Really. Let's do it. It'll keep me good."

I can't exactly say how many times this very thing has not worked out—maybe not as many as I think since we've simply learned not to make too many plans. Still, the idea of Hawaii sounded fabulous. I kissed his chin.

"Lucy, I swear I'll make it work."

"How 'bout this," I said to my looming husband. "We save the money. We make the reservations, I buy the bikini. And three months from now on my birthday, with or without you, I go to Hawaii."

"Oh, I'll be there. You're not going without me."

"I know you'll be there, but just in case . . . you still get to keep your promise."

He draped his arm around me and we strolled the grounds, dreaming and planning, until Mickey's medication made him too thirsty to talk. When we got back to the third floor General Psych and Substance Abuse unit, Peony was there to check us in. "Lucy! It's good to see you, honey. How are you?"

"Not too bad."

"You finished with school for the summer?"

"I am, and it feels good."

The old nurse chuckled. "People think I got a hard job, but I wouldn't work with teenagers if they paid me double."

I smiled. I felt the same way about her job. She handed Mickey his pills along with a paper cup of water and then watched him take them. After he swallowed, she checked under his tongue, and this small intrusive act always surprised me. In our regular life, Mickey was a bright, funny, successful business owner. He was laid-back and conversational. He was the guy who cooked dinner if he got home before me. Whined when I asked him to run to Mosely's for tampons. He rotated my tires and paid the light bill. He was the guy I still couldn't resist fresh from the shower. And he was this guy, too. The one who periodically slid off his carefully maintained course far enough that Peony had to make sure he hadn't cheeked his medication. I squeezed his hand and he squeezed mine back.

After years of patience, perseverance, and expertise, Gleason—Dr. Gleason Webb—had finally pinned down an effective prescriptive cocktail to treat Mickey's bipolar disorder. A cocktail that my husband sometimes abandons for reasons that make sense only to him but that always lead back to a gradual reintroduction of said cocktail, where we are now. It takes a small handful of pills a day to keep my husband even. He takes a mood stabilizer, usually lithium, sometimes Depakote, frequently both. Sometimes Risperdal, to keep him from hearing voices. Neurontin, which keeps him from having convulsions—a side effect of the Risperdal. Symmetrel, for Parkinson-like symptoms that can occur secondary to the Depakote, Propranolol for tremors and Benadryl for muscle stiffness secondary to the tremors. Klonopin for bad anxiety, and Ambien to help him sleep. That doesn't count the antidepressants thrown in when needed. But all of it works like magic to normalize Mickey's behaviors and moods and reactions, but only if he takes what he's supposed to when he's supposed to, which is frequently a crapshoot.

That is the background music to our life: is Mickey taking his medication? If I were a different kind of wife, one who counted out pills and watched Mickey swallow the way his nurse did, the answer would be a resounding yes. But I couldn't fathom taking that responsibility from him, that dignity, so I've tried never to encourage Mickey's reliance on me. In sickness or in health, I liked him empowered, not dependent. That doesn't mean I don't keep track of him, and it doesn't mean I don't take care of business when he gets nutty. That's what you do when you love someone like Mickey. I'm not whining. Not when I'd been warned about living this life. Not when I'd had a dozen chances to change my mind. The truth is I think I loved Mickey a little the moment I saw him. And thank goodness, because now I can't imagine loving anyone else. Or, being loved by anyone else. Despite the pitfalls (and the occasional missed cruise) I know I'd choose Mickey all over again.

three

*She gave me her phone number, and even though I knew I
would never call her, I memorized it anyway. I couldn't help
it. No one ever saw me the way she did. I'm sure that sounds
odd, but looking at me and seeing me are two very different
things. And I know the difference since I've been looked at
by women, and not a few men, most of my adult life. But
Lucy seemed to view me not through a young girl's prism of
attraction, but a much less forgiving light, rawer and more
revealing. First of all she totally disarmed me as I sat flirting
with her sister, who, I have to say, was pretty hot herself—
blond, smart, and definitely interesting, though not really
my type. But as the crowd gathered for a birthday party at
my club, I was just enjoying myself in her company. And
then this girl—and she was just a girl—walked in the door
and the mood immediately changed, it elevated. Everyone
knew her, and she was clearly adored. It's cliché I know,
but I couldn't take my eyes off her as she worked the room.
She had a hug for everyone and an easy laugh. She had on
a tight black sweater with a short skirt and boots—and she
was just my kind of pretty. I thought she might have caught
me staring because when finally she walked over to us, I got
a little anxious. But it wasn't me she came over for. She came*

for the girl I'd been flirting with, and you could have knocked me over when I found out they were sisters. She smiled at me in an openly appreciative way and said her name was Lucy Houston. It fit her perfectly. She was smaller than her sister and had amazing chestnut hair that I just wanted to touch. Where her sister Priscilla struck me as a showpiece—carefully and beautifully maintained—Lucy was more effortless, and believe me, she needed no enhancement: clear skin, big green eyes, little upturned nose, full kissable lips. Add all that to her seeming to be just plain nice, and little Lucy Houston was practically irresistible.

Well, it turned out we were celebrating her twenty-first birthday, which made her much too young next to my twenty-nine. But something happened when she came onstage with me. I was just trying to do my thing, crack a few jokes, get a few laughs, business as usual. I called her up to do a little sparring and she didn't hesitate. Then the world just sort of fell away and it was just her. I don't know what she did, but somehow she drew me out from behind the careful persona I showed the world and got a look at the real me. And she didn't flinch. When in pure fun I kissed her, and she kissed me back, I think I simply recognized her in some cosmic way, like a missing part of myself I didn't know was missing. I don't know if that kind of thing really happens to normal people, but it was pretty undeniable for me. And for someone standing far beyond the blessing line, it was shocking to the degree that it terrified me. And it terrified me to the point of stupidity. That gorgeous girl gave me her phone number and I let her walk away.

*　*　*

I met Mickey Chandler in 1998 while I was a student at Northeastern University in Boston. Lily had lured me home to Brinley for my twenty-first birthday, where she had cooked up a party and invited everyone we knew. The occasion may have been my birthday, but I knew she needed a break, too; my sister and her husband, Ron, had just been through an adoption gone terribly wrong.

I didn't think poor Lily would ever recover from waiting and waiting for that precious child. She'd named him James Harrison Bates after our dad and Ron's dad. We were all in love with him, that big, healthy, bald, adorable baby boy. Then we lost him when the fifteen-year-old mom changed her mind. That girl—with her idiotic mom and their attorney—just knocked on Lily's door and asked for her son back. The legal term, of course, was *adoption revocation,* and in New York where the mom was from, she had forty-five days to file her intent to revoke consent. She filed on the last possible day, and it tore a gaping hole in Lily that I didn't think would ever heal.

My sister vowed that she would never try again. No one could blame her. Not after two miscarriages and tedious procedures to fix the problem—incompetent cervix. Now another failed adoption. The first mom changed her mind before the baby was born, so it was tough on Lily, but not as tough as losing Jamie. After Jamie, the subject of babies became completely off-limits. And later, the topic simply became unnecessary—I swore never to reproduce, and Priscilla married her career, insisting she had no interest in a family. But back when Lily first lost her son, Ron was so desperate to heal her heart, he bought her a dilapidated Victorian on our historic Brinley Loop, and their "baby" became an antique store they named Ghosts in the Attic. They closed the deal the day before I turned twenty-one, so my big night out was their celebration as well.

Lily had gone to great lengths to make my twenty-first birthday completely fabulous. She found the venue and recruited the owner to make a fuss. Then she invited all my friends and even some of my surrogate moms. I'd had several of those over the years, since I was only seventeen when our mother died and—in the eyes of Brinley's womenfolk—not fully grown. Three women in particular had stepped up to the plate, and they were all at Colby's that night for my party—Jan Bates, Lainy Withers, and Charlotte Barbee. Of the three, I was probably closest to Jan. She was a gifted artist who'd once painted a portrait of Lily, Priss, and me with our dad and surprised Mom with it out of the blue. Jan had pieced it together from photographs taken when we were young, but you'd never know we hadn't posed for it. It had hung in Mom's bedroom until she died, and now Lily had it over her fireplace. Jan and Harrison Bates had been my parents' closest friends, and they couldn't have been more loving or supportive of us if we were their own flesh and blood.

Lily pried me from Jan's hug and swallowed me in a hug of her own, and I swallowed her right back. My sister had grown bony and there was a thin ring of pain around her eyes, but she was doing a good job of hiding it, especially when Ron sang out an off-key "Happy Birthday" that hurt our ears. Priscilla—our glittering jewel—was in the corner draped over a good-looking man who seemed a little in need of rescue. I walked over and she flashed her brilliant caps at me. My oldest sister looked utterly tantalizing in her tight jeans and an even tighter T-shirt the color of Fuji apples. She was flirting like a courtesan, but Priscilla was a study in contrasts. To look at her now one wouldn't guess she was doggedly climbing the ladder of corporate law and could rob an opponent of his ability to speak in full sentences. She was a hard-coated triple threat: beautiful, brilliant, and driven. But Priss had a soft underbelly few besides Lily and me even knew existed.

"Hey," I said.

"Hey, back," she said, unclasping her hands from the toned arm of her friend long enough to give me a hug. "Happy birthday, Lu," she whispered quickly in my ear. Then she resumed her place next to the handsome man, who was now looking hard at me.

I smiled. "I'm Lucy."

He stood up. He was tall with very broad shoulders and a tapered waist. I, on the other hand, am quite small and boyish, and I had to lift my gaze to meet his. He extended his hand and I took it.

"This is . . . well, to be honest"—Priss grinned—"I don't even know your name."

"I'm Mickey." The man smiled his nice smile that seemed to hold a little something extra for me. I glanced at Priss, whose look warned me that she'd seen him first, which was a shame, because he was very cute. He had the most wonderful hair, dark and wavy with a wide silver thatch that fell over his forehead and made his age tough to determine—I'd say thirty. He had a great mouth and beautiful dark eyes that didn't stray from me once as I took him in, thinking, *I could get used to this*. But I'd never competed with Priscilla for men, and I wasn't about to start now, so I pulled my hand away and simply said, "Nice to meet you."

His eyes held mine long enough that I knew if I *were* competing with Priss, she'd be in trouble. But my sister was clearly in her element, and I left her to it as I worked the room and caught up with my friends.

Colby's, a club in the next town over from Brinley, was rocking that night with music and beer and chatter. I was having fun catching up with my friend Chad Withers, whom I'd known since kindergarten and who now ran Brinley's only funeral home with his father. He was filling me in on his anemic love life when someone thumped on a squealing microphone and said, "Is this thing working?"

Everyone stopped and turned their attention to the small stage at the corner of the room. I figured Ron would have given management the heads-up on my birthday, and that at some point the occasion would be acknowledged. But I was surprised when Priscilla's hunky friend with the great smile did the honors.

He said, "Welcome to Colby's! It's good to see you. Having fun? You're all from Brinley, right?"

Chad whistled between his fingers.

"Good. Good. They say Brinley is known for fun. I know this is probably a step down from bingo at the town hall, but . . ." Mickey laughed, then put his hand on his heart in mock apology. "Just kidding. I love Brinley Township. People are real nice over there. And rich, I hear, which is even better, so . . . you know, feel free to spend lots of money. Howie's over there making specialty drinks, and he's working on one tonight called the Lucy Comes of Age in honor of our special guest."

Whoops of laughter echoed through the club, and I felt a little heat rise in my face.

"Yeah. It's twenty-one bucks a pop, so drink up, I'm late with my mortgage payment." He chuckled and slipped his hand in his pocket and out again. "Soooo, anyway, I'm Mickey Chandler, and we love special occasions here at Colby's, especially birthdays, and tonight we're roasting Lucy Houston." He patted down his shirt and pulled out of piece of paper. "I want to thank her sister Lily for providing me with all the dirt on Looooosy—if you know what I mean. Where is she, anyway? Anybody seen the birthday girl?"

In the dim room, a spotlight found me and I bowed dramatically as my friends erupted with cheers.

Mickey clapped a couple of times. "There she is. Lucy is now twenty-one years old—so watch out. So let's see . . . you're a student, right?"

I nodded.

"Going to school in Boston, living the good life with roommates, I suppose. So let me ask you something. Is your fridge cordoned off in neat little roommate sections? It is, right? And I bet your name is on your cheese and each one of your eggs. Admit it, Lucy." Mickey chuckled. "Guys are so not like that. It's all community property, right, guys? Food, beer, girls. It's all up for grabs. Am I right?"

Chad hooted as if he knew exactly what Mickey was talking about, and I laughed just because he was so cute! But more important, Lily laughed, which she desperately needed to do, so I was an immediate fan.

"Lucy, c'mon up here," Mickey said. "Help me out before I screw this whole thing up and y'all leave me and go back to bingo."

Not shy, I was on my feet before he finished asking, passing Priscilla on the way. She looked a bit peeved, but there was nothing I could really do about that. Onstage, Mickey's smile was back—the good one from when we first met—and without my sister blocking its warmth, I marinated in it. My sisters are beautiful blondes, but I'm the one with the really good hair—thick and reddish brown—from my dad. That night it was loose, and Mickey reached over and ran his hands through it, coming close to inspect it. He smelled terrific.

"How come you're not blonde like your sisters?" he said away from the mike as he rubbed a handful between his fingers. Then he caught himself and let go. "So, uh, Lucy . . . twenty-one. What do twenty-one-year-old girls like to do for fun?"

"Well, Mr. Chandler, I'm pretty sure the same thing dirty old men like to do for fun."

"Was that an *old* joke?" he said with mock offense. "You're killing me, here. But I'll cut you some slack since you're such a hot little birthday girl."

"Why, thank you. You're not too bad yourself." I reached over and patted his solid chest, and when I did, his eyes shifted in a way that I would not have let go of for money.

He quickly recovered. "Don't you love college girls? Guys, am I right? Young, gorgeous women? But you gotta catch 'em at just the right moment. You know, in full bloom but just dumb enough still to give us a chance. After they get serious about their lives, forget it. It's over for guys like us. Right, Lucy?"

"Are you talking about me personally?"

Mickey looked around theatrically. "I don't see anyone else up here." Then he lifted another handful of my hair. "I better check again for blond. Yes, I'm talking about you," he said, standing close to me.

"Well, I'm pretty sure *you'd* stand a chance with me."

Again, he was flummoxed, and my friends were now egging him on. I grinned.

"It's pity, right?" he said. "You're an honors student who feels sorry for a guy who graduated magna-cum-nothing and wound up working stand-up in a comedy club?"

"You kidding me?" I sang out. "A comedian with a *degree*? I'm sold!"

His laughing eyes held mine as he decided what to do next. Finally he said, "Well, all right then! Let's go!" Mickey Chandler pulled me close and made a big production of giving the little college girl a birthday kiss. I think it was meant to be a harmless little peck, but I went for it—it was my birthday, after all—and to be fair, he went for it, too. Something in the way our tongues danced and our teeth clanked together was almost familiar. It was delicious, and I wasn't the one to break it off.

When we finally pulled ourselves apart, I was breathless and a little embarrassed. Mickey's mask had slipped again, and he looked as if he couldn't believe what had just happened. I laughed and tripped off the stage to a bawdy rendition of "Happy Birthday," and to the crowd the whole thing had just been good fun. Well, Priss looked a little annoyed. But I wasn't sorry. It was my night, and Mickey's act. He kept looking over at me, trying to be nonchalant about it, and that made me happy. As I headed back to the bar, Priss intercepted me. "What was that?"

"Nothing. It was nothing, just some fun."

"It looked like more than that," she said, miffed.

I laughed as I glanced back at the stage where Mickey Chandler was still looking my way as he told a funny story about a couple of dogs and an ATM. I tried to picture what he was seeing. Tall, stunning, blond Priscilla, man-made voluptuousness spilling out of her top, getting mouthy with her smaller, considerably less voluptuous—but nicely put together in a skirt and boots—younger sister, who was having none of it.

When Mickey was leaving the stage, I said, "Now's your chance, Priss."

My sister took a beat to weigh this, but then glanced over my shoulder. "I have some catching up to do. So consider the funny man my birthday present."

I turned to find Trent Rosenberg staring at my sister like she was a meal and he hadn't eaten in about a year. Trent was an old boyfriend from high school, and he and Priss were the oldest running rumor in

Brinley. I wanted to believe my sister was better than the likes of him. Especially since he was married with children. "Don't be stupid, Priss."

"What? It's nothing."

I would have said more, but just then Lily wedged between us and asked Ron to take a picture. She pulled me in front of her and Priss and we all smiled; the Houston girls in our traditional pose; me flanked by my big sisters, each of us holding tight to one another.

After that, Chad grabbed my hand. "C'mon, Lu, they're playing our song." And indeed, Wang Chung poured from the jukebox, transporting me right back to the senior prom.

When nearly everyone else had called it a night, I decided to look for Mickey Chandler. The bartender pointed down the hall, where I found an office with the door slightly ajar. I cleared my throat and knocked. Mickey Chandler looked up from his computer. "Hey."

"Hey, I just wanted to thank you for the fun."

"My pleasure." He grinned.

I'd scribbled my phone number on the back of a napkin and I handed it to him with my best smile. "I had a great time."

He took the napkin and looked surprised that I'd offered it. "You were a natural up there," he said with a self-conscious smile. But then he didn't say another word. Nothing. So, before it got too awkward, I just said, "Well, thanks again," and walked away. I was confused and a little disappointed, but I refused to believe that I'd misread him.

Mickey Chandler intrigued me. While I was teasing with him onstage, I knew I'd caught a glimpse of something very real behind his clown's mask. He knew I'd seen it, and I could tell he wasn't sure how he felt about that. But it was this glimpse of the man I saw hiding in the buffoon that so affected me. I tried not to dwell on it, but I have to admit he crossed my mind a few times over the next eight months.

It was late May of 1999 when Priscilla showed up at my apartment near campus at four in the morning. I answered the door bleary-eyed, but the sight of her standing there trembling woke me fully. Her hair was wet. "Priss? What are you doing?"

"I need you to drive me home," she said, hurrying past me. She wasn't wearing any shoes. "Where are your keys?"

"Priscilla, what are you doing?"

"Can you take me?" She lifted pillows and moved quickly around the room. "Where the hell is your purse!"

I grabbed her hand and she tried to tug it away, but I yanked. "Priscilla, stop! What is going on?"

"I found a lump!" she shouted. Then softer, terrified: "I found a lump."

I looked at her and didn't breathe.

"Please, Lucy. Can we just go?"

We drove home to Brinley in our pajamas, Priss in quiet panic and me wondering if I'd missed something. I'd seen my sister fairly often while I was in Boston, but I'd never seen Death looming anywhere near her. Now I was afraid to look. We'd driven more than halfway in silence when I reached for her hand. "Priss, talk to me."

She squeezed and let go. "Just drive, Lu."

Charlotte ordered a biopsy later that morning. Then we waited. We were all in her office when the results came back, Lily and I each holding one of Priss's hands. Thank goodness the news wasn't terrible. The lump was malignant, but it was completely encapsulated and would be removed in its entirety—practically cause for celebration. But not quite. The area near the growth would need to be thoroughly examined for abnormal cells. If any were found, that would be reason for concern. So Priss went into surgery and we waited again. It was a long day of hand-holding for Lily and me. "I don't think I can watch her go through this," Lily said more than once.

"She's too ornery for this thing to bring her down," I replied.

Late that night we finally got the report that the surrounding cells were clean. We nearly melted with relief, especially Lily. Ron took her home around eleven, but I stayed because Priscilla was so restless.

It was close to midnight when she finally got to sleep—thanks to a hefty dose of Demerol. I needed a break, so I walked down to the cafeteria for a drink. It was dimly lit, and quiet. Most of the chairs had been placed up on the tables so the floor could be mopped. Just one little man was working the counter. I asked for an order of fries and a Coke, and he told me he'd bring them to me. I looked around the big, empty room for a seat and discovered I was alone except for a couple of doctors in the corner, and one guy sitting by himself.

I recognized the silver streak in his hair immediately and locked eyes with Mickey Chandler. When he didn't look away, I walked over and said, "Hey, Funny Man. Remember me?"

He looked at me as if he were seeing a ghost. "The birthday girl."

"Yeah."

"How ya doing?"

"It's been a long day, but I'm good. You?"

"I'm swell."

"Swell?" I said. "I've never actually heard anyone use the word *swell* before. You really are old, aren't you?"

Tonight, Mickey had no witty comeback for me. His grin was gone and his eyes looked a bit haunted.

I cleared my throat. "Well, it was nice to see you."

The cafeteria worker was on his way over with my fries. Mickey pushed a chair out from the table with his foot. "Do you want to sit?"

"You sure? I don't want to disturb your brooding."

This time he chuckled. "I do remember you. Sass all the way."

I sat down and the little waiter placed a humongous plate of fries between us. "Hungry?" Mickey teased.

"I ordered these for you."

We tap-danced a little, talking about Northeastern, the weather in Boston, my studies.

Then he asked, "What brings you here in the middle of the night?"

"My sister is upstairs recovering from surgery. You remember my sister Priscilla. She wanted to eat you for dinner."

"Oh, that sister. Is she okay?"

"Yes, thank goodness. We're very relieved. It was cancer but they got it."

"Well, that is good news then."

I nodded. "It's great news. And you, Mr. Chandler, what are you doing here in the middle of the night?"

He looked around and came back to me. "Looks like I'm just sitting here with a pretty little college girl."

"Yeah, yeah. That's cheating. What's the real story?"

"It's funny, actually. I was just walking by and thought, 'I bet I could get a good table in the hospital cafeteria without a reservation.'" It was weak humor and he knew it. I waited for the real answer to my question, but it was not forthcoming.

I cleared my throat. "Do you live around here?"

"Just over in East Haddam. I have a house on the lake. You?"

"I live over in Brinley. Well, not at the moment, actually. I'm still in Boston for another year, but I'll be moving back as soon as I graduate. Do you have a wife that lives with you in that house on the lake?"

"No."

"No?"

"No."

I smiled and it felt good after this day. "Tell me about your house."

"It's ancient. Actually it's a freaking money pit that's been in my family for years. It has a lot of original wood and glass and I'm restoring it, then I'm going to sell it. I like doing it. It's good for me. Very physical, and I can work at it all night if I want."

I nodded.

He smiled. Not a full smile, but something more vulnerable, more stripped and without pretense. It invited my boldness. "How come you never called me?"

He looked sideways at me. "I don't know."

"You don't know?"

He shook his head. "I had fun with you that night, Lucy. I remember that." Then his gaze drifted somewhere over my shoulder. "But it wasn't real. That guy's not who I am."

"What do you mean?"

His eyes came back to me. "I mean you wouldn't have liked the guy I really am."

"Oh? Are you sure it's not something easy, like you're already in-volved? Or gay? Are you gay?"

"No. That's not why."

"Well, that's good. Did you think you were too old for me? Was that it?"

"Hadn't thought of it, but now that you mention it, I am too old for you."

"What are you, forty?"

"Hey, don't let the hair fool you. I'm not even thirty until next month."

"Thirty's not bad. Are you an ax murderer?"

"Not yet." He grinned.

I watched this incredibly handsome man sitting there in his white T-shirt and a hospital gown he was wearing like a jacket. *Hospital gown?* I watched his face and listened to his voice and was struck by how sad he seemed. "You're serious? You thought I wouldn't like you?"

"Dead serious."

"Why? What is there about you I wouldn't like?" When he didn't answer, I got bold again. "I only ask because I'm still interested."

He tried to look embarrassed but didn't seem to have the energy for it. He laced his fingers together and looked at me with steady eyes. I didn't look away, and it took a long time for him to say anything. Finally, he cleared his throat. "I have a lot of problems, Lucy."

"Don't we all?" I said, taking a sip of my Coke. When he didn't respond, I put down my drink. "What are we talking about here? Ex-wife? Debt? Criminal record? What?"

"That's nothing you couldn't live with."

"You're right. So what is it?"

"A long history of mental illness, for starters."

I swallowed. Hard. *Mental illness?* "That's it?" I said shakily. "That's all you got?"

"Believe me, that's enough. You should get up and run away right now."

I leaned back in my chair and folded my arms.

"You'll be sorry." He laughed. "I'm a sick man."

When I didn't react, his smile faded and he looked down at his hands.

"What?" I coaxed softly.

He shook his head and didn't look up. "I'm a patient here, upstairs on psych."

I paused, more than a little taken aback, and trying to cover it, I blurted, "Did you try to kill yourself?"

He looked at me and shook his head. "Not this time. I wasn't rational enough."

I took a moment to digest this and at the same time do a little inventory of the room: shadowy lighting, industrial furniture, doctors discussing something serious in the corner. But nothing else. No familiar apparition looming. I looked into his sad eyes. "Do you want to tell me about it?"

He shook his head. "Nothing to tell, really. My chemistry gets out of whack and I go nuts. End of story."

"Why?"

"It's complicated."

"I'm pretty bright. I'm sure I can follow."

He chuckled. "Sass."

"I'm sorry. I'm awfully nosy, aren't I?"

"Yes, you are." There was an awkward silence and I thought it might have been a good time for me to leave, but then Mickey Chandler locked me in his gaze. "You really want to know?"

I nodded.

"Okay. My deal is I never know who I'm going to be when I wake up in the morning, and I hate that. I hate not being able to count on the guy in the mirror."

"I don't blame you. Why are you like that?"

"There's a problem with the chemicals in my blood, or the lack thereof, so I have to take a lot of pills to balance me out. If I don't, I'm pretty much all over the place. I'm only considered stable when I'm chemically altered, and sometimes even the pills don't keep me in check." He looked at his hands. "So, I get frustrated and just stop taking them, and then everything blows up and I end up back in the hospital."

"That stinks. Is there a name for this condition?"

"Bipolar disorder."

"Have you had it a long time?"

He nodded. "Yes."

I looked at him. "For what it's worth, you look normal. How do they treat it?"

"Therapy and medication. Depends on what symptoms I'm presenting. Lithium. Sometimes antipsychotics, but mostly mood stabilizers and sometimes antidepressants, but that can be tricky because they can push me into mania. Sometimes all of the above. More pills for the side effects. They experiment with me a little because I'm a rapid cycler—I move pretty quick between the highs and lows and they want to keep me in the middle."

"Is that your safety zone?"

"Yeah. Safe but boring." He shrugged. "It's hard to explain, but when you know you can feel invincible, flooded with so much energy you could take over the world, then safe and stable just don't cut it. I self-medicate some to keep myself a little on the edge."

I nodded. "I can understand that."

"Really? You get that?"

"What's not to get? Who doesn't want to feel good?"

"Yeah well, my 'good' gets out of control really fast. Then I stop thinking right, and I don't take my medication, and I climb higher and higher. I don't eat. I don't go to bed. I work out like a maniac. I get hyper and irrational and I do bizarre things because I'm thinking bizarre things. And then I crash." He tapped his knuckles on the table a few times. "Eventually I realize what I've done. And I get depressed about it. Then I get more hyper and irrational, and sometimes, if it's real bad, I just want to . . . I just want it to be over." Mickey Chandler took a deep breath and shook his head. "I can't believe I'm sitting here telling you all this."

I wanted to cry for him. He was so exposed, so unprotected. "Who takes care of you? Who helps you stay on your pills, and tells you if you're . . . I don't know, off? Who picks you up when you crash?"

"Well"—he shrugged—"my doctor, Gleason, is always there after the crash. And he's usually there while I'm not doing what I should be doing. But it's pretty much just me."

"No family? No girlfriend? Nobody to help you?"

"No. I mean there have been plenty. But they don't usually stick around for this part." He sighed. "Before I got smart and bought Colby's—when I was just doing stand-up—I would get very valuable feedback from my employers because when I was crashing, I wasn't very funny, which is sort of important in my line of work. I tended to get fired." He ran his hands through his hair. "But when I'm manic, I'm a pretty funny guy—and it's intoxicating. I want to be more productive, funnier, better, and I can do all that while I'm climbing. But I can't sustain it. I have to crash. And I know the crash is coming, I can taste it, but I can't stop it. Well, actually I can, but I always think I have more time to stop it, until I don't. And then I fall—fast and hard—and disappoint just about everybody." He shook his head. "It's why most of my relationships are short-term. It's a very unstable, sick, stupid way to live."

I nodded. "I don't know what to say to you."

"I've freaked you out, haven't I?"

"No. Well, a little maybe. I just can't believe you have to live like that. You do have a family, right?"

"I have a brother in Denver, but we're not close. I talk to my dad once in a while, but he's been in New Orleans for years and I don't get down there much." Mickey shrugged.

"Do you have a mom?"

"No. She died when I was a kid."

"I know a little something about that," I said. "But at least I have my sisters."

"I've got a great business partner who's beyond understanding, and I've got Gleason—Dr. Webb, my psychiatrist."

"So you've been fighting this bipolar thing pretty much on your own? For most of your life?"

"Pretty much."

"I think that's amazing. You're amazing."

He shook his head. "No. I'm not. I'm just a guy trying to play out the hand I was dealt. And, you may not believe this, but I'm a lot of other things besides mentally ill."

I smiled. "No doubt." Mickey Chandler was breaking my heart. I was trying to maintain perspective because it didn't make a lot of sense to be so profoundly attracted to a *mental patient*. "So, are you supposed to be down here in the middle of the night or did you escape?"

He grinned. "Actually I'm pretty good tonight, so I have cafeteria privileges."

"Well, then, congratulations on your good behavior."

He laughed and I remembered the way his smile had sucked me in on my birthday. I found myself looking for evidence of his illness in that smile, but I couldn't see it. It was there in his eyes, but not in his smile.

"Tell me about *you*, Lucy Houston."

"Oh, it's late, maybe another time." I started to get up from my chair, but Mickey grabbed my wrist. "I don't think so, missy. I spilled my guts, now it's your turn."

I sat back down, intensely focused on his hand. I didn't want him to let go, but I pulled away from him anyway. "Well, okay," I said, finger-combing my hair. "I go to Northeastern—well, you know that already—I'll graduate next spring. Then I'm going to teach world history. I have two sisters, Lily and Priscilla—you met them. I was born here in Brinley and I'll come back and teach at Midlothian."

"Parents?"

"I had great parents. Unfortunately, my father was killed when I was little. He was a policeman. And my mother died when I was seventeen—of cancer. Cancer also got my grandmother and my aunt, which pretty much wiped out my entire maternal line." This came out sounding a lot glibber than I'd intended and I struggled to correct my tone. "That's why Priscilla's here. They caught it, thank goodness, but we Houston girls are always steeled for the worst." I was still playing with my hair, which I tend to do when I'm anxious. I stopped, feeling self-conscious. "That's *my* demon. That's the unknown I wake up with every morning. Am I healthy today? Did a cellular uprising take place while I was sleeping? Any cytoplasmic rebellion I need to be aware of? It's hell. And if I do say so myself, my hell is worse than yours, because I not only have to worry about me and my cells, but I have to devote serious anxiety to my sisters as well. It's exhausting, worrying like that. It's a very unstable, sick, stupid way to live."

Mickey Chandler laughed as I threw his own words back at him. I laughed, too, not even realizing how badly I needed to laugh, and the rush felt so delicious after a day of worry over Priscilla that I couldn't catch my breath.

Mickey leaned forward. "Well, at least now you know why I didn't call you."

"You should have called me."

He looked me over and smiled. "I remember everything about that night. I couldn't believe you kissed me. I couldn't believe you gave me your number."

"Why? I liked you."

Mickey Chandler shook his head, suddenly serious. "You liked *him*."

"I liked *you*. I still do." He looked hard at me, and I thought in my whole life I'd never met anyone like Mickey Chandler. He was real and seriously flawed. No pretense of perfection. The package was open and damaged and sitting here staring at me, and I found it all incredibly refreshing, if a little frightening.

I was the first to break away and glance at the clock. "I really have to get back to my sister," I said, pushing the plate of fries closer to him. "She'll spit nails if she wakes up and I'm not there." I stood up and graced him with my most sincere smile. "But just for the record,

Mr. Chandler, *you* kissed *me*." I suddenly wanted very much to revisit that moment despite everything I'd learned tonight.

Mickey grinned.

"You haven't scared me," I said. "I just want you to know that. I can see that despite your diagnosis, you're a good guy. And the way I see it, we both have problems—stuff beyond our control—although you could stay on your medication and control some of yours."

He kept on grinning.

"I don't see the big deal," I said, "about two people, with what basically boils down to just health issues, sharing a pizza sometime. If I give you my number again—"

"I know your number, Lucy. I know it by heart."

The look he gave me made me shiver, and I hoped it didn't show. And then I hoped it did.

"Then use it sometime," I said. "I promise I'll say yes."

four

There's a genetic link to bipolar disorder. My mom had it and I have it. I'm not sure about my brother. I've found that some people think knowing that about a person, explains everything, excuses everything, or rebukes everything. That's not fair. A person is infinitely more complex than that. I like to think of my mental illness as supplemental to the rest of me, like emotional diabetes. Depakote is my current insulin, mood is my blood sugar. Like any good diabetic, I have to work hard to keep my chemicals aligned. If I don't, I get sick.

It takes some skill to navigate this disorder. It takes some grit to control it so it doesn't control me. Sometimes it takes a guide. For me it takes a destination. Lucy is my destination. Whether I'm cowered in a dark corner or perched on a blindingly bright plateau, my aim is always to get back to her. Gleason tells me this is how I differ from my mother; she had no destination, nothing was more important than her illness. She trusted nothing but it. Not my father, not me or my brother. Her world revolved around the pain—dark, thick, encompassing emotional pain. It came to define her; I refuse to let it define me.

But I've known pain like hers; it's why I cheat with my pills.

After she'd given Mickey his medication, Peony Litman dismissed us, and we walked to the common area hand in hand. "So," Mickey asked, looping his arm around my shoulder, "what are you doing tomorrow? Can you come in for my session with Gleason?"

"I would, but it's Celia's memorial service. Remember?"

"Oh, right. How could I forget that? Have you seen Nathan?"

I shook my head. "I called earlier this week, but he didn't answer." Both Mickey and I were quiet for a minute, lost in the cruelty of a life ended in midswing. Celia Nash had been watching her son's soccer game last fall when she was stung by a bee that killed her. At the time they were living in Phoenix, where Nathan had a thriving orthopedic practice. But after the death of his wife, he decided to bring his kids back home to be nearer his and Celia's parents. Now, six months later, the family was having a memorial service for Celia and burying her ashes in River's Peace Cemetery. I hugged Mickey's arm, remembering how happy Celia and Nathan had been.

We were about to sit down when a lab technician claimed Mickey, who needed his blood drawn for a Depakote level. As I sat waiting for him, a cell phone rang and it took me a minute to recognize it as my own. I missed the call, but the screen flashed Charlotte Barbee's number. My heart did a little thudding. I had left her office only three hours earlier. Three hours was scarcely enough time to discover anything amiss, right? As I sat there wondering what Charlotte could want, Peony walked in to say I had a call at the nurses' station.

It was Dr. Barbee, and she wanted to see me.

Charlotte was with her last patient, and I'd been told by her receptionist, Bev Lancaster, that she wouldn't be long. Bev could see I was a little anxious and did her best to reassure me with a sympathetic smile. "Would you like some candy, Lucy?" She gestured to the crystal bowl she kept stocked next to the phone. I shook my head but took a Hershey's Kiss anyway. Naturally, Bev knew my medical history, so she could probably imagine the source of my angst. "She shouldn't be much longer," Bev said, gathering her things. It was five o'clock and her workday was over.

I had stayed at the hospital as long as I could, nodding as Mickey spoke, but having no real notion of what I was nodding to. Probably lots to do with Hawaii. Finally, I'd told my husband I had a headache and needed to go home. I promised to call him later. Now I was here, sequestered in Charlotte's plush waiting room, trying to let go of the queasy feeling her call had induced. On her way out, Bev squeezed my shoulder. "Everything will be fine, hon. You'll see."

"Oh, I know," I said, sounding not one bit convincing.

Then I was alone. I looked around Charlotte's waiting room, which was soothing by design: dark paneling, overstuffed furniture, soft lamplight. It didn't look like the last place on earth a person would want to be—it just felt that way at the moment. I was sitting in a cushy chair upholstered with black and ivory toile. The fabric depicted French ladies drinking tea and probably discussing lovers with bad teeth.

The door to the outer office opened and Charlotte followed Elaine Withers into the waiting room. "Remember what I said," Charlotte boomed. "Rest. Rest."

Lainy looked at me and rolled her faded blue eyes toward the ceiling. "She's so darn bossy, Lucy. I don't know why I put up with her."

I stood up and smiled at my neighbor. "Yes, you do, Lainy."

"Well, I hope she's nicer to you than she was to me, sweetheart," Lainy said as she left.

I watched the door shut behind her and waited for Charlotte to say something. When she didn't, I took a deep breath and turned to find her looking at me just as my mother would have. She smiled. "Let's sit out here, darlin'. Everyone's gone and it's quiet—not so clinical."

"Do I have something to worry about?"

"That depends."

I sat back down gingerly in the midst of the tea drinkers, and as Charlotte took the chair across from me, I felt my heart pound. The conversation I'd been imagining hung unsaid between us as I looked into the eyes of my mom's dear friend. Every line in Charlotte's face was beautiful to me, maternal and tender. And I did not see pity in her dark eyes, which I found profoundly reassuring.

"What is it, Charlotte? Why am I here?"

Charlotte brought a hand to her face and contemplated me. "Lucy, it's not what you think. I have no oncological results back yet."

"Then what's going on?"

"Well, I do have results from one test I thought you should be aware of."

"Is it serious?"

Charlotte looked at me and smiled. "Lucy, you're pregnant."

Minutes, maybe hours, passed. What had she said? I'd seen her mouth move. I'd heard something come out, but the words had frozen on impact and never actually penetrated, so they couldn't actually be true.

Charlotte was nodding. "Are you okay, darlin'?"

"I don't think I heard you."

"Yes, you did. I said you're pregnant. Pregnant."

That single word had a visceral effect on me, like fire spreading through my blood. *Pregnant*. "No."

As Charlotte nodded, all the reasons that this was an impossibility poured through me. Mickey's mental illness, the cancer that seemed magnetically drawn to my bloodline. All the women in my life who'd been taken by that heartless disease. Including me, almost. Despite the fact that Mickey and I would have loved a family, we'd long ago accepted the reality of these undeniable factors and made the hardest decision of our lives. "How can that be, Charlotte?" My vision blurred, not with tears, but because I seemed incapable of blinking. "Check again, because it's just not possible." Even as I rambled, I was trying to remember when I'd had my last period.

Charlotte reached over and took my hand.

"I don't understand. My tubes . . ."

"It happens," she said softly. "Sometimes—granted it's rare, but sometimes—a valiant little swimmer gets past the knot."

"After all these years, I have a knot that can be swum through?"

"A knot or tubes that reattached. It's hard to say, but it happens."

"Charlotte . . ." My mind was reeling. This was too big. How long had it been since I'd had a period? They weren't regular and I didn't really keep track, but, dear Lord, *how long had it been?* Charlotte smiled her reassurance as I sat there shaking my head. I didn't know what else to do. "I can't even remember when I had my last period."

"It doesn't matter, Lucy. It doesn't change a thing."

"It matters to me, Charlotte. What am I going to do?"

"How 'bout this: for tonight, let it be. Just be. You are a woman doing what women do. You're pregnant. Natural, beautiful, normal—"

"Unbelievable. Insane."

"Not tonight, Lucy," Charlotte said calmly. "Tonight just go with it. We'll think about the hard things tomorrow. This isn't the end of the world."

"Really?"

Charlotte took my hand. "Really."

"Why now? Why after all this time? What happened?" A dozen feelings screamed through me.

As the numbness dissolved, I found I was profoundly relieved not to have been told I was sick again, but *this* news filled me with fear and such anxiety I could hardly breathe. Anxiety and—if I'm being honest—a sudden, incomprehensible joy. I was pregnant? I was pregnant.

When I finally left Charlotte's office, I drove around for a while and tried to follow the advice she'd given me: Just be pregnant. Don't worry. Don't horribilize. It wasn't working. I drove down the old country road that connected Brinley to the next county. It was sunset, quiet and familiar as old shoes, and I ended up crying so hard I had to pull over.

Pregnant.

I should have gone to dinner with Charlotte as she'd suggested, but I had to get away. Now I was sorry I was alone. Pregnant?

Despite everything, I started imagining things I had no business imagining. Me, a mom. Me, with a baby. Oh, how I love the way new babies smell, and those great big eyes in an itty-bitty person. A toddler with curly hair. I imagined a little one who'd had a bad dream, screaming for me in the middle of the night: "Mama." I started my car, turned up the radio, and drove home.

I grew up in the house Mickey and I now live in. It's an old Victorian cottage with lush trees my dad planted before I was born. Sometimes when I pull up to it, I am fifteen years old again and my strong, healthy mom is waiting for me in the gabled sitting room. I'd give anything to have her there now. I get the mail and fiddle through the bills, appearing to anyone who might happen to be looking as if nothing was on my mind but the envelopes in my hand. I pick up the paper and unlock the front door. A robbery at the Nicklecade made the front page. I imagine it saying LUCY CHANDLER PREGNANT! WHAT WAS SHE THINKING?

Then I hear it again, in my mind, a little voice calling me, crying, "Mama, Mama." She's had a nightmare. She? I barely make it into the house before I'm overwhelmed all over again.

The same thoughts follow me up the stairs and into the shower. They're with me as I open a can of tomato soup and there when I dump it, untouched, down the drain. A baby. I could put her—I am now somehow painfully certain it's a *her*, which only compounds my angst—in Priscilla's old bedroom. It's just a catchall room now with a treadmill, computer, and lots of ironing that never gets done. All that junk could be moved downstairs. Growing up, Priss had the best room in the house. Right next to Mom and Dad, with a big window seat and lots of delicious light. Perfect for a nursery.

It became my room when it was just Mom and me, and Mom was dying. Close enough to hear her cry out for me in the middle of the night when she needed a pain pill or had to go to the bathroom. The room was definitely close enough to hear a baby who'd had a bad dream. No. What was I thinking? This wasn't happening.

The phone rang and the caller ID said Edgemont Hospital. Mickey. I couldn't talk to him now. Not yet. Not now. Mickey might be ecstatic about this turn of events. He'd forget about our agreement, our oath, our reasons. Oh, how he'd love to be a father. Despite his many, many liabilities, he would love this news. He'd be no help at all.

When the phone stopped ringing, I went to the ancient armoire in our bedroom and opened the creaky door. On one side, the mirror screamed back my battered reflection: tangled, wet hair, Mickey's old 49ers T-shirt—the one I always slept in when he was gone—and my puffy, shell-shocked eyes. On the other side hung the framed contractual agreement I had with my husband. It was our bible, the Geneva Convention of our relationship. Scripted in various inks—as over the years we had added conditions as circumstances dictated—and framed in flimsy brass, hung the practical provisions we placed on our commitment to each other. It was inviolate. After I got sick, we'd penned the sad addendum: *No children*.

We'd come to this heartbreaking decision after a particularly brutal breakdown that landed Mickey in the Connecticut State Hospital for seven weeks. It happened smack in the middle of my cancer hell. After he got out, we put it in the contract. No kids. We'd written it in bold blue ink, underlined it, and sealed it with our tears. I never told Mickey that later, after that hellish year of almost dying—later when we were both back on top—I'd had second thoughts, but only fleetingly.

I pulled the contract from the peg where it hung. The very fact that this child would have parents who required a written document to safeguard their marriage was probably a good enough reason not to have her. What would she think if she ever stumbled across the terms of our agreement?

Mickey Chandler agrees never to hit his wife or abuse her in any way.

Mickey will never have sexual contact with another human being. Neither will Lucy.

Mickey will not use illicit drugs. And he will try not to drink alcohol.

Alcohol is sometimes a challenge during his periods of instability. After one particularly bad manic episode he handwrote this promise: *Okay, I will try harder not to drink. Especially when I am mad and do not get what I want. Especially when I'm losing it!*

Mickey will make a constant and concerted effort to take his medication . . . exactly as prescribed. Try. Try. Try Harder!!! (He'd added these *trys* on three sequential occasions.)

Lucy will not nag Mickey to take his medication.

Lucy and Mickey agree to see Mickey's therapist every week even when Mickey is doing well.

Lucy will see Gleason, or a facsimile, before she has any major fight with Mickey.

Lucy promises to be patient and not expect perfection from Mickey.

Lucy will not overreact.

Lucy will not get fed up and sleep around or seek friendships with attractive men. Mickey added this line after an insane fight we had when I told him I thought Bruce Willis was cute in his *Die Hard* movies.

Lucy will take a break when Mickey gets overwhelming. And Mickey will not take it personally when she needs to vent or cry to Lily or Jan or Charlotte.

Lucy will employ the 10-second rule when she gets angry at Mickey. Cranky okay. Bitchy no.

Lucy will not hover.

Lucy will not blame Mickey for what he cannot control.

Mickey will not pretend to not be in control.

Lucy will never be cruel in reference to Mickey's illness.

My gaze fell on the last agonizing handwritten line of our contract added after I didn't die: *No CHILDREN!!!*

Due to circumstances beyond what we are able to control, we agree for all parties involved—especially the child—that we will not bring babies into this marriage. Not because we wouldn't love you, but because our love would never be enough. (Tubal ligation the day I turned 27. Happy f—ing birthday!)

Nothing had changed. Tears melted the words as I read the last addendum again. Nothing had changed, except a valiant little swimmer had made it through the knot. I crawled into bed wondering just *how* valiant, and why I was pregnant after all this time.

five

Gleason Webb holds open group therapy every other Thursday for the bipolar population of the Lower Connecticut River Valley. I attend when I can and I've been going for years. As we are all different men (Gleason meets with BP women on opposite Thursdays) with different presentations, we make up quite a group. Collectively we are a gathering of mentally ill men, some of whom have destroyed marriages—and not just their own—some have hurt and alienated their kids, some have lost that privilege, some have dishonored their parents, abused their friends, betrayed their employers, stolen, lied, and manipulated. Some blame God for all their problems. For some it's all her *fault. Some have brought their careers to ruin; others have squandered their life's fortune. Some are drunks, addicts, flat broke and homeless. Some have burned every bridge to every loved one. Some are obnoxiously entitled and blameless one week, and guilt-ridden and suicidal the next. I've been there as well. We are all damaged men, but we're rather interesting.*

In this setting Gleason is our instructor. He's a brutal confronter and has always warned that if we are to survive our diagnosis, we must understand it—this is our number one responsibility. We must respect it, and we must attend to it. He also recommends having someone in our life we can trust to tell us when our feet have left the pavement.

I can't speak for my compatriots, but I've always thought that's a lot to reveal about yourself, and the chance of finding someone actually willing to look beneath all this symptomology to the man was slim to none.

So, to say that I was blindsided by Lucy Houston would be a vast understatement.

The night I met Mickey Chandler in the cafeteria, I'd left him with an invitation I really didn't think too hard about . . . until later. It was probably best if he didn't call. Mickey was a sick man—*mentally ill* if I believed what he'd told me. I couldn't see it, but then I didn't know what it was supposed to look like. I dwelled more on the look in his beautiful eyes when he'd said, "Believe it or not, I'm a lot of other things besides mentally ill." Because of those words, every day that passed found me thinking about him more.

A few weeks later, I was putting together a presentation packet for my ethics class when my phone rang. I didn't recognize the number but I knew it was him.

"Hey, birthday girl."

"You called," I said, certain my smile had reached my voice.

"Yes, I did."

"How are you?"

"I'm doing great now," he said. "You?"

"I'm great, too," I said, feeling it.

"So, against my better judgment, I'm wondering if you'd like to go out with me."

"Hmmm. I'm not sure I've ever been asked in such a flattering way."

He chuckled. "After the other night, I think you know what I mean."

"What did you have in mind?"

"Well, you'd think we were ahead of the game with everything we know about each other, but I don't know if you like surprises or if you like to know what to expect . . ."

"I love surprises."

"Great! How does Thursday look?"

I had a class that night, but it didn't matter. "Thursday's great."

"I'll pick you up at six. We'll be outside and it will probably start out warm and get cool, so bring a sweatshirt. And I wouldn't do stilettos."

"Sweatshirt. No stilettos. Got it." I gave him directions to my apartment and hung up feeling giddy and ignoring my previous qualms. Three days later he showed up right on time, looking fit in jeans and a henley, sunglasses pushed back in his great hair. He looked me over, and my jeans, white T-shirt, and ponytail all seemed to pass inspection.

"Hi," I said.

"Hi."

"You look great, like you're feeling better," I said.

"Thanks. You look good, too."

"You found the place okay?" I said.

"Drove right to it," he said.

"Good."

"Good directions," he said.

"Good," I said again.

Mickey shook his head. "This is why I hate first dates."

"Me, too. Let's get out of here." I grabbed my jacket and my house key. "Do I need anything else?"

"I don't think so." He chuckled as I locked the door. "Low maintenance. Who would have thought?"

If our conversation started out stilted, it didn't stay that way for long. As he drove, I learned all about Mickey's business. He and his partner, Jared Timmons, not only owned Colby's, but two other clubs as well, and they were looking at another one. "I'm very lucky," he said. "Jared works around my mental health, and I work around his commitment to overpopulate the world. He has three kids and his wife is pregnant."

I laughed. "Sounds like a great arrangement."

Mickey parked the car and looked over at me. "Ready?"

"Absolutely."

We'd driven to the pier at Pemberton Point, the ferry launch for the Boston Harbor Islands. I was excited because I'd lived in Boston for three years but I'd never seen any of the islands. I was invited to a party on Spectacle my freshman year, but I'd missed it because Lily got married and I had to give her away. I looked at Mickey. "So far I'm loving this surprise!"

He smiled and took my hand as we walked to the ferry. The air was soft on this warm June evening as we stood at the rail. I felt safe, protected, with Mickey's broad shoulders shielding me from the wind. I caught him staring at me with those same dark eyes I'd encountered when I first met him . . . kind of stripped. He liked me, but wasn't quite sure he should. I gazed out at the harbor. "I love the water."

"Do you sail?"

"Not as much as I'd like. My sisters and I inherited an old sailboat. A Catalina. I remember going with my dad when I was little. I've always loved it."

"You'll have to show me your stuff sometime."

I lifted an eyebrow at him. *Sometime* implied a next time. "Do you sail the Connecticut River?"

"I have a few times. But I spend more time on Bashan Lake. I do a lot of fishing."

I smiled. "I love to fish."

"I wouldn't have bet on that." He grinned.

"I might surprise you yet."

The ferry moored at the Georges Island dock, where we got off and waited for the shuttle. We were the only ones in line, and when I looked over at Mickey, he was smiling. "Have you ever been to Bumpkin Island?"

"No. Have you?"

He shook his head. "Looks like we get to discover it together."

"I hear you can see the Boston skyline from it. Maybe we'll get lucky and see the sunset."

"Maybe."

The shuttle dropped us off on the island, and Mickey and I made our way to a path that was bordered with wild berry bushes.

"We better pick some of these for dinner," he said.

I wasn't sure if he was joking, but I popped a big fat blackberry in my mouth anyway. In the distance, Boston's lights were just starting to flicker. "It's beautiful here," I said.

"Yeah, it is. There's supposed to be an old farmhouse around here . . . or the ruins of one. Let's find it." He reached for my hand.

"There's an old hospital here, too," I said as I put some berries in his palm.

"Are you hungry?" Mickey asked me.

"A little. Do you have a peanut butter sandwich in your pocket?"

He laughed. "I could win you over with a peanut butter sandwich?"

I didn't want to tell him he probably could, so I just smiled. "Low maintenance, remember?"

We found the ruins at dusk, and the fading sun made them seem very gothic. I was kind of lost in the moment, imagining who used to live here. I turned to say something to Mickey, but he was standing off to the side, watching me. When I caught his eye, he shifted uncomfortably. I walked toward him, noting that the first stars were starting to glint over the harbor. "It's so quiet here."

"We might be the only two people on the whole island, Lucy. Does that make you nervous?" he said, still drinking me in.

I stopped in front of him. "Do I look nervous?"

Mickey smiled and shook his head, then took my hand. "C'mon, we have to be someplace."

"Where?"

In the last moments of twilight, just before night took over the wheel, we came upon the true surprise Mickey had planned. He helped me down an embankment and into a clearing, where a candlelit table was set for two under an arbor. I was stunned. The picnic table was covered in white linen and china and flowers and stemware. The best part was the tuxedoed waiter standing there with a napkin he snapped loose and placed on my lap. I looked at Mickey and shook my head. "Oh, you're good."

He sat down across from me and grinned.

The waiter was just a kid, but all business as he introduced the menu: rack of lamb, new potatoes, spinach salad, and fresh fruit. He removed the silver lids from the serving trays and placed a basket of rolls between Mickey and me. "And for dessert, fresh pastries from Maria's." He looked at Mickey. "Anything else, Mr. Chandler?"

"No. It's perfect, Ryan. You've done a great job." As the kid disappeared in the shadows, I watched Mickey, who suddenly seemed a bit bashful.

"This is the best surprise ever," I said.

"Better than peanut butter?"

"Way better. In fact, you must be psychic because these are all my favorites."

"Or I just had your sister's phone number."

"You talked to Lily?"

"We're old friends since she booked your party at my club. When I told her what I was thinking, she said food was the way to your heart. I sort of took it from there."

I stared at him. "I don't know what to say. It's lovely."

We took our time and everything was delicious. While we watched the bruised sunset, we talked about art, which led to books we loved and hated and movies we'd seen. At one point, Mickey asked me if it was true that Priscilla was a lawyer.

"Yep."

"Is she a good lawyer or a great lawyer?"

"I don't know. What's the difference?"

"A good lawyer knows the law. A great lawyer knows the judge."

I laughed. "Oh, she'd love that."

Mickey leaned his elbows on the table. "You two seem very different. Kind of hard to believe you're sisters."

"Sometimes we can't believe it either." I smiled. "But Priscilla always has my back—mine and Lily's. She's sort of the parent—mom and dad rolled into one big, bad, bossy sister. She's very career-oriented, success-oriented, smart, gorgeous, and only as nice as she has to be."

"She'll probably get just what she wants."

"I hope she does."

"And Lily? She seems real nice."

I nodded. "Oh, Lily's my touchstone. We're very close; almost like we're extensions of each other. She's a worrier, but I'd trust her with my life. She married the guy next door—you met him, Ron. He's a fabulous brother-in-law. They live in Brinley Township and own an antiques store." I leaned over and lowered my voice. "Lily knows all my secrets."

Mickey smiled. "And I have her number . . ."

He was so easy to be with, no stumbling around for words, no second-guessing if I was holding his interest. "Now you," I said. "Tell me something I don't know about you."

"I'm having a great time looking at you in the candlelight." He winked.

I swallowed. "Backatcha," I said, meaning it. The light playing in his dark eyes and his easy smile could have held my interest all night. I cleared my throat. "What kind of kid were you?"

"Tall, I was tall. Gangly. Shy. I liked to read joke books when I was a kid."

"Well, that explains a lot."

"It probably does. Laughing saved me because my life was very unfunny."

"Why?"

"My mom had terminal depression, and my dad dealt with it by drinking too much. I wouldn't wish that on any kid," Mickey said matter-of-factly, with no trace of self-pity.

"I'm so sorry."

He shrugged. "You're lucky to have your sisters."

"I know. We sort of cling to each other since our parents are gone."

Mickey nodded. "You do what you can to fill the loss, no matter when it happens. I had a gig a few weeks ago. It was an eighty-fifth birthday party for a little old lady. Her good friends—the youngest was seventy-nine—found me on the Internet and hired me to make her laugh since she'd just lost her husband. They were married sixty-seven years. He was a circuit court judge."

"Did you make her smile?"

"Oh, yeah. Lots of lawyer jokes. I had so much fun with those ladies, I didn't even charge them."

I shook my head. "My first impression of you still stands, Mickey Chandler. You are a good guy."

We were quiet for a moment, then Mickey stood and came to sit on my side of the table. He straddled the bench, facing me, and my heart sped up as I looked at him.

"Thank you for a fabulous evening," I said. Then I softly kissed his cheek. When I pulled back, Mickey almost said something, but then thought better of it. Mostly he just looked unsure, and I was glad when the boy waiter emerged to clear our table. He made a big production of checking his watch.

"You told me to let you know the time, Mr. Chandler. The shuttle will be here in twenty minutes."

Mickey nodded. "Thanks, Ryan."

"Yes, thank you," I said. "Everything was perfect."

The boy beamed and Mickey stood up and handed him a couple of bills, hundreds if I could trust the candlelight. Then he took my hand and a flashlight Ryan offered him and we walked back to the shuttle.

When we got back to my apartment, I wanted to invite Mickey in, which was probably a good reason not to, so instead I just looked up and thanked him again.

"I had a great time, Lucy."

"Me, too. I hope we can do it again sometime."

He looked at the floor and I started to get the same vibe I got the first time I thought we were on the same page, but weren't. It took him a minute to meet my eyes, and when he did, I saw pain there.

"What?"

He shook his head. "I'm not sure."

"About what?"

"About this. About again."

I swallowed. "Oh. Really? I thought it was great. Did I misread something?"

"No. No. It's me. I think I have."

"What does that mean?" I said, a pit forming in my stomach.

"Lucy, I have no business doing this."

"What are you talking about?"

Once again, words were right there but not said.

"Mickey, I know you like me. And you have to know I like you. So what's the problem?"

He shook his head. "I don't know how to do this."

"Do what?"

"I'm a pretty superficial guy, Lucy. I've survived this long because I've learned to just enjoy the moments and not expect much in the long run. I don't think you're like that."

"You're right. I'm more of a jump-in-with-both-feet kind of girl. My world is full of guys just living for the moment, and I gotta tell ya, I've had my fill of them. It's fun for a while . . . but in the end, it's nothing—empty calories. That's not what I want."

"What *do* you want?"

"I want someone interesting and real in my life. Someone who doesn't pretend."

He was very close to me, and I was getting lost in his eyes when he whispered, "I'm not that guy, Lucy."

"Really? Because you seem like exactly that guy."

He shook his head, his expression unimaginably sad.

I was 5' 4" to his 6' 3", 100 pounds to his 215, but I could feel

Mickey Chandler quaking in the palm of my hand. I moved closer and touched his face. When he didn't move, I kissed him, one side of his jaw and then the other, then I gently kissed his lips. "If you want to take a chance on me," I said softly, "I'm right here."

He swallowed. "I'm afraid you're being a little naive, Lucy."

"I guess that's possible," I said, bristling.

"I didn't mean to imply—"

"It's okay. I'm young and you're probably right—where you're concerned, I might be naive. But here's breaking news: you might be, too. I don't have any answers, and as much as you think you do, you don't either. I don't know if I want to be with you, Mickey, but I think it's okay to find out. So . . . I guess you just need to decide if this thing is worth exploring." I put my key in the lock. "If you decide it is, meet me on my roof tomorrow night. You bring your answer. I'll bring the sunset." I opened the door and walked into my apartment, and when I turned to face him, there was such anguish in his eyes that I didn't know what else to say. "Think about it, Mickey."

When I shut the door, my heart was pounding and I just knew I was not going to see him again. I got my one fabulous date, and because of it, the girl in me wanted to open the door and run after him. But another part of me, seasoned well beyond my age, still knew Mickey was a damaged man, a frightened man. But as true as that was, I could not deny our connection. I may have been young, but I'd felt old since the day my mother got sick. Mickey was older, but he was filled with such vulnerability. I leaned against the door completely frustrated because none of it mattered. None of it mattered because I was not going to see him again.

The next day I went through the motions of what I was supposed to be doing, every minute focused on the time. This day had to end so I could get on with my life. Until it was over, there was possibility. Tomorrow that possibility would be dead. I'd call Lily, and we'd have lunch. I'd tell her all about the wonderful date she'd had a hand in, then I would rehash all the details of how it ended and let go of each one as I described them to her. But I had to get to tomorrow first.

Finally, at twenty after seven, in shorts and barefoot, I went up to the flat roof of my apartment building. It boasted incredible views of Boston and Cambridge across the river. A big equipment shed was in the center, and chimney pipes protruded all over the place. A table and a spattering of lawn chairs were bolted down in the best corner, but I wandered to the opposite edge and sat down.

I was alone for the time being, but that could soon change because the roof was a popular place at sunset. I sat down and let my legs dangle over the edge as I watched night drain the blue from the sky. A couple of times I thought I heard the metal door open behind me, but with so much city noise I couldn't be sure. I just knew Mickey never showed up. Finally, when I realized it had to be past nine, I gave up and said hello to tomorrow. This was probably for the best. I got to my feet and walked across the roof.

I was just about to the door when I saw someone sitting at the table. He stood up and for a minute I wasn't sure it was him. But as he walked toward me, the moon came out from behind a cloud and dispelled any doubt. His eyes bored into mine, and in three long strides he was in front of me. His face held his every hope and fear, urgent and unsaid, but completely evident. For a moment we just looked at each other.

Then Mickey pulled me roughly to him, found my mouth, and kissed me like he'd invented the concept.

six

Today my friend Nathan Nash will bury his wife. I don't know how he hasn't imploded. I know hell, but the prospect of losing my wife was unparalleled torment. Reality, I've learned, is much crueler than insanity. Insanity can be medicated, subdued, sedated. Watching Lucy dissolve, be ravaged from the inside out, was a wall I couldn't push through. I could do absolutely nothing but hold her and breathe. Just breathe, as her beautiful hair fell out in my hands. Just breathe, as she lay in my lap whimpering, the poison intended to save her burning a path through her. All I could do was watch and breathe until cancer gave up and let go of her. But it did let go of her, a siren prayer was heard, a miracle granted. Lucy got better. And then I got worse. My relief turned to mania, then delirium. Insane irony. I'd just held on so tightly to my anxious hope that when it was no longer required, it seemed I had no outlet. The timing was unforgivable. My wife recovered slowly without me on an oncology ward while I recovered slowly without her, miles away at the state hospital. We were almost strangers by the time it was over, altered, weak with gratitude, tentative in our trust of life and second chances. I think we held each other for a solid week.

I woke with a start, realizing I'd fallen asleep with the framed contract pressed to my chest like the portrait of a lost lover. As I lay there, I realized I had spent most of the night recalling our history and imagining our future, and now I absolutely understood what Mickey meant by not being able to shut down his brain.

This morning, I couldn't seem to stop thinking of us as parents, myself as a mother. I saw me chasing a naked, slippery little girl down the hall after she'd escaped the bath. I saw me pushing her in a grocery cart down the aisle at Mosely's Market, little legs swinging from the child seat, one red sneaker untied. I saw myself trying not to laugh when she cut her own bangs. I saw Mickey reading to her in the big window seat in her room. Our daughter, in Cinderella footee pajamas, snuggled in the crook of her father's elbow, both of them hunkered behind a big picture book.

I was simply not prepared for this.

I'd put away the idea of being a mother years ago out of sheer necessity. By the time Mickey and I made it official, and I finally went in for my tubal ligation, I had pretty much accepted my life and buried any self-pity so deep it eventually stayed there. I settled for being a surrogate mother five days a week at the high school and put away what was never meant to be. I never once imagined a determined little swimmer would get through the knot.

But every time I thought of this baby—this baby that was never supposed to be—she grew more and more real. Today my entire life looked different.

The phone at my bedside rang and I knew it was Mickey. I picked it up and groggily said, "Hi, are you mad?"

"Yeah. You didn't call."

"I know. I'm so sorry." I yawned, then coughed. "I think I'm getting a cold. I just came home and went to bed."

"Call Charlotte."

"It's nothing," I said, getting to my feet. "But I'll see her today at the memorial and I'll mention it. So what are you doing this morning?"

"Lucy, what's wrong? I hear something in your voice. Tell me."

"Mickey," I said, surprised as always that he read me so well. "I think it's just Celia," I lied. "She's been on my mind, you know. I wish you could be with me today. That's all."

"I'm sorry, baby. I'd be there if I could, you know I would."

"I know. . . . But, hey, Friday is just three days away."

"And Lily and Ron are with you today, right?"

"Yes, they'll be there."

"And, Lu, I'll be thinking of you the whole time I'm making my papier-mâché birdhouse in crafts group."

Despite myself, I had to laugh.

He did, too, his big, booming, wonderfully normal laugh. "I know I'm better when everything here starts to feel like *material*."

"You're so much better. And you're coming home. We're going to have such a great weekend." *We have so much to talk about*.

I showered, blew my hair dry, and put on my only black dress, a loose, flowing shift with elbow-length sleeves. As I stood in front of the mirror, I was thinking I looked pretty good in black. It complemented my auburn hair, fair skin, and green eyes. Of the three of us Houston daughters, I looked the most like my dad. Though I only knew him for a little over five years, I always imagine that, had he lived, we'd be close. I know I've idealized a father where none has been, but, oh, how I would love to talk to *that* man today. How I'd love to be the same kind of parent I remember him being, answer the hard questions in the same magical way that has stayed with me all these years.

Then I did a dumb thing. I don't know what I was thinking, but I wadded up a pillow from the bed and stuffed it under my dress. There I stood, maybe a tad disproportionate—maybe about fifteen months pregnant. Even so, as I looked at myself in the mirror, I took my own breath away. It would be okay, wouldn't it? I knew we hadn't planned for this; we'd done what we could to prevent it. But here it was. It would be okay. I'd be so careful. I'd see Charlotte every month, so that if anything in my chemistry changed, we'd be right on it.

And who knew? Maybe a baby would snap Mickey out of his bipolarity. Anything was possible, right? And Mickey almost always rose to the occasion. Mickey, my wonderful Mickey, was the same man he'd always been. But that didn't necessarily mean he couldn't be a great father, did it?

I rubbed my manufactured belly until I heard the train whistle, which in Brinley was more reliable than the kitchen clock. It was 10:30. With a final look at my pregnant self, I tugged the pillow out from under my dress and dragged myself back to reality. What had Charlotte told me to do? Just be. Just be pregnant. I ran a brush once more through my hair and leaned into my reflection. Somehow it would be okay, wouldn't it?

I was just shutting the front door when Ron and Lily pulled up in front of my house.

Ron waved.

"You lazy suburbans," I shouted. "You live just around the corner."

Ron shrugged as Lily hopped from her side of the car. "Ron's going to meet us there," she said. "I need to borrow some shoes." My sister was wearing a white blouse and a black skirt and was indeed barefoot. "Can I borrow those pointy, red mules?"

"They're hard to walk in."

"No, they're not. I've worn them before."

We went back upstairs and I waited on my unmade bed for Lily to rummage through my closet. She came out wearing not only my shoes, but my favorite necklace and some earrings she'd given me for Christmas. She picked up the framed contract that I'd slept with and looked at me. "Which rule were you thinking of breaking, Lucy?"

I wondered when I should tell Lily about me—or, *if* I should tell her. Of course I had to tell my sister—we're so close I was surprised she didn't already know—but of course I couldn't. Not until I'd told Mickey. So even though I was bursting to tell her, I just looked up at her and shrugged.

River's Peace Cemetery sits on the border between Brinley and Ivoryton, less than a mile from my house. It was a beautiful day so Lily and I walked. We passed the grand old English Tudor that was Withers' Funeral Home and spotted Lainy Withers just pulling onto the street. She rolled down her window and offered us a ride.

"We're going to walk, Lainy," Lily said, clearly trying to prove a point about the shoes. "But thanks."

"Dr. Barbee says I should be walking, too," Lainy shouted. "But I just don't want to."

We laughed as she drove away. Earl Withers and his son, Chad, were probably already at the cemetery, having been put in charge of the graveside service. The Witherses handled most of the funeral preparations in our township. They had taken care of both of my parents.

At the cemetery, cars lined both sides of the narrow lane leading to Celia's gravesite, where an accumulation of well-wishers surrounded Nathan Nash. Celia and Nathan had grown up in the area and married and raised their family here until last year, when they moved to Arizona. They were beloved in our small community, and no one expected to see them back so soon. Especially under these circumstances. Celia Nash had been vibrant and successful in her own right. She'd put Brinley on the map as a bestselling author of children's books.

I spotted Muriel Piper getting out of her Cadillac. She looked like the definition of ancient sophistication in her ivory linen suit and tasteful jewels. She was with funny Oscar Levine, her beau of the last quarter century. Oscar was also dressed to the nines with his signature ascot, and when they saw us, they waved.

"How goes the flower planting?" I asked when we got closer.

Muriel laughed. "My knees can't take it. I've hired the Story twins to finish for me."

I shook my head as she eyed me critically. "Lucy, this dress is lovely on you. It's a rare woman who looks good in black, but you pull it off swimmingly. And you," she said, turning to Lily. "Just fabulous. I love the shoes!"

"Why, thank you, Muriel," Lily said, jabbing me with her elbow.

We followed them up the path, where we found Ron and Nathan talking to Earl Withers near the makeshift podium. Celia's husband looked subdued and a bit overwhelmed, standing a few yards away from a brass urn that held the remains of his wife. When I hugged him, he trembled against my neck.

"Thanks for coming, Lucy."

"Wouldn't have missed it," I murmured lamely.

"Is Mic with you?"

"No, I'm sorry. He's still at Edgemont."

"Oh, I did hear that," Nathan said. "Let's get together when he's feeling better."

I kissed his cheek. "It's a date."

Standing just past Nathan with a large basket of African daisies were George and Trilby Thompson. Whenever someone in the township died, gruff old George always ordered in the most beautiful annuals and made sure everyone got one as a memento. They'd been doing it for years. I hugged Trilby. "I heard you broke your foot, how are you doing?"

"Oh, it was just a sprain, but that'll teach me to dance around in a room full of clutter."

"Here ya go, Lucy," George said, handing me a flower. I took it and kissed his cheek.

As I turned away, my neighbor Wanda Murphy pulled me into

her chest, which was as cushy as a down pillow. "I heard your Mickey was doing better."

I thought of my husband working over his papier-mâché birdhouse. "Yeah, we got through another one, Wandy."

"Yes, you did, sweetheart."

I squeezed her hand as Lily tugged me toward Jan, whom she'd just spotted. Jan Bates looked elegant in her black suit and white-spiked hair. She patted our faces, and I could see she'd been crying. Lily and I wrapped our arms around her.

"I'm such a mess," she said. "I knew she was gone, but this makes it so . . ."

"Oh, Jan, of course this would be tough on you," Lily said to her mother-in-law.

I nodded, unable to add anything. Jan had illustrated all of Celia's books, and the two of them had been good friends.

Jan pulled us both closer. "And I can never come here and not think of your parents."

I'd thought this same thing as Lily and I passed our parents' markers and instinctively reached for each other.

Over Jan's shoulder, I saw Jessica Nash standing all alone. Celia's daughter had her mother's strawberry blond hair and her wide-set eyes, which were now swollen with sadness. I excused myself from Jan and Lily and walked over and put my arm around her.

"Oh, kiddo," I said. "There's just nothing in the world meaner than losing your mom. I bet you miss her every day."

She nodded. When I was pretty sure I wouldn't cry, I said, "I was just a little older than you when mine died."

"Did it happen all of a sudden, Lucy, like my mom?"

"No. She got sick and it took her a long time to die."

Jessica swallowed her emotion. "Which do you think is worse?"

"I think they're both terrible and we should both still have our moms."

We shared some tears until Jess's grandmother motioned her to a seat near the graveside. I walked back over to Lily, a little lost in my own hurt, remembering things about my mother's death I hadn't thought of for a while. The train waking me up when I'd fallen asleep in the chair next to her bed. Her sunken eyes steady and unafraid as she asked me if I was ready. Her warm, warm hands.

I slipped my hand in Lily's and let the soft hum of our small community temper my old sadness, even as we gathered to say good-bye to another of our own. It was soothing, and I remembered how it had wrapped me in peace when I'd been here burying my own family. I'd been a little girl and curiously detached at my father's summertime funeral. I was a teenager and much more emotional when we all gathered here for Mom. But I remember every detail of both days and the strength I drew from these same people.

"Oh, she made it," Lily said, jolting me back. I followed her gaze to a familiar BMW parking at the bottom of the hill. A moment later, our sister's long legs preceded her out of the car. Priscilla wore a formfitting black suit and ridiculously high heels, so she was careful on the gravel path. Once she reached level pavement, she waved at us and walked over to Nathan, who was, I could see, touched that she was there. He hugged Priss, and his big shoulders shook as he buried his chin in her loose blond hair. They'd all gone to school together. Nathan, Priss, and Celia had been great friends. Priss said something in his ear and hugged him again, then walked over to us, fingering away tears beneath her dark glasses. Lily and I each took a hand and Priss kissed us both, then whispered to me, "You didn't call me back."

"Sorry," I said, grateful that Nathan had started to address the gathering.

He was tender in his remarks as he recounted what had happened to his wife, and how painful it had been to be so far from loved ones when it happened.

"Without her," he said, "anywhere is too lonely, but she's part of Brinley Township, and this is where she would want us to be." He shrugged. "We'll all be okay because of you, our dear friends. Thank you. Thank you for everything."

The memorial service was beautiful but utterly devoid of the spirit I'd felt when my parents died. We hadn't been religious per se, but the minister was unequivocal in his assertion that there was a God and that He was in charge. Just hearing that had somehow softened the loss, at least for me. That, and my dad's promises.

When Nathan finished, Jan and Harry came over to bestow hello pecks on Priscilla, then Trent Rosenberg snagged my sister. Years ago, my mother and Priss had fought bitterly over Trent, and I knew if Mom were here today, she wouldn't be any happier. I left the ever-present speculation over their relationship and walked along the path to the big oak that spread its shade over my parents' headstones.

The year my father was buried, the Brinley police force—four officers—donated the marble bench engraved with his name. It was per-petually cooled by the shade of the hardwood trees, which were prob-ably centuries old. I sat down and breathed in the crisp air that floated off the cove. It was beautiful; the sky was summer blue and so was the Connecticut River, which lapped onto the shore not ten feet from where I sat. As final resting places go, this one wasn't bad. On a little hill at the far edge of River's Peace, just above the shore of the placid Connecticut, my parents were separated from the masses by a gravel path.

I had only been there a moment when Charlotte rounded the corner. She was wearing a silk suit the color of coffee. It fluttered in the breeze, and her long, gray hair hung in loose waves. She sighed as she looked at the large headstone with my mother's name on it. "I still miss her every day," she said, sitting down beside me.

I nodded. Charlotte and my mother had been friends since be-fore friends were invented, as Mom would say. Certainly before I was born.

"So, how you holding up?" Charlotte asked me.

"I'm okay. Thanks for yesterday. After all was said and done, I did just what you told me. And it worked pretty well except that now I keep imagining things I probably shouldn't."

"Like?"

"Like I just can't believe how this baby—who I've known all of five minutes—has so completely taken over my heart. How can that be?"

Charlotte smiled. "Have you told Mickey?"

"Not yet. I'll do it this weekend when he gets home. For now it's my little secret." I shook my head. "I had no idea it would feel like this. I don't know what to do."

Charlotte took off her dark glasses. "I know the decision you and Mickey made and I understand it. And you did your part, Lucy. I don't know what could have happened after all this time, but it seems you have one very determined little embryo on board."

I sighed. "Charlotte, what would my mom tell me?"

"Oh, please! She'd have it named and already be quilting the bunting."

Tears sprang from nowhere. "Are you sure? I don't know. Not if she knew everything Mickey and I could pass on to this baby."

"Or not." Charlotte patted my hand. "Lucy, for all your predictions and nightmares, you don't know what the future holds."

"I know enough. I mean, look at me. I may never get sick again. I know that. But what about her? And don't forget Mickey up there in a locked psych unit."

"It is a dilemma, Lucy. I don't argue that."

"But?"

"But what, darlin'? Do you honestly think your mom would have done things any differently? If she'd known she would lose her husband the way she did, or that she would die when she was so young, do you really think she would have done one thing different?"

"It's not the same, Charlotte. She *didn't* know. I do."

"If you say so."

I coughed over the lump in my throat. "This was never supposed to happen. And now, I . . ." I stared at my mother's headstone and thought of the strange space I occupied: caught between parents who were gone and a child that I simply should not have. The breeze caused Charlotte's earrings to chime, and when I turned, I found her watching me. She was serenely beautiful, her sun-touched face lined with wisdom and understanding.

"So it's a *her*, huh?"

I shook my head. "That's another terrible thing! I can't tell you how I know, but I know it's a girl. And with these genes to pass along, a boy would be so much better. But she's a girl. I just know it." I dropped my head and palmed my forehead. "Charlotte, what am I doing?"

"Worrying about things you have no control over."

"I have *some* control."

"Do you? If we're talking abortion, I can't quite see it."

"Me neither," I sighed. "But nothing has changed. Every reason we were never going to do this is still relevant."

Charlotte took my hand and patted it. "I know. So how do you think Mickey will feel about a daughter?"

"Oh, Charlotte, I don't think anything could make him happier." I stared out over the river and let Mickey's likely reaction play itself out in my mind.

This was how Priscilla found us, and when she came around the corner, she looked a little alarmed. "What's happening?"

I shook my head, grateful she couldn't have overheard us. "Nothing."

Priss walked over to us, clearly unconvinced, and I realized what she was seeing: me holding my doctor's hand, looking somber the day after my physical.

Charlotte stood up and put her arms around my sister. "We were just chatting about your parents."

"Really?" Priss looked over at me and I nodded.

"Well, I'm off," Charlotte said. "It's always lovely to see you girls. Hopefully next time we'll meet up under happier circumstances."

We watched her leave, then Priss sat down and took my hand. "Don't scare me like that."

"I didn't mean to scare you."

"You couldn't call me back?"

"I'm sorry. I forgot to, and then by the time I remembered, I realized I'd be seeing you today so I figured I'd catch you up in person."

"You did not. I didn't even know until this morning that I'd be able to come. Work's been brutal lately."

"Well, I'm glad you made it. I'm fine. Everything's fine. And I know Nathan was happy to see you."

Priscilla shook her head, a deep furrow between her brows. "I wish we had fewer occasions to meet up here."

"I know."

We were quiet for a few minutes, lost in our own memories. Finally Priss sighed. "So, how is he?"

"Doing better. He'll be home Friday."

She nodded. "I don't know how you do it."

"Yes, you do," I said, squeezing her hand.

My sister kissed my cheek. "Call me when you get your blood work back." Then she stood up and walked down the path. She was a good person, my sister, but only if you could penetrate the walls of the panic room that was her personality. Few things left Priscilla vulnerable, but my health was one of them. Her health was one. Once it was her health *and* a man.

It was the night Mickey and I had talked away the hours in the hospital cafeteria. After I left him, I went back to Priscilla's room, where I found my sister crying.

"What is it, Priss?" I'd asked. "Are you in pain?"

"No."

"Do you want me to leave?"

"No! I've been waiting for you."

"What? What do you need?"

"I just need not to be alone, is that all right?" she snapped.

I sat down and listened to her sniff back emotion, knowing if I turned on the light, I would see her tears. "It's not the cancer, is it, Priss? Charlotte said we got the best possible news."

"It's not the cancer. But that is such a relief."

She didn't say anything else for a long time, but she was still crying. Finally I ventured, "Talk to me, Priss. What's happened?"

It took her a minute, but she was able eke out, "He's married."

"Who?" For a selfish second I thought she was talking about Mickey, that she'd dragged herself downstairs to spy on me and knew something about him I didn't. "Who's married?"

"Does it really matter what his name is? He's a client, he's married, and I'm an idiot. I'm a walking, talking cliché." She groaned. "How could I have been so stupid?"

"Priss, honey, what are you talking about?"

"I broke my own cardinal rule and fell in love with a client."

"How long has this been going on?"

"Almost a year."

"A year? Do you love him?"

"Oh, Lucy," she squeaked. "I love him like there's no me without him, and I don't know what I'm supposed to do now."

I'd never heard my sister talk like this. She was the last person I could imagine letting herself be wounded by a man. The world knew her as self-contained, ornery, ambitious. She was the youngest-ever female partner at her firm. Her friends knew she loved neoclassical music, and that she believed macrobiotics would keep her young. Lily and I knew she hated the elliptical but still put in forty-five minutes a day. We knew she made cookies just to eat the dough, and that she had a stash of cashmere she would someday knit into scarves on expensive bamboo needles. But men to Priss were kind of like dessert (which she rarely indulged in), and what you had for dessert last week or last month wasn't usually report-worthy. So how did this one get so special? And a married client, what was she thinking?

I'd climbed up on the bed and put my arm around her, surprised she didn't push me away. But she just whimpered against my shoulder until I thought my own heart would break with the sound of it. When she'd quieted, I said, "Start at the beginning. And talk slow."

Her married client was Kenneth Boatwright, at the time, forty-one to her twenty-eight. She'd met him when he signed his company on with Priss's firm. She'd been the team lead on his account, and he was brokenhearted and in the middle of a bad divorce. *Sure he was,* I thought, but to say it would have been suicide. She described him as mouthwatering, but not one to flaunt it, whatever that meant. Priss said it took four phone dates where they just talked all night, mostly about him—a sure sign that Priss was smitten—before they ever went out. After that, they couldn't stay away from each other.

His company had offices all over the place, and he was open-ing offices everywhere else, so naturally they had to travel together. Their love affair was inevitable. So was the ending, because like so many other upstanding men just like him, Kenneth Boatwright was perpetually going *through* his divorce, but was never quite able to make it to the other side where Priss was waiting to start her own life with him.

My sister had crashed into the reality of her situation within that last twenty-four hours when she was being diagnosed with cancer. Scared and vulnerable—two completely foreign states of being for Priss—she had tracked Kenneth down at his vacation house on Maui to tell him what was happening and beg him to come be with her. The charming Mr. Boatwright said he was sorry about everything she was going through, but he couldn't help her. In fact, he said the timing was bad, but apparently good enough to let Priss know he and the little woman were going to give it another go . . . for the sake of the kids. His boys were fifteen and twelve.

I would never say it to her, but my sister was right. She was a cliché—brokenhearted, lied to, used up, and traded in for the kids. "I'm so sorry, Priss."

"He loves me," she bawled. "How can he do this to me?"

"I know," I said, running my fingers over her hair.

I'd wanted to kill Kenneth Boatwright that night. He'd devas-tated my tough and savvy sister. To my knowledge, no one had ever done that.

I watched her now, saying good-bye to Nathan Nash at the bot-tom of the hill. She touched his face and kissed his cheek, and he watched her walk away, probably seeing what we all saw: a beautiful, seemingly invulnerable woman. Only Lily and I knew about the scar on her heart.

We'd never spoken of Kenneth Boatwright again. Not seriously, anyway. I'd tried once, but Priss just gave me a look that made her meaning clear. I think she changed the subject with something rude about my hair.

seven

Lucy was a package deal, I probably knew that the night I met her. She was part of a trio of sisters who watched over each other—at times like lions at the gate, and I knew I had to win majority approval if I wanted to be part of her life. Lily was the first to put me to the test. It was a couple of months in and I thought I already loved Lucy. One night Lily knocked on my door and I was surprised to see her. She just walked into my house and didn't even sit down. "Lucy is on her way to falling in love with you, Mickey," she said. I nodded. Then she laid it on me— she wanted to know what I (meaning I the nutcase) was planning to do about that. Then her bottom lip quivered and I knew my answer would make or break me. I needed Lily. I could do without Priss if I had to, but I needed Lily. I told her she had every right to be worried; on paper, I'm a bit of a nightmare. She said she knew that. I couldn't think of what else to do but assure her that having bipolar disorder didn't mean I couldn't love her sister. Lily's eyes filled with tears and I worried that I'd said the wrong thing. I told her my disorder didn't mean I wouldn't give Lucy everything I had to give, and I told her I would never intentionally hurt her. I told her this, holding my breath and keeping the details to myself. For instance, I didn't tell Lily about the place in me where I'd buried my dreams; the wadded-up list of things I'd always wanted but was certain someone like me would never have. I didn't tell her I'd started the day my mother died just filing away wishes, hopes, all things unreachable. But I'd told Lucy.

One night we were sitting on my porch swing, and we'd talked away half the night and were about to talk away the other half. Her bare feet were in my lap and I was stroking her smooth calf when I told her about my list and how and why it had come to be. When I was finished, she smiled up at me, her eyes glistening in the moonlight. She said, "You realize you have no choice now but to love me, Michael Chandler."

"Why's that?"

She kissed me then and whispered in my ear, "Because I can answer every single thing on that list."

Thinking of the moment she'd made me believe that choked me up, and now Lily was asking how I planned to love that woman. What was there to say? Could I be trusted not to screw up? No, and I was completely sorry for that. But I promised Lily that she could trust my love for Lucy because it was the reason for everything I'd been through to get here, and it was the reason for all I would go through to stay here—right here, in Lucy's life. I looked at Lily and tried not to bawl, didn't quite make it. She stepped close to me then with tears brimming in her eyes and just stared at me, hard, as if she was looking for a lie.

Finally she put her arms around me and said, "No wonder Lucy loves you, Mickey. Just please promise me you'll be good to her."

I hugged Lily tighter. "If I'm lucky enough to win your sister, I promise you I'll give her my all."

Having Lily as a sister is kind of like walking through life next to a mirror that reflects back only my best self. I should be so lucky to actually be the girl my sister sees in me. But that's Lily's way. She told me once that when I was born, she thought I was a present that Mom had given her, a new doll she could pour her bottomless love into. And I, apparently, was a willing and obedient toy. Family legend has it that my sister used to gather her stuffed animals and dolls in a circle and place me in the center of them. She would then teach this rag-tag "classroom" the alphabet, simple addition, songs, numbers, and poems. Mom told me when I went to first grade and could already read that I could thank Lily, who had sounded out, with great gusto, her words and sentences, insisting I repeat them. I do remember this, though I must give my early-morning phonics practice with my dad some of the credit as well.

I've always thought Lily and I were a little like twins in our synchrony of souls. She knows me in an eerily unexplainable way. She feels my joy, my anguish. She hopes my hopes, cries my tears, laughs my laughs. And I know her the same way. I see Lily's strength where she insists there is none.

As sisters we'd shared the death of our parents, my dad's sudden and tragic, my mom's drawn out and agonizing. Then Lily had lost the baby she'd poured her life into. And she'd nearly lost me back when cancer almost won the war. Lily hates to talk about any of this, and I know at times she's afraid to breathe. But there's more to Lily than fear and loss. At the bottom of everything wrong, there was always right, too. There was Ron, who had been in our lives forever.

I remember Thanksgiving night just three months after Mom died. We were all in our parents' bedroom. Lily had just gotten home and had plopped down on the bed where I was reading the ads in the huge sale section of the newspaper. Priss was in Dad's chair painting her toenails, and Leno had just started his monologue. "How was your date?" I said, circling a Crock-Pot I thought Jan would like for Christmas.

"I don't know," Lily said, preoccupied. "Ron's been so weird lately. Nervous. I think he's trying to break up with me."

"Ron? Break up with you? Don't make me laugh," I said.

"It wouldn't be the worst thing that could happen," said Priss. "There are other guys, you know."

"I've been out with other guys, Priscilla," Lily snapped.

"Oh, yes, I forgot your year of trial dating."

"Thank goodness that's over," Lily muttered. "But now Ron's so . . ." She looked pained and I was surprised.

"Lily . . ."

"Maybe there's someone at school he wants to get back to." She blew out a big breath and shook her head. "I don't want to think about Ron anymore. What were you guys talking about?"

"Christmas Eve," I said.

"I still think it's time to let the party go." Priss started up again on her side of the argument we'd been having. "Some things just have to end."

"No way," I said. "Too many things have ended; we can't let this one go, too. We have to do it . . . for Mom."

"I have to side with Lu on this, Priss," Lily said absently. "It's tradition."

"Big surprise," Priss said, but she knew we were right.

When my parents moved to Brinley, Mom was pregnant with Priscilla and Dad had just been hired as the number two man on the two-man police force. They didn't know anyone so they decided to open their home and introduce themselves, using the holiday as an excuse. The party had happened every Christmas Eve since, and I couldn't imagine Christmas without it. When it came right down to it, Priscilla didn't really fight us because whether she would admit it or not, Brinley was where she kept her yesterdays. No matter where she went in life, this was where everything had started, right here in the soul of this community.

She gave in with a hearty sigh, and an hour later we'd hashed out all the details. I'd slipped into Mom's bed, and Lily had put her pajamas on and slipped in beside me. Priss was the only one really paying attention to *Perry Mason*. But we all heard it. Downstairs, the front door had opened and closed, and in a few seconds there were footsteps on the stairs. I reached for Lily's hand and locked eyes with Priscilla, who had tensely risen to her feet. She inched to the door and peered out, then relaxed. "What the hell are you doing here?"

Ron Bates walked into the bedroom looking ashen. Lily sat up and put her hands to her face. "What are you doing?" she said from behind them.

"Lil . . . can . . . can I talk to you? Alone?"

"No. No! This isn't happening."

"Lily, please."

"I'm not going anywhere with you, Ronald Bates!" she shouted. "You're going to have to break up with me right here, in front of my sisters."

Priscilla folded her arms, lifted her chin, and stared at Ron, who looked shell-shocked. "We're not going anywhere, you little weasel, so break up and leave. We're trying to watch *Perry Mason* here."

Ron opened his mouth in astonishment. "I don't want to break up with you, you idiot girl! Lily, I want to marry you!"

He might as well have asked me, because my reaction could not have been more bride-to-be-like. I leaped up and started screaming and jumping on Mom's bed while Ron kissed Lily and Priss turned up the TV.

Ron Bates has loved my sister since they were children, and to be loved that purely had to be the secret dream of every woman I knew. Lily had it, and I wanted it. So as I fell further and further into Mickey, I would call my sister and tell her just about everything. She was dutifully curious and patient with my blow-by-blow descriptions of our dates. Since Mickey and I couldn't see each other often—I was still in Boston and he was in Connecticut—when we did get together, he always made it special, which made Lily gush. Whether it was spending the day on Bashan Lake, which I called Mickey's lake because his home was on the shore, or when he surprised me with tickets to the Boston Pops at the Hatch Shell, or the time he told me to meet him at the airport and we flew to New York because he'd scored tickets to *Letterman,* Mickey gave it his all. Once he rented out an entire theater in Colchester for just the two of us to see *As Good as It Gets*. When Jack Nicholson's character was at his most obsessed and Helen Hunt had thrown up her hands, Mickey had leaned over and whispered, "Behold our life." When they ended up together, I repeated the same thing to him.

Lily called us sickeningly romantic, and I guess we were. I just loved being with him. I loved his big productions as much as I loved his quiet moments. I loved that I could keep up with him—we biked and hiked and fished and bowled—he couldn't hit a tennis ball and I couldn't golf, but other than that we were pretty compatible. I loved to look at him looking at me. I loved that he seemed in awe of my feelings for him. I loved the sweet things he did for me. When I couldn't see him because I was pulling an all-weekender with my study group, he always had food delivered—pizza, pastries, subs, sometimes even flowers. I adored his many facets, which he insisted were part of his disorder. But I didn't see disorder; I saw a beautiful tapestry unfolding before me.

"Just be careful, Lu," my sister would say. It was good advice, and she gave it to me every time we talked—nearly every day.

By comparison, I seldom thought to share any of this with Priscilla. Bad as this might sound, it wasn't really that unusual. Priscilla was a different type of sister altogether. She left Brinley—and Lily and me—when she was seventeen, screaming her good riddance to my weeping mother, with whom she'd been fighting for the last year. I was ten at the time and Lily was nearly fourteen, and we were relieved when Priss left. Even then, the two of us knew that we were never leaving Brinley Township. Priscilla headed full throttle into a corporate, cutthroat, succeed-or-die life, determined to run as fast and as far from Brinley as she could. Lily stayed and married the boy next door, and so as far as Priss was concerned, her life was over. The jury was still out on me, since Priscilla refused to believe I would actually return to Brinley to live in the house we all grew up in and teach at the high school we'd all graduated from. But that was, in fact, exactly the plan. She loved us, but we didn't make it easy for her. Priscilla opted for sophistication, which Lily and I were rather sadly indifferent to. And with so little in common, it was hard to imagine Priscilla ever taking much interest in my love life. Except that my love life was Mickey Chandler.

I suppose it was because Priss had seen him first that I never got around to telling her about our relationship. Though they never got together, I was pretty sure the idea of *him and me* would never compute. Still, I imagined that at some point I would take Priss to lunch, spend an hour catching up, then casually mention that I was seeing Mickey. I would get it out there where it belonged, defend it, and offer not much more than that I was falling in love with him.

But I never got around to telling her, and when she found out, it wasn't pretty.

It happened at a fund-raiser in Cambridge, a black-tie event for the Greater Massachusetts Children's Aid Society. Mickey was one of the entertainers. We looked fabulous if I do say so myself—Mickey in tails, me in a wine chiffon gown, floor length and strapless, jewels dangling from my ears catching the light. Mickey was onstage talking about an invention he was working on—a wall made of Velcro you could toss kids onto when you needed to get them out of your hair.

I was laughing at him when Priscilla materialized at my table in a gunmetal-gray dress so tight it looked shrink-wrapped to her curves. Her hair was lighter than the last time I'd seen her, her tan darker, and she looked like she belonged on the cover of a magazine. A naughty magazine. Surprised to see me at such an exclusive function, she swooped in to air-kiss my cheek and to ask what I was doing there. But before I could answer, Priss had made herself at home in Mickey's chair, her attention decidedly on the stage.

"Can you believe this, Lucy? You know who that is, don't you? Was this meant to be or what? Kenny Boatwright can kiss my fabulous butt. And this time, Lucille"—she met my eyes with a teased warning—"you stay out of my way."

"Priss, I need to tell you something."

Mickey had just finished his set to rousing applause and the crowd was on their feet. Priscilla stood up, tugged at the bottom of her dress and tucked herself back into the top of it, then walked away in search of her prey. My boyfriend.

"Priscilla, I really need to tell you—," I shouted, but she shooed me away with a flick of her wrist. Mickey was on his way back to our table, but an appreciative fan had delayed his progress. I held my breath knowing this was a disaster waiting to happen and I could do nothing about it. Mickey didn't stop when he saw Priscilla. He just walked on past her to me and planted a quick kiss on my lips. The crowd was still clapping and Mickey waved in gratitude.

Priscilla was embarrassed; I could see it on her face. Her eyes flashed humiliation, hurt, and annoyance, but whether it was from Mickey's affront or his being with me, I couldn't tell. I dropped Mickey's hand and hurried over to her. I know she would have preferred to walk away and forget she'd ever seen us, but I caught her arm before she could do that. "Priscilla . . ."

Mickey was suddenly at my side, confused. "Hey . . ."

"Mickey, you remember my sister," I said, squeezing his hand like a vise to convey the importance of his answer.

But his blank look delivered the final blow to Priss's porcelain ego. Priscilla nodded, incensed. "Nice to see you again, Mickey," she said behind a stiff smile. "We met at Lucy's birthday party last year."

If this reminder sparked anything beyond what he'd already displayed, Mickey's expression didn't say so, but he covered with "Of course. How are you?"

"I'm fine. And you're still very funny." Priscilla then turned and walked away without a word to me.

"That's your sister?"

"Yes! Surely you remember Priscilla."

"Priscilla? Was she always that blond?"

"What?"

"I'm so sorry, Lu. She doesn't look like the girl from your party. I'm sorry. I'm so stupid. I hurt her feelings, didn't I? What can I do?"

I looked at Mickey and let go of all my angst when I saw the earnest expression on his face. He was sorry he'd hurt my sister. He didn't make fun of her, which he could have done in a dozen ways. He didn't try to defend himself for his unintentional rudeness. He just owned it with an integrity Priscilla would never have displayed if the tables were turned. I smiled up at him. "This is why I like you, you know." I kissed him and he looked confused. He had no inkling what I was talking about.

The next day, I finally put my lunch plan into play, even though it was way too late for it to turn out the way I'd hoped. I was sitting in Maggiano's and Priss was forty-five minutes late. I'd eaten the rolls and was working on my third iced tea, but I knew she'd eventually turn up. She'd told me she might be late, which was Priscilla-speak for *I'll be there when I feel like it*.

I was halfway through my chicken Caesar when she finally arrived. She eyed my plate as she took off her jacket and smoothed her skirt. "Nice, Lucy."

I looked at my watch. "Backatcha, Priss."

She ordered a green salad, dressing on the side, and ice water. When the waiter walked away, she sat back, folded her arms, and hardened her jaw at me.

I sighed. "Would you please just get over yourself?"

"I don't know what you're talking about."

"Yes, you do."

"I'm busy, Lucy. Why did you want to talk to me?"

I pushed my lunch aside and leaned over. "I should have done this before, and I'm sorry, Priss. But, about the other night . . ."

"What about it?"

"Well, I'm with Mickey Chandler. I've been seeing him for a few months now. I think I'm in love with him, and if he asked me today, I would probably marry him." When her expression did not change, I had no choice but to plow on. "I know you scoped him out for your-self . . . and it was kind of awkward last night, and I'm sorry. But . . . anyway, that's what's going on, and I have important things to tell you, so again, please, can we get past this?"

Priscilla's eyes bore into mine. "First of all, Lucille . . . what makes you think I care?"

I leaned back in my seat and sighed.

"Second of all . . . congratulations."

"Thank you, Priss," I said with caution.

Her salad arrived, and as she picked up her fork, she continued, "For the record, after I got a good look at him the other night, I found I was not even remotely interested."

"Well, that's great. That'll make things easier, right?"

"I suppose." She shrugged as she popped a tomato into her mouth. "So what important things do you have to tell me about the two of you?"

This was the part I was dreading, but there was no way around it. I cleared my throat. "Have you ever heard of bipolar disorder?"

"Yes. It's a mental illness. Why?"

"Well . . . I thought you should know that Mickey's been diag-nosed with it."

She stopped chewing and put her fork down, but she didn't say anything for so long that I felt compelled to fill up the silence. I told her about Mickey's regular therapy and what the medication did for his mood. I told her how productive he was when he was manic. But I didn't say anything about his depressions or past suicidal thoughts. Priscilla heard me out and did not interrupt, but when I was finished she stared at me for a full minute before responding. I should have known what was coming.

"Are you really that desperate?"

"What?"

"I mean it, Lucy. Are you? That desperate? Because I'm sure, if you tried, you could attract a competent, intact man. Why would you even consider this?"

I glared at her. "Stop it, Priscilla. I mean it. This is my choice and my relationship."

"Well, honey, you need to find another relationship. You don't need this one." Her tone wasn't particularly unkind but the words stung.

I shook my head.

"Think about what you're doing, Lucy. And figure out a way to end it. You can do better than this. You're worth more than this."

I looked hard at my sister. "I think I'm done here." I tossed my napkin on the table. "I don't have to answer to you for what I'm doing, and you're not allowed to criticize me for it."

"Excuse me?" my sister said, looking honestly surprised.

"I mean it, Priss. This might be a deal-breaker between us. You have to accept this and be nice or we're done. You've got your career, you're not around, so it won't be much of a leap if that's how you want it. But if you want a relationship with me, you have to accept my life, and that includes Mickey." I placed a twenty on the table and stood up.

"Where do you think you're going? We're not done here."

"I've said everything I came to say. I'm leaving so you can think hard about your next move." I walked out then, more angry than I wanted to be.

Late that night, Priscilla showed up at my apartment. I'd already gone to bed, and though she had doctored her face, I could tell she was exhausted. She walked in wearing the same suit she'd had on at lunch, still looking fairly crisp except for her blouse, which was untucked.

"Have you been working? It's two in the morning."

"Yes, I've been working," she barked. "That's what I do, remember?"

"Do you want to come in?"

She looked hard at me and her tears betrayed her. "Dammit!" she hissed.

"Do you want to sit down?"

"No, I don't want to sit down!"

"Priss, why are you here?"

My sister brought a hand to her forehead and sighed. "I'm here because . . . because I want us to be okay."

"What?"

"You heard me. I want us to be okay, and if I have to be sorry, then I'm sorry, and if I have to be quiet about Mickey, then, well, I'll do my best."

"Really?"

"Don't be so shocked," she snapped. "I'm not the heartless bitch you think I am."

I walked over and put my arms around her. "Oh, Priss. Yes, you are. But I love you anyway."

She laughed a strangled little laugh and then we were both crying.

When we finally pushed away from each other, Priscilla's face was a disaster. "Do you want a drink? Have you had dinner?"

"I'm fine. I'm going home to shower. I have to be back at five."

"You're kidding."

She shrugged. "Anyway, I just wanted to tell you he seems nice."

"Who?"

"Your boyfriend. He sent me two dozen roses. Fire and Ice."

"Mickey. Mickey sent you roses?"

"You really didn't know? You didn't put him up to it?"

"No. But I might have if I'd thought of it."

"Huh. Then I like him better than I thought I would." Priss held a small card out to me, but pulled it back quickly. "Just for the record, Lucy, I will always be concerned about you being with a crazy person. And I don't think concern should be a deal-breaker."

"Don't start, Priscilla. We just had a moment."

She handed me the card. "Anyway, it's hard to believe he's all *that* crazy."

I opened the note and recognized Mickey's handwriting.

Dear Priscilla,
   I'd like to apologize for not recognizing you the other night.

I'm very embarrassed. But honestly, the reason I didn't recognize you is that you are even more beautiful than when we met last year. You looked familiar, but as you walked away, I thought Lucy had introduced me to another sister, not one I had met before.

I love your sister. That being the case, we may cross paths again and I wanted to repair any hurt feelings I may have caused before we do.

Again, my sincere apology.
Michael Chandler

Priscilla took the card from me and kissed my cheek. "Please be careful," she said as she walked out.

eight

I said good-bye to the gals at the nurses' station, and Peony buzzed me out of the security doors. "You be good now, Michael," she said. I saluted her. I've been hospitalized five times during my marriage and four times before that; Peony knows I'll do my best.

I like to walk home from Edgemont. It's not far and I like turning my back on the hospital. It's symbolic. I've come here in various stages of mental disruption. I've been terrified, and I've been too far gone to be terrified. I've been so lethargic I couldn't stand, and I've been so wired I couldn't sit. They always take good care of me, but I'm still a little frightened at the thought of being here.

I remember one time when I was little, my mother had been in the hospital for weeks—it seemed like weeks—and we'd gone with Dad to pick her up. He wouldn't let us go in, so we waited in the car. David was reading a comic book and I was watching the front entrance for my parents. "You know they fried her brain, don't ya?" David said to me.

"What does that mean?"

"Electric shock. They sizzled her. She probably won't

remember our names . . . so, you know, don't expect much."

David was five years older than me and I believed whatever he told me. But he was wrong that time. Mom was walking a little bit funny, like she was dizzy and Dad was helping her, but when she saw us, she cried. She crawled right in the backseat and hugged us and kissed us and cried her eyes out. She knew our names.

She didn't recognize our house, but she knew our names. . . .

I woke up early feeling incredibly optimistic, and as soon as I realized this, I tried to rein it in. I had serious business to attend to: Mickey was coming home. Still, it was a beautiful day and wouldn't it be wonderful to forget everything and just go sailing? I called Lily to see if she and Ron had made plans to use the boat. Lily said she was having a sale at Ghosts that promised to keep her busy all weekend, so it was all mine.

She then asked if I'd seen Priscilla. I hadn't and suddenly thought it *was* a bit odd that my sister hadn't been in touch since the memorial service. "Well, if you see her," I said to Lily, "tell her I've gone sailing."

"Have fun," Lily said, but before I could hang up, she surprised me with another question. "Have you heard from Charlotte?"

"Why?" I asked, mentally clamoring for a fib.

"I just wondered if your tests came back."

"Oh, not yet. But it should be anytime. I'm not one bit worried."

"Well, I guess I won't worry either, then."

"Good girl. Have a good sale."

"You have a good sail, too." She giggled.

Just as I hung up, I heard the train whistle and knew Mickey would be home any minute. He always walked home from Edgemont, which is only a few blocks from our home. For Mickey, there's great significance in walking away a free man. A new man.

I was waiting on the porch when he came around the corner in his jeans and white T-shirt, his backpack slung over one shoulder. Looking at my husband's hard body and easy smile, one would never guess what demons play poker under his skin.

He saw me and grinned, and I could not contain myself. I ran across the street in my bare feet and jumped into his big arms, wrapping my legs wantonly around his waist. He felt absolutely delicious. He kissed me hard, and all was right with the world.

I can gauge the degree of my husband's mental health from the way he kisses me. When he's manic, he's rough—very rough—which isn't always a bad thing. I just know he's percolating. When he's truly depressed, his lips have virtually no life, initially. There's no elasticity, no passion—but then his kisses turn scarily desperate. When he's completely mad, filled with delusions, he doesn't even taste right. But, when the stars are aligning, like right now, the two of us are cosmic perfection, our lips, teeth, and tongues playing raspy music in the back of our throats.

Mickey finished kissing me with a bunch of small breakaway kisses that traveled down my jaw and onto my neck. Just when I would have pulled down my panties, he set me down and laughed. "I missed you, baby."

"Me, too," I said, a little breathless. I picked up his backpack and wrapped his arm around me and we walked across the street. "How 'bout we go sailing and never come home," I said dreamily.

"Is this because I screwed up the cruise?"

I laughed, having forgotten completely about the cruise. "Of course."

"Sounds good to me."

We packed the cooler with ice and drinks and ham sandwiches and threw a change of clothes into a leather tote, just in case we decided to stay overnight. While we worked, we chattered about everything that had happened while he was hospitalized: Celia's memorial service, Peony Litman, the phone bill, the sale at Lily's store. I knew I was avoiding the conversation we had to have, but there was anticipation, too. I was excited to tell Mickey our news even as my *rational* self kept the hard facts in my field of vision.

In the meantime, I could hardly stop staring at my husband. Every time he did something normal, such as look through the bills or take a glass from the dishwasher and fill it with milk or wink at me when he caught me staring, I just felt this crazy tingle that after all this time should probably be gone. But it wasn't gone. Far from it.

"I have a present for you, Lu. Do you want it now?"

"Absolutely."

"Close your eyes."

I heard the zipper from his backpack and a distinct rustling of paper. Then I felt his lips soft on my forehead. "Okay, you can open them."

In the palm of his hand stood a birdhouse, painted in the same muted colors as our home—sage green with coral accents. I laughed because we have a small collection of these little projects. And each one represents yet another storm that didn't destroy us and is therefore very meaningful. The inside of this one was meticulously made to mirror in miniature the room we were standing in: overstuffed red furniture, a massive wall of books, two floor-to-ceiling windows shuttered in wood grain. I pulled Mickey to me and kissed him with completely impure intent.

This is my favorite time—this fresh newness that comes right after a hospital stay. I'm not so foolish as to imagine he's fixed, but what being in the hospital does is change the direction; it gets his feet pointed back the right way. Mickey calls it a do-over. We just bag up everything that led to that particular breaking point and toss it away. Gleason taught us to do that. He taught us that no good can come from wishing things were different. He says no good comes from blaming or resenting what is clearly worthy of both. So, it's a do-over, a clean slate, bright with promise and renewed commitment. And we always start over by making love, which I knew would be the first matter of business once we cleared the marina.

We were at the intersection of Foster Pier and Main, waiting for the red light to turn green, when I spotted Trent Rosenberg's Jeep Cherokee. Mickey saw it at the same time. "Isn't that your sister with Trent?"

They were directly across from us, waiting to go through the intersection in the opposite direction and having what looked like an intense conversation. When the light changed, they sailed past us, having apparently never seen us. I looked at Mickey, who said, "Poor Shannon."

I stupidly hoped when I hadn't heard from Priss after the memorial that she'd gone back to Hartford. Seeing her now with Trent just made me sad. What was Priscilla thinking? Shannon Rosenberg was pregnant with Trent's third child. I was glad to be leaving town. I didn't want to think about what my sister was doing.

It was just past one when we got to the harbor. Since it was Friday, more than a few tourists had gotten a jump on the weekend, so it took us a minute to find a parking place. Casey Noonan, the harbor attendant, helped us with our gear, and while he and Mickey did our safety check, I went belowdecks and discovered where Priss had spent the night. My sister had left the little cabin rumpled. The bed was unmade and an empty wine bottle and food wrappers were in the trash. An overnight bag and cosmetics were on the tiny counter.

That's Priscilla for you. Just waltzes into town and takes over the boat without checking with anyone. No phone call, no conversation, she just moves right in! It looked as if when she was through with whatever she was doing, she planned to come back. Well, too bad! I stripped the bed and scooped her things back into the bag, then asked Casey to make sure Priss got it when she came back.

He laughed. "Oh, she'll be a hellcat when she sees you took the boat."

"She might. You can tell her I'm sorry, if you want. You could say a little discussion would have avoided this whole thing." I laughed. "Tell her whatever you want, Casey. We're going sailing."

"Oh, sure, I'll tell her."

"Are you just about ready?" I said to Mickey with a little too much edge. "I want to get out of here."

"Don't be barking at *me*, Lucille. I think we should stick around. Wait for your sister and the fireworks. It'll be fun."

I was tickled by Mickey's sarcasm, but not enough to stay and risk an ugly confrontation with my big sister. We filed our route, then eased out of the slip. When we had completely cleared the harbor with no sign of Priscilla, I breathed a big sigh of relief. I don't mind a good argument with Priss, I just wasn't in the mood today—not on this absolutely perfect, cloudless day.

The air was so clean and soft and the water was so blue that thoughts of Priscilla simply evaporated. I drank in every delicious sensation as we made our way up the Connecticut, Mickey at the helm, his hair blown back.

As we headed lazily toward Hollis Cove, our cares melted away. In this isolated bubble of time, we were just two absolutely normal people: I was pregnant with a dark-haired daughter who had enormous eyes, and my husband was a regular guy whose recalibrated synapses were firing at regular-guy intervals. I hugged Mickey from behind as he steered us upriver. Life was good.

It was just dusk when we sailed into the marina at Hollis Cove. We'd made love, eaten the sandwiches, and made love again. Now I was just sitting on the bow of our boat, watching the stars come out, the night air warm and soft against my skin. Mickey dropped anchor and slid back beside me. I leaned into him and he wrapped me in his arms, his hands slipping beneath my shirt. "I love you, Lu," he whispered, making my eyes sting. I knew he loved me. If I didn't know anything else, I knew that.

I watched a trio of blue herons on the shore, their sleek, graceful, efficient beaks taking care of the business of dinner. Then, pulling Mickey's face into my neck, I said, "I have something to tell you."

He said what he always says to statements like this. "Is it good or bad?"

"I'm not sure."

"Talk to me, Lucille."

I squirmed around to face him, to see his eyes. I knew I could see in Mickey's eyes how sound he was. I decided, all things considered, that I couldn't have chosen a better moment.

"Baby, I'm pregnant."

Mickey laughed, quick and easy. "Right."

"I am, Mic. I'm pregnant."

Mickey's lips parted just a little. "What?"

"I'm pregnant." We were so close, I could almost see those two little words being metabolized in his pupils.

"I . . . I don't understand."

I leaned up and pulled my T-shirt down over my breasts and looked at my husband. "I don't understand it either, Mic. Charlotte says she doesn't know how, exactly, but"—I shrugged—"I'm pregnant." I held my breath waiting for him to fully comprehend my words and react.

Finally he said, "You're sure?"

I nodded.

"What do we do?"

"I don't know."

"A baby? Really?"

I nodded. I couldn't tell what he was thinking, and it was making me tense. Slowly he sat up, his eyes never veering off mine. He stared at me for a long time, then he cupped my face with his big hands and shook his head as if he didn't have the words.

"Are you okay?" I said.

Still shaking his head, he asked, "Are you?"

"I don't know."

"Lucy, I can't believe it." His voice was barely a whisper.

"Me neither."

"Oh, Lu."

"I know."

"A baby. A baby. I'm not sure I've ever really imagined a baby.

Look at me. I just don't know what to do with this." He lifted my hand to his chest. His heartbeat was a palpable thud.

"I know."

Pure emotion was in his eyes when he slowly started kissing me all over my face. "This isn't necessarily a bad thing, is it?"

For a moment I was swept away by his affection, but his words were stones. "Of course it's bad. But it's wonderful, too. What are we going to do?"

"Looks like we're having a baby."

"We are? Mickey, stop kissing me." I pulled away from him. "We have to think about this. We have to get serious. Remember our agreement, our contract? Our decision *not* to procreate? We're unfit, remember? How can we have this baby?"

"Doesn't look like we have a choice, Lucille."

"Mickey . . ."

"No." He shook his head. "That's not us."

I slumped. "I know, but, Mickey, how can we do this?"

"How can we not?" But then his own question somehow made supreme sense to him. "How can we not, Lucy? Good or bad, right or wrong, this is our baby. It already *is*. And everything will be fine. We'll make it fine."

"Mickey, stop it! It's never going to be that easy. Nothing's really changed. Look where you've been this week. And me. I just had my physical. My lab work isn't even back yet—I know everything is fine, but this is the blade we live under. There are reasons we were never going to do this."

"Why didn't you tell me you went to the doctor?"

"I'm telling you now."

Mickey looked at me skeptically.

"Honey, it was just my regular checkup. You were in the hospital. I didn't want you to worry. I'm telling you now, everything I know. I'm pregnant and a little tense about it, because this is us we're talking about here."

Mickey nodded. "I get that, Lucy. This *is* us. And you're right. It's never going to be fine, *all the time*. But somehow it's worked so far."

"Mickey . . ."

"Shhhh. We did what we did to prevent this. But here it is anyway. Doesn't that tell you something?"

"What? What does it tell me?"

"That this baby was meant to be."

"Mickey."

"I'm serious, Lu. This baby, our baby, is *supposed* to be. I just don't believe after all this time it's an accident."

Infuriatingly, Mickey was winning me over. But then, I so wanted to be won over.

"C'mere," he said softly, pulling me to him. He wrapped his arms around me and held me for a long, long time. The deceptively strong beat of his heart lulled me into believing in miracles, and I started feeling like I had when I first married him: like we *could* make this happen. Mickey was right. Wasn't he? We'd made it for nearly eleven years. Obviously we were stronger than I'd given us credit for. And wasn't *the determined little swimmer* who'd made it through the knot further evidence of our genetic fortitude? Well, of course it was.

I couldn't think about the downside anymore. It was out, this awesome news, hanging beautifully and frighteningly between us. I was too excited to fight it. And Mickey was there looming over me with his awestruck smile and contagious optimism. We were pregnant, and for the time being that's all I wanted to think about.

Before I knew it, it was dark and Mickey and I were still huddled under a blanket on the bow making plans to transform the junk room into a nursery. I had never seen my husband so moved, so humble. Long after I was sure he had fallen asleep, I turned to find him staring at the stars, his eyes glistening. When he caught me watching him, he pulled me closer. We finally fell asleep under those almost perfectly aligned stars, holding tight to one another as we swayed to the mood of the river. By the next morning we were full and equal participants in the fantasy that life had handed us. Right or wrong, it seemed we were having this baby.

Right there in Hollis Cove, anchored to hope, we ignored the statistics. We ignored our history. And we ignored logic.

Well, it's not like we hadn't done that before.

nine

Theoretically, being mad, it's hard to be driven mad . . .
but apparently not impossible. I say this because I did not
know what was happening to me when I was with Lucy. I'd
known a lot of women, but I didn't understand the power
this girl had over me almost from the moment I met her.
I used to wonder how falling in love—real love—worked
for people who didn't have to worry about madness. They
probably didn't have to try as hard as humanly possible not
to fall into it in the first place, or feel like they had to reject
it because it couldn't be trusted, or have to imagine the
scalding rejection that would come when the full extent of
the madness was revealed. Despite all this, I was a goner by
the end of our first date and it terrified me . . . for her. When
we started peeling back our layers, I couldn't quite believe
she wasn't repelled by me. I'd never opened myself up to
that much scrutiny, I'd never wanted to. But with Lucy I
found I could not resist her desire to see inside me.

Her fearlessness scared me a little. But then maybe
fearlessness is what happened to a person when the worst
things that could happen, actually did. Whatever Lucy
went through with the loss of her parents, it left a deep

well of something extraordinary. But could I trust it?
Could she?

Lucy honestly believed she could deal with anything as
long as she knew what to expect. She liked all the unseemly
possibilities piled on the table where she could survey the
mess and prepare a strategy. What she didn't know was
with a guy like me, the pile was a shifting landscape, sub-
ject to the elements and hard to predict. I tried to warn her.

I was falling in love with her, but it seemed like a bad
idea. The thought of having Lucy, hurting her, scaring
her, losing her—all of it overwhelmed my psyche. I tried
to save her from a life with me—a few times. But she
never really blinked.

Not even when she should have.

The year I fell in love with Mickey was not the typical romance most
girls fantasize about. In the throes of it, I would sometimes step back
and try to see myself analytically. Did I have some hidden personality
quirk that made me see Mickey as a project? Was I using him to fill
a dark place in myself? I was loath to think these things because my
feelings for him were growing so strong.

All I knew for sure was that I was falling hard for a man who could
tell on his eleventh birthday that he was different from the rest of the
world. A man who'd grown up frightened of the way his mind worked.
I was falling for a man who was doing everything he could to make
me understand how immortal he sometimes felt, how expansive and
entitled and unapologetic he could be.

Sometimes it scared me. But then Mickey would give me an out.
One night he just held my face and forced me to look at him. "It's okay
to doubt this, Lucy. I'm a lot to take on, and you have to be sure."

The permission he gave me only intensified my feelings for him.

"We can't really help how we feel," he went on. "If you're scared, you get to be scared. And you get to decide what to do about that. I see you, Lucy. I see who you are. You're strong and smart and you can handle whatever life throws at you, as long as you can see it coming."

I felt stripped under Mickey's gaze because he was not wrong.

"I want you to take some time. Let all this uncertainty about me, about us, let it settle." Mickey kissed my nose, then he walked out.

I took a day to see what it would feel like to not see him or talk to him or touch him, and I didn't like it. I didn't like it at all. He was right; I was pretty okay with whatever was going to happen as long as I had some lead time. Being true to that, I decided that perhaps growing attached to a mentally ill man called for a different kind of falling-in-love protocol. I wanted to understand Mickey's illness; I wanted to see it from a clinical perspective. So, I called him and asked if I could meet his psychiatrist, and he seemed almost relieved that I'd suggested it.

I liked Gleason Webb immediately. A round man, balding and unassuming, warm and appreciative, he took my hand in both of his. "This is a rare pleasure, Lucy. I feel like I already know you."

When I told him why I was there, he said that I was a smart girl to look under this rock. I laughed, but I knew he was serious, and after that first meeting, we got to work. In fact, after that, most of my dates with Mickey started out in Gleason's office.

Dr. Webb thought it was imperative that I understand the black depressions that could completely immobilize Mickey. So he chronicled Mickey's descents to this dark hell where he could not move, could barely breathe, and did not care if he lived. Dr. Webb made sure I understood how hypomania could quickly lead to a psychotic break. Gleason gave me pharmacological handbooks so I could gain a working knowledge of Mickey's medications. Mickey gave me journal entries he'd written when he was manic so I could comprehend his inability to rein himself in when he was spinning off the planet.

He was determined to make me understand his disorder. He explained that his thoughts sometimes moved so fast, he actually perceived himself as outrunning whatever the next moment held. He described his psychotic need to race past the day, determined to get so far ahead of it that he could actually look back on it and adjust it to his own specifications.

During these therapeutic *dates,* Mickey was like a laid-back professor who expounded on his illness in the sympathetic third person—completely rational, a gifted orator. He made no excuse for who—or what—he was, and I was absolutely crazy in love with the man explaining the man. But of course it was the man being explained that I needed to be sure of. I shared this thought with Gleason privately, and his advice to me was to do my best to merge Mickey's many nuances into a single entity. He had me diagram all of Mickey's unequal parts, everything from his magnetism to his charm to his cruelty, the neediness that came with his depressions, the irrational self-confidence that was part of the mania, the tenderness and vulnerability. I told Lily at the time that when I looked at all these components, it felt as if I were dating a fraternity.

As his life unfolded before me, Mickey could not comprehend my ability to love him. He backed away from me more than once in an effort to save me. One time he did it for a hellish ten days. I was in the last stretch of finals week with graduation right around the corner, and Mickey's timing made me furious. My life was on track, I was in love, I was graduating, I was moving home and getting ready to start a new job teaching summer school. Maybe it was everything else I had going on, but my heart couldn't take his withdrawal, and our conversation quickly turned into a screaming match on my front porch.

He stood there vomiting up what sounded like a speech he'd been rehearsing for weeks. "Lucy," he'd shouted. "Can you even begin to understand what it's like to hide the fact that you're mad from the world? Can you imagine a man who's taught himself to command his weirdness? I do that all the time. I wear a mask. I'm insane behind it, but I know how to look like a fully functional person to the world. I've trained myself not to yell out loud at inappropriate times by promising myself I can do it later. I know how to command my irritability. I morph it into something socially acceptable by promising myself that I can unleash it later. Later, when I'm alone!

"But don't you see, Lucy? I'll never be alone if we do this. You'll be there. You'll be there when I can't keep it in anymore, and I'll scare you and you'll leave."

"I won't leave."

"You don't know that. You don't know me!" He was yelling, and I tried to put my arms around him, but he backed away and started up again. "Lucy, you're not hearing me. I know how to fake it! I know how to look completely sane when I have to. But I can't keep that up for very long. I have to let it out when I'm by myself."

"So what? You'd rather be by yourself than deal with me?"

I saw my question had stung him, but he was on a roll. "Yes. Yes, dammit, I think that's what I want!"

I nodded, my head aching, tears stinging my eyes. "I'm in love with you. And you standing here being an ass doesn't change that. But you need to decide. It's your life that you keep trying to push me out of, so the decision is yours. There's nothing else I can do to prove myself. If who I am is not good enough, and you really want to be alone, then I guess you gotta do what you gotta do."

Mickey looked as if I'd slapped him, but I was so tired and so mad I didn't know what else to try.

"Go home, Mickey. Go home and be alone and be nuts if that's what you need to do."

"Lucy . . ."

I looked at him and did my best not to cry. I didn't quite make it, but I lifted my chin and looked him square in the eye. "Mickey, I really think everyone should be important enough to just one other person on this freaking planet to be fought for. Even me. And nobody's fighting for me. So I'm done." I walked in and shut the door, the pounding of my heart a hammer in my head. I shoved my piles of notes off the table and threw my textbook against the wall, spilling my Coke. I looked at the mess, thought of the exam at seven thirty in the morning that I was not prepared for, and started to cry in earnest. My head was throbbing. I took three Excedrin PM and went to bed.

Somehow I got through that next week. I passed my last final, picked up my cap and gown and honors ropes, made sure my sisters knew what time to be in their seats the next morning, and then, because I was moving back to Brinley, I set to work packing boxes. Anytime Mickey crossed my mind, I simply turned up the radio. He must have been serious because I had not heard from him.

I had to be at the Matthews Arena and lined up by nine thirty to be ready to march in at ten, and it took everything I had to drag myself there. I'd worked hard and I should have been excited. I was graduating magna cum laude. This was the period at the end of my formal education, and it should have been thrilling, to file into that giant gymnasium to "Pomp and Circumstance." But I just wanted it over. The arena was massive, but I still had this notion that I could scan the packed-to-capacity seats and find my family. Didn't happen.

The addresses were blissfully short, and before I knew it, we were graduating. It seemed to take forever to get to my row, but finally I was on my feet. For the most part the crowd had been respectful—a few exuberant whoops, a few cowbells, but mostly just shouts and applause from dignified well-wishers when familial pride got the best of them. Finally, it was my turn. Lucy Houston. I took one step and heard my sisters screaming and above their noise a man shouting, *"I love you, Lucy."*

I stopped, stunned, and turned in the direction of the voice, but couldn't see where it had come from. I'd stood there long enough to disrupt things, and the next graduate had to propel me forward. I accepted my diploma cover thinking I'd imagined it. But then as my dean was hugging me I heard it again, louder. *"I LOVE YOU, LUCY."*

The dignified head of the department smiled and said, "Someone very loud and obnoxious loves you, Miss Houston. Good for you."

Somehow I got back to my seat, where I planted myself and looked straight ahead. I knew he was watching me—I could feel it—and all the emotions I'd tried to keep at bay since he walked away broke loose inside me. I ventured a look a few times in the direction he'd shouted from, but I couldn't see him. I don't know how I got through the rest of the ceremony. When it was over, I just sat there, numb and a little afraid of what was happening. Lily found me and wrapped her skinny arms around my neck. "I'm so happy for you."

"Thanks, I can't believe I made it."

She laughed. "Not that. I'm *happy* for you. He's wonderful."

I started to cry all the tears I'd refused to cry since our fight. "What's happening? What do you mean?"

Then Mickey was there and I was in his arms and he was kissing me and I was crying and Ron was taking pictures and Priscilla was shaking her head, trying not to look concerned.

We got engaged to be engaged that afternoon at lunch with my sisters and Ron. Mickey asked me between the salad and the main course and told me wrapping a string from my tassel around my finger was just a place-keeper until I picked out the real thing. Mickey said I couldn't really say no since my family had already given us their blessing, something he had apparently obtained that morning in the overflow parking lot.

Mickey told me later that falling in love with me wasn't just his destiny, it was his crusade. He had taken to heart what I'd said about being fought for and spent the last ten days fighting his demons for me. In the end, he'd won. I was pretty sure it didn't get better than that. And after sifting through the minutiae of his strangeness, and identifying all his known parts, I simply couldn't find a good enough reason not to love him. We pledged our imperfect selves to each other and vowed to form something bigger than either of us alone, utterly certain we were capable of our dreams.

We made it official the next week and ordered matching silver bands. I moved home and started my new job teaching history to summer school students. I was in love and life was fabulous. I thought I knew all there was to know about Mickey and that anything I'd missed couldn't possibly be that important. But I soon learned that knowing and experiencing are two very different things. Despite everything I thought I knew, I had still fashioned the man I was marrying from my own selective notions. Not until a few months later was I forced to see his condition in its shattered totality.

On a Saturday in early June, we'd made plans to go sailing with Ron and Lily. My sisters and I had inherited my father's most prized possession: a thirty-three-foot Catalina cruiser—*The Rose of Sharon*—named for my mom. We'd had her restored a few years after Mom died, but it pretty much fell on Ron to keep her sail-ready. Now Mickey would help him.

Mickey had been working like a madman on his house, and because he'd had to let his manager go, he was pulling the swing shift at Colby's, which meant he usually worked until after two in the morning. I had to be in the classroom by eight, so we pretty much lived for the weekends. We did manage to grab dinner together most nights, and we never missed an appointment with Gleason. Except for that week, when Mickey canceled it. He was swamped, trying to finish the staircase at his house for a showing the next Tuesday, but he was on schedule to finish up in time to go sailing. Besides, he assured me, he was completely in love and all was well in his world. I giggled and didn't think anything of it.

I should have.

I was home putting groceries away when he called me five times in less than an hour. First just to tell me he loved me—he sounded out of breath. Then to ask me where the paintbrushes were—I had no idea. Then to laugh and tell me he forgot why he called. He rang back a minute later to remind me again that he still couldn't find his shorts. Again? He hadn't mentioned it once. The last time he called was to rather desperately demand that I quit calling him.

"Lucy, I'm serious. I'm trying to finish this up, what are you trying to do to me?"

"Mickey . . . you called me," I said, my heart skipping a beat.

"What? Oh, sorry. No. No."

"Mickey? Honey?" He didn't answer me. Instead he dropped the phone, and I could hear him groaning. Or maybe laughing. Either way, he sounded hysterical.

"Mickey!" I shouted. I threw the milk in the fridge and drove straight over to make sure he was okay.

When I was in the third grade, we had a fire that burned down the school. We'd been trained with a fire drill every month and we knew what to do, but we never imagined it would actually happen. That was how this felt to me, as if everything I had learned to this point had been a kind of drill for what was never supposed to happen.

East Haddam was twenty minutes away but I was determined to make it in ten. I thought I was pretty calm until I hit Smith Road and realized I was flying at sixty-six miles an hour in a thirty-five-mile zone. I was shaking, but I forced myself to slow down. Mickey's house was on the shore of Bashan Lake. He'd bought it from his grandmother when he was twenty-five so she could move into an assisted-living center. Naturally she gave him a good deal, and that good deal pretty much cost him his relationship with his brother. He told me once when we were stripping the wallpaper in the guest bedroom that he planned to surprise David with half the equity when it finally sold. But the massive colonial was a never-ending project. Especially the foyer and the grand staircase Mickey had meticulously restored down to its original mahogany.

The house had just come into sight when I saw the red and blue flashing in my rearview mirror. I slapped the steering wheel but kept driving. I swear I would have stopped if anyone had been on the road, but there was not a soul and I had to get to Mickey, so I gunned it instead and prayed the cops would let me by. I turned down the gravel drive and slid to a stop, then ran around to the back door. It was wide-open, but Mickey was nowhere to be seen.

"Mickey?" He was not in the mudroom. "Mickey!" He was not in the kitchen either, but he'd obviously been there because it was an absolute mess. Several pages of crooked scrawl were scattered on the table and the floor. I gathered them up when I saw that it was a letter to me.

Then I heard him. "Where are you? Mic?" I shouted as I stuffed the pages into my back pocket. I hurried down the hall to the foyer, where he'd been working for weeks on the staircase. When I rounded the corner, I wanted to cry and scream and wake up from what I was sure was a nightmare in primary colors. The beautiful floor that last week had carefully been papered to protect it was exposed and splattered with blue paint. Orange paint had seemingly been thrown against the wall and left to pool at the baseboard. Vivid footprints were on the wooden stairs Mickey had been oiling to a high sheen, and several balusters were glopped with a tragic combination of several colors.

Near the top of the staircase was Mickey, naked and covered in paint.

I gasped. "What are you doing?"

He stood quickly and knocked over a can of yellow paint, and I watched in numbed fascination as it trickled down the stairs in a slow stream toward me. Mickey's laughter brought me back, but it wasn't a laugh that I'd ever heard before.

"You're early! Come in. Are you from the Realtor's office? I told them three, but, well . . ." He introduced his project with a flourish. "You get the idea. I think when you walk into a house it should make a statement, don't you? Did you bring juice by any chance? I need fuel. Grape juice is a great antioxidant. I saw it on the health channel. They delivered a two-headed baby on that damn show. I swear. You alone or did you bring your office?"

"Mickey, it's me. Lucy."

"Lucy? That's my girlfriend's name. Shit, am I bleeding?" He seemed to notice for the first time that he was covered in what he presumed to be blood, and he started to dance around at the top of the stairs trying to find its source on his naked body. I ran across the foyer, doing my best to avoid the slippery puddles.

"Mickey! Honey, it's okay. It's not blood. Mickey, can you hear me?" He was now slapping his face with both hands, and I was afraid he would slip in the mess and fall down the stairs. When I got close to him, I tried to take his hand, but it slid out of my grasp. "What's happening? No, no. No!" he sang in breathless and escalating panic. "What is this stuff?"

"Mickey! Honey!" I didn't know what to do. I couldn't get his attention, and I was standing right there screaming at him. I ran into the bathroom and grabbed a towel, then threw it over his shoulders and wrapped my arms around him. "Mickey? Mickey! Look at me, baby!"

He was shaking and grunting like an animal. I held him as tightly as I could, but he was stronger than I was, and whatever he was afraid of made him that much more of a force.

I heard footsteps downstairs and wondered if Mickey had actually called a Realtor. But it was a police officer with his hand on his gun. Drawing it, he said, "I'll need you two to come on down here."

That seemed to stop Mickey for a second. As for me, I couldn't put the moment in context. But then I remembered the flashing lights and speeding faster away from apparently this very officer.

"Thank God!" Mickey boomed. "Look at me! I'm bleeding like a stuck pig. I've been shot, and in my head I imagined I needed a cop and here you are. What are you doing here? Don't you know to knock? You can't just break in here with your little gun and your little badge. I got rights! I got a right hand and a right foot. You probably do, too!"

"Mickey, be quiet!"

Mickey jerked around to me and flung off the towel. "Who the hell are you, woman! Get out of my house."

"Sir, now." The policeman had taken a few steps across the foyer and was trying to stare Mickey into cooperation, but Mickey had assumed the posture of a cat getting ready to pounce. I took a deep breath and ignored my hammering heart. I stepped in front of Mickey and said to the officer, "I need you to call 911. My fiancé is not dangerous, he's just naked and delusional and I need to get him to the hospital. Can you please help me?" To his unwavering stare, I said, "Look, that's why I was speeding back there. My name is Lucy Houston. This is Mickey Chandler. He lives here. You can arrest me later, but right now he's having an episode. He's not bleeding. He's not shot. He has bipolar disorder, and as you can see, he's not doing very well at the moment. Please." I shouted all this over the expletive-laced mutterings coming from Mickey as he resumed his ruining of the balusters.

The police officer apparently found enough logic in my explanation to lower his weapon and call for an ambulance.

"Thank you," I said, suddenly aware I was shaking.

An hour later, in the same hospital where we'd talked away the night a year before, Mickey was tied to a bed, smeared with paint, bathed in sweat, and psychotic. He didn't know me. I was a stranger in the world he'd fallen into. I'd watched the making of what was now culminating, completely unaware of what I was seeing. I'd naively enjoyed his endless energy. Now I was appalled at where it had led. Somehow, Mickey had hidden the extent of what was happening to him. It seemed that, despite his promise, he'd been wearing the mask he'd told me so much about.

A crabby nurse was doing her best with him, but Mickey was spitting at her. He was yelling obscenely, and the cords in his neck protruded like stiff ropes. The rage—the terror and desperation, the utter loss of control—took my breath away. I remember feeling like I was going to faint and running down three flights of stairs to find a place where I could breathe. *What was I doing with this man?*

Gleason Webb found me on a bench outside. Not prone to emotional displays, he simply sat down next to me and placed a reassuring hand on my shoulder. We sat like that for several minutes before I turned and asked, "What's happening to him?"

"This is what happens when mania gets out of control."

"I don't understand."

"Full-blown mania turns quickly to psychosis. Mickey crossed the line."

"I didn't see the line. What's the matter with me?"

"You didn't know what to look for. And I'm not sure if Mickey recognized it himself until he couldn't turn back." Gleason shrugged. "He's been so happy since he met you, Lucy, but for him, there's a fine line between joy and exhilaration. Crossing it can lead to this."

"I never imagined he could be like that. I don't know if I can do this."

Gleason looked at me. "It can be very overwhelming. But this is what happens, Lucy. Mickey's been here before, and he'll probably come here again. It's the nature of his illness."

"How many times has he been like this?"

"A few."

"And there's nothing we can do?"

"*We* don't have any power, Lucy. The power is Mic's. It's how *he* manages his disorder. And the bottom line is, he wants to feel good—like anyone wants to feel good—so he tries to balance on the edge without falling off. When he's down, or he thinks he's headed down, he self-medicates to stay on the upside. And sometimes that leads to irrational thinking and trying to correct that can make it worse. Mickey has a chronic illness, Lucy. And even when everything seems fine, the possibility of an episode like this can be just under the surface."

"Why didn't I see it?"

"It takes a long time to know someone like Mickey. He's a great big onion, and it's an extraordinary task, peeling back the layers of his illness, his personality, his character." Gleason looked hard at me. "You can't fix him. And if you're having second thoughts, it's completely understandable." Gleason's thick, gray brows were knit together, watching me.

"I had no idea."

"Then it's good you got to see this, Lucy. Next time you won't be so surprised. Assuming you're around next time."

"I don't know what I'm doing."

"I believe you."

"Gleason, I'm afraid," I said, fighting tears. "I love him . . . but . . ."

"Fear is healthy." He patted my shoulder.

After a while I said, "Could he hurt me?"

"I can't say. Right now he'd probably hurt his nurse if he wasn't restrained. But that's the psychosis. You'll learn to recognize the signs before he gets to this point."

I was quiet for a long time thinking about this. Gleason was quiet, too. After a few minutes, I turned to him. "Tell me what my life will look like if I marry him."

Mickey's doctor considered me for a moment, then took a deep breath. "Lucy, every marriage is a dance; complicated at times, lovely at times, most the time very uneventful. But with Mickey, there will be times when your dance will be on broken glass. There will be pain. And you will either flee that pain or hold tighter and dance through it to the next smooth place."

I let his words sink in as my tears fell. "I can't imagine my life—my future—without him, but I don't know." I pushed the tears away and ran my hands over my hair. "You're right, though, Gleason. It was good for me to see this now." Then I looked at him. "Do you think I can do this?"

"Only you can answer that, Lucy."

"But . . . I can learn to recognize the line?"

He nodded. "Mic will help you. One of the best things he's got going for him is he doesn't want to be sick. He doesn't want his illness to dictate who he is. He tries to be compliant, and for the most part he succeeds. And when he slips, *this* is what can—but certainly doesn't always—happen." Gleason looked at me, clear intensity shining in his eyes. "All that said, Lucy, no one could love you more."

I tried to smile. "Why are you so devoted to him, Gleason? You can't possibly care this much for all your patients."

Mickey's longtime psychiatrist looked wistful as he sighed. "I lost a patient a long time ago. It was a bad suicide, one of the hardest of my career." He shook his head. "I just couldn't do enough to save her, and it devastated me. So much so that I almost left the profession. I went to her funeral and I remember I was sitting on the back row thinking of replacement careers when this skinny kid found me. He just sat down next to me, and for the longest time he didn't say anything. Not a word. Then he looked at me with big tears in his eyes and he said, 'It wasn't your fault, Dr. Webb. My mom just really, really wanted to die.'" Gleason nodded. "Two weeks later he showed up at my office and asked me to check him for crazy. He said he'd do anything, have any kind of operation, take any kind of pill, if it would keep him from turning out like his mother. It was his birthday. He was twelve years old." Gleason shook his head at the memory. "We've been together ever since."

I pushed more tears off my cheeks. "He never told me that."

"He will."

"He really is incredible, isn't he?"

"Lucy, I've never known anyone who tries harder not to be sick, or takes it harder when he is. Mickey's an extraordinary man who just so happens to be mentally ill. If I were to give you any advice, it would be to make sure you focus on *that* Mickey."

I nodded.

"Weed through all his fine print. When you find a man you truly love beneath all his symptoms, *memorize that man*. And know *that man* will, at times, be missing in action."

I cried like a baby all the way home, mad that love couldn't fix the mess I was in. Madder still that I thought it was a mess. As I got ready for bed, the papers I'd found at Mickey's fell out of my pocket. I smoothed them out and didn't recognize the writing; the uneven scrawl looked like a child's, written in haste, maybe desperation. It had no periods, and by the end, no spaces between the words.

My Lucy,

I'm speeding I did a bad thing when I first started to notice it I didn't tell anyone I didn't tell you or Gleason or anyone because it just feels so wonderful to have this much energy and this much faith in myself I feel invincible like I can do anything Now I'm going too fast to stop on my own and something is going to happen that I want to warn you about so you won't be afraid I never want you to be afraid of me I would die if I scared you Lucy I'mjumpy and losing it even as I write this I can't sit still I can't stop thinking of what I can do to hold onto this feeling go back to yesterday which was a good day and look forward to today which was a better day until right now The working part of my brain knows I'm going to crash am crashing I'm seeing things move that aren't supposed to move Im in a cloud andit islaughingI see thingsfalling dripping from cracksIts redthen its blueand I know its notreal I'm trying to hurry so Icantell youIm sorry This hasn't happenedfor so long I forgot to be careful You make me so happy andmyhappy is not to be trusted No thatsnotwhat I mean You are happinessYou are everyhappy beautifulwonderful thing in the world and I amsoworried that I will make you hatemebecauseI screwed up again and pretended I was good whenItold you I wouldn't pretendI can't make you understand whatshappening to me You don't want to know I'mtrying to stayawayfrom the edge, but I cant I'mfloating above theholeandIm going tofall I'm sorry I love you I love you I love you If my love came in a better packageitwould drown you That's how big it is Don'tbe afraid of me Pleaseplease please don't be scared ofme Whatever I do or say the next time youseeme I'm sure I don't mean Except if I say-Iloveyou Because that's theonlysolid unshakable thing I have If they call you to come to the hospital don't come Please don'tcome Idon'twant you to see melike this I neverwantyouto seemelikethis CallGleasonhecan explain I'll call you when I get my headbackonstraight Ilove you IloveyouMic.

I sank to my knees and read the letter again. In it, I could hear Mickey's voice, which by the end was screaming off the page. And I saw him. In my mind's eye I saw Mickey writing this to me, trying to outrun his illness, trying to capture every word before it overtook him. In the center of Mickey's madness, in the eye of his horrible storm, *here* was his heart, open and aching. For me. I couldn't imagine not loving him. And I couldn't imagine not being loved by him.

I knew then and there that a life without Mickey Chandler would not be worth living. I loved him with my whole heart. And I loved him broken.

ten

A baby. The idea lifted me to a place completely unfamiliar. A place where I could almost imagine the small heft of an infant in the arms of someone else, anyone else, not me. Little head, tiny hands and feet, all alien to my experience. A baby. A family. Our shot at immortality.

Before Lucy's cancer, a family was our down-the-road plan, put off indefinitely until stability could be achieved. But after she got sick and cancer took its toll on us, our future seemed too precarious for babies. So we made the option impossible, or so we thought. We climbed back from hell to regain our footing, and life again became a small haven, safely two-dimensional. Until today. Today it seemed a place of miracles.

A baby. A little family. The thought blew through my chest and filled me with terror. Would I be a good father? Would I love and protect and behave like a good father? I thought of my own dad—distant at times, drowning in my mother, beaten down. I know he did the best he could. Who could ask more of a man? How could I be any better at it than he was? I trembled thinking of all the ways I could screw up. All the damage I could do. What was I doing?

Lucy found me in this panic and slipped her hand in mine. We're both going to make mistakes, she said, but we will balance each other. Then she settled my racing pulse with these words: "You will be a wonderful father. You will tell your child every day how much she is loved no matter what. And she will believe you because it will be true. And because she believes that one truth down deep in her core, it will be enough to temper everything else."

When we got home from sailing Sunday night, a note from Priscilla was sitting on the counter. It said she had slept on our couch since we'd taken the boat. She sort of halfway apologized for not talking to anyone about using it, which I appreciated since sorries were not my sister's strong suit. She closed by letting me know I was out of milk. All things considered, Priss could have been madder. I'd call her tomorrow.

While Mickey caught up on the mail, I lit candles and ran a bath. I had just eased into the suds when I felt the tickle in my throat and started coughing. I wished I had remembered to grab something to drink. But as if on cue, Mickey showed up with two glasses of ice and a liter of bottled water. He said he knew I would have preferred wine, but of course there would be no wine until after the baby. Then he joined me in the tub, and my plans for a relaxing bath became a bit less relaxing, but I couldn't complain.

For the longest time, we just lounged in the water and continued the conversation we'd started on the boat. I was amazed at the way this baby had so quickly come to dominate our every thought. How completely she'd become the new point of reference in our marriage. I had a feeling the conversation that had started yesterday would be the conversation we'd have for the rest of our lives. I supposed that's what it meant to become a family.

❅   ❅   ❅

I woke up early the next morning not feeling too well. My stomach was queasy, and virtually nothing sounded good to eat. I wanted Mickey to feel bad for me, but when I looked over at his sleeping, solid, peaceful form, I didn't have the heart to whine. This is how he sleeps when he's stable. No restlessness, no terrors. Of course, the increase in his Ambien didn't hurt. I kissed him on the nose and crawled out of bed.

While I boiled water for some tea, I checked the changes Gleason had made to Mickey's psychotropic recipe. I dug through his backpack for his drugs. It looked like he'd started him on Tegretol again, and bless his heart, Mickey'd taken what he was supposed to while we were on the boat. The teakettle whistled, and I steeped a bag of herbal mint. As soon as I felt better, I planned to start the laundry, then maybe make a big fat breakfast for Mickey, but I got sidetracked. I found myself in the junk room, sitting on the window seat.

I looked around Priscilla's old room, now bathed in the sun of a brand-new day. Sipping my tea, I wondered how on earth anyone could wake up in this room in a bad mood. But somehow Priss had frequently managed to do just that. She'd even taped a threatening sign on her door when I was a little girl: TRESPASSERS WILL BE SPIT AT, AND IF YOU DON'T BELIEVE ME, JUST TRY IT!!!

I looked around the room and imagined where I would put the crib, tried to picture the best color scheme for a baby girl. Maybe pink and moss green, maybe pale yellow and bright orange. Gingham and flowers for the bumper pads. Maybe when she was older, I could resurrect my old four-poster. I sipped my tea. Consciously, I wanted to imagine this room as a nursery, but my thoughts willfully veered off to a time when the room was mine.

Priss had long since moved out and Lily was in college, so it was just Mom and me. I had always been in the little bedroom behind the kitchen. But while I was away on a summer trip to Washington, DC, she moved my things upstairs to Priss's room. When I got back, Harry and Jan had papered the walls and laid carpet over the wood floor. Jan and Mom had made me a quilt, and there was a new bedroom set—a four-poster canopy bed with a double dresser. It was pretty over-the-top, and I wasn't sure we could afford it, but it was beautiful.

When I hugged my mom that day, it was the first time she felt small to me. I knew she was starting to shrink, to waste away, but until then, when she put her arms around me, she still felt the way she was supposed to. Substantial—like she was in charge and her child had nothing to worry about. But I clearly remember that day as the day my mother started to die. Four months later, right after my seventeenth birthday, she finished.

Priss's old room was next to Mom's, and I knew I'd been put there because Mom needed me to be close. She didn't want to be alone, but I don't think she wanted me to know that. I know I didn't have a full night of sound sleep for those four months. Near the end, I was no longer sleeping in Priss's room at all. I slept in the chair by Mom's bed. Even on her good nights.

Sometimes, waking to find me there, she would scold me, remind me I had school. But those were just words she whispered through parched lips. Rather than answer her, I'd give her a drink or help her suck some ice. Sometimes she would reach for my hand and pull me next to her, and I would feel how terribly warm she was even though she said she was freezing.

In a way, it was as if I'd been a new mom, responsible for a person who depended on me for everything. Sitting there on Priss's window seat, rubbing my still queasy stomach, I realized I'd already had lessons in mothering. Hard lessons. I was there when Charlotte spoke those terrible irreversible words to my mother: Cancer. Aggressive. Resistant. Poor prognosis. Mine was the hand she reached for to steady her when the current of those terrible words threatened to drown her. Mine were the tears I would not let surface in her presence, for fear of making her fear worse.

I was there alone when Dr. Barbee gave me my instructions, told me what to expect. And the pep talk she gave me that informed me

I had officially left my childhood. At sixteen, *for all intents and purposes,* she'd said, I was an adult in an adult world.

Dr. Barbee taught me how to drain my mother's catheter and measure her urine output and told me at what point I needed to call her to start an IV. She taught me to give Mom the injections she would plead for when the pain was unbearable. I was the caregiver, Dr. Barbee had told me. I was in charge. Mature beyond my years, people whispered. Old soul. But what other option was there, really, but to grow up and get ready to let go of her? None that I could see.

I couldn't have faced what I was facing without the utter belief in what my father had told me about death when I was little. If my father's words were simply meant to console a little, frightened girl all those years ago, they served the same purpose twelve years later when I steeled myself for Death to claim my mother.

My tea was cold by the time I realized how deeply I'd been contemplating the hereafter. Staying in the present required discipline. So I pulled away from thinking of my mom and focused my attention on my plans for this room. What would Mom have suggested? Maybe red and white. Maybe yellow and blue. I'd call Wanda Murphy. She was president of the Brinley Quilters' Guild, she'd have some great ideas. But then I scolded myself. I couldn't tell anyone about this baby until I'd told my sisters.

It was almost noon when I walked into Ghosts in the Attic. Lily was behind the counter with a phone tucked under her chin, ringing up some china for a woman poised to hand off her credit card. I sat down in the parlor and helped myself to a pumpkin cookie. Lily has fresh pastries delivered twice a day by Matilda Hines, who owns Heavenly Hines Baked Goods, two doors up. Lily does this so she can set them out on the obscenely ornate Regency sideboard, which also sports a Tuttle Silversmiths tea service and dozens of hand-painted teacups.

Lily and Ron had transformed this crumbling Victorian two-story (and attic) into a prosperous business. Every inch is utterly inviting, starting with the parlor. Deep-wine-colored walls and floral carpeting set the tone. An Adam-style settee, some Queen Annes, and a Victorian nursing chair offer seating around a mahogany coffee table. Lily keeps her reference material in here—when a serious collector wants to know if Lily's prices are fair, they can consult one of her myriad pricing guides while noshing on an éclair.

Supposedly, nothing is for sale in this room, though the turnover in furniture is almost monthly. Lily's parlor has an ambience that people yearn to emulate in their own home. They are seduced in the parlor, then shop the remaining fourteen rooms for tapestries and art, pottery and Lalique crystal, furniture and lace. Lily's theory is that if she can make shopping at Ghosts an event for the customer, the customer will keep coming back. The theory has proven itself; Lily's patrons come from all over the place. She keeps in touch with them with note cards, always thanking them in writing for their purchases, and alerting them when she's acquired something that fits their taste.

I watched my sister bid good-bye to the china buyer and tell her she expected a call when her grandson was born. The woman trilled a delighted promise as she walked out. Lily checked the monitor on her counter and looked up at me. "Let me just look in on these ladies shopping for linens upstairs. I'll be right back."

I finished my cookie and, realizing I felt better, reached for a brownie. Then it hit me like a hammer on the head: I'd had morning sickness. The thought exhilarated me! This body of mine was doing exactly what it was supposed to do.

"What is that dumb grin on your face?" my sister said, rushing into the parlor. She startled me and I dropped my brownie. Lily poured herself a cup of hot water, and while she squeezed a lemon quarter into it, she said, "Remember that obscene lamp I was telling you about? The one I bought for five hundred bucks from that kid over in Woodbury?"

I didn't, so I shrugged.

"Turns out it's a Daum Nancy, worth about fifteen thousand dollars. And I have a buyer." She looked up from her lemon-squeezing and grinned at me. Her green eyes, the one trait that links me to both my sisters, were dancing. "Oh, I'm sorry. Look at me prattling on without even asking how you're doing. Did you ever meet up with Priss?"

"Kind of. Did you?"

"No. There was a message on my machine Sunday that she'd gone back to Hartford and was sorry she missed me. Like she even tried. I'm right here. I'm always right here. And like you, she was a no-show at the Shad Bake."

"Oh, sorry. We stayed on the boat, and I completely forgot about it."

"Well, it was great, like always. So, what's up?"

I looked around to be sure we wouldn't be disturbed and took a deep breath.

"Oh, no," Lily said as she sat down, alarm filling her face. "You've heard from Charlotte, haven't you?"

"Well, as a matter of fact, yeah. But it's not what you think."

Lily set her teacup on the coffee table with a trembling hand. "What?"

"Lil . . ."

"Just tell me, Lucy. Don't beat around the bush."

"I'm pregnant."

Dead silence. I'm not even sure she inhaled.

"What?" she finally asked.

All I could do was nod.

She stared at me.

"I know," I said.

"You . . . you're pregnant? Really? Oh, Lucy."

"I know." When Lily didn't say anything else, I had to ask, "You're happy for me, right?"

She smiled then, but her heart wasn't in it. Still, she came over and put her arms around me. "Of course I'm happy for you, Lu. You just took me by surprise." When I pulled away from her, there was something in her eyes she was trying to hide, and then there were tears. I knew what it was, and I was suddenly mad. I wanted this to be about me, not the baby she lost thirteen years ago. I shook my head and wouldn't look at her. "I'm sorry, Lil, I have to go," I snapped.

"Lucy, don't leave. I'm sorry. I just—"

The front door chimed, and Lily quickly wiped her face with her hands, but it was just Ron. He took one look at us and said, "Oh, this can't be good. What's going on?"

Lily stood up too quickly, knocking her teacup to the floor. Her tears had surfaced again, and she ignored the lemon water on the rug as she said, "Honey, Lucy has some news. I'm just going to check on Mrs. Flowers." Then she was gone.

I felt like I might vomit.

"Are you and Lil fighting?" Ron asked, picking up the teacup.

I looked at my brother-in-law in his crisp khakis and chambray shirt. He hadn't even taken his sunglasses off.

"I think we might be."

"Is it bad?"

"I'm pregnant, Ron."

He slid off his dark glasses, slowly, and stared at me for a few seconds. "Oh, wow. That's a surprise."

"Yeah."

"And she's upset?"

"Apparently." I shook my head, growing even more annoyed with my sister.

"Ahhh, Lucy," he said, glancing down the hall after his wife. He stared in that direction for a long moment, clearly weighing the situation, then he looked back at me. "She'll be okay," he said, putting his arms around me. "She'll be fine. But are you okay? I thought no Houston girl was allowed to get pregnant. What's the deal?"

I shrugged. "A failed tubal ligation, a determined little swimmer . . . you do the math."

He chuckled. "Is this a good thing or a bad thing? I need to tailor my response."

Despite myself, I laughed. "I'm pretty sure it's both."

"How's Mic?"

"He's good right now. He's happy about it."

"Well, then I'm happy for you. Both of you." He looked me in the eye and nodded. "Everything will be fine."

"I don't know what I expected, Ron. I just really wanted her to be happy for me. But . . ." I trailed off.

He was still nodding. "I better go check on her. You okay?"

I waited for several minutes, long enough for the wine-colored walls to close in on me. When it was clear that Lily wasn't coming back, I walked out. What had I expected? That Lily would fall all over herself with joy? I knew something in Lily had shattered the day she had to give that baby boy back. She'd cried every time we had talked about it, so I should have known how tender this would be for her. But was I so wrong to just want her blessing? Yes! Apparently.

After I'd sat in my car for several minutes, I decided to call Priscilla and get the rest of the unpleasantness out of the way. Her assistant put me through, and my sister answered with a professional "Priscilla Houston."

"Hey, Priss."

"Who is this?"

"It's me, and you know it. I called to tell you sorry about the boat."

"Really?" Sarcastic tone.

"Yes. And to tell you I'm pregnant."

Silence.

"Well, that's all I called for. I'm having a really crappy day so I won't keep you."

"Lucy, wait while I shut my door, I want to talk to you." I heard a slam, then she picked the phone up again. "Start from the beginning. Are you okay?"

"I'm okay. But Lily's not."

"She didn't take it well, huh?"

"No."

"Lucy, what are you doing pregnant? Aren't your tubes tied?"

"Apparently they came untied, or grew back together. Something happened. Obviously."

"Do you want it?" Priscilla said bluntly. "I thought—"

"Yes, Priss, I want it. We want it. It wasn't planned but we're going to do it."

"Really? Are you sure?"

"Priss . . ."

"I'm sorry, sweets, but really? Has some miracle happened to change your situation? Is Mickey cured, or is he still . . . ?"

"Priscilla, I have to go now. I just wanted you to know." I snapped my phone shut and threw it on the floor of my car. What did I really expect from either of my sisters?

Almost immediately my phone rang and I nudged it toward me with my foot. Of course it was Priss, and I was tempted to let it go to voice mail, but I forced myself to answer.

"I'm sorry, Lucy. You didn't need that from me. You just caught me off guard—completely off guard. Are you sure you're okay?" Priss asked in absolute sincerity, and I wanted to cry.

"I don't know. I only found out a couple of days ago, and I just told Mickey this weekend, on the boat—that's why I took it. I wanted to tell him in a place where he couldn't run away."

"Well, then I'm glad you took it. But, Lucy, are you sure you know what you're doing?"

"No, I don't. But I'm doing it anyway."

"How pregnant are you?"

"As near as we can tell, about eleven weeks."

Priscilla sighed into the phone. "I'm worried."

"I know and I love you for it."

"I love you, too, you know I do. But, Lucy, it's not too late to *not* do this."

"I have to go, Priss." I hung up the phone, remembering the last time she said those exact words to me.

eleven

Not long after I'd recovered from the manic episode that should have scared Lucy away, Priscilla told me to meet her at Colin's Grill. I really don't like being ordered around, but I knew whatever Priss had to say was inevitable, so I met her. When I got there, she was in the corner booth and she was not smiling. I sat down.

"Priscilla."

"Hello, Mickey. Thanks for coming."

The waiter brought me a Coke that I hadn't ordered and Priscilla thanked him, then said, "We don't want to be disturbed." He handed her the bill and walked away. With no preamble, she said, "This thing with my sister can't happen. I'm sure you realize that now."

I didn't say anything.

"I should have stepped in sooner, but I really thought it would burn itself out by now. You're a decent guy, Mickey, and this is nothing personal."

Priscilla paused, but I let her words hang between us heavy and unanswered. She cleared her throat. "Lucy has no idea what she's doing with you. She's young and naive and you're . . ." She shrugged. "You have way too many problems, Mickey. If you really love my sister, please just walk away. She's not prepared to take you on and this isn't fair to her."

I took a drink and kept listening.

Priscilla became agitated and leaned over the table to drive home her displeasure at me. Then she said, "My sister is not a fully formed person yet, Mickey. She's not even twenty-three years old, and she's not being rational. She thinks she wants to teach high school in Brinley, which is ridiculous! She graduated magna cum laude! She's better than that!" Priss pinched the bridge of her nose and sighed. "Lucy doesn't even realize there's a world out there; she needs to grow up and see it. You need to man up and do the right thing."

I took a bracing gulp of my Coke. "My turn?"

"Of course."

"I think the right thing to do, Priscilla, is forget this little conversation ever happened."

"I beg your pardon!"

"I'm serious, Priss. I'm grateful for your devotion to Lucy, but apparently you don't know her at all. And you don't know me. Do you honestly think she and I have not looked at absolutely every aspect of this? We have. I can be a lot to deal with, everyone knows that. And I guarantee that there will be times when you like me even less than you do right now. But I can live with that, Priscilla, I'm not marrying you. I'd like for us to be friends, but that's completely your call. I love your sister."

"Then walk away," she hissed. "Because you will ruin her life."

I slid to the end of the booth and stood up. "I'm leaving, Priscilla. You're very important to Lucy, so I'm not going to tell her what you've asked me to do here. We both know it would damage your relationship with her."

"Walk away from her, Mickey."

I shook my head. "You get to choose your life, Priscilla, not Lucy's. The only way I'd ever walk away from her is if she asked me to. So, I guess you'll have to work your magic with her. You get this one shot, Priscilla, so make it count, because if you ever dare to interfere after we're married . . ."

"Are you threatening me?"

I smiled. "No. I'm just strongly advising you not to cross a mentally ill man who evidently has the power to destroy lives."

Lucy's sister glared at me, and I did my best to glare back. And I'll be damned if a single belligerent tear didn't roll down her face and melt the ice. I blew out a breath and slumped down next to her. For a moment neither one of us spoke. Then Priscilla whimpered, "You scare me, Mickey. You really do."

"I can understand that." I put my arm around her. "I scare me sometimes, too. But no matter how hard I try, I can't seem to scare your sister."

Priscilla looked up at me, and I was deeply moved by the raw concern in her eyes. I pulled her closer, and over the knot in my throat I said, "I'll take good care of her, Priss. I promise."

After I found Mickey's letter, I knew there was no turning back. I loved him, but I didn't know what my love should have looked like during that awful time. The hospital wouldn't let me see him, which filled me with so much anxiety I could barely function. But Gleason assured me it was best because Mickey was still grossly psychotic. So, though I couldn't see him, I stopped by the hospital each day on my way home from school anyway, just to leave him a note. I left the same note every day: *I love you. Call me when you get back.*

And one day he did. Sort of. My phone rang but there was no sound on the other end, and then he hung up. I knew it was Mickey and I immediately called the nurse on duty, who told me he was improving, that he was better but exhausted. "Less than twenty hours of sleep in a week will do that," she said.

I drove straight to the hospital. Thankfully Gleason was there. He gave me a fatherly hug and said Mickey'd had a good day. To simplify things for me, he described Mickey's journey as *falling*—which he'd been doing for some time, but started in earnest seven or eight days ago, *landing,* which had prompted his admission to the hospital, and then the *climb back,* which he was apparently slowly doing now. Gleason told me the time it would take to complete the climb varied depending on Mickey's response to the medication.

"Can I see him?"

"Of course."

I was only planning to stay a few minutes, but when I saw him, I couldn't leave. Mickey was sound asleep on his bed, covered with a thin, worn sheet. He had showered and I could smell his shampoo when I bent to kiss his cool forehead. He didn't stir as I ran my fingers lightly down his arm and over his hand, where I could see he was holding my notes against his chest. I must have sat with him for an hour and a half, maybe longer, just watching him. I'd missed him and I so wanted to be there when he opened his eyes. What a week he'd had, what a contrast to find him so still and peaceful tonight.

Up the hall, the patient phone rang and someone yelled for Terrance. They yelled for Terrance three times, each time louder than the last, and I hurried to shut the door so Mickey wouldn't be disturbed. But when I got back to his bedside, he was awake. "Hi," I said.

He didn't move, but his eyes widened as he looked around, and I read the confusion and fear in his expression. "Mickey? Honey?"

"Lucy?" he whispered.

"I'm right here, baby." I touched his arm. "Can you feel my hand?"

He looked so intensely disbelieving I wasn't sure what to do.

When his eyes filled with tears, I thought my heart would break. "I can't believe you're here," he whispered.

"Why?"

He opened his hand and showed me my crushed notes. "I called you, but I didn't know if you . . . I didn't know what to say."

I bent down and ran a finger over his cheek. "How about you just say you still love me, and we'll call it good?"

Mickey looked at me like I had spoken in tongues. He sat up with some effort, and I could tell he was extremely medicated. Again he didn't seem sure of what he was seeing as he searched my face. "Are you real?"

I took his hand and held it in both of mine. "I'm real."

He shook his head. "Lucy, I'm supposed to be the crazy one."

"What does that mean?"

"Did . . . did I write you a letter?"

"Yes. I got it."

He stared at me, confusion again filling his face. "And you came back?"

"Baby, I never left. And I'm not going anywhere."

Mickey stayed in the hospital for five more days and I watched his odyssey, from psychotic to less psychotic to fragile sanity and slowly back to my Mickey, albeit very subdued. He told me he remembered just about everything and said it felt like not being able to wake up from a nightmare. He explained that the line between crazy and sane for him was a fine one, and that when he was falling into psychosis, they both felt real.

"The difference," he said, "is that when I'm sane, I realize the nightmare is psychosis, and when I'm psychotic, I don't know that. And I don't trust what's happening when I'm moving from one to the other. That's why it takes a while for me to believe what I'm seeing."

I smiled at him, but he shook his head. He wasn't done explaining.

"I don't know how to thank you, Lucy."

"For what?"

"For showing me how to do this. How to love you. How to be loved by you. Lucy, no one's ever really taught me how to do this before. My mom never crawled out of herself long enough; my dad tried but he just wasn't capable; and my brother was doing whatever he had to do to survive." Mickey shook his head. "Don't look at me like that. Don't pity me. Just understand that's the reality I grew up in. It's why this—what you've given me here—is so foreign to me. It feels solid. I've never had solid."

I nodded. "Mickey, no matter where you go when you get sick, this—us—is real. I will always be here when you come back."

After that, there was no more doubt about our being together. We decided we were ready and very anxious to get married, so we got back on track and made a wedding plan.

We invited my sisters to dinner. Mickey barbecued steaks and I tossed the salad, and we laughed around my kitchen table for most of the evening. Ron and Mickey had become fast friends who were planning to go fishing the next Thursday. Since Lily and I would be joining them, Ron teased Priscilla, telling her if she could get a date, she could come, too. She didn't think that was funny, but retorted, "Some of us have to work, you know."

"Why don't you start your own firm and be your own boss like Mic, here? Then you can call the shots," Ron told her.

"I just made partner, I think I should hang out for a while. But who knows, maybe someday." Then she turned to Mickey. "Lucy said you were looking at a club in Bridgeport—did you buy it?"

"No, we passed on that one. We decided to stick to within an hour radius so we can stay more hands-on. And Jared found an opportunity about two minutes from here."

"Where?" Lily asked, surprised.

"The inn right across from your antiques store."

"No way! The Brubaker?"

"Yeah. We approached the owners last week with a proposal for turning their dining room into a club. We think it will attract the locals more than the restaurant."

"I heard they were closing their restaurant. Not enough traffic," Ron said.

"Which is great for us. We want to create a place to hang out, have a drink, enjoy some entertainment—some comedy. And we're buying the space, so that helps them out."

Priss nodded. "I'm impressed, Mickey. Brinley doesn't have anything like that. You've got a good eye for business." With that she stood up and started to clear the table.

I took the plate from her hand and told her to sit down.

"What?" she said. "It's late and I don't want to leave you with this mess."

"It'll wait. We have something to tell you." I looked at Mickey, then at my sisters, and I couldn't keep the dumb grin off my face as I blurted, "We're getting married."

Lily squealed and clapped her hands. "Oh, Lucy! When?"

"Six weeks," Mickey said.

Ron laughed. "Welcome to the club, my friend."

For a moment I basked in their happiness. But then I looked at Priscilla, who wasn't even trying. I watched her stand up and carry her plate to the sink. Then she walked out of the room.

Ron—bless him—chuckled and said, "And welcome to the drama, Mic."

Lily leaned over. "Don't pay any attention to her. Either one of you. She cannot be surprised by this. We were all worried when Mickey had his episode, but you got through it together, and now look. I'm so happy for you."

"*We're* happy for you," Ron echoed. "Especially me. I need the support."

Lily elbowed him and Mickey laughed. He seemed completely unfazed by Priscilla's reaction. I leaned over and kissed him, then went in search of my rude sister. I found her on the front porch taking an aspirin. She looked at me with no joy in her face. "You're really going to do this?"

"You know I am."

She shook her head. "Why? I mean it, Lucy. Three weeks ago he was certifiable and now he's worth marrying?"

I sighed. "He was always worth marrying."

"See! That attitude is exactly what concerns me."

"I understand your concern, Priss, and I appreciate it. But I love him."

Priss rubbed her forehead like a frustrated parent. "Love isn't a panacea, Lucy."

As I looked at my sister, I thought of the crash course on bipolar I'd been taking all these weeks. If anyone knew there was no panacea, it was me. It was Mickey. "Why are you giving me a hard time about this? You knew we were engaged."

"People get engaged all the time, Lucy. Doesn't mean they have to get married in six weeks. He just got out of the hospital, what's the rush?"

"I love him, that's the rush. And I'm going to marry him, and it would be nice if you could be happy about it."

Priscilla dumped her water over the railing and handed me the glass. "Well, that's not going to happen." With that, she dug the keys out of her purse, walked off my porch, and headed to her car.

Later, I was getting ready for bed when the phone rang. As soon as I heard her voice, I steeled myself. "What do you want, Priss?"

"Lucy, I didn't mean to ruin your big night."

"You didn't. You should have stayed, we had a great time."

She cleared her throat. "At any rate, if you're going to do this . . ."

"Priss, don't start again. Please . . ."

"I'm not starting. I'm just saying, if you're going to do this, then let's at least do it right. Let me take care of the wedding."

"What? No. Priss, we were thinking something small. You and Lil, Ron, Mickey's dad, lunch."

"Oh, please, Lucy. It's your wedding, not the early-bird special at Chuck-A-Rama."

Despite myself I had to laugh. "I'll talk to Mickey and let you know."

"Well, let me know by nine o'clock in the morning. Because that's when I'll be there to pick you up."

"Priscilla . . ."

"We'll start with the dress and see how far we get."

"Priss . . ."

"Let me do this. Please."

I sighed. "Okay, but I'm bringing Lily."

"I've already called her."

I had a blast. We all did. We drove into Manhattan, where Priscilla had made us an appointment at Kleinfeld Bridal. I must have tried on twenty dresses. In the end I chose the first one I tried on—a Romona Keveza, which meant nothing to me, but seemed to mean a lot to Priss. To me it was just an empire waist, tip of the shoulder, A-line, silk and taffeta, flat out most gorgeous thing I'd ever seen in my life. Lily cried when I came out of the dressing room. Priscilla said it was nice but tried to talk me into the Amalia Carrara—another designer lost on me. That was a lovely dress as well, but overwhelming, covered in beads and weighing more than I did, not to mention costing more than I was worth dead.

In the end, of course, I won. Priscilla begged me to wear a veil, and she was being so nice about buying the dress that I almost gave in, but then I just couldn't do it. I decided on a jeweled headband I could wear with the pearls my dad had given my mother the day they got married. Lily said it was very *me* and Priscilla relented. Like she had a choice.

Because we were in New York and there was no fighting it, Priscilla and Lily bought dresses, too. It was a great day, an exhausting day. But it was nothing compared to the next week, when Priss dragged me to caterers, decorators, photographers, a printer, and some place she'd found on the Internet that would set up an ivy-covered arbor in the backyard. She had an appointment in Hartford for us to pick out a wedding cake and seemed a bit crestfallen when I suggested that Matilda Hines right here in Brinley would do just fine. I also mentioned that she made a mean quiche and that we could put her in charge of the catering. Priscilla cackled like I'd said the funniest thing she'd ever heard.

Mickey was working hard on his house—the mess he'd made of the foyer had required industrial cleanup. But it had finally sold, contingent on his refinishing the hardwood floor. He'd already started moving his things into my house. Mickey wanted to gut it and make it ours, but we compromised and agreed to start by breaking down just one wall between the downstairs bedroom and the kitchen so we could have a formal dining room.

Thankfully where we would live had never really been a question. I asked him if we could stay in Brinley and he said yes, and I told him thank you every day for a year.

On August 12, two days before my wedding, the forecast said intermittent wind and rain throughout the week, and I thought how silly of Channel 8 not to consult Priscilla on the issue. She wasn't worried. The tables had arrived the night before and were set up around the perimeter of the yard. Ten rows of chairs were arranged in the middle, each with a bow of white tulle tied around it. The arbor was a thing of beauty, but I could hardly admit that to Priss since I'd given her such a hard time when she'd suggested it.

In a matter of a few hours, my kitchen filled up with boxes of linen and crystal that Priss had rented. On the big day, huge pink boxes arrived full of open-faced sandwiches, éclairs, macaroons, and chocolate-covered strawberries. Crates of champagne were sitting on my sofa, and when I looked through the living-room window, I saw my cake headed up the walk. I hugged its guardian, Matilda Hines, and truly thought I'd never seen anything lovelier: four square tiers covered with shavings of white chocolate, big orange gerbera daisies adorning the top.

The ceremony was planned for four. At one thirty, when I got in the tub, the sky was blue. Not so when I got out.

I was still in my bathrobe when there was a knock on my door. "Come in," I yelled from my closet, thinking it was Priscilla there to reassure me for the eleventh time that it was not going to rain. But it was Mickey with a man who looked the way Mickey would in about forty years.

"Hey, baby," he said, kissing my cheek. "I wanted you to meet my dad before the show started."

I don't know what it was, but seeing Mickey with his father brought tears to my eyes. He'd said his dad would never make the trip, yet here he was, a gentle giant with a shock of white hair. "I'm so happy you came, Mr. Chandler."

He seemed a bit timid or maybe just not sure what to do with a woman in her bathrobe, but he stuck out his hand. I bypassed his hand and hugged him, and bless his heart, he hugged me back. "I feel like I already know you, since you're all my boy here can seem to talk about."

I reached up and kissed Mickey's chin. "Well, he's a great guy. I'm very lucky."

The old man nodded and something like pity passed through his eyes. I hoped Mickey didn't catch it.

"How was your flight?" I asked.

"It wasn't bad. I lived through it."

"Dad hates to fly."

"Well, then it means all the more that you're here."

"Wouldn't have missed it."

Priscilla barged in just then, dressed like royalty in her silver halter dress and matching five-inch heels; her crown: two curlers on the top of her head. "Lucy! What are you doing? Do you know what time it is—you're getting married in fifty-one minutes! Mickey, you can't see the bride, what are you thinking?! Get out of here!"

"Nice to meet you, Lucy," Mickey's dad said. "Sure hope it doesn't rain on you."

"It's not going to rain! The clouds are moving toward the coast.

Everything is fine. Go get dressed." Priss shooed the men out, but Mickey caught my eye before he shut the door and whispered, "We should have eloped."

"I heard that," Lily said, walking in just as they were walking out. She looked gorgeous in a tea-length, navy-blue silk dress, a corsage of wildflowers pinned to her strap, a daisy clipped in her short hair. My sisters helped me into my dress and fussed with my makeup. Lily clasped the pearls Dad had given Mom on their wedding day around my neck, and Priscilla helped me with the matching teardrop earrings. As I appraised myself in the full-length mirror, Lily put her arm around me. "You look so beautiful, Lu." She pushed my hair off my shoulder, and I watched tears fill her eyes.

"You're going to make me cry, Lily."

"I just . . . I just want to tell you how proud I am of you," she said, hugging me. "You really are amazing, Lucy, and Mickey is so very lucky."

I shook my head. "Thanks, Lil, but I'm the lucky one."

Priscilla finished with the final inspection of my hem. "Just lovely," she said, stepping up to the mirror with us. But her expression quickly turned mortified when she saw the curlers still in her hair. There was a knock at my door and we all said in unison, "Come in."

It was Jan, and when she saw us, her hands flew to her chest. "Look at you! Look at all of you. You are stunning women!" She walked over and held me at arm's length, then pulled me close. "Oh, I wish your mom could see you. She dreamed about this day."

I smiled through the threat of tears.

"Are you ready?" she said.

"I'm so ready."

"Good. It's time. Everyone is seated, the musicians are playing, Judge Doyle just arrived. We're a minute early, but we should start. It looks like it's going to rain."

"It's not going to rain!" Priscilla boomed.

"Maybe not. But we moved the cake back in the house, anyway," Jan whispered.

I looked at Priscilla glaring at the sky from my window and smiled. Whether it rained or not, I was going to bed tonight Mrs. Michael Chandler, and that was all that mattered.

Jan kissed my cheek. "We'll see you downstairs, sweetie." She walked out with Lily, and it was just Priscilla and me, and Priss looked like she would cry.

"What?" I asked her.

"You know I love you, Lu."

"I think you've proven that this week."

She walked over and took my hands. "That's true, I have. . . . But, Lucy, it's not too late to *not* do this."

I pulled her into a big hug. "Yes, it is, Priscilla. I love him way too much. Now get out of here."

"You're sure?"

"I was born sure."

She sighed as she fingered Mom's pearls, then she kissed my cheek. "I'll see you downstairs."

I was alone and about to get married. I picked up the picture of my parents that had sat on my nightstand since I was a little girl and walked to the window. I could see Mickey and Ron standing by the arbor, laughing. My dearest friends were all dressed up and seated, some with umbrellas at the ready. My sisters were huddled together in back, waiting for this to happen. I would remember this moment forever, gazing out on the day my life changed. I looked down at the picture in my hand. The only thing missing was my parents. But I could feel them here with me. I could feel their blessing. I ran my thumb across their faces, then walked down the stairs.

Harrison Bates, my stand-in father for all these years, was waiting by the door. When he saw me, tears sprang to his eyes. "You look very handsome, Harry. Thank you for being my dad today."

"It's an honor, sweetheart," he said softly. "Mickey's a very lucky man."

When I heard the quartet begin Pachelbel's Canon in D, I shivered. "This is it."

The backyard looked like a fairy tale. Priscilla had absolutely out-done herself, and there was even a double rainbow in the sky above the arbor that was framing Mickey. He looked wonderful standing there next to Ron, solid and elegant and nervous in his gray tux.

When I'd reached Mickey's side, Judge Doyle smiled and wel-comed everyone, then cleared his throat and recited a poem. He'd been speaking only a moment when I felt a raindrop hit the tip of my nose, and it almost made me laugh as I wiped it away. Then I felt another. And another. Mickey, who seemed to be leaning forward, hanging on every word, squeezed my hand. As we stood there listen-ing to the judge, who seemed oblivious, the sky opened up, and I heard a shrill "Lucy!"

Priscilla was holding a limp napkin over her head, and next to her, Lily was trying not to laugh. Several of our guests were huddled under our covered patio. I shook my head. My kitchen was full of food and boxes, my living room was cluttered with gifts and wedding parapher-nalia. I shrugged at Priscilla, who looked utterly flabbergasted that we were letting it rain. I turned to Mickey. The way this was going to go, and be remembered, was decided in a split second when Mickey looked up at the sky and laughed out loud. He asked the judge, "Is a wedding performed in the rain legally binding?"

"I don't see why not."

Mickey took off the jacket of his tux and draped it over my shoul-ders. "Well then, let's get on with it."

As Judge Doyle wiped water off his face, I heard my sister groan over some quiet laughter behind me. Lightning split the sky and the judge quickly wrapped up his poem and turned to ask Mickey that life-changing question: *Do you take this woman . . .* Thunder obliter-ated some of the important words, but Mickey nodded anyway. "I do. I do."

The judge then turned to me. "Lucy, do you take this man to be your lawfully wedded husband, to love and honor, to cherish and respect, in sickness and health, in good times and bad, forsaking all others for as long as you both shall live?"

I looked at Mickey, my eyes filling with happy tears. "I absolutely do."

We slid our rings onto each other's wet fingers, and the judge invited Mickey to kiss his wife. Mickey lifted my face to his and kissed me in the middle of a rainstorm, and every drop felt like a blessing. Nothing mattered but him. Not the ruined backyard, not our wet finery, not all our friends running for cover, not even Priscilla's fury with the weather gods. Just him. I wrapped my arms around Mickey's neck and his coat slid off my shoulders and fell to the ground. The rain poured down on us like we were standing in a shower, and all we could do was laugh and laugh. He scooped me up in his arms, spun me around, and someone snapped a picture that made the front page of the *Brinley Gazette*. (They got a picture of Priss, too, soaked to the bone, which she threatened to sue the paper for printing.) After that everyone crowded into the house and spent the rest of the afternoon eating the delicacies Priss had ordered. They ate standing up and laughed and stayed for hours.

Sometimes my wedding still comes up in conversations and it always makes me smile. And every once in a while, when the weather is just like it was that day, Mickey and I go outside and dance in the rain.

twelve

There's a picture by the lamp downstairs of a little girl sitting on the lap of a big man. She's laughing, her entire face alive with joy, eyes squeezed shut, mouth wide-open, she could be screaming. I think she's being tickled. The man's expression overflows with adoration. You can almost hear Lucy's laughter lifting off the photograph; you can practically hear her father's promise that he will always love her.

I want to take a picture just like that when my child is two or three. I want to see that same love in my face and in my child's. What I really want is to be the kind of man Lucy's father was.

I had big plans to tackle the junk room this afternoon, but as soon as I looked at it, I knew I was too tired. It was the kind of tired I'd told Charlotte about at my checkup a few days back. At the time, I was worried, but now I knew it was just the exhaustion of being pregnant. I walked into my bedroom, hoping Mickey was having a better day than I was, and dialed the club. Mickey's partner answered. Jared Timmons sounded upbeat, which was not at all unusual. He was unflappable, and that made him the perfect business partner for my husband. That had been the recipe from the beginning—Mickey brought the energy, the ideas, the creative juice. Jared brought the good attitude, the organization, and the follow-through. This combination of business acumen had made the two of them very successful entrepreneurs. They now owned five clubs and served as backup entertainment for each of them often enough that they had a following.

"How's he doing?" I asked.

"He seems great. We had a meeting this morning with the Connecticut Rotary Club—their bigwigs anyway—and Mic was terrific. They'll probably use us for their convention next spring."

"So you think he's back?"

"Getting there, for sure. Right now he's handling some auditions we decided to hold back before he went into Edgemont. Looking for some new blood, you know. Hey, he told me your news. Wow, girl. A baby. I have to say it's about time. Kids are the best!"

"Oh, well, that's what I hear," I stammered, not realizing I wasn't quite ready for open congratulations.

Jared laughed. "I'll tell him you called, Lucy."

I lay down, planning to rest just until Mickey called back. But when I woke up two hours later, it was as if I hadn't slept at all. I left Mickey another message and went to work on the junk room. First I decided to take the accordion doors off the closet. I wanted to wallpaper the inside and fill it with shelves and wicker bins for baby paraphernalia the way I'd seen in a magazine. Once I started to clear the space, I realized it was a near endless task.

I filled one Hefty bag with empty boxes, papers, and garbage, and another one for Goodwill with old shoes, and a pile of sweaters I hadn't seen in years. I thought I was done when something on the top shelf caught my eye. I'd never seen it before and figured it must have belonged to Priss. The dusty leather bag was full of ancient papers that, at first glance, I figured were old school assignments. When I looked closer, however, I saw they were love letters written to my mother by my dad.

I was dumbfounded. I could still see my father clearly in my mind's eye: a big, sturdy man with a good-size belly and a gruff laugh, strong, gentle hands. He wore a heavy gunbelt and a silver badge on his pocket. And he'd written love letters? I sat down, right there in the middle of the rubble, and started to read. I couldn't believe his beautiful prose. I even found a poem I recognized. Not because I'd ever read it, but because when my mother was dying— just before she died—she was a bit delirious and these beautiful words came dripping out of her. A phrase she said over and over: *Your smile is my rainbow, your laughter is my home, your touch is my heaven* . . . Now I realized that she was quoting the poetry my father had written for her on paper now yellowed with age and fragile in the fold.

In the midst of all these letters, I found a thick envelope addressed to an editor at Doubleday, stamped and ready to go, but never sent. I opened it and smoothed the pages. *An Angel for the Princesses: A Fairy Tale* by James Houston.

What? Love letters, poetry, and now a fairy tale. Who *was* this man?

It started the way they all do . . .

Once upon a time, there lived a king. He was married to the queen, of course, who was beautiful beyond description. She woke with an enchanted smile each day of her life, which was certain proof of her royalty.

And the joy was redoubled because the king and his queen had been blessed with three green-eyed daughters. None could compare to these emerald-eyed beauties: Princess Priscilla, Princess Lilianne, and Princess Lulu. My eyes blurred over when I saw my dad's nickname for me.

The king's heart soared when the first princess, Priscilla, was born. Such a beauty. Who could be this fortunate? When the second princess, Lilianne, came to be, he wept with the immensity of such a blessing—two princesses! But then a third? The king could not comprehend being worthy of such treasures, or the responsibility of keeping such treasures safe and loved.

Soon the king was losing sleep with worry over his daughters, for though he was a powerful king, he was but a humble father who knew he would die to see even one of them harmed or unhappy.

So the king did what any king would do in circumstances such as these: He commissioned a protector to guard against the dragon bats and wanton wizards that lurked outside the castle walls. He sent word far and wide and promised great rewards. And when all were rejected, worry stirred his royal soul. Night and day the king sent pleas heavenward.

He waited patiently—then impatiently—for a response to his urgent petition. He roamed the halls of his castle nightly. He drank hot milk and read dull books and even considered potions that were said to induce slumber. The good queen rubbed his royal feet, but to no avail. Finally, when he could worry no longer, he wept, and while he was in this state, an angel appeared.

She was small and impish with large eyes the color of the ocean at midnight.

"I'm Abigail," the angel said.

"I know you," said the king, though he knew not how he knew her. "You are the protector I seek? Have you the ability to bind the princesses with devotion to one another? Have you the needed magic to salve broken hearts and despair?"

The angel bowed. "Majesty, how can I serve thee?"

"Oh, angel, I would that you bless and keep my daughters. Fill them with my love and guard them in my absence. Can you do this for me?"

"It will be my honor."

The king considered the small angel, who settled his heart with calm. "Come," he said. "You must meet the princesses while they yet sleep, for they are purest when they dream."

In the first bedchamber, Princess Priscilla slept, long limbs splayed over her bed. She had thick lashes and a tiny, upturned nose, and a look of peace that belied the many thoughts that burdened her when she was awake. "This is my beautiful firstborn, on the cusp of womanhood. She is brilliant and driven to perfection, but prone to overlook goodness," said the king. "Angel, you must work to soothe her soul, for she is easily hurt and hides her tender heart behind a razor tongue."

The angel smiled, knowing such things take time and pain to cure.

In the next chamber, there were two beds, one of which was curiously empty. In the other, Princess Lulu was nestled in the arms of the Princess Lilianne, who nightly stole into her sister's bed on the pretense of protection. The king scooped the middle princess into his arms and carried her to the bed near the window. As he drew the coverlet up over her small shoulder, he said, "This princess has the purest heart and the gentlest disposition, but she does not trust her nobility. She worries far too much, angel. I would that you unbridle her laughter. Give her courage to act upon truth."

"I will help her find her strength," said the wise angel.

The king then moved to the next bed, where the tiniest princess slept, dark curls spilling over her pillow, a royal thumb in her mouth. The king knelt by this bedside and stroked the child's smooth brow. "This one, angel, only appears fragile, but she has a tempered soul and a determined nature. There is promise in her that will surely save us all." A single tear rolled from the king's eye, and the angel caught it in her palm. He kissed his tiny daughter on the nose and said, "My wish for this princess is that she find the hidden joy in an imperfect life."

"She was born to do so, sire."

The king considered this lovely cherub surely sent from the land of gods and dreams. He knew that she alone could relieve his torment and make well his worry. He knew this in his royal heart, but he knew not how he knew. He would ponder it all later when the waiting day dawned. For now, he bid Abigail *a good night and crawled in bed beside the beautiful, smiling queen.*

Then, and only then, was he able to sleep. . . .

I heard my front door open and Lily called my name. I hugged my dad's pages to my heart, a chill driving up my spine. My big, strong dad-in-a-uniform had written us a fairy tale. I couldn't believe how well he knew us, then and today, and how much he loved us. I wiped my eyes and put his story back in the envelope, missing him in a way I hadn't missed him in years.

When Lily walked in, I looked up at her from my nest of first-edition James Houston. "Lucy, do you hate me?"

I shook my head, as if hating her were even possible, all thoughts of being angry gone.

For a moment she just stood there, looking down at me. From this angle, she looked so thin. She was holding a colorful bag filled with tissue paper, and her bottom lip quivered. "Lucy, I'm awful. I can't believe how I treated you."

I patted the floor beside me and she sat down.

"It just knocked the wind out of me, Lu. I'm so sorry." Lily had been crying. A lot. Her eyes were swollen and red and her nose was raw. She put her arms around me and I said into her neck, "Are you still mad at me?"

"I don't want to be, Lucy. I'm trying not to be."

"What should I do?"

"Nothing. It's not your fault. I'm going to be happy for you any minute now. I *am* happy for you. Just not all the way yet." She sniffed. "I just didn't realize this monster was still in me after all this time."

"What monster? What are you talking about?"

She shook her head. "After we lost our baby, I didn't get out of bed for weeks. I almost destroyed my marriage. I couldn't get that little face out of my mind." Lily's tears were running down her cheeks and she was struggling to catch her breath. "You were away at school, so you don't know how bad it got, but if I couldn't have that little boy,

I just wanted to go to sleep and never wake up." She wiped her nose on the back of her hand.

"Lily . . ."

"It was awful and I hated myself for what I was doing. To Ron. To myself. But I couldn't help it. I try never to think about him, Lucy, because part of me died that day. But now, you with your news . . ."

I looked at my sister. I thought we'd shared every experience in life, but I'd had no idea how much she suffered when she lost Jamie. I'd been totally caught up in my own life.

Lily wiped the tears from her eyes. "I have no business telling you all this. I just want you to understand. It isn't you. It isn't your baby. It's me."

"I'm sorry, Lil. I didn't realize."

"I don't want you to be sorry! I just wanted to explain."

"You don't have to explain anything. It's okay. It will be okay."

Lily pulled back and looked at me with teasing fury in her eyes. "How do you do that? How do you stay so good and so nice? There's something wrong with you, Lucy, and I really hate you for it."

I laughed a little.

"It's not funny, Lucy. I want you to fight with me. I've been horrid to you. But you never argue. You wake up and Mickey's done something to mess up your life, and you never complain. Mom dies on you when you need her most. Awful things happen and you just adapt! I rain on your good news, and you won't fight with me. What's wrong with you?"

There was nothing to say, so I said, "It's Priscilla's fault."

"It *is* her fault." Lily slumped. Then she laughed. Then we both laughed. Whatever we couldn't pin on anything else, we pinned on Priscilla.

Lily handed me a present. Two actually. Two of the teeniest pairs of shoes I had ever seen: basketball high-tops. The boy's were bright orange, and the girl's were powder-puff pink.

After Lily and I had cried and laughed and had tea and read some of dad's love letters, she went home to put on a pot roast. She'd invited us to dinner and I told her I'd bring a salad. Lily was trying—she was trying to be happy for me despite her pain. She'd always been like that. She had always been the girl in my father's fairy tale, the gentle one who worried too much and didn't laugh enough.

I never showed Lily the fairy tale. The afternoon slipped away from us as we read Dad's letters, and by the time we realized how late it was getting, I'd had a better idea.

After Lily left, I was scooping up all of Dad's papers when I heard Jan pull into her driveway. I ran across the yard and knocked on the screen door, and Jan sang out, "Come in." She was at her kitchen sink rinsing off a huge cluster of grapes, her purse still dangling off her shoulder, her dark glasses still resting in her white-spiked hair. She turned off the water and looked at me. "Well, hello, missy. Want some fruit?" She laid the grapes on the counter and pulled a carton of strawberries from a plastic bag. "Sit down, let's talk."

I watched her at the sink looking like a model who had wandered into a gingerbread house. Regal and polished all the way down to her red nails, a modest tennis bracelet hanging around her bony wrist. She grinned at me, and that grin held a secret.

"You know, don't you?" I waited for her to deny it.

"Know what?" she said, feigning ignorance—and not very well.

"Where were you just now? At the store? At Ghosts?"

"I just dropped in to see my son . . ." She smiled a big, motherly, warm smile. "I'm so happy for you, honey."

"Are you really?"

"Yes! Of course I am." She set the bowl of fruit on the table and put her arms around me. "I'm worried, too, but Lucy . . . A baby? It's wonderful news!" She stood back and cupped my chin in her hand, and I could see her happiness was genuine. As was her concern. She knew all about my contract with Mickey. I tried to thank her, but my throat had closed and it came out as a squeak. "Did you see Lily?" I finally managed.

"No."

"She's having a hard time with this."

Nodding, Jan pulled a grape from the cluster. "I'm sure she is. Be patient with her, sweetie. Her heart was truly broken over that baby boy."

"I'd give anything not to hurt her."

"She knows that."

I looked around Jan's whitewashed kitchen, one end of which currently doubled as her art studio. Not because she didn't have a studio—it was down the hall—but because the light in here was remarkable this time of year. Summer light: ideal for portraits. I moved to the easel and admired the rough sketch of what promised to be a beautiful young woman.

"That's Jessica Nash," Jan said.

"Oh, Jan. How is she doing?"

"Poor baby's struggling. But I think she's happy to be home with her friends and grandparents. She came over the day after the memorial service to look at my paintings for her mother's book, and we ended up talking for the longest time. I just couldn't resist sketching her."

"She's beautiful."

Jan nodded. "She asked about your mom. I hadn't realized she knew."

"I told her at the cemetery. I thought it might help a little to know someone else had gone through it and survived." Again I was kissed by memories of my parents, and I remembered why I had come over. I took the envelope from my pocket and handed it to Jan. "I have a favor."

When I got home, there was a message from Gleason, who said, "I understand congratulations are in order. Mickey sounds very happy. Mic, I guess I'll see you later this week. Lucy, why don't you come, too."

I listened with a little mass of discontent churning in my gut. I couldn't even put my finger on what he'd said to turn my mood. But it wasn't anything he said. It was that Mickey had called him. Why did Mickey do that? Why couldn't he have waited until his appointment to tell Gleason about the baby? Was he afraid?

Suddenly I remembered sitting in Gleason's office all those years ago, cranking out our bloody contract. The No Babies clause hadn't even been drafted. That didn't happen until after my cancer and Mickey's big breakdown. After that, Mickey and I had written the addendum ourselves. Was Mickey having second thoughts?

The evening didn't get any better. Mickey was annoyed that Gleason had called, so we arrived at Lily's already a little off. My sister was stiff and hard to be around, and the whole dinner was painful and awkward. I couldn't wait to get out of there.

Mickey and I walked home in silence, but we were holding hands. As we turned the corner off Gambol Street onto Chestnut, Mickey squeezed my fingers, "Are you okay, Lu?"

"I'm fine."

Mickey pulled me close. "Are you mad at Lily?"

"How can I be mad at her? It was just a dumb night. We'll be okay."

Mickey kissed my forehead. "I'm sorry about Gleason. It just bugged me that he called."

"Why?"

"I don't want anyone thinking I'm going to fall apart over this. Not you, not him. I just called to tell him the good news because I'm excited."

I looked up at him. "You sure?"

"Yes, I'm sure. But he knows me . . ."

I ran my hand down Mickey's arm. "Please don't keep secrets from me, Mic. This is way too important. Too big."

"What do you mean?"

"I mean, if you're afraid, I want to know it. Are you afraid?"

He shook his head. "No."

"Are you sure?"

"I didn't call Gleason because I'm afraid, Lucy. I did it because

I want to do this right. I don't want to blow it. I don't want to let you down. Or it."

"Then don't."

Mickey chuckled.

We walked the rest of the way in silence, and when we got home, we sat down on the front stoop. It was a calm night with a sky full of stars. I could hear the faint noise of a TV over at Jan and Harry's and the small sound of a softball game going on in the park. I breathed deep and snuggled next to Mickey. "It?" I said.

"What?"

"The baby. You called it an 'it.'"

"I guess I did."

"It's a she."

Mickey turned to me. "Charlotte told you it's a girl?"

"No. I just know."

Goofy amusement played over his face. "A mini you? How great would that be?" He ran a finger down my face, then he kissed me, soft at first, then more hungry. When he pulled away, his eyes had turned all soft around the edges, stripped bare of whatever fear I had imagined. "I love you, Lu."

"Backatcha, Michael."

He kissed me again. "Let's get naked," he murmured.

"What a fabulous idea."

thirteen

*I was riding a natural high and it felt delicious; the baby and
all its attendant excitement, planning, growing closer to Lucy,
making room for our budding family. Every time I saw a
baby in a stroller, I felt giddy and then like I should rein it in.
Every time I walked into our bedroom and saw the car seat
we'd bought, I laughed and then scolded myself for laughing.
And it wasn't just the baby. I couldn't get enough of my wife—
touching her, breathing her in, watching her, and I worried
about the fine line between joy and pathology that I seemed
to be tap-dancing on. A normal man doesn't have to question
his sense of well-being. But a mood-disordered man trying to
balance on a pinhead of stability really needs to pay attention.
Obsessing over all of this was starting to make me nervous. I
talked to Gleason about it. He prescribed Lamictal.*

We were in Deep River Center having lunch with Gleason Webb—a
little impromptu checkup over lunch. We'd discussed Mickey's meds
and how much sleep he was getting, and now Gleason was smiling at
us over the pizza we'd ordered. "I feel like I'm going to be a grandpa!"

"Well, you should, Grandpa Gleason!" I said.

He laughed. "So you're both happy?"

"Absolutely," Mickey said, and I nodded.

"Well, you wear it well," Gleason said as the waitress refilled our drinks.

I liked the sound of that—*we wore it well*. It was true; despite sisters who weren't sure how to feel about all this and a doctor who tempered his concern with happy wishes, life had felt so right since Mickey had gotten out of the hospital. The small tiff we'd had over Mic's calling Gleason was the last time we'd argued. Since then, we'd totally immersed ourselves in making room for our baby. In fact, after our appointment/lunch with Dr. Webb, we were on our way to get some more paint samples for the nursery. And next week I was going to drag Mickey to a crib sale at the Baby Depot in New London. I'd fallen in love with a pricey little number in the Pottery Barn catalog that Mickey was trying to talk me out of. Now he'd have his chance.

In the meantime, we'd worked hard cleaning out Priss's old bedroom, and I was shocked at how much junk we'd accumulated. It had all translated to eight bags of trash to the curb, six boxes of odds and ends for Goodwill. A broken desk and the carpet we'd pulled up was headed to the dump. But now we had a clean canvas. I'd even taken the old curtains off the bay window, though now when the sun poured in it highlighted the terrible shape of the wood floor. Mickey promised to sand it down, and after it was refinished, I'd find a plush rug, one colorful and soft enough for a baby to crawl through the sunbeams—

"I'm sorry, what?" Mickey had poked me in the ribs, interrupting my thought, and I was a little embarrassed. "Sorry, Gleason, I was just imagining the baby's room. We're duking it out over buttercup yellow or cotton-candy pink for the walls."

He chuckled and put his hand on his heart. "Well, I can see truly epic decisions are to be made, but I was just saying how proud I am of you two." Gleason nodded. "I really think life has handed you a gift, despite yourselves. I know you didn't plan for this, but you've made room for it. And it looks like you're doing well in the process."

"We are," Mickey said. "For whatever reason we've been granted this little miracle, and we're just going to trust it."

I smiled at him. Sometimes my husband just took my breath away.

"That's good to hear, Mic." Gleason took a last gulp of his coffee. "You two will get through your challenges together, just like always. And of course I'm right here if you need me." He stood up. "I've got a one forty-five, so you two enjoy the rest of the pie. Call if you need to, otherwise I'll see you in two weeks and you can buy *me* lunch." He smiled at me and palmed Mickey's shoulder as he walked away.

Mickey looked at me. "See? He thinks it's great."

I kissed his cheek, thinking it was so much more than that. Gleason knew we could handle it, and that was even more comforting to me.

It was amazing how having this singular focus lifted Mickey and me. Maybe it was because we'd been by ourselves for almost eleven years, which neither of us thought was a terrible thing, but now it was like we were getting ready for royalty. We'd been having so much fun these last few weeks; it was like falling in love all over again over paint and hardwood.

It certainly felt that way the morning Mickey finally found time to sand the floor in the nursery. We were so thrilled to find honey-colored birch under the grimy layers of time and neglect that we almost danced. "Just clear-coat it," I told him on a cough. "It's beautiful just the way it is. Except," I said with a wry smile, "it's way too light now for buttercup. We need a color with more depth."

"Not pink," Mickey insisted. "It's too . . . girly."

"Well, hello . . ."

"Something between the two, but not pink. Besides we don't even know it's a girl yet, and I don't want my son's eyes to burn out when he wakes up to Pepto-Bismol. He could be a boy, Lu."

"He's not a boy. I'll bet you everything in the checkbook, he's a girl."

"You know there's only one hundred and twenty-nine dollars in there. Not too confident, are you, Wife?"

Mickey was covered with a layer of fine dust, and as he teased me he shrugged off his shirt and wiped his face with the inside of it. The sight of his hard chest glistening in the sunlight made me smile.

"What are you doing?" I said as he unzipped his pants.

"I'm getting in the shower, and I don't want to leave a trail from here to there. I have a meeting with Jared and the new talent in half an hour."

"Hmmmm," I said, following him down the hall and into the bathroom. "I didn't know you had a meeting."

"Pretty sure I told you," he said, turning the water on.

"Pretty sure you didn't."

He dropped his boxers and stepped into the shower still talking—something about the talent—but I wasn't listening. I was unbuttoning my blouse. When I opened the steamy glass door, standing there wearing just my smile, Mickey grinned and lifted an eyebrow. "What do you think you're doing, missy?"

"A bad thing," I said, stepping into the shower.

He swallowed. "How bad?"

"Pretty bad, I think. I'm gonna make you late for your meeting."

"What meeting?" he said as he ran his soapy hands over me.

A couple of weeks later, I had to attend a state teachers' conference in Hartford. I was gone all day, and when I finally got home, Mickey, who I thought would be at the club, was sitting on the front porch. His shorts and bare feet made it look as if he wasn't planning to go anywhere, and I got out of the car happy. "Hey, what are you doing home?" I asked, planting a kiss on his forehead.

"I had a project, so I took the night off."

"What kind of project?" I said, trying not to sound anxious.

He laughed. "Don't be nervous. Come with me and close your eyes."

He guided me into the house and made me promise not to peek, which was impossible with his big hands over my face. I half expected to smell paint fumes, but apparently painting the nursery had not been his project. "Okay, Lu. Open them."

I squealed. In the center of my living room sat the crib that I had wanted since I'd seen it in the catalog. It was even more beautiful than the picture; off-white, thick slats, and it would convert into a twin bed for her when she was older. I looked at Mickey and just threw myself at him. "I love it! Oh, baby, thank you! Thank you. Thank you!" I kissed him all over his face.

He'd done a beautiful job putting it together, and it was everything I wanted. I ran my fingers over it and imagined the way the puffy, pink bedding I'd found would look in it; the dark-haired baby girl that would sleep among all that pink. I stepped back to take it all in. Then I laughed because it did take up quite a chunk of space.

"I know," Mickey said, reading me. "I meant to put it together in the nursery, and I would have if it had been delivered when it was supposed to be—next Thursday. But it came today and I couldn't resist. We'll paint this weekend—because by then we'll know we're having a boy—then I'll haul it upstairs." I kissed him as I slipped out of my shoes. "You are a fabulous husband even if you are pathetically wrong." I plopped down on the couch to admire Mickey's handiwork. He still refused to buy paint until after Charlotte proved me right, so for the time being it looked as if the crib would stay right here in our living room. I didn't actually mind that. "Have you eaten?" I yawned.

"No, I waited for you."

"What should we have?"

"I think we should have the lasagna I made."

I looked at him and wanted to cry. "Oh, you are sooo my hero!"

The next weekend I figured out a way to surprise Mickey back when I found a rocking chair at the Dunleavys' yard sale. It was solid and ancient and oversize, and I didn't even know I was looking for one until I saw it. I fell in love with it, knowing it would be perfect for my great big husband to rock his tiny daughter to sleep.

*　*　*

After much pleading, Charlotte had agreed to do our gender check at eighteen weeks. So on August 1, the day that had forever been circled in pink and blue on our calendar, we headed to Charlotte's office. The $129 bet still stood, but I was certain she was a girl. I knew Mickey secretly wanted a girl, even though he would at random times give my baby bump a little squeeze and say, "Feels like a boy, Lu," and I'd say, "No, she doesn't."

What I really wanted him to feel was what I'd started to feel: the butterfly wings, so faint at first that I'd completely dismissed it for what it was—our baby coming to life. I couldn't wait to lift Mickey's hand to my stomach so he could feel her kick.

Bev Lancaster showed us into the examination room and told me to climb on up on the table. Ten minutes later I was still there, now with my shirt pulled up, my lovely bump on full display, willing my baby to move. Mickey was studying a plastic model of a birth canal with a funny look on his face when the door opened and Charlotte walked in. She was pushing a little cart, on top of which was a computer screen. There was also a white paddle trailing what looked like a phone cord.

"So . . . how are the Chandlers today?" she said. "Mickey, you look wonderful. How are you feeling?"

"I feel great, Dr. Barbee. A little nervous at the moment."

"Why?"

"He hates to lose money," I said, reaching for his hand.

Charlotte laughed and bent to plug the machine into the wall. "All right, let's get this show on the road and see who's going to collect." She pulled a bottle of gel from a sleeve in the cabinet and squirted it onto my exposed belly. Where I had expected cold, I was pleasantly surprised by warm. She turned on the computer, then smiled down at me as she placed the paddle low on my stomach. "Let's see what we have here."

Immediately the screen came alive. I didn't know what I was seeing but it looked like snow, like bad reception on a black-and-white television. I glanced at Mickey, who was closer to it than I was, trying to decipher it as well.

"Where are you, little one?" Charlotte said under her breath, slowly sliding the paddle over me. It looked as if something was coming into focus, but then I had to cough and it was lost. "Do you want some water, Lucy?" Charlotte asked.

"No, I'm fine."

Charlotte resumed her sliding, and in a moment a form took shape. "There you are," Charlotte said to the screen. "And we have a baby." She adjusted a knob that somehow amplified the image. "Can you see the head?"

"Where?" Mickey and I said at the same time.

"Right here." Charlotte pointed, and as she did, the image started to make sense. "Full on like this, the face looks a little strange."

"How can you tell that's a face?" Mickey said. "All I see are black holes . . . or . . . is that . . . what am I seeing?"

"Those are your baby's eyes, but you're only seeing the sockets. Let me see if I can get a profile." Charlotte slid the paddle around, pushed it deeper into my skin.

"Is that an arm? What is that?" Mickey let go of my hand and bent closer to the screen.

"Yes. There's an arm and there's the other one, and a leg and . . . Oh, there you are; another leg. I'm looking," she said. "Not seeing . . . Nope. I don't think so." She adjusted the paddle and zeroed in on a specific angle. "I'm sorry, Mic, but I can't seem to find a penis."

"Are you sure?"

"Well, you tell me. This is the glass-table view. We're looking between the legs, but from underneath. Sorry, Dad. If this is a boy, it looks like it's the girl kind."

"Yes!" I squealed.

Mickey looked over at me and grinned. "I told you he was a girl," he said. Then he bent to kiss me full on the mouth, lingered a second. "A mini you . . . ," he whispered, all awe and joy.

"And you don't look disappointed at all, Dad," Charlotte chuckled.

"Well, I'd feel better if she had a face," Mickey said on a laugh. "But other than that . . ."

I laughed, too, and then I was crying, but not because I was surprised. It was suddenly all so very real. We were having a daughter.

Charlotte winked at me. "You were right, darlin'."

I don't know how I'd been so sure, but now it felt as if I'd always known her. My daughter. Charlotte kept talking as she pointed out the chambers of the heart, the hemispheres of the brain. Mickey was fascinated, asking all kinds of questions, and as I watched him, it was as if I'd stolen this moment from someone else this was supposed to happen to. Not us. Never us. Through my tears, I watched my great big husband looking utterly awestruck at his daughter's clenched fist. "Look, Lu, you can see every little bone in her fingers."

Charlotte printed several screen shots for us, and Mickey said he was going to run over to Partners and scare Jared with the pictures while I finished up.

"Jared has five kids," I said. "These won't scare him."

Mickey kissed my forehead. "I'm going anyway. Just come over when you're done and we'll have lunch."

I'd gained a total of six pounds, which didn't seem right, but Charlotte assured me that my weight would catch up with me. As for everything else, all was well; my blood pressure was good and my heart was beating away at a normal clip. She examined my breasts in her usual manner and totally disregarded that they were tender. She seemed especially hard on the left one, and before she let me go, she decided that, since she had the machine, she'd do a breast ultrasound. Charlotte was thorough, first one, then the other, then back to the first one and none too talkative as she worked. I watched the computer screen and had no idea what I was seeing.

"Do you see something, Charlotte?"

"Ummmm. I don't think so, mostly just a lot of engorgement. I think they probably look pretty much the way mama-to-be breasts are supposed to look." She turned off the machine and handed me a towel. "A little messy, but easier than a mammogram, huh?"

"Much."

"All right, Lucy, I'll let you get on with your day. If you don't hear from me, come see me again in two weeks."

"Okay," I said, sliding off the table. "But I'm not going to hear from you, right?"

Charlotte smiled. "Not if I can help it, darlin'."

I was almost skipping as I walked up the street to the Brubaker Inn.

Mickey's club was through the hotel lobby, and when I got there, Mickey had ordered sandwiches for us off the room-service menu. While we ate in the office he shared with Jared, we pored over the pictures of our daughter. It was awesome to consider this little *life* was inside me. Jared popped in and acted dutifully impressed. He picked up one of the pictures. "This one looks like you, Lucy."

I laughed, but he was serious. "Check it out, Mic, that's Lucy's profile. Am I lying?" They made me turn just so. Jared held up the profile of our baby next to my face, and Mickey got a strange look on his. "That's unbelievable. It is your profile, Lu."

I would have loved to run across the street to Ghosts just then and get my sister's thoughts on the ultrasound, but I didn't trust that it wouldn't be awkward or, worse, hurt her. I missed her horribly. I missed sharing everything with her and I didn't know how to get that back.

I think Mickey must have read the change in my mood, because he gathered the pictures and handed them to me. "Okay, Mom, that's enough staring at our faceless daughter. We have paint to buy."

"Have fun," said Jared as he walked out.

"Finally," I said, standing up. But then Mickey's phone rang and I could see that he wanted to answer it. "I'll wait in the lobby."

"I'll only be a minute," he promised.

I walked out of the club and headed into the hotel lobby, where a plushy sofa faced the big fireplace. Just as I rounded the corner, I saw Lily walk into the Brubaker. When we saw each other, for a split second I think we both wanted to turn the other way. Instead, she offered me an anxious little wave and bit her lip as she walked over to me. "I saw you come in here a few minutes ago," she said. "And I just . . . I just wanted to see how you were doing."

"I'm good, Lil. I'm glad I ran into you, I was going to come over. At least, I thought about it."

"What's new?"

My eyes filled with tears because hers did. And because she was brave enough to come find me, I didn't hesitate. "I want to show you something, Lily." I took her hand and we walked over to the sofa.

"What is it?"

We sat down close to each other, and I pulled the ultrasound pictures from my pocket. "I want you to meet your niece."

Lily coughed out a little squeak as she took the pictures from me, her hands shaking.

I put my arm around her and leaned my head into her shoulder. "She's not much to look at right now, but I think she's beautiful."

Lily nodded and I saw her tears fall as she studied the images. For a long time she was quiet. "She is beautiful," she finally said. "But . . . where is she, Lu? What am I looking at?"

I laughed. Lily laughed even though she was crying.

"This is her profile." I pointed. "Here's her legs and that's her *I'm a girl*. There's her little clenched fist."

"Oh, she *is* beautiful." Lily shook her head. "I didn't know until this very minute how much I've always wanted a niece."

"Really?" I rasped.

Her arms came around me. "You're having a baby. A baby girl. How wonderful is that?" she said into my hair. "No more of this avoiding each other, I can't stand it. I can't. I want every single detail, every single day. Can I please have that?"

"Well, that's the second-best sight I've seen today," Mickey said, walking across the lobby toward us.

Lily and I unhugged, and my sister pushed the tears off her face.

"I've just had the pleasure of meeting your daughter," she said, as she stood and put her arms around Mickey. "Nice work, Mic. Congratulations."

"Thanks, Lily. You okay?"

"I'm just fine. I'm gonna be an aunt for heaven's sake!" She kissed his cheek. "I have to get back to the store now. I'm pretty sure I'm being robbed blind this very minute by Muriel's sister—don't be fooled by the walker, that old gal can get around." She chuckled as she wiped her nose. "I just had to come over when I saw you." She turned to me. "Remember, Lucy: every detail."

"Okay," I promised, relief washing over me.

She kissed my cheek and walked out.

Mickey's arms came around me from behind and he pulled me to his chest. "It's a good day, Lu," he said into my ear.

"It is. It's a very good day."

fourteen

The cycle. Familiar in every way. Part me, part my medication. It's been almost two months since I was discharged from the hospital and I'm recovered from my ascent. I'm so grateful I didn't fall too fast or too hard back to level ground, because if that happens, I can dive through it and into depression, a place dark and draining where nothing matters and I don't care. But life is too good right now for this to be a concern. Even if it weren't, my serious depressions have been blessedly few and far between. This is probably because I am highly responsive to antidepressants—so much so that with little warning I can be pushed into mania. I am a brittle bipolar. I strive to live in the pocket of sanity known as the safe edge of hypomania. If there's an upside to bipolarity, that's it—the energized state of being that unfortunately can't really be sustained. It's not static, it has a destination. Eventually—if left unchecked—it leads to what Gleason calls "the point of undeniability," a state in which I am helplessly psychotic but don't know it.

For me the cycle goes like this: a small disruption in my sleep pattern, moods that begin to bleed together, a subtle shift in my reality, ideas that strike me as unusually brilliant, more disruption in my sleep, more brilliant ideas that flow fluidly, slowly at first, deceptively so, but then gush through the sieve of my brain, thoughts I try to catch because they are so good, but which slip through my fingers like water. More disruption of sleep, not tired, wired, still thinking clearly but starting to second-guess myself. My course can be corrected when I'm standing here, right here—not one inch further in. But it feels so good here, to work like a demon, no time for sleep, no desire for sleep, alive to the extreme, I need more hands to get it all done. All what? It slips away. Muddled thinking, but aware that I'm losing it. I need sleep, but I am now incapable of sleep because I am incapable of shutting off my brain. This is the edge. Another step is to fall, lose touch with reality but not know it, angry because everyone seems critical of me, telling me how to live, what I should be doing, what I shouldn't be doing. What do they know? I can fix this on my own with pills that for some reason have stopped working. In my brilliance, I double up on some and eliminate others that are surely the reason for this spiral. The edge of sanity: one foot in, one foot out.

I know this cycle: the fall and rise, the leveling out. I've learned trust is the secret. I can't trust me, which has taken a lifetime for me to grasp. But I trust Lucy and I trust Gleason. Ron and Jared have not lied to me either. All of them tell me to trust the pills to get me back to the speed limit. Back to level ground or hovering just above level but not lower; if at all possible, not lower. I do what I can to not dip below the fault line into despair. But then that, too, is part of the cycle.

I looked around Charlotte Barbee's inner office and tried to control my shaking. It had been three days since I'd been here with Mickey, gushing over a perfectly normal ultrasound. Charlotte hadn't even been the one to call this afternoon. She'd had Bev Lancaster do it, and Bev said she had no idea why Charlotte wanted to see me. It took my breath away, and now I was waiting, filled with dread. What had happened in the last three days to fill me with this much anxiety?

Finally Charlotte came in and took her seat across the desk from me. She cleared her throat a couple of times and avoided my eyes. "Thanks for coming in, Lucy."

My hands stiffened around each other. "Charlotte, what's going on? Is there a problem?"

She took a deep breath. "I don't think so. I really don't, Lucy." Her tone was clear and confident, all business. "It's just that I've been comparing your mammograms with this most recent ultrasound, and I think this last one might be just a bit off. I'd feel better if a colleague of mine could double-check it."

"Okay," I heard myself say.

"Lucy, I'm almost certain it can be explained by your pregnancy. I've looked at the images a hundred times and . . ." She shook her head. "I just want to be sure we have nothing to worry about. It's only because of your history, which is the reason we're checking so often anyway. I'm just going to be suspicious until I know otherwise."

"And you're suspicious now?" I wanted to be clear.

She shook her head, but said, "Just a little. I sent your films from last week to another radiologist; one more specialized than the doctor we usually use. I just wanted a second interpretation, and he agreed with me that what we see can probably be attributed to your pregnancy. Here, let me show you." She hung three sets of images on the white screen behind her desk and flipped a light switch. "These are from a year ago, these are from two months ago, and these are from last week."

"What am I looking at?"

"It's hard to see, but this area is just a bit darker." She pointed. "Do you see that?"

I leaned over to get a closer look. "Maybe."

"It's probably nothing, Lucy. Pregnancy imposes a number of physiological changes that naturally result in the enlargement of breast tissue—increased glandularity, water content. But those normal things can also make it difficult to evaluate small changes that might be serious. When you came for your regular checkup two months ago, when we found out you were pregnant, I didn't see anything problematic.

"And then, just to be on the safe side, I ran the comparative ultrasound when you came in on Monday. That's this one." She pointed to the third picture.

I stood up and leaned over Charlotte's desk. "I'm not sure I see a difference."

"I know, me neither. But I felt something the other day."

My legs tingled and I had to sit back down as I took in the sight of my doctor—serious features, capable bearing, white lab coat over a black linen dress. "You felt something? Why didn't you tell me?"

"Because I really didn't think it was anything outside of the norm, and your labs didn't indicate a problem—in fact, nothing really points to a possible problem except your history. That's why I want another opinion. It's just a little thickness in the area that coincides with this dark area." She pointed again to the bottom of one of the images. "Lucy, as I said, if it's just tissue engorgement, it's a completely normal finding."

"But?"

Charlotte flipped off the light and turned back to me. "But we want to be sure, right, darlin'?"

"Okay, yes," I said shakily. "So now what?"

"I'd send you back to Dr. Stevens who treated you last time, but he's moved to Fort Worth, so I'm sending you to Dr. Matthews over in New Haven. He's at Women's Oncology, specializing in everything we've been talking about. I know him. He's very good." Charlotte scribbled an address on a slip of paper and handed it to me. "Can you go this afternoon?"

"Today? I thought you weren't worried."

"Lucy, he's there now, and as a favor to me, he said he'd squeeze you in. He's just going to look at these pictures and examine you, maybe run a test or two. It might take a few days for him to get back to me with his findings. And when he does, we can all just get on with this pregnancy breathing easier. Okay?"

I stared at Charlotte. She was not smiling. I tried to read her. "Charlotte, do you think I should tell Mickey? Should I have him go with me?"

Charlotte's gaze stayed steady. "That's up to you, Lucy."

If I called, I knew Mickey would drop everything to go with me. He would be here now if I would have asked. Charlotte came from behind the desk and put her hands on my shoulders. "Lucy, this is just a precaution. And we're not going to worry about this until we know if there's anything to worry about." I nodded but couldn't seem to find my voice.

Charlotte handed me a large manila envelope that contained my images, and I somehow got myself out of her office and into my car, her words echoing in my head. My first impulse was to call Mickey. I wanted his strength right now. But he was in such a great place, relaxed and stable, so excited about everything. Did I really need to disrupt that before I knew anything? Wasn't that just selfish? It was probably nothing and I would have worried him for no reason. This is how I rationalized the decision not to call my husband.

I leaned my head against the headrest, closed my eyes, and tried to stop trembling. Surely this could not be happening to me again. I replayed everything Charlotte had said, and all that she hadn't said, and I couldn't make it any softer.

I sat in my steamy car wondering if anyone else would be up for a drive to New Haven. Lily was as big an impossibility as Mickey and for nearly the same reasons. For a fleeting moment, I thought of Ron. As brothers-in-law go, I couldn't be luckier. Ron was not an alarmist, nor did he overreact. He was laid-back and solid and real and he wouldn't ask me any questions. He'd just hold my hand and share all the silent possibilities with me. But then we'd have to tell Lily, and she might not forgive him for being a better candidate than her. I couldn't put him in the middle.

In the end, I just drove my perfectly capable, big-girl self to the New Haven Center for Oncological Research Hospital. The huge, multibuilding complex was sterile and unfriendly right down to the receptionist in Building D, Suite 410, Office of Reproductive Imaging Studies. I walked into a crowded waiting room and told the girl at the desk who I was. She scanned her computer screen and told me I didn't have an appointment. I said I knew that. I told her I'd been sent by Dr. Charlotte Barbee in Brinley—I might as well have told her I'd come from the moon. Tina Pulsifer, according to her name tag, told me that there was no way I was going to be able to see a doctor today. "No one has a free second for a walk-in," she said, like I was there for a haircut.

"Not *a* doctor—Dr. Roland Matthews."

Her mouth fell open. "You're kidding."

"If you knew why I was here, you'd know I wasn't kidding, Tina. Dr. Charlotte Barbee spoke with him directly. I don't mind waiting, but please tell him I'm here."

Her perfect little lips parted again, and a perfect little sigh escaped as she picked up the phone. "It's going to be a while. Dr. Matthews is in surgery. Do you have your films?"

I handed her the envelope. "Surgery? I thought he was a radiologist."

"He's not a radiologist—he's the head of the department."

Panic, formerly swaddled in cotton, stretched awake in me.

"Please sit down, Mrs. Chandler. I'll have him paged," Tina said, dismissing me. I stumbled, just a little, over to a chrome-and-leather chair, ultramodern, uncomfortable.

As I sat for an interminable amount of time in that awful chair, I replayed the suddenly questionable calm in Charlotte's voice. I retraced her words and tried again to hear her tell me I had nothing to worry about. Somewhere in the midst of this exercise, I heard my name and looked up to find a tall, thin boy coming toward me. "Lucy Chandler?"

I nodded.

He smiled. "I'm Owen Peters, Dr. Matthews's PA. If you'll come with me, I'll take you up to surgery."

"What?" I said, suddenly unable to get to my feet. "I'm not here for surgery."

"Oh, I'm sorry, no. I meant I'm here to take you up to Dr. Matthews. He's in surgery, but he wants to see you." Owen was holding my images.

"I appreciate him squeezing me in like this," I said, trying to tamp down my anxiety. I followed the tall physician's assistant to the elevator. Neither of us spoke as we ascended the six floors to the surgical suites. I studied Owen's indifferent reflection in the smooth doors and wondered why he wasn't nicer, more talkative, why he hadn't been trained in ways to put nervous women at ease.

When the elevator stopped, he escorted me to an office and told me Dr. Matthews would be right with me. I looked around. The bare office didn't seem to belong to anyone; it was cold and impersonal and felt hard against my nerves. Thankfully, I was only there a few minutes before Owen Peters returned. He smiled his insincere smile again and said, "Mrs. Chandler, if you'll come with me? Dr. Matthews looked at your images and he'd like to examine you."

"Really? Did he find something?" I asked, trying to match his stride.

"I don't know, ma'am."

I suddenly regretted not bringing Mickey. Owen deposited me behind a curtain and politely asked me to take off my blouse and put on a hospital gown; then he was gone again, and I broke out in a sweat.

I waited in the exam room for nearly a half hour, imagining the unimaginable. When I didn't think I could stand to wait another moment, I decided to leave. I was reaching for my blouse when the curtain parted and a short man in surgical greens walked in. "Mrs. Chandler?"

"Yes."

"I'm Dr. Matthews." He extended his hand and I shook it. "Dr. Barbee had some concerns and asked me to take a look at you. Would it be okay if I examined you?"

"Oh, okay."

The doctor lowered the gurney until I was positioned to his liking, then he kneaded my tender breasts with his ice-cold hands. He was thorough, I'll give him that, but not one bit gentle, and not talkative. He spent what seemed like an inordinate amount of time pushing my engorged tissue around in a circular motion. He apologized once when I grimaced but continued without adjusting his pressure. He seemed to zero in on the backside of my left breast, close to my ribs. He kneaded and flattened and pushed and dug with his nimble fingers. I was left to concentrate on his breathing, attuned to concern. Finally, he sighed and let go of my breast.

"Hmm. I can see the dilemma." He sat down on a rolling stool and seemed to be organizing his thoughts. "How is Charlotte these days?"

"What?" I asked, taken aback. "Fine. She's fine. She's a good doctor."

"One of the best. We were in medical school together." He tapped his chin. "Well, I can understand her concern, given your history. And I agree with her that nothing *seems* all that out of the ordinary."

I exhaled a lungful of relief.

"But we don't want to overlook anything, either." Dr. Matthews's demeanor changed ever so slightly. "Lucy, as long as you're here, I'd like to do a biopsy. Just a fine-needle aspirate. Let's make sure there's nothing to be concerned about." He stood up. "I'll send Owen in to get you prepped and I'll see you in a few minutes."

I nodded dumbly as the room grew smaller. As he disappeared on the other side of the curtain, I was suddenly cold and a bit lightheaded.

As if in slow motion, I got off the exam table, walked to the trash can by the sink, and threw up. All my substance came up hot and violent until there was no strength in me; not in my legs, not in my arms. It was such a strange feeling to step aside and watch myself slump to the ground as the cold, white room shrank to the diameter of a quarter. I just shut my eyes and let go.

Owen Peters and a woman, probably a nurse, were suddenly there, talking loud as I inhaled the biting stench of ammonia. They helped me into a wheelchair and the nurse spoke sweetly to me. "Put your head down, hon, and take some deep breaths. Are you feeling better? Are you okay?"

"I think so. I'm sorry, I don't know what happened."

"No problem. Here, you're shaking." She covered me with a warm blanket, and I pulled it close around me. Owen then handed me a consent form. "Um, I'm pregnant and don't want any medication that could hurt my baby," I said as I took the clipboard.

"I understand, ma'am," he said without looking at me. As he wheeled me into Operating Room One, the robotic PA provided me with an impressive explanation of the local anesthesia that would numb my left breast. He was a font of information.

I was transferred to an operating table, then covered with a drape, except for the breast in question. I imagined the aerial view of me lying there. I imagined how I must seem, completely reduced to just that breast, nothing more. Through a fog of anxiety, I gave Priscilla's telephone number to whoever might be listening and asked them to call my sister.

As I lay there helpless to do anything else, I imagined crouching over my baby, pulling her to me, protecting her with the meager shield of my body. I was so lost in this image that Dr. Matthews had to address me twice to tell me it was over. I was then suddenly aware of the feeling of heaviness on my chest. Ice. I was quickly wheeled into another room and left alone. I closed my eyes.

"Are you in any pain, honey?" I looked into the warm eyes of a woman I assumed was a nurse and shook my head.

"Can you sit up? I have some juice for you." She helped me, telling me to take deep breaths so I wouldn't faint again. "When's the last time you had anything to eat, sweetie? Are you hungry?"

The juice tasted wonderful. "This is fine. Thank you."

"Well, some crackers then." She placed some saltines in my hand. "Now, do you have any questions for me?"

"Where do I start?"

The woman shook her head. "You poor thing. I can just imagine your day." She sat down and smiled. Her name tag said GAIL and she was probably about Charlotte's age. She was blond and top-heavy in her blue scrubs. "I understand your doctor sent you over with some slides, and the next thing you knew, we were doing a biopsy."

"That's about it. Did they find anything?"

Gail shook her head. "Dr. Matthews performed two biopsies, a fine-needle and a core-needle aspirate on a small area at the back of your breast. He collected several hundred cells and is running some tests. He'll be in touch with your doctor."

"Why two?"

"He's just very thorough. And he must really owe your doctor a favor to have seen you on such short notice. You're in very good hands."

"Well, that's good to know."

"Now, his PA is something else. We think he runs on batteries." I chuckled, and Gail helped me back into my blouse. "Thank you," I said, amazed at the power this woman had to calm my fearful heart. "I mean it. Thank you."

"You eat some more of these." She filled my hand with crackers. "And if you feel okay in ten minutes, I'll let you leave."

As I sat there in my curtained enclosure sipping my juice, I heard a commotion in the hall. Priscilla was whisper-shouting my name. Apparently she was searching behind every curtain for me. Finally she found mine.

"Lucy, are you okay?"

"I'm fine, Priss."

"What are you doing here? Tell me what happened."

"Charlotte felt something. She saw a shadow on the ultrasound and sent me over. But it's probably just because I'm pregnant. It's probably nothing." I heard my own voice crack and felt Charlotte's promise break. I stared at my sister, lip quivering, tears stinging my eyes, feeling foolish and exposed.

Priscilla put her arms around me. "It's okay, Lu. I'm here."

It felt so good to hand my turmoil over to my sister; let her hold it for just a minute while I pulled myself together. Priss stroked my hair as I pressed my face into her silk blouse and tried not to cry. I was scared and tired, but better now that she was here. After a few deep breaths I convinced her I was okay. Priscilla smoothed my shirt and combed through my hair with her long fingers.

"Lucy, you're a mess."

"I know, and I've got to get it together before I see Mickey."

Priscilla groaned, "Oh, of course. Where is he? Is he here?"

"No, he doesn't know anything about this."

"Well, that's just great, Lucy. So what now—you'll pretend life is fine? Is this the next big secret Mickey won't be able to handle?"

"What are you talking about? Mickey's not here because I didn't want to worry him."

"I'll never understand. Never. What's the point of—"

"Priscilla, please. Don't start."

She shook her head. "And you're pregnant. Lucy, what are you thinking?"

Now I was mad at myself for calling her in the first place. "I'm thinking you should be quiet now and take me to get something to eat."

Priscilla has always punctuated her harsher statements with body language—a disapproving slump, lengthy looks of reproach, eye-rolling. But this time an alien softness transformed her face and she took my hand and kissed it. "I'm sorry, honey. You don't need a lecture right now. I'm just so glad you called me."

We drove separately to the Olive Garden down the street from the hospital. I was hungry, but suddenly the smell of Italian food turned my stomach. I ordered soup and a breadstick and sipped my water as Priscilla flirted with our waiter. She flashed her gleaming caps and rubbed her diamond-studded earlobe. I kicked her under the table, and she glared at me.

When he came back with our food a few minutes later, clearly expecting a reprise, I felt bad for him because Priscilla was checking the messages on her BlackBerry. When she didn't even acknowledge him, he walked away, looking wounded.

After a lengthy monologue about Priscilla's incompetent assistant who'd left her four messages, she threw her phone in her purse and looked back at me.

"Are you scared, Lu?"

"A little. But I'm just going to assume everything's all right until Charlotte tells me it's not."

Priscilla looked pointedly at me and shook her head. "You've been here before, Lu. So have I. We both know the empty sound when they say it's probably nothing. It stops your heart."

Her blunt appraisal felt like a kick in the stomach and I had to work not to cry. "I'm trying not to be afraid, Priss. Not now. I'm pregnant, and I don't want to be scared!"

Priscilla narrowed her eyes at me. "What are you going to tell Mickey?"

I looked at my untouched soup. "Hopefully nothing. Hopefully I won't have to tell him anything."

My sister looked like she had something to say, but she swallowed it and reached for my hand. She stared hard at me through her dark-green eyes with an expression that could be intimidating. It wasn't working. Especially when tenderness crept into her icy glare. "What have you been thinking about?" she said softly.

"To be honest, mostly Mom. All the way here, I just kept thinking how hard she tried to stay with us. How hard it was for her to leave her daughters."

"I sometimes still blame her."

I sighed. "Why do you do that to yourself, Priss? You've been mad at Mom your whole life. She's been dead for sixteen years. Let it go already!"

"I just don't understand her. Why would a woman have kids only to leave them this legacy? What she's done to us, in my opinion, is almost unforgivable. Look at our lives. Look what we have to go through."

"And the alternative, Priscilla?"

"I know. I know. But she *knew* she came from a long line of cancer and still chose to have three daughters."

I shook my head. "I swear, sometimes I think you are mentally ill."

"That's not funny. But if it were true, I could probably attribute that to Mom, too."

"Well, at least you're luckier than most menopausal women," I snarked. "At least you can identify the exact person responsible for your misery. But it's cruel to blame Mom, and you *are* mentally ill if you can't see that."

"You might be right. But at this moment—*this moment* that none of us ever wanted to revisit—I just need to blame something . . . someone. Cut me some slack, Lucy."

I slumped. Being loved by my sister took a lot out of me. Priss paid our bill and took my hand as we walked outside where we were parked next to each other. When we got to my car, Priscilla turned to me and squeezed my fingers. "So, Lucy, tell me the truth. Have you seen your *friend* lately? Have you seen her today?"

"No." I shook my head.

"No pretty specter? You promise me?"

"I promise."

Priscilla pulled me close. "I'll call you tomorrow." She walked over to her car and shouted at me above the roof of her Beemer, "By the way, you little snot, I am *not* menopausal."

I waved at my sister and we parted ways at the intersection. The drive back to Brinley took about forty-five minutes, and I drove straight to Partners. I just wanted to see Mickey, bask for a minute in his lazy smile. But when I walked into the club, I could see he was having a bad time of his own. By the look on his face, I realized I must have looked as bad as Priscilla said I did. "What's the matter, Lucy? Are you sick?" he asked, his voice gravelly with irritation.

His tone caught me off guard. "Yeah, maybe. I think I'm getting a cold on top of all my regular complaints," I said hesitantly, placing his big hand on my belly. "But other than that, we're fine." I stood on tiptoe and kissed him on the chin. "Just came by to see you and give you a kiss."

He settled down and gave me a half grin as he bent toward me. "Why don't you stick around, and we'll have some dinner. It looks like I'm going to be here until closing. One of the bartenders called in sick and we're short an act tonight, so I'm filling in."

"Really? You don't look like you've got much comedy in you right now." When more annoyance surfaced in his eyes, I cut my losses. "Where's Jared?"

"On the phone with the damn faking-sick bartender."

Mickey's looking ornery and overwhelmed gave me the perfect excuse not to tell him where I'd been. I'd tell him tomorrow when Charlotte called with the good news. "I guess I'll just see you when you get home. Are you good?"

He nodded. "I'm okay. I'm sorry to grouse. I just need to figure this out."

"It's okay." I kissed my big, ornery husband again and headed home to put this day behind me. I took a bath, gingerly sponging around my tender breast, and went to bed with a bag of ice. If I was awake when Mickey got home, maybe I'd tell him about it. But probably not. I fell into my pillows hoping to drift quickly to sleep, but something was nagging me, something annoying and indistinct, but familiar. I ignored it until I couldn't stand it another minute, then I got up and turned the bathroom light on.

I'd been avoiding it since before Priscilla had asked. Now I stood looking at myself in the mirror, scrutinizing all the space around my silhouette. It was the mirror I had watched my father shave in every morning. It was the mirror my mother's face had grown pale and gaunt in. Now it was the mirror that would warn me of what was ahead, so I looked hard for the messenger.

I searched, not wanting to see her. Not now, not when the world was lovely and my future held a little girl. And I didn't *see* her—I hadn't even seen her when I was sick before. But for the first time since I'd met Death all those years ago, I had the distinct feeling she was en route. That knowledge settled on me like a cool night on a garden. And the longer I stood there, the stronger the feeling grew. I ran a hand over my face, where a cold sweat had appeared, and told myself I was being paranoid.

I turned the light off and got back into bed where I rubbed my swollen belly. I was imagining things. Surely, I was imagining. But unbidden, warm tears dripped down my temples and into my hair. It took everything I had to tamp down the foreboding and push myself above it. I finally fell asleep in a much softer place, a place that smelled like a baby right after her bath. A place where the background music was a little girl's giggle.

fifteen

Lamictal is used in some to lengthen the stable time between bipolar episodes, so I was happy it seemed to be working. But I still felt a little brittle, and for the past few nights I'd gotten by on fewer hours of sleep. I'd have to watch that. Last night I crashed on the couch a little after two, and by five I was in the shower. But I felt great, focused, tracking, my thoughts lined up in a nice straight line with no random ideas jumping ahead or sideways, which was good. Lucy was still asleep and I was ready for the day, but since it was too early to go to work, I pulled out my laptop and the newspapers I'd been saving. One of the things that helps ground me is watching my investments. I like to follow the stock market, the Dow Jones, the NASDAQ. I like to graph the activity; I like straight red lines tracking numbers across a perfectly white piece of paper. To me, it represents order in economic disorder. Lucy worries a little when I start doing this, but it's just an interest, not necessarily the precursor she thinks it is.

When I woke up, I realized Mickey had already showered and gone downstairs and I wondered what time he'd gotten home. On the surface his getting up early may not sound like a bad thing, but when Mickey has a diminished need for sleep, it's a rather large red flag. I threw back the covers and rubbed my stiff eyes. In the bathroom, I splashed cold water over my face and pushed thoughts of unseemly visitors away. More pressing issues were at hand than what may, or may not, have happened last night in this bathroom. For instance, I was seriously nauseated.

After I retched absolutely nothing into the toilet and brushed my teeth, I went downstairs. Mickey was in the kitchen, the newspaper spread out in front of him, MSNBC mumbling from the little TV on the counter. I kissed his head, and he looked up at me sheepishly. "I got up early."

"I know."

He stood up, knocking a red pen onto the floor. "Lucy, you don't look good."

I reached for the oyster crackers and took a handful. "I'll be fine in a minute."

Mickey put his arms around me, and I just wanted to crawl into that hug and never come out. "Are you okay, Lu?"

"I'm not too keen on this morning sickness, but other than that . . ."

Mickey held me at arm's length and studied me. "Lucy, I'm sorry about last night. I was mad at the bartender and I took it out on you."

"You did?"

"I thought I did. And I thought you were still mad. Is it this? Are you upset about this?" he said, referring to the current props at hand: some graph paper, a red Sharpie, and a big stack of newspapers. "It's nothing to worry about, Lu, I was just curious," he insisted. "It's been a while since I checked on things."

I nodded as I walked out of his grasp and put some water on to boil. "Don't dance with me, Michael. Should I be worried?"

"Absolutely not." He returned to the project spread over the table.

When he was spinning, his "curiosity" about the economy had to be satisfied immediately, and his mood was dependent upon the numbers. When the indexes were up, his excitement could take over all reason. If they were falling, fear and catastrophe could do the same thing. Some days he checked the Dow Jones Industrial more than a hundred times.

It was too soon to be alarmed about this, I told myself, even as I wondered if Mickey was taking his medications. I shot for nonchalant when I asked him, steeling myself for the most telling sign of a problem: an eruption. But Mickey just looked at me and grinned.

"I'm right on, Lu. And I'm having my levels checked this afternoon." When I didn't respond outwardly, he got up and tousled my hair on his way to the fridge. "Don't pretend you're not relieved," he chuckled. He knew me so well. I was relieved that since his discharge from Edgemont he'd pretty much maintained his gains. Still, changes in sleep usually forewarned of bad things to come, so I made a mental note to pay closer attention.

Mickey has always had compulsions to do strange things—feverishly tracking the seven-day weather forecasts across the nation or the price of gas and airline tickets. Sometimes he counted things—the blades of grass stuck on his shoes after he mowed the lawn, the number of commercials in a half-hour sitcom, red cars on the road. As many times as he's appeared to escalate, he's de-escalated, so these idiosyncrasies were not always reliable markers of his level of stability. Still, by the time he's so compulsive he's counting red cars driven by women with short hair and pierced ears wearing hoop earrings, he knows it's time to have his meds adjusted. I could have it so much worse. Seventy-five percent of the time he takes care of business. You gotta love a guy like that. You just have to live always knowing that 25 percent of the time there are things that will push him toward the edge.

I smoothed my robe over my tender breast and decided *this* was one of the things that would do it for sure.

"You okay? You look worried." Mickey reached over and kissed my wrist. "I'm good, Lu. I really am. But if I don't sleep tonight, I'll call Gleason."

"That's why I love ya." As I sat there waiting for my stomach to settle, I watched him graph the nation's economic activity, remembering a couple of years ago when he went all the way back to Reagan's last year in office.

When the kettle whistled, I unwrapped a cinnamon mandarin tea bag and had a little internal debate with myself. What good could come from telling Mickey anything about yesterday until I knew there was actually something to tell? Probably none. But we'd made that pesky promise never to hide what we were going through. On the other hand, we'd already broken one promise for the better. . . . I steeped my tea bag and arranged the words I could say into the gentlest configuration I could muster. *I haven't been completely honest, babe. I'm really not okay, and something happened in the bathroom last night. Charlotte found a thick place and a shadow and sent me to Dr. Matthews, who thought it looked suspicious, so I had a biopsy. We won't know for a few days what the results are, but, I gotta say, I'm a little terrified about what it could all mean. So, no, I'm not doing so great this morning, Mic, but it sure feels good to give some of my worry over to you, my big, strong, wonderful husband.*

I took a bracing sip of tea. "Mic, honey, I need to talk to you before—"

The ringing of the cordless phone at Mickey's side cut off my words. Harry, next door, had a dead battery. Mickey was out the door to give him a jump before I could exhale. A half hour later when Jared called with another problem, Mickey's mood turned so quickly that I began to doubt my prior reasoning. He was gone in a flurry of promises that we would talk when he got home. And though I worried about it all morning as I shopped for a rug for the nursery, it became a moot point by that night.

I was setting the table when Mickey came in the back door. He didn't look good. "Honey?" I said. "You okay?"

He came up behind me and buried his face in my neck, which I misinterpreted as his wanting to fool around. "What are you doing?" I giggled. But then I felt him shudder against my back. "Mickey? What's wrong?"

He was quiet for a moment, then said, "Lucy, do you have anything to tell me?"

I felt myself get a little tingly and my mind raced to find the excuse again for not telling him about yesterday. But I was given a reprieve when my front door opened and Lily yelled my name. Mickey let go of me as my sister walked into our kitchen.

"Ron's picking us up some chicken and I brought some leftover—Oh, hi, Mic. I hope it's okay that we're crashing here for dinner—" Lily stopped when Mickey didn't say anything. "Is everything okay?"

"Mickey?" I said.

He looked pained. "Charlotte called."

I felt the tingle again start around my jawline. "What did she say?"

"What's wrong?" my sister said.

The chimes sounded at the front door, and for a few seconds we stood dumbly looking at each other. Then I pushed past Lily and went to answer it. When I found Charlotte standing on my front porch, I felt an unseen hand at my throat. "What's going on?"

"Hi, darlin'," she said, with no lilt as she walked into my house.

"Charlotte?"

Charlotte Barbee smiled falsely at me, then looked at Mickey and Lily, who had followed me into the room. "Sit down," she said to them. "I need to speak with Lucy for a moment." Charlotte took my elbow and led me back to the kitchen.

"What's happening? Charlotte?"

She took a composing breath. "I heard from Dr. Matthews."

I felt one knee buckle. "Oh, Lord."

Charlotte put her hands on my shoulders. "Now, now, none of that. He has some concerns, and I came to talk to you and Mickey. But Lily being here probably isn't a bad thing." Charlotte nodded, her grip on me tightening. "You didn't tell Mickey about yesterday, did you?"

"No . . . ," I squeaked. "I was going to, but . . ."

"Okay then, I'm going to ask you to allow me to speak to all of you about this. Let's just get it out there. Are you comfortable with that?"

A breath shuddered out of me. "It's that bad?"

"We don't know that yet, darlin'. But it needs to be talked about."

"Okay." I nodded.

Charlotte took my hand and led me back into the living room. Neither Lily nor Mickey were talking. I'm not even sure they were breathing.

With trepidation in her voice Lily said, "What's happening?"

Charlotte walked me to the couch and patted the seat on the other side of her for Mickey. Lily was in the wingback leaning over so she could see us around the crib that we'd pushed against the wall. I looked at my doctor and said, "So this is about yesterday?"

She nodded.

Tears sprang from nowhere and Charlotte's grip on my hand tightened, just slightly.

"What happened yesterday?" Lily and Mickey asked in unison.

My hand went limp as Charlotte cleared her throat. "I want you both to try to stay calm." She breathed deep and looked at me. "I'd like to start at the beginning, Lucy, because I know you haven't." She searched my eyes for permission, and I nodded.

Charlotte looked at Mickey, then at Lily. "Yesterday I sent Lucy to see a colleague of mine. I sent her because the ultrasound she had five days ago indicated some changes from her last mammogram. It suggested some minor concerns, and I wanted her to be evaluated by someone more specialized than me."

"What?" Mickey said on a breath. There was also a squeak from Lily, but Charlotte didn't acknowledge either of them. She looked at me. "Dr. Matthews did a biopsy yesterday, and he found some unusual cells, which has created more questions than answers."

"Oh, no," Lily whimpered.

"I'm worried about Lucy because it's her nature to try and take care of each of you. . . ." Charlotte turned pointedly to my sister. "I don't want to frighten you, Lily. I want to give you the opportunity to be supportive here." Charlotte then looked at Mickey for a long moment, then turned back to me and squeezed my hand.

"Is it back?" I whispered. "Be straight with me, Charlotte."

"It's too soon to know that, Lucy."

Lily sniffed.

Charlotte turned back to Mickey, whom I couldn't see. "I found a little abnormality in Lucy's breast the other day. Mickey, I was almost certain that it was pregnancy-related. But I wanted to eliminate any possible question, so I sent her to see Dr. Matthews."

Mickey ripped his hand from Charlotte's and leaned forward enough to make scalding eye contact with me. "And you didn't tell me?"

"I didn't want you to freak out," I said weakly.

"Please don't be angry with her," Charlotte said in an even tone. "She knows how frightening this can be for you, Mic. I know she was only trying to protect you. And you have to believe this was the last thing anyone expected." She patted his hand, but I couldn't see his reaction. "Yesterday, when we were dealing in favorable probabilities, I didn't think there was a reason to worry. I honestly thought another evaluation would clear up my concerns, not create more. So be angry with me, not Lucy. I didn't present this to her as a huge concern, I'm sure that's why she didn't mention it to you."

Charlotte then sighed. "Today, however, we have no choice. Mickey, you'll have to rise to the occasion here, and I know you will."

Charlotte then turned to my sister. "I had no idea you'd be here, Lily, but the same goes for you, darlin'. I can imagine the pain you've had to confront over Lucy's pregnancy. But, sweetheart, that, too, has to be put aside. Your sister needs you. And, Ron, well, he'll need to calm the waters whenever they need calming. He's very good at that."

Mickey bent over and pushed his fingers through his hair. For a long time he just stared at the floor. None of us moved. Finally, he looked over and fixed me with eyes layered in emotion—fear, anger, confusion. I'm pretty sure he saw the same in mine. He got up and came to sit by my side.

Charlotte turned toward us. "Roland found some unusual cells, which he is going to evaluate further. Let's just go that far for now."

I looked around—there was Lily holding back tears, Mickey holding on to me like a lifeline, and Charlotte squeezing my fingers. I had been in this very place before. I felt hot tears sting my eyes. "What do we do now?" I croaked.

"Dr. Matthews will need to do more tests to determine what we're dealing with."

I nodded. "When?"

"He can do an excision on Monday. Then we'll know exactly what we've got."

"What about my baby?"

Charlotte looked hard at me. "We're not going to think about the baby right now."

"We're not?"

Charlotte shook her head, then kissed my forehead. Her refusal to say anything more about my daughter sent a black chill through me. "Charlotte?"

"Sweetie, you are the priority right now. We're going to take care of *you*."

I thought I might faint and I leaned my head into my lap. *What was she telling me? What exactly was she saying?*

Mickey palmed my neck for a moment, then I heard him say, "Charlotte, can I talk to you in the kitchen?" He stood up and Dr. Barbee said, "Of course," and followed him out of the room.

I sat up to find Lily looking helplessly at me. When my eyes filled with tears, my sweet sister walked over to where I was and gathered me into her arms. I wanted to be strong for her; my getting sick again was her worst fear. She surprised me though, my sister who's afraid of all uncertainty. "Let it go, Lu," she crooned in my ear. "You don't have to be a hero tonight. Just cry and let it go."

So I did. Not over the terrible prospect of a second go-round with this monster, or even a second go-round with Mickey's crushing fear, and not even the dark possibility of dying from all of it—these specters were not strangers to me. Instead, I sobbed over the tiny life now threatened by the betrayal of my chemistry. I wept uncontrollably under the sudden pall imposed by Charlotte's awful words: *We're not going to think about the baby right now.*

sixteen

Can't sleep. In the kitchen the full impact of the words that were never supposed to be uttered again had slammed through me and I started to shake. I've been shaking ever since. Charlotte followed me as I'd asked and she took my hands in hers. "You're okay, Mickey." It was not a question.

"I can't blow this, Charlotte." I looked at her and almost pleaded for her to lie to me. I needed her to lie. I needed her to tell me my wife was going to be okay. I couldn't breathe. I shook my head and whispered, "I can't fall apart here, but I'm afraid I can't stop myself."

"Yes, you can," Charlotte said firmly. She put her hands on my face and forced me to look at her. "We're not going to make this worse than it is, Mic. We only know that we need more information. We don't need to imagine anything past that. Take a deep breath." She nodded. "I have faith in you, Mickey. I know you're scared. But as scared as you are right now, Lucy is more scared. So, you need to put yours away. Take a break, go for a run, and pull yourself together. Your wife needs you to be strong. Are you hearing me? Look at me. She needs you to be solid and reassuring. Let her lean on you. If she needs to

cry, you let her cry. If she needs to scream, you let her
scream. You can do that, Mickey. I know you can."

After Charlotte left, none of us really said anything, and if I hadn't been so lost in my own thoughts, the silence might have felt awkward. But I was so self-absorbed I barely registered Lily's hug or her leaving. *Why?* was the only thought in my head. That and begging *it* not to be what it might be. Not again. I could not imagine it. I leaned into Mickey and his arms came around me.

"We'll get through this, Lu," he said on a shaky breath.

"Will we?"

"Yes."

"I don't think I can do it again," I croaked. "I can't go back there and be that sick again. I can't."

Mickey said nothing, and I knew he was thinking the same thing.

I breathed deep and pulled my hand free. "I'm sorry I didn't tell you. Honestly, I would have, but Charlotte didn't think it was serious. I should have told you, though."

"Am I really such an invalid, Lu, that you couldn't have trusted me?"

"It wasn't that. I promise you it wasn't that."

"Then why?"

"I didn't want to pop the bubble we're in," I said thickly.

Mickey's eyes softened. "We're in this together, Lucy. You had to face it, and I should have been there. You have to trust me."

"I know, baby. I'm sorry."

We sat in silence for a moment, then Mickey stood up. "Will you be okay if I go for a run, Lu? Clear my head."

I nodded.

"You sure?"

"I'll be right here," I said, not unhappy that he was leaving. It would be a chance to be alone with my thoughts. Not his or Lily's or even Charlotte's. Just my own voice. But as Mickey left and the opportunity presented itself, it turned out I had nothing interesting to say.

I pulled my knees to my chest. It was dim thanks to light glowing from just one lamp, and I looked around the room that I had grown up in. My father had played poker around a wobbly card table in this room. I'd caught Lily and Ron making out in here when they were in junior high. Priscilla had screamed her good riddance to my weeping mother in this room.

These walls had witnessed it all, the evolution of my family. I so wanted the chance to see my little girl come into this room on a Christmas morning with eyes full of awe, Mickey catching it all on video. She deserved to grow up in this rickety, creaky, cozy house that was filled with so much history. And I deserved to raise her here, dammit!

I'd almost fallen asleep on the couch when I heard a soft knock on my front door, too soft for it to be Mickey. The old door slowly opened, and Harry Bates, bedecked in a robe and cotton pajamas, walked in. He didn't say a word. Ron's father is just like Ron. Quiet, strong, dignified. He's tall and commands your attention, reassures you with his confidence even when it's apparent he's ready for bed.

"Hi, Harry."

He smiled and walked over to sit beside me on the couch. Harry looked at me without fear, without any annoying overblown solicitousness. He was solid. "What can I do for you, kiddo?" he whispered.

I didn't know what to say, so I just leaned my head into his.

Harrison Bates had stepped inside my family when I was five years old to help us, never attempting to fill shoes that didn't belong to him, and at that tender age I would have known. Just as I knew now. But as I looked at Harry tonight, I so missed having my dad. I shook my head. "Be the one person that doesn't assume I'm going to die."

"I think I can do that," he said, taking my hand.

I sighed. "What are you doing here? It's after midnight."

"Your sister is still over at the house bending Jan's ear. I got tired and decided to see for myself if you were as bad off as she said."

I smiled despite myself. "I haven't been given a death sentence yet."

"Well, then, why is everyone crying?" He hugged me. "Where's Mic?"

"He's gone for a run."

"Should I go look for him?"

"No. I just think he needs a little time. This is hard for him to hear again."

"What about you?"

I nodded but couldn't find my voice.

Harry and I sat in the quiet for a few more minutes, neither of us speaking. When my eyes were too heavy to hold open another minute, I told him I was going to bed. He kissed my hair and offered again to look for my wayward husband. But as if on cue, Mickey walked in the door. He looked awful. His eyes were swollen and his hair was wet. He'd run hard. He nodded at Harry but didn't say anything.

Harry walked over and patted Mickey's shoulder. "You kids take care of each other," he said as he left.

Mickey looked at me from across the room and we stared at each other for a long moment. Then he came over to the couch and wrapped me in his arms. He didn't say a word. And when we were both finished crying, he carried me upstairs.

Mickey and I held hands in the office of Roland Matthews, waiting for the doctor to come in and talk to us. Mickey was in a dark mood and trying to hide it. But his deep sighs and the way he chewed the inside of his mouth gave him away. He'd had a bad night despite a second dose of Ambien. I reached over and stroked his cheek and he managed a tight smile. I found myself fantasizing about a man who looked just like Mickey stroking my cheek, telling me with a straight face that everything would be okay. And fantasizing that I would believe him.

I looked around the cold, bare space. The snotty receptionist had called first thing this morning and set up this procedure with the same put-out tone she'd used to greet me a few days ago. "Please don't be late, Mrs. Chandler," she instructed. "Again, you are being squeezed into a very full day." Mickey and I had now been sitting in this exceptionally impersonal office for nearly forty-five minutes, and the tension he was emitting made me want to crawl out of my skin.

Finally, the door opened and the doctor burst in, head down, studying my chart. "Mrs. Chandler, how are you doing this morning?"

All I could do was nod, and Dr. Matthews briefly met my eyes with an apology, then offered his hand to Mickey. "You must be Mr. Chandler." Dr. Matthews was pudgy and bald, but he still managed to pull off a fair degree of panache in his crisp white shirt and pleated trousers. The brisk scent of cologne followed him into the room and settled around his person as he sat down in front of us. Small, rimless glasses perched at the end of his nose as he scanned the pages of my chart.

He looked up at me. "If my calculations are correct, you're nineteen weeks pregnant. Is that right?"

I nodded.

"General anesthesia can pose a mild threat to the fetus at this stage, but you will be monitored very carefully and we'll do our best not to jeopardize the baby. I know this is upsetting for you, Lucy."

He handed me a consent form. I scanned it, realizing that it exonerated him from any liability. I swallowed. "Can't this be done under local anesthesia?"

"I don't know what I'll find, and I don't want to be limited if I run into more than I expect. I'm going in surgically to evaluate the size and extent of the problem, and I anticipate the procedure to be quite intricate." He shook his head. "I'm just not comfortable with the limitations of local anesthesia under these circumstances."

"Just sign it, Lucy," Mickey said sharply, then apologized for his tone.

He asked more questions and I heard Roland Matthews answer most of them, but I couldn't process what he was saying. I remember Mickey kissing me, and I wanted to cling to him, to beg him to take me home. I remember him reassuring me, but he spoke with a voice that was too shaky to trust. I was taken to another room, where I undressed and got into a gown. A girl who looked no older than twelve came in and drew three vials of blood, after which someone else came in to start an IV. I was cold, and when I was secured on a gurney, someone else covered me with a warm blanket, but I don't think the person spoke to me. Then I was wheeled into an operating room, where I rubbed my stomach until I went under.

It was my first thought when I came out of the fog, but my hand was too heavy to move to my belly. The familiar voice of a kind woman nudged me closer to consciousness. It was the nurse who'd plied me with crackers the last time I was here. "My baby?" I managed to ask.

"We monitored the heartbeat throughout your surgery. Everything appears to be fine with the baby." She offered me ice chips. I looked at her then, my expression urging her on. *What about me? Does everything appear fine with me as well?* She looked away, and a terrible heaviness settled over me as she injected something into my IV.

I woke up sometime later, alone in a pretty room. My head was still heavy with medication, but I was able to look toward the hall, where I thought I heard Mickey's voice. It took a moment for him to come into focus, but there he was with Lily and Priscilla. Ron was there, too, and Dr. Matthews. Mickey's back was to me and he kept pulling his hand out of his pocket to rub his neck. He did that when he was anxious. When Lily patted him on the shoulder, I saw both his hands go to his face. Priscilla was pushing tears away as she listened to the doctor. Ron must have sensed my gaze because he turned and peered into the room at me. When his eyes met mine, I saw no soft news there. We stared at each other for a weighty moment, then he dropped his attention to the floor.

My little family blurred as the tears came. I thought of my mother and the calm way she had accepted the terrible news she received, and suddenly I was furious at her. I had been scouring the sink, swirling designs in the gritty suds, when the phone rang. My mother, who'd been washing the windowpanes on the back door, pulled off her yellow rubber glove to answer it. It was Charlotte. I'd stopped scrubbing but didn't dare look up at Mom. Not even when she said, "We'll be there in fifteen minutes." My mother had had several different tests done that past week and the results were back. Now we were going to Charlotte's office on a Saturday. My mom let the yellow glove drop as she hung up the phone. Then she turned to me and said, "Well, that's that, then." I remember how slowly she walked up the stairs. I remember how I couldn't do anything but stare at that lifeless rubber glove sitting on the floor.

I closed my eyes, distancing myself from the reality of my situation. With excruciating effort, I found my belly with my limp hand and kneaded the firm bulge I could feel beneath my gown.

Later—I don't know how much later—I simply refused to respond to Mickey or anyone else when they tried to coax me awake. I wasn't ready for what waited on the other side of sleep, so I stayed there, locked in pretense, for as long as I could. When finally I ventured a peek through the slit of my eyelids, I found Mickey staring into the distance through wet eyes, and my heart seized. I couldn't watch him go through this hell with me again. I was not strong enough. And neither was he.

It was nighttime and the room was dark except for the fluorescent light coming from the hall. There were distant voices—a nurse on the phone ordering dinner for a new admission, visitors in the next room discussing bowling scores, someone wanting a drink. But in my room, the silence was deafening.

"Mic?" I croaked.

He leaned over and rubbed my ear. "Hey, beautiful. I thought you were going to sleep forever. I was getting worried." He stood up and kissed me gently on the lips. He looked beaten up, but he forced a thin, transparent smile that I knew came with great effort.

"I had a dream," I said.

Mickey laced his long fingers into mine.

"I dreamed the doctor found bad news."

The tears in Mickey's eyes threatened to fall on my face as he loomed above me. He sniffed and pushed back the blanket. Then he got on the bed beside me and pulled me into his arms. I felt him shudder.

"Tell me, Mic," I whispered.

It took Mickey a long time to respond, and his silence seemed confirmation enough. Finally, he spoke. "I didn't understand everything he told us, but I do know he found a mass. And it's—" Mickey swallowed a sob. "It's spread to your lung, Lu."

His words rolled over me, crushing me. A mass? Spread? Lung . . . My tears made no noise, but they soaked Mickey's shirt as he held on to me.

Much later that night Roland Matthews came into my room. Mickey had finally gone home to shower, and it seemed no accident the weary doctor found me alone. He looked at me for a long moment, and a sad knowing passed between us in that silence. When he started to speak, his words had a practiced, but not unkind, ring to them. He had excised a small portion of a mass approximately six centimeters in size. It was atypical and flat and had attached itself to my chest wall, far enough behind the breast for it to elude a mammogram's detection until it had grown to this size. The fullness and discomfort I'd experienced were symptoms identical to the pregnancy-induced changes that were naturally occurring, and this further allowed its escape from medical scrutiny. In short, Roland Matthews told me the perfect set of circumstances had allowed this mass to develop and flourish. And spread.

I realized, in that moment, that the most overwhelming word in the English language is not *cancer*, as I had long supposed, but *metastasis*. *Metastasis*. That horrid word ripped through my brain like shards of glass, slicing patches of hopelessness along its path. The word stopped time as Dr. Matthews offered up his discourse on pathological markers and advanced staging, not to mention the unnecessary litany of my laboratory values. Strangely, my blood work, which had been followed so closely for so long, showed no rise in my CA scores. But today they did find the marker that made the diagnosis of metastasis to the lung a certainty. This, he said, explained my annoying little cough.

It was a lot to take in, and as the doctor babbled, I simply retreated inside myself until the rush in my head drowned out his voice. I did, however, hear him when he presented my treatment options—a brutal regimen of radiation and chemotherapy. The atypical tumor in my breast was inoperable, and the best we could hope for was to shrink it from within. He had excised what he could for the purposes of pathology, but even a radical mastectomy wouldn't totally capture the lesion. He explained something about the proximity of the tumor to my lung that made it sound almost as though he were describing a single tumor from which growth was taking place in two areas. Roland Matthews informed me that his colleague would be by tomorrow to further evaluate me, then apologized unnecessarily for the lesion in my lung being outside of his area of expertise. He finished, "I'm sure Dr. Gladstone will agree that we need to begin aggressive chemotherapy and radiation as soon as possible."

I stared at this man as he politely delivered this devastation without emotion. He didn't seem to notice that his rhetoric bounced off me, fully unabsorbed. It didn't matter. I'd heard it all before. I knew it when I was a girl hearing it all explained to my mother. I'd heard it again seven years ago when I was diagnosed the first time. But no matter how I tried, I could not comprehend the timing. Not now. Not when I was pregnant. Why not last year? Or six months from now?

"No! I won't do it!" I shouted, fully aware of how childish my protests sounded.

He breathed out a heavy sigh and wasn't able to look directly at me when he said, "Naturally, we'll do all we can to achieve the most positive outcome."

"What about my baby?" I asked through clenched teeth.

He was silent for an eviscerating moment, then finally he met my eyes. "I'm ordering a therapeutic termination, Lucy. You have advanced-stage breast cancer with metastasis to the lung. The prognosis is poor. But it's nil without pronounced and aggressive treatment beginning immediately. If it goes well, perhaps a baby can come later."

"No. No." My voice was barely recognizable as my own.

"I'm sorry, Lucy."

When there was nothing else to say, the doctor left me to digest all that he'd told me.

Despite my fury, I teetered on the brink of panic. But before I could fully give in to it, my father's words wrapped around me as tangibly as an embrace. Once again, I was five years old and he was kneeling at my bedside, his soft breath on my face. I heard the same gravity in his voice, accepted his logic with the same unquestioning trust. *Death is not the end, Lulu, and it doesn't hurt. And if you're not afraid, you can watch for it and be ready. . . .*

But I *was* afraid.

The wall of my fury crashed down then and emotion gushed out of me. Loud, obnoxious sobs that prompted a passing nurse to check on me. I cried long enough to wear myself out, long enough that it took a while for my heart to stop pounding.

When it did, I imagined my father's gentle, calming hand on my head, and the thought of him so near cradled my sorrow. As my breathing grew quiet, I canvassed the room slowly with teary, swollen eyes but found no comely visitor lurking anywhere. Good. Good. Surely she knew she was not welcome here tonight.

seventeen

There's a deadness about me, I'm slow to move, heavy and paralyzed. Maybe it's the calm before the storm. Maybe it's sanity—maybe this is how normal men, stable men, are able to absorb their crises. It wasn't like this last time. Last time when they said that dreaded word, an electric fear shot through me and pretty much stayed put until it was over. This was a suffocating weight. I could think all the terrible thoughts; I could process all the terrible information. I just couldn't reach the emotion that was supposed to go with the news of the day. I could think how cruel this timing was, how obscene fate was to choose now, when a baby was in the works, when we were bursting with happiness. I could think these thoughts, but they just floated on top of the deadness and never sank in. Maybe the deadness was a blessing because I couldn't reach the pain through it, only the words. Stage 4. Inoperable. Metastasis. Poor prognosis. Situation grave. Abortion. Abortion. Abortion. Lucy would abort our daughter. Then chemo. Radiation. Surgery. After all this, she might recover. He said it was a long shot. But a shot we had to take, right? This was a hostage situation; if we followed the rules and did exactly what we were told, there was a chance, a slim chance, he'd said, that Lucy

could get better again. And then who knew, maybe we'd be in
line for another baby that was never supposed to be.
　　Maybe. But probably not.
　　All these thoughts floated through me as I dismantled
the crib in our living room.

Living in a small town, among people who have always known you and cared about you, there is no such thing as a secret. It started when Elaine Withers noticed Jan and Lily crying in a corner booth at Damian's. It continued when Mickey gave Jared the barest explanation for not coming to work. When Ron delivered the inlaid mahogany sideboard Muriel Piper had bought at Ghosts, she grilled him until he broke down and told her everything. From there, the news of my condition turned into a mushroom cloud of scuttlebutt.

By the time Mickey brought me home, a mere two days after my surgery, my living room was empty of a crib, but filled with flowers from well-wishers. Lainy Withers had left soup on my stove and Jan had covered my bed with a new comforter. Diana Dunleavy had left a bundle of bestsellers tied together with raffia on my porch, and Nathan Nash had dropped off DVDs of the *Lord of the Rings* trilogy for nine hours of diversion. There were notes and cards and sweet messages on my machine. Priscilla even moved onto the boat to work from her laptop and cell phone so she could watch over me. I sat on the couch and did not move. Mickey must have kissed me a hundred times that day. He kissed my hand, my head, my cheek, my wrist. Always followed by the sound declaration that everything would be okay.

But he lied. How could everything be okay when we were losing our baby? He wouldn't talk about her. And he wouldn't let me talk about her.

As my friends and family surrounded me with tender consideration, Mickey grew moody and frightened . . . and desperate. He hadn't slept much, but then neither had I, and this of course led to edginess in both of us. One night we had a terrible fight that we both knew was really just a loud and nasty expression of all the things that were breaking our hearts. But it didn't stop us. It was late when Mickey stomped out in his running gear, and I hate to admit it, but, after the screen door had bounced against the wooden frame for the final time, I was relieved beyond words.

As I sat in the dim light and let the silence cushion me, I felt my daughter softly roll over—the feeling as natural as the gentle turn of a wrist. I felt her and I thought I'd never known pain like this. It was unbearable what I was facing, what we were facing. We had fallen in love with her. And now . . .

I thought back on a night years ago when I didn't die. I think I was supposed to—cancer was dangling me over my grave, and I believe everyone was steeled for it. Dr. Barbee, though she wasn't attending me on oncology, was there taking care of my family. I know she had prepared Mickey. Lily. But then I didn't die. The body's miraculous healing resources can only be explained as God's hat tricks, and for some reason He changed His mind. It took a long time to recover from my attempted murder by cancer. But tonight, I almost wish I hadn't because then I wouldn't be facing the loss of the most precious thing in our lives.

I loved this baby with my whole heart. And I loved Mickey with a whole other heart, and tonight both of them were breaking.

More than an hour later, Mickey finally came home. He looked wounded and in pain. "Oh, baby," I said as I walked over to him. He put his arms around me, and mine came around his waist. It was so nice for a moment. But before I knew what was happening, Mickey was kissing me with an alarming urgency, rough and hungry and insistent. Suddenly he was holding me so tight it hurt. I tried to pull out of his grasp, but he held tighter. "Stop," I said into his mouth. "Stop it, Mickey. Stop!" I shouted as I pushed him away. "Jeez, what are you doing?" I said, rubbing my bruised mouth.

Mickey ground the heels of his palms into his eyes as a terrible groan erupted from his throat. I watched him for a minute. I watched him writhe and swear and cry, his pain tangible. Finally, he looked at me through tortured eyes and took a step toward me.

I backed away. "Don't. Don't."

He stopped, injured.

"Can you just stop making this so awful?" I said. "What are you doing?"

"Lucy, I can't lose you. I can't. I don't know how to be without you," he whimpered.

I slumped against the wall feeling as if every one of my bones was melting. "Well you might have to lose me, Mickey," I said meanly. "That's the reality, and we have to face it. But it's not going to happen tonight. Right now, can't I just *need* you?" I cried. "I'm sorry, but I don't want to have to take care of you right now. I'm tired, Mickey. And if you can't just stand up straight for one minute and let me lean on you, then what the hell are you good for?"

His beautiful face folded in on itself and my heart cramped at his pain, but I couldn't take back my words. After a moment of silence, Mickey rubbed the horrid expression of fear off his face and replaced it with a look of forced calm. He took a deep, shaky breath and nodded. He didn't say anything, and I don't know what he did after that because I went upstairs.

I always tried to give Mickey's roller-coaster moods a wide berth, but right now I was at a loss. I couldn't do anything but get out of his way while he did battle with himself. His mental illness was braided with his natural impatience, and right now everything was colored by his anger and fear and unavoidable grief. He erupted at random moments without provocation, then was quick to apologize. I just let it all fall around me unanswered because I knew hiding under all that was a man desperately trying to be strong. I gave him an A for effort. I always do.

Over and over, he promised it would be okay. But that was Mickey's way. In a crisis he always scoped out the one thing he could grab on to; the one sure thing that, would, in his mind, fix whatever was broken. Last time I had cancer it was my treatment. Mickey placed all his hope in the massive doses of chemotherapy I was drowning in. He held my hand and watched the rise and fall of my T cells like a frenzied day trader. In the end, they did not let him down.

This time he glommed onto the abortion that had been scheduled for next Tuesday. That would fix everything, he knew it. Without a pregnancy to contend with, every conceivable anticancer strategy could again be safely executed, and *of course* I'd recover. He survived this solution by making himself forget how much he already loved our daughter.

As for me, every time the thought formed in my head, I went numb. There had to be another way. How could I lose this baby and not lose myself? I had no idea, so I opted for avoidance. I didn't dare look even an hour into my future because I knew I would then be an hour closer to what was waiting for me. When I started to feel overwhelmed by it all, I would find myself protectively stroking the bump that was expanding my midsection. But then Mickey would lift my hand away and lace his fingers safely—and firmly—into mine.

I passed the time mechanically, refusing to process what was happening. People came and went, called and said nice things, showered me with affection and encouragement. I made my face do all that was expected of it. My voice instinctively found the words needed to soften the discomfort of those around me. None of them seemed to recognize the charade. But I could only keep it up until we pulled into the parking lot of the abortion clinic. Of course that wasn't what it was called. It had a more palatable name: The Montrose Center for Women's Health. But when Mickey came around the car and opened my door, the reality of what was happening hit me like the face of the devil, and I couldn't get out.

Mickey bent down. "Lu? Honey, we're going to be late." He tugged on my arm and I looked up at him.

"I can't do this."

"Lucy, c'mon. It'll be over before you know it."

He was lying, but I didn't dare argue. I got out of the car.

The clinic's waiting area was dark and plush with leather sofas, and lots of current magazines. I sat down while Mickey signed me in. The only other person waiting was a young girl reading a *People* magazine who popped her gum as she turned the pages. She was wearing cute shoes and never once looked at me.

I looked over at Mickey, who was signing insurance forms, hunkered over the reception desk, reading intently. He looked substantial, like he could carry me across the state and not even break a sweat. His wonderful hair was still damp from his shower, and he was freshly shaved. He was wearing a blue, button-down shirt, dress pants, and a tie. I think the tie inspired an element of trust in me. Mickey always dressed with style, but when he had something challenging to face, he wore a tie.

When he finished, he sat down next to me. We didn't look at each other. We just stared straight ahead into the saddest day of our life together until a nurse called my name. Then I stood up. Mickey stood up, too, and gave me a hug. I could feel his heart pound against my face. "It'll be okay, Lu. I love you."

I nodded and followed the nurse into Procedure Room number three. An instrument tray was covered with a white towel, a suction hose, and a large bowl. An enormous light was positioned directly above the place where I would lie with my legs spread open. A nurse with a pleasant smile handed me a paper gown. "Don't be nervous, Mrs. Chandler. It's really not so bad." She patted my shoulder, and her expression said she'd uttered those words a million times. "Get into this gown and climb up onto the table. Everything off but your bra. Dr. Hale will be ready in just a minute. You okay, hon?"

I nodded, not much in the mood for conversation.

I struggled out of my T-shirt, careful of my bandaged breast, and stepped out of my sandals. The paper gown was stiff and scratchy and I couldn't believe I was actually wearing it—that I was actually perched on the end of this custom-made abortion table, that the baby that had grown to be the most significant thing in my life would soon be gone. Suctioned into a stainless steel bowl, examined to be sure they'd gotten all of her, and dumped down the stainless steel sink.

Every image of her that I had conjured up over these past weeks flashed into my mind's eye. I could see her big dark eyes. I knew the touch of her silky hair. I could feel her soft, warm skin on my cheek.

After a light knock on the door, a white-haired man poked his head in and asked if I was decent. I nodded dumbly.

"I'm Dr. Hale." He offered me his hand with a smile. "And you're Lucy?"

I nodded again.

"So, let's see here, it says you're about twenty weeks, is that right?"

"Yes."

"And, I understand we're doing a therapeutic abortion due to a recent diagnosis of cancer. I'm sure sorry to hear that."

"Thank you."

"Well," he said, sitting down. "Do you have any questions for me?"

"I've never done this before. I don't know what to ask."

Dr. Hale smiled again. He was a bit too chipper for my taste. "Well, let's start at the beginning here." He cleared his throat and asked me to lie down.

His hands were cold as he measured and palpated and frowned, muttering concern about the substantial growth of my fetus. "This could take a while." Then he explained the procedure as if he were reciting the weather report—I wasn't paying attention, I was counting the ceiling panels. When he was done, he opened my chart. "Your doctor sent over your lab values so we don't need to repeat those," he said, pleased.

I nodded.

"I'll get our technician in here to start an IV, and then we'll begin." Dr. Hale stood up and clapped his hands together. "I'll check on you soon," he said, then walked out.

A minute later a short man in a white lab coat hurried in with an IV bottle and what looked like yards of clear tubing. "Sorry to keep you waiting, hon," he said in a high voice. "We're just a bit short today." He pulled my arm taut as he thumped around looking for a cooperative vein. I started to cry.

"I'm sorry that hurt. It's in now, hon," he said, misreading my sudden tears. He was securing the needle under my skin with about a foot of tape and babbling off something to do with dilatation. I wasn't listening; I was begging to wake up from this nightmare. He patted my shoulder and said the nurse would be right in with the medication that would start the process, and then he left.

I looked at the wall as I felt my baby move. She'd been very active these last few days, and I wondered why. I cried out, I couldn't help myself. I couldn't stand it! I knew this horrible abortion made sense, even if it was far from a guarantee, but every breath I took was agony because she was moving inside me. Today would be the day Mickey might have been able to feel her. She was strong, and every moment she was getting stronger and becoming more and more my daughter. Our daughter. I knew I had to stop thinking about her. I had to wrap my head around the fight. My fight. I had to fight. For Mickey. And then maybe later . . .

I closed my mind against this thought and tried to rein in my hopelessness. Dr. Matthews had told the lie best: perhaps a baby can come later. I didn't believe him then and I didn't believe his words now as they echoed in my head. I squeezed my eyes shut and pushed my hands into my hair and sobbed. Everything I'd buried beneath my numbness came gushing furiously to the surface. The way I felt about this baby. The fear of being sick again. What I absolutely knew about myself. And I knew, despite everything that had brought me here, that after today I was never going to be the same. I would leave this horrible place damaged beyond repair. "I can't do this," I wept. "I can't."

As I lay in this clutch of agony, something fluttered against my eyelids and I gasped. Against the throb of my emotions it was no more than a sigh, as uncanny and untraceable as sound against skin. It was *her.* And for just a breath, I let go of my angst, or it let go of me.

But then her being there made terrible sense. *Of course, a baby was dying!* Of course Death would show up! My baby was dying.

But my reasoning was quickly reproached as clearly as if I'd been spoken to. *What?* It took me a moment to trust the sensation, but then undeniable certainty filled me. *My baby was not supposed to die. I was not supposed to do this. I did not have to abort her.*

I stopped crying and my frenzied heart calmed. For a moment I just basked in a spirit of complete assurance, complete relief. But . . . if she wasn't here for my daughter, why then was this apparition holding me like a gentle parent calming a nightmare?

And then I knew.

If I opened my eyes, I would see the same being that had looked at my five-year-old self, but had seen into my grown soul, into *this* soul. So I opened them. And the gentlest, kindest, softest *impression* looked *into* me and filled me with pure knowledge. It was as though the whole world, the entire unabridged design, was explained to me in a microsecond, and I not only understood, but I had the vague sensation of having always known it. And I knew then that none of this would matter. None of everything that was anticipated to save my life would actually save my life. Not this time. As emotion threatened to engulf me, my father's wisdom surfaced to keep it at bay. *Death is not the end, Lulu, and if you're not afraid, you can watch for it and be ready. . . .*

Watch and be ready.

I sat up and looked around this terrible room, barely able to breathe. *I wasn't supposed to be here. I wasn't supposed to do this.* I felt *her* reassurance and broke down, again. And as she held me, I looked my small future straight in the eye and didn't blink.

I was going to die. *I* was going to die.

Me.

Not my daughter.

There was no reason I should be pregnant. A tubal ligation years ago. A knot that could miraculously be swum through after all this time? She was a baby that was never supposed to be. And yet . . . *for some reason we've been granted this miracle, and we're just going to trust it.*

Trust it. Trust the miracle.

I didn't hesitate another moment. I tore at the tape plastered along my forearm and winced as I pulled the needle from my vein.

eighteen

How could she do this! How could Lucy refuse to have the abortion? How could she refuse treatment—any treatment that might save her life—until after the baby was born? Where were her promises! How had it come to this? I screamed this betrayal at the sky as I ran, speeding my pace, lengthening my stride. I ran to the end of my strength, but the rage was stronger than me. I had no power to subdue it. I'd been running for nearly an hour and my heart was an iron barbell clanging inside my chest and still I was fueled by this clot of unbearable emotion.

It was nearly dawn and I had run down the country road that separated Brinley from Ivoryton, my breath ragged and harsh. I slowed my pace and gulped in the air as the color in my head faded. I breathed slow and deep and felt it pour through me—the real stuff that was beneath the rage, the stuff that hurt like hell.

That's how it works; sometimes I can outrun rage, but I can never outrun fear.

Mickey went off the deep end in the wee hours of the morning. He was furious with me, and nothing I could say made him feel any better, so I gave up. I stopped trying to explain. I stopped trying to reassure. I stopped promising him that I would subject myself totally to whatever the experts recommended after the baby was born. I don't think he believed I would last that long. That was the bright fear I saw in his eyes.

He'd left before dawn, supposedly to work out. I never slept. Every time I shut my eyes, all I saw was one of two images: the horrible gray hose, or Mickey's expression when I told him what I'd done—hadn't done.

This morning, my eyes felt coated with sandpaper and I knew I looked like shit. I didn't care. Today I wasn't getting out of bed. I was just going to lie here, finish my senior-class outline, and gestate. At that thought, my eyes started to sting again and I tossed my papers on the floor and pulled the sheet over my head. I was thus ensconced when I heard the furious pounding on my front door. I didn't care. Whoever it was would eventually give up and leave. They'd have to, I wasn't moving.

Not so. The rapping was rude and insistent and seemingly endless. It had to be one of my sisters. I burrowed farther into my bedding, but pretty soon Priscilla was under my bedroom window yelling at me to let her in. She punctuated this demand by throwing handfuls of sand against the glass.

I endured her boorishness as long as I could, then stomped downstairs and angrily threw open the front door. Then I flung myself onto the sofa in a huff, arms crossed against my chest, a bitchy scowl on my face. It was only Priscilla and there would be no obligatory courtesy for her.

My sister slammed the door and came to stand before me, her hands clamped tightly on her hips, her toe tapping. *Tapping!*

"Stop that, Priscilla!" I shouted. "You are not going to barge into my home and stand there tapping your foot at me! What do you want?"

"What are you *doing*, Lucy? Why didn't you have the abortion?"

I groaned. "Do I not have one private matter in my whole life?"

"If you do, it's not this baby. And if you ever did, it was before you married Mickey."

I looked at my sister. Priss had an infuriating way of glistening like a new penny, no matter the time, no matter the occasion. It was early—well, eleven—and she was utterly complete. Hair, makeup, skinny jeans, polished toenails peeking out from her sandals. It was nauseating. "When did you talk to Mickey?"

"He called at the crack of dawn, thank you very much, and begged me to talk to him."

This was a stretch for both of them since they could barely stomach each other. For my sake, they lived a tacit truce and grudgingly agreed not to kill each other in my presence. Yet Mickey had called her? I ran my hands through my tangled hair. I looked at Priss, my bark evaporating, her toe now still. "What did he want?"

"What do you think? He wants me to talk you into going back to that clinic. What are you trying to do to him, Lucy? The man's insanely afraid of losing you. And you're refusing to save your own life because of this baby? You're killing him. You know that, don't you?"

"I couldn't do it, Priss," I croaked. I closed my eyes and saw Dr. Hale's insincere smile, felt the crunch of the paper gown—disposable for easy cleanup. "I couldn't do it."

"Of course you can do it! It's not that hard. It's a simple procedure."

I gaped at my sister. "It's a baby, Priscilla. It's *my* baby."

"It's a gob of cells, Lucille. It's *not* a baby. Grow up. Your own life is on the line here. What on earth are you thinking?" Priscilla looked at me incredulously, and I'm sure I mirrored the same. "Now get in the shower," she said, instructing me slowly as if I were a child. "I'm driving you back to the clinic. Oh, stop looking at me like that. You'll get it done and we'll go to lunch. Easy, end of story."

Emotion hardened in me. "How easy, Priss?"

My beautiful sister narrowed her gaze at me. "I don't like that tone, Lucille."

"Exactly how easy is it to have an abortion, Priscilla? I need to know. *Mentor* me through this process. *Shaaaare*," I sang, my words dripping with sarcasm.

A telling flush made its way up Priss's jaw, and I watched a tic start near her eye. But she quickly subdued the color and commanded the tic. "Watch your tone, Lucille. Stop turning this around. You should be focusing on your husband. I swear, for the first time ever, even *I* feel sorry for him. He's going to self-destruct when you get sick again. I hope you're ready for that."

Rage exploded through me. "This is none of your business!"

"No? You need to face the facts. It is selfish to keep this baby under these circumstances." Priss sat down hard in the armchair facing me. "I want to know what's changed. What happened to the attitude you had before you got pregnant? The wonderful legacy Mom left us in her DNA. Did you forget that's why you never planned to get pregnant in the first place? Have you lost your mind because now you have this . . . this . . ."

"It's called a baby, Priss."

"Lucy! It is nothing more than a parasite!"

"Oh, Priscilla," I sighed, incapable of making her understand. "Just go home."

"It's okay to get rid of it, Lucy," Priscilla said with sudden softness. "You didn't want it there in the first place. Remember? Lucy, use your head. It's not worth your life."

"I can't do it."

"You could die."

"I know. But for every moment that I lived, I'd never forgive myself."

"Lucy, do you have any idea how childish you sound?"

I gawked at my sister. "Did these arguments work for you? Because you're sounding awfully experienced, Priscilla." I could see from the look on her face that I had hit a nerve. Lily and I had always speculated that our sister had gotten into trouble with Trent Rosenberg back in high school. It had been the reason for the terrible gulf between her and Mom. But of course neither of us ever had the courage to broach it with either of them. All we knew was that whatever happened back then ruined their relationship. Then Priscilla was gone.

"We're not talking about me, Lucy. What I have or have not done has nothing to do with this."

"Excuse me?"

"I mean it. You could lose your life, Lucy. You could die!"

"I'm not doing it, so go home, Priscilla."

"Lucy, are you crazy?"

"I'm sure that will be debated long after I'm gone."

"Then use your head, I'm begging you. Call that clinic back. I'll take you myself."

"Priscilla, stop it. I'm having this baby." I ran both hands over my sweaty face and pulled my hair tight.

"Why? Give me one good reason, Lucy."

I doubled over not wanting to cry. The tears showed up anyway so I pushed my palms into the sockets of my eyes.

"You don't have one, do you? There is no earthly reason not to do this."

"I've seen her," I shouted.

Finally she was quiet.

I looked at my sister. "I've seen her. She's a beautiful dark-haired, dark-eyed little girl." I sat up and my hands instinctively went to my stomach. "And I've felt her."

"What are you talking about?"

"I know exactly what she looks like. And you're right, Priss, at this moment my daughter only loosely resembles a baby. But she is as real to me as you are. Her heart is beating inside me. She moves inside me. She gets the hiccups inside me. Aborting her now is no different in my mind than waiting until she's born and smothering her with a pillow, or throwing her in the lake on her third birthday, or shooting her in the head when she's twelve."

Priscilla slumped. "Oh, Lucy."

"It doesn't matter what you say, Priscilla, this baby is real to me. I can't make her unreal now because I have the right to, or because the timing is off. I can't do it. I won't. And even if I could, Priss, there's a part of me that knows I would never be able to face—"

"*God?*" Priscilla cut me off. "Is that where this is going, Lucy?" She spit the word *God* out as if a bug had landed on her tongue.

"I was going to say Mom and Dad, but God works, too."

Priscilla's mouth opened but nothing came out. She bore her eyes into mine until hers filled with tears. "Lucy, please. I get that you are in love with your baby. But next to you, she doesn't mean anything— she's not real. She's not real to any of us. *You're* real, Lucy. Don't you get that? You beat this before and you can beat it again, but you have to fight. How can you not fight for your life? How can you not do that for Mickey, for Lily . . . for me? Lucy, you're going to die!"

"I am, Priss," I said, looking deeply into her eyes.

"So you need—" My sister stopped breathing.

I nodded.

"No, Lucy. You don't know that."

I got up and put my arms around my sister. "Yes I do. I *know*."

"What?" For a moment she did not move, but then she drew back. "No, no, no. We're not leaving this to a dream, a ghost. Lucy! I'm not listening to this!"

I looked at my sister, held her eyes, and made the same promise I'd made to Mickey. "I'm having this baby, Priss," I said softly. "And once she's here, I'll do everything I can to save my life. That's the best I can do."

Priscilla opened her mouth, but closed it, defeated. I didn't move.

"So that's it, Lucy? That's it? What if you're wrong?" She shook her head. "If you die . . ." I watched my sister try to swallow back emotion. "If you die, Lucy, I'll never forgive you."

I said nothing.

Priscilla got up and walked out of my house.

nineteen

It's been a long time since I lost myself completely. But it's coming. I feel it. When I'm like this, Lucy alone has the power to ground me. But we're not talking at the moment.

Gleason refuses to see my side of things. He's accused me of using my condition as an excuse for bad behavior. He says the sadness I'm feeling isn't pathological. It's just life. That I have no business self-medicating my way out of it.

"I am ashamed of you," he says. "Have you really got nothing more than this for Lucy?"

I sat there and let his words rain on me like stones falling from the sky.

"Get off the stage, my friend," he told me. "This is not about you, or being bipolar. You are like any other person in this sad situation—no more than a spectator forced to endure a tragedy. What you're doing is an issue of character, Michael, not pathology. You can't hide your sins behind your diagnosis. If anything drives you to self-destruct, it will not be losing Lucy, but your own behavior as it happened."

I was so angry that I refused to finish my session with him and slammed the door on my way out. Then I went

over to Colby's for a drink. Then I went home and fought
with Lucy, the one person I hated to hurt but did so well.

After his desperate faith in Priscilla's powers of persuasion failed him, Mickey had no choice but to be mad at me. But, bless his heart, he tried to be civil, tried to quell his mounting resentment. He even feigned support. But, like a man trying to paddle an ocean liner with a spoon, it yielded no result.

I would catch him looking at me sometimes, his eyes moist with condemnation. He'd hold my gaze long enough to make his point, then turn away in disgust. Or sometimes he would come up behind me and wrap his arms around my waist. He'd lean his face into my neck and I'd wonder if he was softening, but then he'd groan and shove himself away from me. Again, making his point.

This was so much worse than last time. When I had cancer before, Mickey's fear and anguish were suffocating. But they were tempered by his faith in my treatment regimen, which was brutal. I could have died from ten complications, but his hope was unyielding because I was actively fighting for my life. This time I wasn't.

The bottom line was Mickey couldn't forgive me for not having the abortion. So we were brittle with each other because we couldn't be anything else.

A couple of weeks after I didn't abort our baby, I came home from a faculty meeting to find Mickey sitting on the edge of the bed with his head in his hands. I reached over to touch him, but he inched away. "What are you doing, Mic?"

"Just thinking."

"Well, don't hurt yourself." No chuckle, so I sat down next to him. "Sorry."

"Do you love me, Lucy?" he said to the floor.

"Of course I love you, what kind of question is that?"

"How much do you love me?"

I shook my head. "Mickey, there isn't an end. You know that."

"I used to know that."

I brought his face close to mine and saw that he'd been crying. "What do you mean, you used to know that?"

"I need an honest answer, Lucy. Do you love the baby more than you love me?"

"No. Of course not."

"I don't believe you."

"Mickey, don't say that. I love this baby as much as you love this baby. She's our daughter."

He pushed my hand away and stood up. "I don't love her as much as I love you. I wouldn't give *you* up for her. I wouldn't leave *you* for her."

I pushed out a breath. "Why are you doing this?"

He leaned over to within an inch of my face to yell, "I just want you to be honest, Lucy. This isn't about me! I was important for almost eleven years, but now you're getting your precious baby even if she costs you your life. That's all you care about. But I don't know what you think is going to happen after . . ."

"After what?"

"Look at me! Do I really look like single-father material to you, Lucy?"

"Mickey?"

"I can't . . . I can't do this right now."

"Mickey, c'mon."

He stood up and grabbed his tie from the foot of the bed. "I'm leaving. Have a nice night."

"Mickey, don't leave like this."

But it was too late. He was already down the stairs, and a second later I heard the front door slam.

Later, I'd been dozing on the couch trying to wait up for him when he called. His words were slurred and I couldn't tell if he'd been drinking, which he rarely does, or if he'd swallowed too many Klonopin, which he takes for anxiety.

"Mickey, come home, it's late. I'll make you some scrambled eggs."

"I just don't feel like it tonight, Lucy. I don't want to come home and watch you die anymore. I'm sick of it. I don't know when I'll be home, but don't wait up." He hung up and I stared at the phone for a long moment before I threw it against the wall. *Watch me die anymore?*

I picked up the phone from where I had tossed it and dialed Partners. "Is Mickey still there, Brian?" I asked the bartender.

"I haven't seen him all night, Lucy."

"When did he leave?"

"I haven't seen him at all."

"Really?"

"You okay, Lucy?"

"I'm fine. If you do see him, will you call me on my cell?"

"I got a backup tonight, Lucy. Want me to go look for him? Just say the word."

"Brian, you're a doll. You just call me if you see him."

"Will do."

I hung up the phone and stormed upstairs to change out of my pajamas. Damn him! It was after midnight. How dare he pull this! Where was he? I slid into my biggest pair of jeans and was buttoning my shirt when I heard the back door slam shut. I walked to the top of the stairs and sat down. Mickey was banging around in the kitchen, and I heard him swear when a glass broke in the sink. I raked my hair and waited.

Finally, Mickey was at the foot of the stairs. He glared up at me, then he pointed his finger and slurred, "I've decided you are the most selfish person I know, Lucy." He took a step up. "I was talking to a woman tonight. She said I looked sad, so I told her all about our little domestic situation. And she pointed out that you are calling all the shots. And I'm just like you said, pathetic enough to be letting you." Mickey teetered as he made a few more stairs. "She said I'm a victim of your whims. That's what she said. She was a smart lady."

"Did she say you were an idiot?"

His eyes hardened. "No, Lucy. She said I was a lot of things, but she didn't say that."

"Did you tell her *she* was an idiot and should mind her own business?"

"Actually, I was rather enjoying her company."

"So where did this stimulating conversation take place?"

"I told you. She was a customer."

"No, you didn't."

"Yes, I did."

"Well, then I'm confused, because Brian said he hadn't seen you all night."

The skin around Mickey's eyes tightened, then his balled-up fist crashed down on the banister. "You checking up on me now, Lucy?"

"Doesn't look like I have much of a choice, Michael."

"Great. That's just great."

"Why are you slurring?"

"Why the hell does it matter?" Mickey was now standing directly in front of me. I looked up at him.

"Don't do this. Don't fight with me. Don't say the stupid things you're thinking."

"Stupid? You mean things like, you're selfish? Or that you're only thinking about yourself?" His voice lifted. "It's always about you, Lucy! No discussion! You're just not going to do what you're not going to do. To hell with me. Oh, who the hell cares?" Mickey moved to step over me, but I stood up and he lost his balance, nearly falling down the stairs. I grabbed him but he pushed me away as he lowered himself to the ground. "Leave me alone, Lucy. Just leave me the hell alone."

"What do you want me to do?"

Slowly, he lifted his face to meet mine. He looked unbelievably sad, his eyes momentarily raw, stripped of hostility. "Have the abortion," he said wearily.

I slumped against the newel and stared at my husband, all folded in on himself. I loved him so much. All I had to do was reach for him and I could turn this moment around. I could put his life back together if I just did what he asked. But I loved him so much more than aborting this baby would prove to him—I loved him so much that I could never leave him alone.

"Forget it, Lucy," he said, getting to his feet. "It doesn't matter because you've already decided." He stared at me for a long time, long enough for me to feel exposed by my thoughts.

I let out a jagged breath. "Mickey, please don't do this. Don't waste this time being mad at me. You won't be able to forgive yourself when—"

"I am so sick of you having all the answers," he sneered. "I just about hate you for this, and until you change your mind, that's just how it's going to be!" He steadied himself against the railing and took a step. He needed a haircut and a shave. His shirt was halfway untucked and he pulled it out. "I'm getting in the shower," he said, walking away.

"I'm going to die anyway, Mickey," I said softly to the wall. I wasn't sure he'd heard me until he stopped, and now I could feel his eyes burning into me. "It doesn't matter if I have the abortion or not, Mic, I'm going to die. And you know it. Whether I have chemotherapy or radiation or surgery or a million IV vitamins, it's going to happen. I don't know when—hopefully many, many months from now—but I won't survive it again." I turned to look at him. His face was hard, impassive, but an unreal calm was in my voice. "We need to face this so we can stop hurting each other and get on with what we have left."

I was so proud of myself for not crying, but then I heard a sob break in Mickey's throat and I couldn't keep my tears back. "Please," I whispered.

A shadow of softness passed through his eyes, and he looked ready to say something, but instead he just shook his head and walked away.

I slumped back against the railing. My whole body was swollen with sadness and I didn't think I had the strength to get up and face it all again in the morning. I just wanted to sleep for a year and wake up in a world where Mickey wasn't sick and I wasn't sick and there was a long life in our future. I closed my eyes and wept.

As I sat there wallowing, I felt the whisper of something lovely and familiar. The sensation, ever so slowly, wound its way around me until I felt cradled in a soft hand of comfort. My heart slowed and my tears dried. I didn't see *her* when I opened my eyes, but it didn't matter. I knew she'd been there because I could feel the peace she'd left in her wake. I sat there for a few more minutes basking in the experience until it evaporated, leaving me with just the lingering reassurance that there was nothing to be afraid of.

The shower was now off and I could hear Mickey rummaging in a drawer for his underwear. When it was quiet, I got up and walked into our dark room, took off my clothes, and crawled into bed. Mickey had his back to me, so I stared up at the ceiling and relished the gift I'd just received. As I lay there, the baby inside me moved. She was stronger than the rolls and flutters of the last few weeks, and now I could feel her with my hand, which excited me unbelievably. "Mickey?"

"I can't fight anymore, Lucy. Let's just go to sleep."

"Mickey, give me your hand."

"Lucy, I'm tired."

"Please."

Mickey grudgingly rolled over and I put his hand on my stomach. For a long time she was still, and I thought Mickey had fallen asleep. But then she moved, and I felt Mickey stiffen. "What was that?" he whispered. She kicked again, a good, hardy jab, and Mickey jerked his hand away and sat up. "What *is* that?"

"It's her." I took his hand once more and he slowly lay back down. The baby kicked again, and again, and Mickey draped his long leg over mine and settled in.

"That's really the baby?"

"That's our daughter."

I felt him start to cry and reached over to stroke his face in the dark. Soon his arms came around me. "I can't do this without you," he rasped.

I had no magic for him, so I just rubbed his head until he fell asleep and prayed for a small reprieve. Before he got out of bed the next morning, Mickey kissed my belly and looked at me with a kind of wonder I hadn't seen since I'd first told him I was pregnant. Tenderness and apology were in his eyes.

Sadly, none of this halted Mickey's approaching downslide—far from it. It simply added a cruel wrinkle as he tried to wrap his head around a baby he knew he loved, but was costing him his wife.

twenty

*My first memory as an insane person was two years before
I was diagnosed as manic-depressive. I was lying in my bed
and listening to my mother die of sadness in the next room.
The anguished note she kept hitting struck me as the absolute
definition of hopelessness. I wanted the sound to stop. I wanted
her to smile and love me and be like my best friend Jonathon's
mom. She laughed and gave hugs. She checked Jonathon's
spelling, and mine if I was over there. I wished my mom could
be like that.*

*I climbed out of bed that night with a perfectly
logical plan for bringing this wish about. Some nights,
my mother shouted her prayers so loud I was sure the
neighbors would know she was crazy. My brother, David,
always brought her water and told her to take her pills.
My dad talked sweet to her for as long as he could stand
it, then he would leave and not come home until late.
On the night when craziness began to bloom in me, I
was convinced that if I begged God, he would grant my
wish. But since it was clear he could not hear my mother,
and would therefore never hear me, I wrote my prayer.
I wrote it in my social studies notebook, certain that he
would see it, because God sees everything. I wrote it for*

hours. I wrote it until my hand hurt. I wrote it all night
*long. Just one word—*please. *9,871 times.*

The most common symptom of cancer in the lung is a cough. I had learned that this is because the lesion causes irritation in the airway tissues. I'd been coughing for several weeks, and Charlotte warned me that my lung might at some point need to be drained of the fluid that was building up in response to my tumors. I understood this. I'd educated myself enough to know that without intervention, the lesions in my *left lower lobe* would continue to grow. I was supposed to tell Charlotte if I began experiencing any chest pain, shortness of breath, or if I started coughing up blood. These, I understood, were signs that things had advanced to a dangerous level.

Charlotte was consulting with Dr. Gladstone, whom I had come to refer to as my lung guy, about my situation. I'd seen him in the hospital and I had an appointment with him the next week so he could evaluate how far I had shifted from my baseline function. Dr. Gladstone would do any surgery after the baby was born. Until then, he would monitor my condition.

In the meantime, Charlotte was treating me with vitamins and pure juices and visualization. Sheer nonsense, according to Priscilla, but I knew enough about nutrition to know that whatever could be done to strengthen the healthy cells in me was a good thing. Besides, I felt pretty good, so I wasn't complaining.

Charlotte's office became my refuge, the only place I could think straight. There, I could study hard data and empirical evidence and breathe the air of absolutes while avoiding the more fluid world of my family's opinions and interpretations.

I spent my time poring through the periodicals that lined her shelves and surfing her Internet. I read everything I could find about having metastatic breast cancer while being pregnant. I memorized case studies and mortality rates on babies that had been conditioned by the stress of their mothers' illnesses. I researched hormone therapy and all the latest chemotherapeutic agents, searching for one that could extinguish my disease but not hurt my baby. I recognized the names of many of the cytotoxic drugs from last time. I learned that some might cautiously be considered in my situation, but none were absolutely guaranteed safe for an unborn baby. I read everything I could find about trastuzumab, gemcitabine, Adriamycin, and paclitaxel. I learned the difference between the anthracyclines and the taxanes, and I held my breath over the promising studies that floated through cyberspace and breathed out my disappointment over their potential effects on a fetus. Some cancer medications were thought to be safe a high percentage of the time when administered late in pregnancy. But in the end, I simply had no faith in any drug whose job it was to destroy cells indiscriminately.

While I was studying, I willed God to grant me a miracle. Nothing too grand. Just more time. I wanted to deliver a healthy baby girl, to hold her, to smell her, to see my Mickey's first reaction to her. Then Charlotte and her cohorts could start an IV in every vein if they wanted to. They could pump me full of gallons of cancer-fighting poison, arrange me on a rotisserie and radiate the hell out of me. I was open to all of that—but only after the baby got here, unharmed.

Until then, I was determined to live as normally as possible. So though I spent much of my time surfing medical sites on Charlotte's computer, I was also working on my class syllabus for the new school year. It had been a long summer, and I was looking forward to going back to work, even if I was a bit worried about my waning energy. I'd had a frank discussion with my principal, Douglas Bunnell, who had, of course, already heard about my condition, but cried anyway when I told him. But bless his heart, he offered up a lovely recommendation: Miriam Brady was getting ready to retire and wanted to only work part-time. He suggested I team up with her, and he didn't care how we worked it out as long as the classes were covered. Miriam's preference was for us to work alternate weeks, which I thought was perfect.

It felt so wonderfully normal to be starting school again. I loved my students, and come the second week in September, I was going to love going through the normalcy of being their teacher. I planned to work for as long as I could, but even if I'd been completely healthy, I'd had no intention of working past Christmas break, since the baby was due January 3. Of course what I considered a wonderful arrangement was decried by my family, who thought the only appropriate activity for me was to rest.

About a week before school started, Lily saw my car in front of Charlotte's office and stopped over to see how I was doing. She fortuitously arrived just in time to hold my hand during my five-month ultrasound—Mickey had blown off the appointment. But all was well, my baby was growing, and Charlotte said she looked perfect. But even as happiness flowed through me, I felt panic creeping up on me. Every reason Mickey and I were never going to have children flew in my face. Ashamed of all that she could inherit from me, I imagined Priscilla's irrational anger at my mother directed at me. I gasped for breath.

Charlotte's arms came around me and soothed my unsaid worries. "A little dark-haired, dark-eyed daughter. That's what you told me, right?"

Holding back tears, I said, "She'll be little like me, but she'll look like Mickey." I found Lily's hand. "But what if she gets sick?" I croaked.

Charlotte shook her head.

"Just because her mother got sick doesn't mean she will," Lily said.

"Easy for you to say, Lil."

"Not so easy. But in my case, it's true. Cling to that, Lu."

More tears blurred Lily's beautiful face. She was right. Lily was healthy . . . knock on wood. So was Priss, in spite of her scare all those years ago. Lily kissed my forehead, and the three of us had a handful of completely normal moments full of happy tears.

I was actually grateful that Mickey hadn't shown up. If he'd been there, he would have seen my doubt and hung me with it. Later that night, when I told him everything looked good with his daughter, I was able to hide my anxiety from him. It wasn't that hard—he was too busy sulking to read between the lines.

Frustrated, I went to bed. But sometime after midnight, I woke to the sound of a basketball bouncing on the back patio. When I looked out, a full moon was shining on Mickey and Harry, who were playing a little one-on-one. *Bless you, Harrison Bates,* I thought. Later, when I checked again, the two of them were sitting on the picnic table, their feet on the bench, just talking.

I don't know what Harry said to my volatile husband. I just know he worked his magic, because when Mickey finally came to bed, he scooped me into his arms. "I've been a jerk, baby," he whispered.

"Really?"

"Really. And I'm sorry. I'm going to be better."

I'm a pushover for any apology, especially from Mickey, and I rolled over and kissed him long and deep for his contrition. We had pretty good makeup sex after that—all things considered—and I fell asleep while Mickey rubbed my hair between his fingers.

But the cease-fire was short-lived. Soon, Mickey began sleeping less and less, and many nights he didn't come to bed at all. One morning I woke to the sound of the shower, and before I was even out of bed, Mickey was already out and dressed. I wandered into the bathroom to find him combing back his wet hair with one hand as he brushed his teeth with the other. He gazed at me through eyes that looked ready for a fight as he rinsed and spit. When I didn't engage him, he checked his teeth in the mirror, gargled, spit again, and planted a cold kiss on my nose, all in thirty seconds. "I'm late, Lu," he shouted over his shoulder. "I left kind of a mess downstairs, but I'll take care of it later." He popped his head back into the bathroom to say bitingly, "And don't freak out, it's nothing."

My heart sank at his words, wondering what he'd been doing all night. But before I could say anything, Mickey was gone. He'd taken the stairs two at a time and was out the door before I reached the landing. He was sleeping less and working more than ever. Or at least he was showing up at one of his clubs. It was also no surprise that Mickey was blowing off his appointments with Gleason, leaving all those orbiting around him powerless against whatever was going to happen. And something was bound to happen because he'd also hidden his medication from me—he was now self-dosing.

I looked in the mirror and sighed. Already my day felt heavy, and I'd just gotten up. I steeled myself for the "nothing" I might find and made my way down the stairs.

When I saw the kitchen, I wanted to cry. Apparently Mickey'd had a yen for chocolate chip cookies in the middle of the night. He'd spilled flour on the floor and walked through it—several times. He'd cracked some eggs, but missed the bowl, and a stream of the slime was dried on the cabinet door. Though the canister was full of sugar, Mickey had opened a new twenty-five-pound bag, seemingly with his teeth. The bag had been knocked over, and a pile of sugar now lay at the foot of the sink.

He'd clearly used every bowl we owned, as well as every cookie sheet, each of which was smeared with Crisco and stacked at the ready. But there were no cookies, just a mountain of cookie dough that had been abandoned, a wooden spoon stabbed in the top of it. A half-empty bag of chocolate chips was sitting on the table in the midst of a tower of newspaper and magazine pages. Magic Markers, glue, tape, and paper clips were scattered everywhere. And there was a cheap, little paper folder, the kind with a pocket on the inside of each cover. I opened it up and found pages—a dozen at least—covered on both sides, with the word *please*. Mickey had cut and taped and glued the word *please* over and over and over until the pages were completely covered with the word. *Please*, in all different sizes. He'd even cut up the cover of a book for the baby, *Please Don't Make Me Come Home from the Moon* and stolen the *Please*.

It was beyond eerie to sit in my ruined kitchen and peer into the disrupted reality of my husband. I fingered the pages he had obviously taken great pains to create. He'd been dedicated. He hadn't allowed himself to become distracted as he had with the cookies. He'd hung in there for eleven pages—twenty-two if you counted both sides. *Please.* For whom had Mickey intended this message? Me? God? Himself? Please don't die. Please don't hate me. Please make me whole. Please help me. Please fix my wife. Please have the abortion. As I tried to analyze what couldn't be analyzed, the ocean of *please*s blurred under my tears.

How long was this spiral going to take? I was ashamed to be thinking this way, but I had to be able to hope for enough time. It could take three months for Mickey to fall off the planet, and it could take that long to reel him back onto it. Then, if we were lucky, he could be stable for several months, or maybe just a few weeks. Sometimes more than a year.

I looked around the kitchen again, then I buried my face in my hands. It was more than Mickey's illness this time. *That* I could handle. It was his illness weighed down with his broken hope that almost did me in. I couldn't love him enough this time, no matter how hard I tried. So I steeled myself for what I knew was coming.

twenty-one

I haven't told anyone about the nightmares I'm having. They happen when I'm fully awake, and they leave me hollow and exhausted and ashamed. In them I am frenzied and desperate and I'm completely alone. God has claimed Lucy and is pitying the freak left behind who cannot find his way. I'm running, as is my habit, convinced in my warped reality that I will find my wife—wherever God has hidden her—I will find Lucy and be whole again.

Then I hear it, this tiny wail that cuts through all the noise. She materializes in my arms, small and completely vulnerable, and I glare down at her through a sheet of tears born of agony and rage. I think I might hate her— she is the thief who stole her mother's life. My life. I don't want her. I don't want to want her. I want God to take her and give me back my wife. From the depths of me I roar down at this helpless infant, the sound something solid and so loud it cracks the sky until shards of it rain down on us, me and my daughter. We're both bleeding and I pull her close, filled with useless apology, but she bleeds more. She needs me, and I am utterly, shamefully impotent. I set her down, gently, this baby girl who stares at me with no guile, no expectation, and I turn my back

on her need and her trust, and I run away. I run until
I am almost flying, but I cannot run far enough or fast
enough or long enough: I can still hear her.

It is taking longer and longer to recover from this
nightmare—and far too many pills to keep it at bay. Even
when I think I'm safely outside of this terrible experience,
I'm still haunted by a core reality that does not change no
matter how many drugs I take: I cannot do this alone. I
cannot do this without my wife.

Labor Day weekend has always been big in Brinley. First thing Saturday morning, the kids parade through the Loop on decorated bikes while the Midlothian High School marching band struts to the cacophony of brass and percussion. Floats and balloons usher in the firemen, who throw candy from the top of Brinley's oldest fire engine. After that there's a serious softball tournament at Pier Park. At five o'clock, the annual art festival takes over the pier, and then it's time for the crown jewel of the holiday: the Labor Day Regatta.

It's our own ceremonial end of summer, and it draws visitors from all over the state. When I was little, my mother and Jan used to work for weeks on a float that all of us kids got to sit atop. My dad, being the police chief, kept order with a big megaphone. That memory comes back to me every year.

I'd told Priss I'd pick her up at ten thirty and we'd walk over to the park for the game. I drove to the Cascade turnoff, where I left my car and walked up Foster Pier Road to the marina. I found my lovely sister sitting on the hull of our sailboat with her legs dangling over the side. She was wearing a linen skirt and a tank top that hugged her shape. She peered over her sunglasses at me, sizing up our standing.

"Hey, Priss."

She glanced at my bulge and nodded, then pulled herself to her feet and climbed down from the boat. "Hey."

We'd talked on the phone a few times, but we hadn't seen each other or spoken of our fight, so we were both kind of testing the water. But the awkwardness melted away when Priss walked over and pulled me into her arms. When she let go, I squeezed her hand. "I'm doing good, Priss. I really am."

"Liar," she rasped.

Our first few minutes together were a little wooden, but the pier, teeming with townspeople, nicely cushioned the stiffness. It was a lovely clear morning for September—the temperature destined for somewhere in the eighties—cloudless, with just enough sea breeze to remind us how close we were to the ocean. A crew was testing the sound system for the string of performers who would take the stage over the next two days. We walked through the rubble of boxes and tables and crates and canvas that were being transformed into booths. Priscilla laced her fingers through mine and squeezed. "I'm sorry, Lucy. I never should have told you how to live your life."

"It's okay," I said, frankly surprised she'd mentioned it. "It's over." I looked up at my gorgeous big sister. "It's forgotten."

"Good, because I need to tell you something."

"What?"

"Guess who I had dinner with last week?"

"The New England Patriots."

"Very funny. Nathan Nash."

"Oh, really? How is he?"

"He's adjusting, he's lonely. We had a nice time, just friendly. We talked for hours."

"You be nice to him, Priscilla. He's one of my favorites."

"Just what is that supposed to mean?"

I shrugged, grateful we had arrived at the park. "Is he here?"

Priscilla looked toward the bleachers. "His son is playing on the school team, so he's probably around here somewhere."

I followed my sister as she eyed the crowd. We found seats on the top row, and she continued to scan the benches for Nathan Nash.

Mickey's softball team, the Loopers, which was composed of anyone doing business on Brinley Loop, was favored to wipe out the competition: the Midlothian Brainiacs, the students and faculty from my school; the Heavenly Choir, which was made up of all the denominations of Brinley clergy; and the Come Back Kids, who were all the Brinians who'd moved away but had come home for this weekend.

For the Loopers, Ron was pitching, Lily was catching, and my Mickey was playing shortstop. They'd been practicing for weeks, and the mock games had kept my husband fairly focused, even if his intractable mood had cost them a darn good first baseman. As it was, Mickey was keeping Ron and Jared busy putting out fires. I looked over and found Lily swinging a bat that looked as if it weighed almost as much as she did. She was wearing an enormous team T-shirt that hung nearly to her knees, and Ron was giving her some last-minute advice, or maybe it was the other way around. She looked up at Priss and me and waved. I gave her the thumbs-up.

The tournament began with Muriel Piper and Oscar Levine, ostensibly the oldest living Brinians, singing the national anthem. Then it was whistles and applause as friendly wagers, and a few serious bets, were placed for our favorites. I was rooting for my beloved Loopers, of course, but I was pretty sure Midlothian was going to win. When the coin toss sent the Loopers to the field, I watched my family and friends take their places.

Mickey turned his baseball cap backward and got serious. He looked amazing in his team jersey. Looking at him, one would never guess how thin his stability was stretched. He still considered himself perfectly functional, but he'd grown disturbingly sure that everyone had a motive to doubt him. Sadly, this paranoia extended even to me and Gleason. Mickey wanted nothing more than to blissfully soar above the reality of our situation, and he was doing it for the most part. I'd found his meds and watched his prescription for Depakote close enough to know he'd decreased the dose, and his Prozac was just about gone—unless he was very depressed, Prozac usually pushed him toward hypomania. When I asked him about it, he'd snapped at me. He apologized later, but wouldn't admit that he'd manipulated his chemistry to such a brittle degree that at this point anything could happen. I watched my husband in his baggy shorts and Looper jersey punching his mitt, grinning at me from the field, amazed that nothing seemed amiss. He waved at me, and I blew him a kiss.

"That's so sweet," Priss said sarcastically.

The whistle blew and the tournament started. After scoring one measly run, the Heavenly Choir quickly struck out. Next, the first three Loopers made a base each, and then Mickey hit their team's first home run. It gleaned them four lovely points. Lily was up next, and Priss and I yelled and whistled our sisterly support. She aimed her hit at the nearsighted Gladys Finney, who taught summer Bible school. Gladys ducked, missed the ball, and Lily rounded second base before the old gal had chased it down and thrown it back in.

From there, things went downhill for the Choir, and the Loopers took the game 13–5, eliminating the clergy from the competition. Mickey joined me in the stands briefly to receive his accolades. I slobbered all over him and Priss bestowed smiles of approval. A pretty woman with a wrist-thick ponytail eyed my husband appreciatively from two bleachers down.

Next the Loopers played the Brainiacs, and it was a long, close game. I was getting hot and uncomfortable and was fidgeting so much that Priscilla commented on my restlessness. I was surprised she'd noticed me at all, now that she had spotted Nathan a few rows over. The two of them were stealing glances like a couple of teenagers in English Lit.

The Loops pulled off a narrow win, and people started heading for the concessions. Priss and I waited for Mickey, Ron, and Lily at the bottom of the bleachers, where Nathan joined us. He gave me a hug. "You're looking good, Lucy," he told me. Considering how I felt, I called him a liar.

I was glad they were taking a break for lunch because I'd had too much heat and sitting on hard bleachers and wanted Mickey to take me back to my car. "You sure, baby? Maybe you just need something to eat."

"No, I'm tired. I need a nap. I'll come back later and we can all have dinner together. Won't that work?"

He kissed me, but there wasn't much warmth in the gesture.

"I'm sorry, honey. Don't be mad."

"I'm not mad, Lu. I just thought we could have a little fun today."

"We are. You were great. I'll go rest for a while and then come back and we'll party the night away."

"If that's what you want to do," he said, lifting me into his arms. "How 'bout a ride for my tired little wife."

Mickey dropped me off at my car. "Call me when you wake up, Lu, and we'll figure out what we're doing." I kissed him hard on the mouth, but he didn't taste right.

I drove home with nothing on my mind but sleep. By the time I walked into the house, I'd convinced myself that a little rest on the couch was all I needed. As I lay there, I found myself drifting back to last spring when Mickey had promised to take me to Hawaii for my birthday. I'd be thirty-four next week, and I'd had virtually no faith Hawaii would happen. But as I was lying there, I thought how lovely it would be to just get on a plane. Just drive to the airport and get on a plane. I knew Jared would happily encourage Mickey to take the time off. I could talk to Gleason about his prescriptions and pick up anything he wanted to add to Mickey's regimen. Mickey's chemistry could stabilize all day long on a sunny beach in Waikiki just as easily as it could here. I picked up the phone. Why couldn't we do this? He'd promised me. And it wasn't like we'd have another chance.

I woke with a start to the sound of my doorbell. The shadows were long in my living room, and it took me a minute to orient myself. I sat up, stiff from sleeping wadded up on the couch. It was a quarter to six and I'd slept like the dead.

I stood up and groped my way to the door. Charlotte Barbee

stood on my stoop, smiling her familiar smile, the one colored with worry. I yawned. "Hey," I said.

"Hello, darlin'. I saw your car in the driveway and thought I'd drop these vitamins off. They came in yesterday, and I want you to start on them right away."

"Come in. I was just resting."

"I know. I talked to Lily a little while ago. I didn't mean to wake you."

"It's okay. I slept too long, anyway." Charlotte followed me into my kitchen, where I offered her a Snapple. She declined, but I opened one for myself and we sat down at the table. I uncapped the bottle of vitamins she'd brought and spilled one into my hand. They were a special blend she'd ordered from an herbalist in San Francisco, and they smelled like dirt. "These are horse pills."

She laughed. "Take one now, then starting tomorrow take one morning and night."

I swallowed one down with a gulp of kiwi-lime and pulled a face. It tasted like dirt.

"So, how are you holding up?" Charlotte said.

"I'm fine. I mean, I feel okay. I can't seem to get enough sleep. But other than that . . ." I shrugged. "I'm thinking of going on vacation."

"Oh, really."

"Am I okay to fly?"

"Fly?"

"I want to go to Hawaii, Charlotte." For a minute she didn't say anything, and I could see the idea concerned her. "I mean, what could it really hurt?" I plunged on. "If I get in trouble, there are doctors in Hawaii, right?"

"I believe there are." Charlotte pushed a strand of hair behind her ear. "But what are you planning, Lucy?"

What was I planning? "I don't know. Mickey promised he'd take me for my birthday, and even though I never thought we'd actually do it, I still want to go. I want to surprise him. Is that crazy?"

Charlotte leaned her chin into her palm. "No, it's not crazy. What about school? Did you change your mind about going back to work?"

"No. But I made a little compromise." I told her about my plan to work alternating weeks with Miriam Brady and that Miriam had chosen this first week. "So I think I can make this work. And it will be so good for Mickey."

I must have looked hopeful because Charlotte studied me for a long moment before she finally said, "I'll get on the web and find some doctors for you. Just in case."

"Thanks." I grinned, relieved. A vacation. Despite my promise to Mickey that I would go with or without him, I hadn't planned to go anywhere since I'd found out I was pregnant. But right now, I couldn't imagine anything more deliciously spontaneous than running away with my husband—running far, far away from all our problems.

Thank goodness Charlotte had agreed since I'd already called Adam Piper. Muriel's grandson owned Piper's Planet, Brinley's only travel agency; I'd told him what I had in mind and gave him my credit card number. He said he'd fix me right up.

twenty-two

A little tutorial: The hallmark of BPD is mood instability that cycles between extreme highs and extreme lows. But there are times when mania and depression coalesce to become the worst of both extremes—highly energized and wicked irritable. That's where I'm at: hyperagitated—a hell of a great place to be! I'm not sleeping, I'm edgy with real-life worry and waking night-mares, and I'm behaving badly. I know I am, and I don't care. I don't know how far gone I am for sure since I'm not imagining the circumstances; my wife really is sick; there really is a baby coming; and at the center I sit desperate to escape it all.

Gleason says this is perhaps actually a crazy-making reality rather than my mental illness. It could be, but I haven't seen him lately to explore that. Gleason gets a little in my face sometimes, and I figure he's just one more stress I don't need to deal with right now. I've got enough on my plate! Leave me the hell alone! I'll keep eating my pills and everyone will be happy, even though I can't feel any difference in my mood. But then mood probably isn't the primary issue. It's the pain. The pain is intractable; so is the fear.

So is the shame. If Gleason's right and I don't have

*my illness to blame, it means I really am capable of this
cruelty.*

When I couldn't get ahold of Mickey, I called Lily to see what everyone was up to, but I only got her voice mail. Then I remembered she
and Ron were in charge of the hot dog concession tonight. I called
Priss, but she said she hadn't seen Mickey since after the Loops won
the championship.

"He must be exhausted," I said. "Three games in one day."

"He did great, and so did our little Lily. Are you feeling better,
Lu?"

"I'm fine. Just needed a rest."

"Well, come down and meet me, and we'll go look for your husband. He's got to be around here somewhere."

"You'd think," I said, a small tingle creeping up the base of my
neck. It was 7:10 and he hadn't called, and he wasn't answering his
phone. *This couldn't possibly be good.*

I brushed my hair, pulled on a sweatshirt, and drove down to
Foster Pier Road. I had to park two blocks away, so it was a little before eight when I finally met Priscilla at the entrance. "Have you seen
him?" I shouted when I was close enough to be heard.

"No, but Ron saw him about an hour ago. Have you tried the
club?"

"Not yet." I pulled out my cell phone and dialed while Priss and
I walked. After a few transfers, I got Jared, who was working the floor
at Partners so his employees could participate in the celebration. He
hadn't seen Mickey since the last baseball game. "Are you expecting
him tonight?" I asked.

"Yeah, but not until later when things die down on the pier."

I nodded. "Well, he's got to be here, then. If you see him, please
tell him I'm looking for him?"

"Sure will, Lucy."

I dropped the phone into my pocket as I took in the glittering sights around me. Thousands of twinkling lights imbued the festival with an amusement-park atmosphere. The noise and the music were evidence that everyone was having a good time.

"What do you want to do, Lucy?"

I linked arms with my sister. "Let's just wander. He's got to be around here somewhere."

We strolled by dozens of booths where everything imaginable was being hawked: tie-dyed dresses, homemade fudge, jewelry, wooden toys. And lots and lots of art, all produced by Brinley's local artisans. We found Jan's booth and I marveled, as I did so often, at what that woman could do with oil paint. Jan squeezed my arm. "Hey, sweetie," she said, patting my belly. "You look so cute. How's our little bun?" Though her words and expression were upbeat, I could see the concern in her eyes. "The bun's good," I said, looking around. "What a crowd, huh?"

"I think it's a record," Jan said.

"I'm looking for Mickey. You haven't seen him, have you?"

"He stopped by around five, I think it was," she said, looking at her husband. "But we haven't seen him since."

I pecked her cheek. "Well, if he comes by again, tell him to come find me."

"I will, honey. And if you get tired, you come back and sit with me for a while. Make her sit down, Priss."

Harry wagged a finger at us, concurring with his wife, then reached over and kissed my forehead. "You heard the boss."

We headed off toward Lily and Ron's hot dog stand, but we didn't get far before Muriel Piper's shrill voice stopped us in our tracks. She shouted at Priss and me from her humongous quilt display on the boathouse lawn and hurried toward us. Muriel wrapped her skinny bird arms around me. "How are you?" she sang. "We've been hoping you would be here tonight. You're doing okay?"

"Pretty good."

"And Priscilla! Heavens, you look like a movie star." Priss preened. "Come, come, you two. Sit with us. We have a little surprise for Lucy."

Muriel insisted I sit in her lawn chair, and it felt good to rest for a minute. Priss pulled up a crate that was part of their pillow display, but they didn't seem to mind. "Close your eyes, now. No peeking. You, too, Priscilla. Okay, Wandy, bring it out," Muriel sang.

I heard rustling and some twitters from my friends, then Wanda Murphy said, "Okay, you can open them."

Of course it was a quilt. A beautiful pink baby quilt.

"Oh my," said Priscilla. "I think that's the most gorgeous thing I've ever seen." The quilt was a jigsaw puzzle of every conceivable shade of pink fabric all fashioned into a scene of a woman holding the hand of a little girl. A brilliant pink sun was rising in the corner, and I had to agree with my sister—it was beautiful.

"Do you like it?"

"I don't know what to say."

"We're going to enter it in the state competition in two weeks. Then it's yours," Muriel said. "What do you think?"

"I love it! And I love you, and I love you." I kissed Muriel and Wanda, two of my mother's dearest friends. Just then Oscar Levine, wearing a pair of khaki shorts and a blue sweater, made his way into the tent with a tray of hot dogs and a bottle of wine. Priss and I got up to leave, but Oscar insisted we stay. He said Lily had seen us and dressed a couple of foot-longs just the way we liked them, so what could we do? We stayed. Even Priscilla, who's not usually too townsy, got comfortable after a couple of paper cups of wine.

My cell phone rang, and Priscilla flashed me a look as I answered, "Hello."

"Lucy? Sorry to bother you. It's Jared."

"Hey." I could hear music and the lively noise of Partners in full swing.

"I think you better come down. Mickey *is* here. I just saw him a few minutes ago. He's been drinking and partying pretty good, and there's a woman here who won't leave him alone. I told her to lay off, but she isn't budging. You better come down. Maybe bring Ron."

I swallowed, my eyes hard on Priscilla's. "Thanks, Jared. I'll be right there." I hung up. It had been a long time since I'd been called to rein in my husband. Usually the presence and friendly discouragement of people who knew Mickey was enough to keep him in line—at least in public.

"We have to go," I said, getting to my feet. I hugged and thanked my sweet friends again, hoping my gushing would keep them from asking any questions.

Once we were out of earshot, Priscilla took my arm. "What?"

"He's at the club. With some woman."

Priscilla stopped and shook her head. "Are you kidding me, Lucy? That stupid—"

"Priss, I need your help, but I don't need *that*." She put up her hands in mock surrender, but her eyes stayed hardened. The hackles on my neck stiffened in anticipation of a snotty comment. "Priss, this isn't really Mickey, you know that. He's just having an unbelievably hard time with all of this. With everything."

Priscilla sighed. "We all are," she said with uncharacteristic resignation.

People were starting to board up their booths for the night. We found Ron emptying his trash at the big Dumpster that had been set up by the concessions. He grinned at us as we approached. "Hey, thanks for all your help tonight. It was wild, and Lil and I really appreciate you lending us a couple of hands." When he saw the look on my face, he stopped the kidding. "What's the matter, Lucy?"

"It's Mickey. Can you come with me to the club?"

He didn't hesitate. He never does. "Let me just lock up. What's he done?"

"I don't know yet, but there's a woman."

He shook his head. "That's not good."

"He's so unpredictable lately," I said. "I don't know what we're going to find."

Lily was leaning out of the trailer window, nodding. She'd heard the conversation as we'd walked up. "It'll be okay," she said. "We'll all go over to the club and deal with him together."

Ron drove Priscilla and me to my car, which was still parked on Foster Pier Road, and from there we followed them up to the Loop. When we got to Partners, we could hear the thrum of the band spilling onto the outside courtyard. There was nowhere to park, so I turned off the engine in front of a fire hydrant. Ron pulled up beside me. "Go on in, Lucy." he said, "I'll park behind Ghosts and come find you." Lily looked nervous, but nodded.

Priss and I made our way through the crowd to the bar, where Jared spotted me and waved me over. He was talking to Chad Withers, who looked at me with concern in his eyes.

"Do you know where he is?" I asked.

"He was outside a while ago," Chad said. "I think he's been hitting the bottle pretty good, Lucy. And this woman just keeps setting him up."

Priscilla and I made our way to the courtyard, where the music was like a hammer against my temples. The dance floor was a crush of bodies, and I nearly lost Priss in the crowd. I passed several of my friends, who obviously knew why I was there. It occurred to me that I should probably feel more embarrassed than I did, but the thought was quickly vanquished. What would be the point? Anyone who knew Mickey and me *knew* us. And anyone who didn't, didn't matter.

When there was no sign of him in the courtyard, we made our way back over the packed dance floor. I looked over at my sister, dread filling me. "I have a bad feeling, Priss."

As we crossed back to the foyer, Ron and Lily were just walking through the front doors. "Is he here?" Lily asked.

"We can't find him." Priss looked at Ron. "Come with me," she said to him. "Lily, stay with Lucy. We'll be right back."

As they disappeared down the hall, I thought how formidable my sister was, and I was so grateful for her strength. As we waited, Lily laced her fingers into mine and I laid my head on her shoulder.

Cory Brubaker, the owner of the inn and a friend, cut through all the layers of propriety and told Priss the woman Mickey had been with was a guest, Hilary Wellington, registered in room 216. She'd ordered an elaborate dinner for two, which had been delivered about twenty minutes earlier. At Priscilla's insistence, Cory handed her the room key.

When Ron and Priss returned to the foyer, I insisted I could handle things from here by myself, but they all accompanied me to the second floor anyway. When we reached the room, I reluctantly pressed my ear to the door. It might have been the TV, but the sound of someone moaning felt like a kick in the gut all the same. I looked at Lily. She leaned her ear against the door and heard it, too. I closed my eyes and knocked.

Instantly a woman's clear voice shouted, "Come back later. We're not finished."

"The hell you're not," Priscilla hissed, jamming the key into the lock. Before I knew it, we were in the room, face-to-face with a beautiful woman I thought I recognized from this morning's softball game. A look of alarm flashed through her blue eyes. She was wearing a loosely belted silk robe, and her thick hair now hung beautifully to her shoulders. Mickey was sitting on the edge of the bed, his arms hanging limply at his sides. His jeans were unzipped and he wasn't wearing a shirt. I forgot to breathe as I tried to make sense of what I was seeing. Confusion and rage each vied for first expression.

"Wh . . . what are you doing? Mickey!"

When Mickey looked up at me and I didn't register in his eyes, fear took the lead. Something was wrong with him.

I took a step toward him and still he didn't react. "What are you doing?" I muttered. "What's happening here?" I stared at my husband, who didn't seem to know where he was, then at the woman. "What have you done?"

Hilary Wellington's stricken look was replaced with cold annoyance. "How dare you?" she demanded. "Get out of my room this minute, or I'll call the police."

"Shut up, you whore!" Priscilla spat, covering the space between them in two long strides. "Just shut up!"

I took in the room and studied my half-naked, dull-eyed husband. It was as though he had collapsed in on himself. He looked utterly pathetic, and I was angry that he was pathetic. An open bottle of wine was on the nightstand, and another on a table in the corner amid the remains of a cozy little dinner for two. Mickey's shirt and shoes were on the floor in a heap, and the bed, though still made, was rumpled. I looked at the woman, then back at Mickey, trying to put this in a context I understood. Mickey was holding something loosely in his fist, and when I opened his hand, I found an empty prescription bottle. "Oh, Mickey," I took his face in my hands and tried to force him to see me, but when his eyes rolled back in his head, I started to shake.

"He's been eating those like candy," the woman said.

"And how much of *this* has he had?" I screamed, picking up the wine bottle nearest me. I threw it at the wall and it shattered in a smear of red glass. The woman jumped. "He can't drink!" I yelled again. "He's taken all his pills!"

"Hey, hey, it wasn't me!"

"Oh, right!" Priscilla barked.

I was shaking when I turned to Mickey. "How many pills have you taken?" I yelled. "Mickey, what have you done?" I wanted to hit him and scream at him and tear his head off, but I was shaking so badly I couldn't think.

Ron took my wrist. "Focus, Lucy. Let's just get him out of here."

I nodded and bent to help Lily, who had quietly begun dressing my husband. She was so gentle, seemingly oblivious to the circumstances as she carefully guided Mickey's feet into his shoes.

"C'mon, buddy, help us out," Ron said as we tried to get Mickey to stand up.

As we tended to Mickey, Priscilla was shouting that the woman was some piece of work. Mickey tried to turn toward the noise but couldn't muster the strength, his head lolling to the side. I was afraid he was going to pass out. "Stay with me, Mic. Stay with me!" I whispered urgently. Despite his near unconsciousness, torture was in

Mickey's eyes, and I couldn't read its meaning. I wanted to cry and slap him at the same time. What was he doing here?

"Priscilla, let's go," Lily shouted from the door she had opened for us.

"Get her purse, Lily," Priscilla barked.

My sister looked at Priss and then at me as she picked up the Louis Vuitton that was lying in the overstuffed armchair. "Take her wallet," Priss ordered. Lily lifted the wallet from the bag, and when Hilary Wellington lunged at her, Priscilla grabbed at her robe, keeping her where she was. The silk slid off one lovely shoulder exposing one lovely breast, which the woman strove to cover while still keeping Lily from her valuables.

"What exactly are we doing?" Lily asked.

We'd gotten Mickey almost to the door when he tripped over his foot. As I helped him right himself, I noticed how dilated his eyes were. "Oh, lord. Mickey," I said, panic rising in me. "Priscilla, we have to go. We have to get him to the hospital."

"Wait!" Hilary shouted. "Where are you going with my wallet?"

Lily took a step toward her. "Look what you've done to my sister! She's pregnant!"

Priscilla shook the wallet in the woman's face. "You can have this back when you get a blood test. HIV. Gonorrhea. Herpes. We have no idea how big a slut you are, so you'll need to be checked out by our Dr. Barbee, here in Brinley. Her number's in the book!"

"You can't do that! Who do you think you are?"

"I'm her sister!"

Ron and I were balancing Mickey between us. "Priss, we're leaving," I said. We were just out the door when Mickey nearly overwhelmed us with his leaden weight. Suddenly, Priscilla was at my side. She disengaged me and slid herself beneath Mickey's shoulder. I took the wallet from under her arm. Again the woman moved for it, but this time Lily leaned right in her face. "We told you what you have to do! Call Charlotte Barbee."

Downstairs, Ron lowered Mickey into a chair and, digging for his keys, said, "I'll pull around front." He realized the same time I did that Lily was not with us and he quickly headed back for her, but she was on her way down the stairs.

"What are you doing?" he said, walking toward her. "Are you all right?"

"I'm fine. She wanted to tell me something." Lily looked at me. "She wanted me to know they didn't have sex. She wanted you to know, Lu. Nothing happened."

"Oh, right," Priscilla groaned.

"I know," I said wearily. "Lily, give this to Cory. Have him return it to her."

"What? How do you know that?" Lily said, dumbfounded, taking the wallet. The collective gaze of my family fell on me.

"Believe it or not, that's the line Mickey would never cross. And to make sure he didn't, he took the pills. They were his safety net." I shook my head. Reckless promiscuity was a trademark of many bipolars, but I'd been blessed not to be married to one like that. No, the woman was the least of my worries; my husband could die from his antics if we didn't hurry. I stared at Mickey, slumped in the chair. I'd seen this train wreck in the making, but there was nothing I could do to prevent it.

twenty-three

I watched myself take the pills. One after the other, sometimes two at a time, swallowed down with wine I shouldn't be drinking. I watched me through a perfectly rational mind's eye. I watched, but I couldn't stop what I was doing. Of course not. I had a point to make, I was sure of it. But the more pills I took, the harder it was to remember. All part of the plan. All part of the plan. What plan? The baby. Right. The baby. The baby? Everything melted together. Lucy's sick again. Long shot. No abortion. Another pill, another drink. Just melt. What a good idea I'd had, just sleep away all the pain. Melt. Just melt. Another pill, more wine. It was almost over, I thought. I was almost over. Then the panic. What? Melting. Wait. Melting.

Dear God, I thought, help me. What have I . . .

And that's the last thing I remember thinking.

When I was finally allowed to see my husband, a physician I'd never met was listening to his chest. When he was finished, he slung his stethoscope around his neck and introduced himself. Dr. Harwood looked tired, but had a nice smile. He told me Mickey's blood work showed an abundance of benzodiazepines and alcohol, and he explained that though Klonopin on its own wasn't necessarily life-threatening, the combination could be deadly. I nodded, I knew. I just didn't understand why Mickey would do it. The only other time he'd ever attempted suicide, he'd been grossly psychotic and so desperately insane that all he'd wanted was relief. But that wasn't the case tonight, and I couldn't believe he actually wanted to die.

If he did, he'd chosen a good way to do it, Dr. Harwood informed me. He said that Mickey's overdose had rendered his central nervous system so anesthetized that he wasn't producing the stimulus to breathe. He was being placed on a respirator so he wouldn't suffocate. The doctor was confident, however, that Mickey's capacity to breathe would return as the toxins worked their way out of his system. He'd put an IV and a catheter in place to flush those toxins through him in a timely manner.

As soon as Mickey was stabilized on the ventilator, Dr. Harwood transferred him to the intensive care unit. Ron, Lily, and Priscilla all left after that, but only because they weren't allowed in the ICU. They'd only let me in there, and I'd promised I wouldn't stay long. That was over two hours ago, and I still couldn't leave. I just couldn't wrap my head around what he'd done. A woman? An overdose? He'd never done anything like that before. I wanted to shake him awake and make him explain it.

But he was asleep, unconscious. He looked so peaceful—the green tubing taped to his face notwithstanding. Sadly, this overdose-induced respite was the most at peace Mickey had been for weeks, and despite myself, tenderness welled up in me.

As I stood there lost in my thoughts, I felt a soft hand on my shoulder and turned to find Lily standing next to me. "I thought you went home."

She ran a hand over my hair. "I came back. I had to make sure you were okay."

"I'm fine. How did you get in here?"

"I told the nurse I was worried about you, and that I came to take you home."

"I'm leaving in a few minutes."

"Why don't I believe you?" She kissed my forehead, then leveled her gaze at Mickey. She stared at him for a long moment, shaking her head. "Is he going to be okay, Lu?"

"Yes."

She leaned on the bedrail and gazed down at my sleeping husband. My sister's demeanor was so earnest with concern, so gentle, so non-judgmental. She tenderly squeezed Mickey's wrist. "What you must go through," she said softly to me. "I don't know how you do it, Lucy."

"Just one foot in front of the other, Lil. There's no magic." I stroked Mickey's cheek and thought back to the day, many years ago, when Gleason had told me what life with Mickey would be like. It hadn't taken me long to understand what he'd meant. Broken glass. At the moment, we were barefoot and dancing over a sea of it. But as true as that was, Mickey knew I would dance with him forever if I could, bloody feet and all.

"I love him so much, Lil. But I'm so mad at him. Why would he do this? Why now?"

"Maybe it's because he feels exactly the same way about you."

I looked at my sweet, wise sister and I couldn't hold back the tears.

"Let me take you home, honey."

"I just need to talk to the doctor once more, then I'm leaving."

Lily eyed me like I was lying. "Lucy, please don't stay all night."

"I won't, I promise." I kissed her cheek.

At about three fifteen, a young, acne-scarred intern checked Mickey's vital signs. He then flipped a switch on the ventilator and evaluated Mickey's respirations without the use of the machine. Apparently he was not pleased with the parameters, because he turned the machine back on and watched the monitor until it was clear Mickey was again being well oxygenated. The young doctor, who wore no name tag and hadn't bothered to introduce himself, spoke in a loud voice, "Mr. Chandler, can you hear me? Mr. Chandler." The doctor looked at me. "He'll come around."

I nodded. "You know my husband has bipolar disorder."

"I didn't know that, ma'am," he said, preoccupied as he tapped something out on Mickey's bedside computer.

"Well, I'm letting you know because when he wakes up, he might be very angry."

"Really?" the boy doctor said, looking up from his documentation.

"Yes. I don't actually know if or why he tried to kill himself last night, but whatever he did do, and the reason he did it, will come flooding back the moment he wakes up. He'll be mad at himself, and probably humiliated, which he doesn't handle well."

"We'll watch him, ma'am."

I nodded, hoping he understood my warning. "He's been hypomanic for more than a month now. And very irritable. He's been self-medicating. I gave a list of his pills to the nurse downstairs. I'm just letting you know."

"Thank you, Mrs. Chandler. I'll pass along the info."

"If you need any verification, call the psych unit. They know him well. His psychiatrist is Gleason Webb. I called him on our way here, but he wasn't home, so I left a message. You might want to try again."

At this point, the intern scrounged up a piece of paper and took down Gleason's number. He was suddenly quite attentive, and when he walked away, it was with an air of urgency. After he left, I leaned over the bedrail and watched Mickey's even, automated breathing. Despite my determination to hate him right now, I couldn't. I was truly sorry for what Mickey would face when he regained consciousness.

When he woke up, he'd learn that his demons had betrayed him, yet again. He'd be livid. I couldn't imagine anything more devastating for my husband than to look upon his naked reflection after he'd pulled a stunt like this. I knew that seeing my disappointment, my tired sadness at his antics, would only compound his pain and quite possibly motivate him to try again to hurt himself. I leaned over the bedrail and kissed his forehead, lingered there a moment. "I love you, babe. But I won't be here when you wake up."

I stopped at the nurses' station and told the same intern I was leaving. "I'd keep an eye on him if I were you," I said. "When he starts to come around, you may need some restraints. He's needed them in the past."

A nurse who'd taken care of Mickey before looked up from a medical chart she was reading and assured me she'd take care of it. I hoped she meant it. "I'll call in a few hours to check on him," I told her.

"Call anytime, Mrs. Chandler," the intern said as I walked out.

It was nearly four o'clock in the morning by the time I got home and so quiet it was like the earth was holding her breath. Even my soft footsteps on the front path seemed a sacrilege to the silence. I sat down on the front step and closed my eyes against the sheer noise-lessness. The air was the perfect weight and temperature and seemingly so compatible with my being that I felt simply absorbed into the night. I sighed as quietly as I could.

The baby inside me stretched vigorously. Despite the ragged shelter I was able to offer, she felt strong and substantial. I rubbed my hard belly and took stock of everything immediately important: Mickey was safe, the baby was active, and I was finally home.

I stood and yawned as I dug the key from my pocket. When I pushed open my front door, I found a large envelope in my foyer that had been dropped through the mail slot.

I stared at it, knowing exactly what it was, and let out a strangled sigh. Then I picked up my airline tickets to Hawaii. As I held them, I became angry, irrationally angry. He'd promised! *We'll go for your birthday,* he'd said. *I'll be good,* he'd said. *I won't disappoint you, Lu.* I dragged myself upstairs holding the envelope. In my bedroom, I fell onto my bed and stared at the blurred ceiling, growing more agitated by the minute. Marinating in my indignation, I decided to keep my end of the bargain and began packing my suitcase.

At LAX, where I was scheduled to change planes, I was already having second thoughts. What was I doing here without Mickey? As I boarded, I honestly considered turning around and catching the next flight back to Connecticut. But I didn't. When I got to my seat, I found a lovely sport coat draped over it, the owner carefully stuffing his carry-on into the overhead compartment. When he saw me, he apologized so nicely I'd have forgiven him for robbing me. He smiled and moved his coat and I slid in and buckled up. I prayed that the seat between us would not be occupied for the flight to Hawaii. I smiled stiffly at the tall, lanky man who smelled like Juicy Fruit gum.

His cell phone rang and he answered it with a "Hi, sweetie." He listened for a moment, then chuckled. "So you found them. Good." He nodded awhile. "Let me talk to him. . . . Okay, I love you, too." He glanced at me, embarrassed. "Scotty? . . . Hey, pal, you remember what I said, right? You're the man this week. I'm depending on you. Don't give Mom any grief, and don't be scaring the girls about flying. Remember our deal: if I get a good report, then it's just you and me. . . . I'm excited, too. I gotta go. Be good. I love you."

He turned his phone off and glanced over at me with a sheepish smile. "Kids."

"Sounds like you have a houseful," I said.

"Four."

"Wow." I rubbed my bump. "I can barely imagine myself with one."

"They're a full-time job, all right." He grinned. "My boy's a job all by himself."

I leaned over, enjoying this man's easy company. "So what do just you and Scott get to do if he's good?"

"Paragliding." He laughed. "To tell you the truth, I'm half hoping he acts up so I don't have to go through with it."

The flight attendant asked for our attention and instructed us on where the exits were and what to do if we went down over the ocean. I wasn't listening. I was standing at the gate of this man's house spying on his family. His wife sounded lovely—she'd said "I love you" first, and I could easily picture his house full of kids. I laid my head back and thought of Mickey. If I squinted, I could imagine him talking on the phone to his daughter just like this man. In that lighthearted tone, telling her to be good, that he'd bring her a surprise if she went to bed on time.

Mickey. Again I wondered what I was doing. I hadn't even seen him since I'd left the hospital two nights ago. I just couldn't go back. Not when Gleason called to tell me everything I'd predicted had in fact come true. After Mickey caused hell in the ICU, Gleason transferred him to the psychiatric ward and put him on suicide watch. He was calling Mickey's benzo-and-booze ingestion a *conscientious attempt*, although he was quick to add that Mickey was not speaking to him and had not therefore actually admitted anything. He told me I probably did not want to see my husband in his current state of belligerence. I didn't argue. Instead, I'd thrown my things together in a bit of a tantrum, feeling completely justified in my indignation. Until now.

That I hadn't had the strength or the desire to see Mickey before I left suddenly felt unconscionable to me. The little snippet of this man's phone conversation—the glimpse I had seen of his life—made me suddenly ashamed of my behavior. But Mickey had overdosed, that was a fact, and I didn't know how to make that fit into what was already happening to us. "We've been here before, Lucy," Gleason had said. "He'll even out." I hoped he would. But I was so angry with him that I didn't have the patience to watch it happen. So, I'd used the e-ticket Adam Piper had left for me and ignored the tongue-lashing from my sisters when I called them from the airport. Now I was sitting at a cruising altitude of thirty-six thousand feet above the Pacific Ocean, wallowing in guilt and second thoughts.

I felt a tap on my arm. "Did you want something to drink?" the man said as the flight attendant looked at me.

"Oh, water with lots of ice, please." She handed me a glass and a bottle of Evian, and when she left, the man turned to me. "Are you all right?"

"I think so. Why do you ask?"

"You just look a little . . . upset."

"Really? No, I'm fine. Well, mostly fine."

The man smiled; he had the kindest eyes. "I'm Thomas Worthington," he said, offering me his hand.

"I'm Lucy Chandler. It's nice to meet you."

We made mindless chitchat for a little while. I asked him about his work and was pleased to learn he'd been a school psychologist for years and also had a private practice in a little place called Alpine, Utah. He'd written a book called *Raising Responsible Kids in an Irresponsible World* and was speaking at a national conference for therapists in Honolulu. I was duly impressed and told him so, making a mental note of the title of his book. He graciously applauded my teaching high school, saying he admired educators of any kind. I smiled. "Utah, huh? Are you a Mormon?"

"Guilty." He grinned. "But I only have one wife, in spite of what you may have seen on TV."

"Duly noted."

Thomas Worthington smiled and looked me straight in the eyes. "So, Lucy Chandler, what does being *mostly fine* mean?"

I smiled wanly and imagined how this conversation would sound to the likes of Mr. Thomas Worthington with his perfect marriage and perfect kids: *Well, Mr. Worthington, my husband attempted suicide the other night so I took off because I'm pregnant and dying, and he promised to take me to Hawaii. And I'm sure I must sound like a jerk to have abandoned him, but, well, you see, you have to understand . . .* I looked at him, ready to answer his question with a meaningless pleasantry, but for some reason I started to cry. Not anything gushing. Just a silent accumulation of tears.

Thomas Worthington did not look away. Instead, he handed me the napkin from his drink and said, "What can I do for you?"

I found his concern so irresistible that my words began limping out of me indiscriminately. I told him about Mickey. I told him more than I had ever told anyone else, and he seemed sincerely fascinated by our relationship, probably because he was a therapist. Looking at me in a deliberate kind of way, he said, "Can you even imagine your husband's life if he'd never found you? He's a lucky man, indeed."

It took me a moment to respond. "I've never thought of it like that," I finally said. "I've just thought of how drab and predictable *my* life would be without *him*."

"I'll bet you have," Mr. Worthington chuckled.

"When I met him, I knew I'd found something I hadn't even known I was looking for. He tried a few times to save me from marrying him. But I think we both just knew we belonged to each other."

Thomas Worthington nodded. "It really is a miracle when we find our other half—that one person that makes our life complete, warts and all."

"It's true. And now I can't imagine my life without him." I turned away to compose myself. Why was I here? What was I doing? I didn't want to be anywhere without Mickey. Not Hawaii, not in my own house, not wherever my soul was headed. I didn't want to be without him, and the thought pierced my heart.

We'd been quiet a long time when I again turned to Thomas Worthington. "Do you believe in life after death?" I said, shocked at my brazen inquiry, but somehow certain I could ask it of this man.

He didn't miss a beat. "Oh, absolutely."

"Really? How do you picture it?"

He seemed to chew on this for a moment. "Perfect. Lovely beyond description. Surrounded by everyone important to us. And in perfect health," he added emphatically.

"That would be lovely, wouldn't it?"

He studied me for a moment, then asked, "Do you believe in life after death, Lucy?"

I thought for a minute. "When I was little, my father told me about death. I couldn't sleep one night thinking about it, and he told me these three secrets so I wouldn't be afraid. He said death wasn't the end, and it didn't hurt, and if I wasn't afraid, I'd have some warning of when it was going to happen. I've carried those words with me like a talisman my whole life."

"He sounds like a wonderful father."

I smiled and didn't speak again until I knew I wouldn't cry. "Just a few days after we'd had that conversation, he was killed. It was like he knew, and he wanted me to know—and I did know—that everything he'd said was true."

"What an amazing story."

I nodded. "I guess it is. My mother died when I was seventeen, and the same thing happened. It was like I knew the secret to death. *I* had the answer, the key, to get through what you have to go through when someone you love dies. And now I think I believe it because I just can't see the point of our lives otherwise. Or maybe I'm just afraid *not* to believe it because it gives me such comfort. I don't know which."

He nodded thoughtfully. "I think it's the separation that frightens us."

"I do, too."

I meant to tell Thomas Worthington about the cancer crawling unchecked through my body. I meant to explain my annoying cough, but somehow the mood seemed too soft, too tender, for those hard realities, so I didn't. It was as though there was no need.

When we landed in Honolulu, I wanted to hug him because I didn't think there was any other way for me to convey my appreciation for his kindness. But I didn't hug him; I just teased him, saying he was probably sorry he'd introduced himself after incurring our lengthy conversation.

Thomas Worthington then looked at me with such earnest sincerity that I was a little taken aback. "I wouldn't have missed sitting by you, Lucy." He smiled. "I've lived long enough to realize there are no accidents. I travel all over. Don't be surprised if I show up at Midlothian someday just to see how you're doing." He handed me his business card. "If you ever want to continue our discussion, you call me, Lucy."

Touched, I took his card and thanked him. When he pulled out his cell phone, I told him good-bye and made my way to the ticketing counter to book my flight home.

The soonest I could get a guaranteed seat was two days away, so I took a shuttle to the Hyatt Regency, where I had reservations, and called to check on Mickey. I wanted only to know that he was safe, and the night nurse told me he was a little better, but still on suicide watch, which, all things considered, made him just about as safe as he could be. I took a long shower, ordered a turkey sandwich on rye, and nearly fell asleep waiting for it. When housekeeping called and woke me up the next morning, I'd been dreaming of a man and a woman in the thirties. The man was lean and wiry and wore a uniform, his face somehow familiar to me. The woman was small, and I had the impression she was crying. There were two little girls, a toddler and a baby. The baby wore my mother's face. As I woke up, the images evaporated until all I could remember was the man who wore the uniform. I felt certain he was my grandfather and certain that dreaming of him now was no accident.

I called the concierge and arranged for a sightseeing tour later that morning, one that I desperately wished Mickey were here to share. Then I called Edgemont. Peony said that Mickey had started to settle down—his irritability was waning, which meant depression lay in its wake. Peony let me know that he was in a session with Gleason at the moment, so I told her just to tell him I had called and would call again. I hung up sick with missing him.

I'm not sure what I expected on my sightseeing trip to Pearl Harbor. I'd grown up knowing my grandfather died on the USS *West Virginia*. But he was just a face in a photo album that had never sparked any particular sentiment in me—until now. I settled into my plastic chair atop a ferry called the *Adventurer V* and found my emotions close to the surface. I was soon numbed by the vivid description of that December morning in 1941, when the Japanese descended on our unsuspecting Pacific Fleet. I was captivated as the carnage and chaos played itself out in my mind, particularly pricked by the mention of the *West Virginia*.

I thought of him. William Dean Butler. Twenty-six years old.

What had he been doing? At the moment he realized what was happening, what was his first thought? Was it of his beloved wife home in Massachusetts with their two little girls—my mom and Aunt Gwen? Did thoughts of him pierce Grandma's heart as he breathed out his last breath? Dead at twenty-six. If everything happened for a reason, where was the reason in that?

The memorial built over the USS *Arizona* was eerie and sobering. I bought a book that listed the names of all eleven hundred men that were entombed in that massive ship. Each one had a life, a story, dreams. It didn't make sense that it could be so *over* for them. Suddenly dead, midsentence, midbreath, midthought.

I could not imagine being *over*. I could not fathom never holding Mickey again, never feeling his hands in my hair, his mouth on mine. I couldn't imagine never laughing with my sisters again, or walking through Brinley Loop, which I could do with my eyes closed. And I could not imagine not knowing the little girl inside me. Not being able to kiss away her tears, bandage her knees, take her picture on her first day of school, the day she got married. Thinking of all this *life* that would go on without me was torment.

It's not the end, I heard my father's echo.

"It's not the end," I breathed out. It had to be true. I needed it to be true. Surely our lives held more purpose than building a posterity we would never know. Our lives had to continue on to something else—if not, what was the point of a twenty-six-year-old husband and father dying at the whim of a Japanese dive-bomber? What was the point of a thirty-four-year-old pregnant woman dying of cancer? Even as I asked, I felt a calm hand on my heart and my father's reassurance.

That quiet comfort was the perfect birthday present.

twenty-four

I did it for her. I should write it all down in detail so she'll
know, but sitting up, holding a pen, moving it across paper, is
taking too much strength, maybe all my strength. So I lie here
and stare at the ceiling and wonder if there was an alternative.
I don't think there was. A man only has his own tools, even if
they're broken. I used mine. I had to. For her.

I called Gleason from the airport as I waited for my flight home. He
told me Mickey was stabilizing, but he'd fought it and had required
some extra medication to manage his depression. "Gleason, be honest
with me. Is he still suicidal?"

"He's not saying. But he's fighting some kind of battle that worries
me. I've kept him pretty medicated until his lithium level evens out."

"I understand."

"I've also thrown in an old medication he's responded to in the
past."

Impulsively I asked, "Do you think he'll even out anytime soon?"

"I sincerely hope so, Lucy. You certainly deserve that."

I sighed again. "My plane gets into Hartford at about noon. Can
I see Mickey when I get home?"

"I don't see why not."

"Thanks, Gleason. Thanks for everything."

"You're quite welcome. Be safe, Lucy. I'll see you soon."

When my next plane finally landed at Hartford/Springfield, I was stiff and sick to my stomach. It was partly the bumpy ride and the stale air, but it was also thoughts of Mickey that had bombarded me during the flight. I was stuck between dread and excitement at the prospect of seeing him. Dread because I didn't know what to expect, and excitement because I'd missed him so much. But then, I'd been missing him for weeks. I claimed my car from long-term parking, tossed the flowered shirts I'd bought at the airport in the backseat, and headed toward the interstate.

Autumn had apparently arrived in my short absence. A nip was in the air, and the sky was overcast—Mickey would call it *a moody day*. It rained the whole way to Brinley, and by the time I got to Edgemont, it was pouring.

When I reached the third-floor nurses' station, I could see *You poor girl* written all over Peony Litman's smile. "Now, honey," she said, "he's not doin' too good, our Mickey. I just want to prepare you. You know Dr. Webb has him on some heavy stuff."

I nodded. "Gleason told me."

Peony sent me down the hall with an encouraging nod, and I went off to find my husband. The combination psychiatric/substance-abuse ward at Edgemont is configured in two long hallways, one for each specialty. Both halls are clearly visible from the central nurses' station, and as I walked, I could feel Peony's eyes on my back. Mickey's room was at the bottom of the psych hall, and I found myself peering through the open doors as I passed. In one room a small, thin man walked around in circles, muttering softly. In another, a woman was balled up in a chair. She looked at me with child's eyes.

I slowed as I reached Mickey's room and took a deep breath. He didn't know I was coming. I hadn't seen him for five days, and I found I was reluctant to walk into the unknown. When I stopped just short of his door, I heard crying, soft and plaintive and heartbreaking. A man crying has got to be the most pitiful sound in the whole world.

The sound was coming from a bed against the wall, but the room was so dim I couldn't make out the face.

Another bed was behind the door, and presently I saw my husband shuffle from that direction across the room to the man crying. He moved slowly, tentatively, his posture bent with the effects of his medication. His back was to me and he was wearing the old maroon bathrobe I had dropped off the day after he was admitted.

"John, it's okay. John, don't cry," Mickey crooned in a soothing, if raspy, voice. He made it to the bed and sat down. "Hey, hey, it's okay, pal. Don't be afraid. Do you need some water?" I watched him pick up a styrofoam cup from the bedside table with a shaking hand. He gently lifted the man's head off his pillow. Though some of the water sloshed over the edge with Mickey's tremors, he got the straw into the man's mouth. I could see now that Mickey's roommate was loosely restrained by a body Posey, a cloth device used to keep him from getting out of bed, or falling out. Mickey had been restrained like that in the past to keep him from wandering when he was psychotic.

I watched him, my beautiful husband, resembling nothing so self-assured and funny as the man he got paid for being. He was tender and kind and quiet, and at the moment he was this man's savior.

True, his mind was frayed and contorted by defective DNA, not to mention the drugs meant to counteract that DNA. His thoughts couldn't always be trusted, and his conduct was frequently driven by conjecture and wrongly processed information. Yet, despite that, here he was, a man of great heart and compassion soothing the fear of a delirious man.

I watched him replace the cup and take the man's beseeching hand in his tremulous one. "It's okay, John. You're not alone, buddy."

"Don't leave me," came the man's gravelly plea, desperate and heart-wrenching.

"Where am I going, John? Dancing? I'm staying right here."

Mickey sat with his frightened friend for several long minutes. He stared blankly at the wall, deep in his own thoughts as he absently patted the man's hand. After a while, Mickey gently disengaged himself and stood to pull the blanket to the chin of his now quiet roommate. When he was finished, he slowly turned around.

When Mickey saw me, he was surprised, like he was seeing me out of context. I stayed where I was, not sure he wanted me there, but then his eyes tried to smile and he said, "Hey, baby."

"Hey."

He held out his arms, and I walked slowly into them and was wrapped in the only real place that felt like home. Still, I sighed, as I remembered the girl in the hotel.

"I was afraid you wouldn't come back, Lu," he whispered.

I pushed myself up on my toes and looked at his face. His eyes were sad, and he looked older than he did five days ago. "Kiss me, Mickey. Then tell me what happened."

He took my face in his big, shaking hands and kissed me like he meant it. When he finally pulled away from me, he took my hand and led me to his bed, where we sat down. His hands trembled, and I wrapped them in mine.

"What's this shaking about?"

"Gleason's been worried, so he's giving me an older antipsychotic for a few days."

"Are you psychotic?"

"I don't know. I was, I guess. I thought it was a bad dream."

I didn't know what to say, so I looked around and avoided his eyes. My gaze fell on a framed needlepoint of an angel, the work exquisite, the colors dull. I picked it up. The caption said CHRISTINA THE ASTONISHING. It was very old.

"Muriel and Oscar brought it to me. Apparently she's the patron saint of insanity. They found it in an antiques store in Greenwich and knew I had to have it." Mickey chuckled with effort. "It's kind of cool. I didn't even know there was a patron saint of insanity."

"Me neither. It's kind of creepy." I put her back on the nightstand, beside a card and a small plant.

"That's from Treig and Diana. They came yesterday."

I looked at him. "You're a popular guy."

"They're just very nice neighbors."

"I missed you."

"I didn't keep my promise," he said. "I missed your birthday."

"I know."

For a long time we didn't say anything, then Mickey whispered, "I love you, Lucy. You know that, right?"

"I think so. But I don't know what you're doing."

"I know. I'm sorry. I acted crazy."

"Acted?"

"Well, maybe not acted. It's just that this is different."

"What do you mean?"

"I mean, I don't think I'm as bad this time as everyone thinks I am."

"I'm not sure I believe that."

Mickey looked at the floor.

"What are you saying?"

He shook his head and didn't look at me.

"What?"

"Gleason's a great doctor, but he can't always tell the difference between my insanity and my regret that I'm insane."

"What does that mean? I don't understand."

Mickey's dull, sad eyes found mine. "I'm scared to lose you. . . . I just don't know how to do any of this without you. And at the moment, *that* is being interpreted as insane." He looked hard at me. "I wish I was stronger, or better at this." He kissed my palms. "But I'm not. Gleason can throw pills at me all day, and it won't change anything. It won't change what's happening to you. To us."

I had no response for this, and I suppose Mickey was able to read that in my face because he lifted my chin. "Talk to me, Lu."

"I don't know what to say."

"Say you understand."

"I don't. You were with another woman."

"No, I wasn't. Not in any way that counts. And you know it."

"You took all your medicine. You tried to kill yourself."

Mickey didn't say anything.

"Right? That's what happened, right?"

"I don't know. It's hard to explain. Maybe. I'm sure it's the reason for all the meds and extra therapy."

"What does that mean?"

"Lucy, I don't know."

"Mickey, I know what's happening to us is hard and not fair, but we have to deal with it. We have to because something more important is at stake here. Can't *you* understand?" The shadows were deep across his face, and I hoped they were deep across mine, because I didn't want him to see my disappointment. "I've been confused about the other night, and I need a straight answer. What happened? Did you really try to kill yourself?"

"I did," he said. "I know the timing was bad, but I meant to do it. There was nothing I could do—no strength in me to stop it."

I stared at him. Something about this too-quick reply suddenly didn't ring true. It was too smooth, too practiced. As I thought about it, I realized it wasn't just his words. I was so stupid! It was that I had never sensed Death anywhere near Mickey. If the love of my life had intended to die, I had no doubt that I would have known! He'd overdosed, but *she* had offered me no premonition, no warning. If she had, I'd never have gone to Hawaii.

I pulled my hands from Mickey's and folded them in my lap, but I didn't let go of his eyes. I searched his bristled, tired, incredibly tormented face. "Something's wrong. You're lying to me."

"What?"

"You're lying to me, Mickey, and I want to know why. I don't know what you were doing that night, but I don't think you were trying to die. What kind of game is this?"

Mickey coughed up a sigh. "You can believe me or not, Lucy. But it is what it is."

"No, it's not. What about the baby?"

A sob broke in Mickey's throat, and for a moment he couldn't speak. His shoulders heaved, and I could see his desperation. "I love the baby," he rasped. "And I hate her. But without you . . ." He dropped his forehead into his palms. "Don't you get it? It doesn't matter! I can't do it!"

"Mickey, you don't have a choice."

"Stop it, Lucy! You're not hearing me. I do have a choice. I used it the other night."

I stood up. Mickey was crumpled and sagging and as tortured as I had ever seen him. I let his words play themselves out again in my head, and as they did, my breath caught. I was such an idiot! Now that I was really looking, I could see it written plainly on his face. How could I have missed it?

A rational man hid in the corner of Mickey's insanity. His entire responsibility was to keep Mickey pointed in the right direction even as crazy tugged at him. He didn't always win, but this man—this voice—was the last thing Mickey let go of when he fell, and the first thing he reached for when he came back. Mickey listened to him. I squeezed my eyes shut and tried to follow the bread crumbs.

Something about this crash felt different. There had never been a woman before, which should have been my first clue. And this one used in plain sight? Where they would easily be found? Why? Slowly it came together, and I gasped with understanding.

"Lucy?"

I shook my head as the pieces fell into place. Mickey's actions that night with the woman had been deliberate, even calculated. But suicidal? I, like everyone else, had mutely accepted what I'd seen because to the naked eye it looked like a legitimate attempt to end his life. My husband had placed himself in the role of exactly what he was—the grieving, frightened, bipolar-ravaged cripple. He'd set the perfect scene to demonstrate his complete lack of judgment. He'd picked the perfect actress to add light and dimension to his performance. And he'd done it all to relieve himself of a responsibility he couldn't fathom.

"Lucy?"

"Don't talk, Mickey." I was so stupid! I'd been so focused on my own decline that I'd completely missed how desperate my husband actually was. I'd seen his despair, but I'd completely underestimated it. So, Mickey had driven his message home with an overdose.

"I have to go, Mickey."

"What? Where are you going?"

"Away from what you've done."

His whole demeanor slackened further, liquefied from beneath, and he slumped against the wall.

"You faked this," I hissed. "You involved yourself with her so you could overdose, so you could almost, but not quite, die. All so you could show the world that you can't be trusted with the baby. It's about the baby, right? You faked this for her?"

He looked at me and didn't deny it.

"You broke your promise!"

"What promise?"

"Mickey will never pretend to not be in control!"

Shock and humiliation filled his eyes.

"Deny it, Michael."

"I had to!"

"You had to? Grow up, Mickey! You're forty-three years old!" I nearly shouted, then checked myself. The roommate hadn't stirred, but I lowered my voice anyway. "I can't do a damn thing about what's happening to me; I'm *sick*. But you . . . We have a baby girl on the way and this—*this*—is your best effort? Staging a Broadway play? You don't deserve her. And *I* sure as hell deserve better." I turned to leave but he grabbed my hand.

"I'll ruin her, dammit! Don't you get it? She deserves better. She needs more than I am. I know what it's like to grow up with a deranged parent. I won't do that to her! We—*we*—could have given her what she needs. But I can't do it alone."

His words hit me like a bullet, and I fought not to cry. With a shaky voice I said, "You're not your mother! And if you don't know that by now, then you *are* nuts!" I roughly wiped at my tears. "I picked you, Mickey. I picked *you* because I believed in *you*, and I've never regretted it. Never! Your daughter needs you!"

Mickey tugged on my hand. "Please, hear me! I'm no different than you, Lucy. You're sacrificing your life for her, and I'm doing the same thing."

Appalled, I leveled my gaze at him. "It's not the same at all. I would do anything, *anything* to stay here, to hold her, to teach her, to kiss her face and be amazed by her every single day of my life. You'd rather manipulate everyone around you, so you can leave her. Don't insult me. We are *not* the same." I burned my eyes into Mickey for a long time, then I pulled my hand free.

The last thing I heard as I walked down the hall was him calling my name, but I didn't turn around. I didn't stop when Peony asked me how it went. I kept walking and was almost to my car before I broke down completely under the weight of it all. I must have cried out a pint of tears before I decided there was only one place I could go. Gleason. My cell was dead, but I decided to risk it anyway, driving to Deep River hoping against hope that he was still at his office. He was just pulling out. I slammed on the brakes and laid on my horn and probably scared him to death, but he stopped. It was still pouring, and the short run to his car soaked me to the skin.

"Lucy! What are you doing?" he called through the open passenger window.

"I need to talk to you."

"Well, get in. Get in. What's happened?"

"He faked it!" I barked. "Mickey's pretending to be nuts so he doesn't have to—"

"Slow down, Lucy," Gleason said, taking off his jacket and laying it across my shoulders. "Start at the beginning."

I told him everything Mickey had said. About our fight, and his pretending to be insane because he didn't think he could live without me. How I'd yelled, and that when Mickey said we were the same, I walked out. Gleason never interrupted. He listened and nodded and looked sad at everything I said. When I stopped talking, he patted my hand. "Feel better?"

He was rumpled and his thin hair was plastered to his wet head, and his expression was as concerned as a parent's. "I shouldn't have gone to see him." I rubbed my forehead. "It was awful! Mickey's been selfish before, but he's never been *this* selfish."

"He's afraid to lose you. He almost lost you before, and he's scared."

"This isn't about me, it's about the baby."

"Lucy, he can't see past losing you to the baby. She's an idea, but she's not real. She's certainly not as real to him as she is to you. The threat of losing you trumps everything."

"So what? He gets a pass for this elaborate . . . *orchestration*?"

"You think he got away with something, Lucy? He didn't. Let's not forget his grand manipulation nearly stopped his heart. That's a bit far to go to prove a point, don't you think? He's sick, Lucy. Whatever he's done, however he's rationalized it, it's all been influenced by his illness. You seem to have forgotten that."

I sighed and dropped my head into my hands. "I haven't forgotten. I've just never seen this side of him before." I rubbed my temples, losing steam. Finally I looked up. "Gleason, do you think he's too sick? Is he really too damaged to be a father?"

"Too damaged? No. Not in my opinion. But too convinced that he's too damaged? Possibly. And that seems to be the bigger problem right now." Gleason turned more toward me, no easy feat in the small car. "He made a sane point in an insane way."

"So what do I do now?"

"Ride it out, Lucy. Just like always. He made a big production of saying he wants better for his daughter than what he had, and he doesn't know he's capable of giving her that."

"So he is capable? I'm not crazy?"

Gleason thought about this. "I think Mickey is capable of being capable. But it's more complicated than that. Right now, his illness and his fear, his anger and you being sick, are all manifesting in irrational thoughts that have led to this behavior."

I sighed shakily. "I guess I forgot that's how it works."

Gleason smiled a grim smile. "Taking yourself to the brink of death to make a point about as irrational as it gets. But take heart, Lucy. Mickey's still in there somewhere, at the eye of this storm. We've just got to clear the crazy, then we'll see what we've got."

For a long time I stared at the gray sky and the rain pelting the windshield. "I was so mean to him," I said softly.

Gleason squeezed my hand. "He probably deserved it. But go back and fix it, Lucy. Your time is too precious to waste it hurting each other."

I nodded as new tears filled my eyes.

Gleason tugged on my hand. "For what it's worth, Lucy, I happen to think Mickey will rise to this occasion. That's not a professional opinion, but it's what I'm rooting for."

I looked at the one person on the planet who knew my husband best. "Tell me the truth; do you think I'll get to see it? Or do you think Mickey will have to lose me first?"

Gleason Webb frowned for an agonizingly long moment, then squeezed my hand again. "I think he'll have to lose you, Lucy. He won't know what he can do without you until he's without you."

I broke down then and Gleason, bless his heart, just let me. No platitudes, just a fatherly hand on my shoulder while I let it all out.

After that, I drove around for a long time with a terrible pain in my chest. What was I doing? What had I done to my husband? He could have died because of me! *Just do it! Have the abortion!* I shouted—my own voice a screeching echo in my car. *Just do it! You're killing him!* I gasped. *No! No!* I started to hyperventilate and had to pull over and roll my window down, feel the rain. I leaned my head against the steering wheel. An abortion wouldn't help me, but it didn't matter; I still couldn't do it. The messenger had been real, so had the message; aborting our daughter would not save my life. I knew it again, as I'd known it then: ultimately, I would not survive this. But that didn't really answer the hard question—*when?*

I drove back to the hospital and walked back to Mickey's room. He was sitting at the foot of his bed and looked stricken. He stood up and took a tentative step toward me. "I'm so sorry, baby," he said, his eyes swollen with tears.

I shook my head. "I've made this impossible for you."

"It's impossible for both of us."

I walked over to him and slipped my arms around his waist. "Mickey, because the future is so full of unknowns," I whispered, "can we just not look at it right now? Can we just grow our daughter and love each other one day at a time?"

Mickey kissed my forehead but didn't say anything. He just held me as tight as he could over the baby that was between us.

I headed home in the rain wishing Mickey could have come home with me. I just wanted to sit on the couch with him and hold hands, lean my head on his shoulder. Maybe in a few days. I sighed as I turned onto my street and down through the lacy tunnel of ancient hardwoods whose branches met in the sky above the road. In four or five weeks, this street would be awash in fallen leaves the colors of topaz and rubies and old parchment. Then, just before Halloween, maybe a bit later, Harry and Mickey and Drew Murphy and Treig Dunleavy would dump the leaves into Treig's garden by the truckload. The little kids would be in the way as always, playing more than helping. Once their dads had yelled at them for the last time to get out of the leaves, Treig would ceremoniously light a match. As the flames roared, we'd sit around with bowls of chili and hot rolls and cider and watch the bonfire. I'd loved it since I was little. I loved smelling the smoke in my clothes long after we'd all gone home.

Surely Mickey would be better in four or five weeks. He'd dress warmly, in deer-hunter flannel and those funny gloves with the fingers cut off. I'd laugh at him as he tossed kids into the leaves. In a few years, he'd toss his own daughter into that same soft mound. She'd be bundled up and giggling, bright excited eyes, little red cheeks. I could see them as clearly as I could see my own house in front of me.

As I pulled into my drive, a white streak of lightning cracked the sky, and I made a halfhearted dash to the front porch. I was soaked before I got there. While rummaging for my keys, I heard a car honking and turned to see my sister pull into my driveway waving madly. Lily jumped out and ran across my lawn, her head ducked against the downpour, her leather bag flying behind her like a wing.

"Lucy!" she shouted. "You're home." She threw her arms around me. "I'm so glad you're back. How are you?" She pulled away to look me over, then once more folded me in her arms. Thunder boomed overhead, and a second later, lightning cracked another jagged bolt through the murky sky. "Let's get inside," I shouted over the torrent. "I'll make some tea."

A few minutes later, the storm raging, the two of us sat sipping herbal tea in front of my kitchen window.

"So, Lu, how was it? How was Hawaii?" Lily asked, leaning on her elbows.

"It was gorgeous. It wasn't any fun without Mickey, but it was beautiful. I slept like the dead, and I even went to Pearl Harbor."

Lily smiled sadly. "Pretty sobering, huh?"

"So sobering."

She reached over and took my hand. "How are you feeling . . . really?"

"It's been a long day, but I feel good."

Lily looked for the lie in my eyes, but gave up. "So, have you seen Mickey yet?"

"I went to Edgemont first thing."

"What did you think?"

I shrugged, not wanting to go into it again. "He's better than the last time I saw him."

"Well, I suppose that's true." Lily shook her head. "You are too good. Does he know how lucky he is?"

"Oh, yeah, we talk about it all the time."

"Well, I've been telling him all week. And so has Jan."

"Thank you for keeping an eye on him. That's so sweet."

Lily chucked my chin. "He's my brother, isn't he? Of course we've kept an eye on him. Ron goes every morning and gets him in the shower, and we both visit after work."

I was dumbstruck.

"What did you think? That we'd just forget him in there while you were gone?" Lily asked incredulously.

"I don't know what I thought. I've never left him before. You guys are awesome," I said, truly touched. I thought of Muriel's heartfelt but eerie patron saint, and the card on Mickey's nightstand from the Dunleavys. "Just awesome."

"Did you know Priss went to see Mickey last night?"

"What?" I gaped. "Are you serious?"

"I ran into Lainy Withers at Mosley's. She said she dropped some cookies off for Mickey and Priscilla was there, so Lainy didn't stay."

My eyes began to sting. "Did you see her, Lil? Did she call you?"

"No. She must have just driven in and back. Maybe she came in to see Nathan."

"Mickey didn't say a word about it." I got up to turn the heat on. Before I sat back down, Lily placed both hands on my belly and bent to kiss it. "How's junior?" she said without a warble.

"To tell you the truth, she's a little abusive," I chuckled. "She's quite the kicker."

Lily smiled up at me with such tenderness in her face.

I sat down, and for a moment we just watched the rain. When the furnace groaned for the first time in months, the smell of a new season filled my house. I knew it was just dust, but the smell somehow always signified the official end of summer—and the beginning of school. As if reading my thoughts, Lily said, "You're not really going back to work are you?"

"Monday morning."

Her shoulders slumped. "Are you sure you've thought this through? Shouldn't you just rest?"

"No."

"But, Lucy . . ."

"But nothing, Lil. I can't just sit around and wait."

When sadness crept into Lily's eyes, I reached for her hand and she gave it to me. For a long time neither of us said anything, just watched the water pelt the window. Then Lily turned to me and smiled through her worry. "I don't know if I ever thanked you for being with Mom. You know, for helping her when she was so sick."

"What?"

"You took such good care of her. You did it all, Lucy. I was at school. Priss had just taken that job in Boston. You did everything and I never even said thank you."

I shook my head. "I've been thinking a lot about Mom lately. Did I ever tell you that one of the last things she told me, the night she died, was that there was nothing to be afraid of."

"Oh, Lucy."

"I can still hear those words in my head."

Lily's eyes watered. "I'll never forget when you called me, Lucy. I can still hear your voice, calm and steady, in charge. You were seventeen, and you said, 'Lil, honey'—you called me honey—'I have some bad news.' And then you told me Mom was dead and you were coming to get me. You were the strong one. You've always been the strong one."

"That's not true, Lil."

"Yes, it is. There has never been anything you couldn't handle. I've never seen you falter. Not when we were babies and Daddy died, not when Mom died, not any of the hundred times when Mickey's been Mickey. Not even the last time you were sick."

"You know that's not true, Lily."

"Yes, it is. I'm not saying you were never frustrated or scared. I'm not saying you never pulled your hair out. I'm just saying you never fell down. You can't be beaten, Lucy. You just can't," she whispered.

I watched my sister, my luminous, green-eyed, hopeful sister. I watched her grapple with her own thoughts, trying to convince herself that my strength would triumph over the ruin inside me. I tugged at her hand and her gaze fell again on my face. "I hope you're right," I whispered.

She cleared her throat, and her doleful expression transfigured itself into a mask of composure. She let go of my hand and pulled a napkin from the holder on my table and blew her nose. The moment passed.

"I'm actually excited to go back to work," I said, meaning it. "I want to live as normally as I can for as long as I can. And before we know it, the baby will be here."

"And then you can start chemo . . ."

I nodded. "That's the plan, Lil."

twenty-five

Gleason says I've stabilized. But I don't feel stable—I feel bridled. The new pills make my fear stop short of panic, and they help me think clearly. They have trapped my impulses in a small jar where they eventually die, which I guess is a good thing. I'm not sure they're working completely. Not when at times I think I can see my wife's cancer. I can almost see it, like it's another woman living right there under Lucy's skin. I watch her take hold of my wife until Lucy can't stand the pain. And I hate myself because I can do nothing but watch it happen. Lucy has no choice but to give in and ride it out until this terrible cancer witch loosens her hold. Then Lucy tries to smile and pretend it's not as bad as I think.

    I've asked Charlotte what these episodes mean. She tells me the cancer is growing. I nod and take another pill.

I went back to work as I'd promised. The second week in September, I geared myself up and walked through the blessedly normal doors of Midlothian High School. Nowhere else is there an environment more replete with undiluted self-interest than the halls of a high school. Because of this, I was able to walk my afflicted self anywhere within its walls and remain nearly unperceived.

Of course, Miriam Brady had informed our shared students of my situation, but the news seemed to have caused them but a momentary hiccup, quickly forgotten, or at least blissfully unacknowledged. It was a win-win for me. Being back in the classroom fed my soul and strengthened my ability to pretend I wasn't sick.

When Mickey walked home from Edgemont a few days later, we started over, the way we always do after he's been hospitalized. At first we were careful with each other. Mickey was quiet, but sweet. And with us both back to work we got into a routine that, from the outside looking in, probably seemed a lot like an ordinary couple going about the business of preparing for a baby. We did fine for several weeks.

But one night in late October, I woke up in a wet panic. I couldn't breathe. As surely as if someone had a clamped a sweaty hand over my face, I could not get air. This paralyzing attack came out of nowhere, and gasping, I slapped at Mickey to rouse him—to save me—to get this building off my chest.

He bolted upright in the dark and flipped on his lamp. When he saw me sucking impotently for breath, he pulled me up by the shoulders and began shaking me so hard my head snapped back. He was yelling at God, I think, as I felt myself start to evaporate. But he must have jarred something, and suddenly a small avenue to my lungs opened up, as thin as a straw, but wide enough that I could inhale. Within a few agonizing moments, I was able to breathe again. But I was left with a terrible pain, like a fresh bruise, inside my chest, and I couldn't stop shaking.

Was this it? Was it happening? I was so scared that I let Mickey swallow me up, and I wrapped my arms around him as tight as I could. I'd been pretending for days—even at home—that I was more okay than I was, and this is where it had gotten me: two thirty in the morning, drenched in cold sweat, my heart hammering, certain I was dying.

Even in this state, part of me was devising some way to soften this troubling episode for my husband. But I couldn't. I was powerless to do anything but hold tight to Mickey's T-shirt and tremble against his solid frame. Mickey stepped up and held me in strong, steady arms instead of the death grip of desperation I was so accustomed to. He rocked me like I was a small child, all the while murmuring composed words of assurance: "You're okay. Just breathe, Lu. Just breathe."

There was no hysteria on the edge of his voice. He knew just what to do and what to say. And in the midst of my panic, it felt unbelievably good to give myself up to the feel of his hand stroking my back. As I started to relax and trust my breathing, I loosened my grip on Mickey's shirt and looked up at him. He kissed my forehead, and then I saw the film of tears in his eyes, the terror that never did reach his voice. I ran a trembling hand down his cheek.

"Should I call Charlotte?" he whispered.

"No, I'm okay," I insisted, knowing she'd send me to the hospital.

"Can I get you anything, some water?" Mickey was out of bed before I answered. He went downstairs for some ice and brought back a roll of cherry Life Savers from my purse. "Maybe these will help," he said, peeling back the paper.

"Thanks, sweetie," I said in a hoarse voice.

"Lu, maybe we should call Dr. Gladstone."

I felt my face crumple. "Can you just come back to bed and hold me for a minute?"

He rolled this request around for a while, then said, "I guess I can do that. But if it happens again, I'm calling 911."

"I'm okay now," I promised, exhausted. "I just want to lie down."

After a few minutes of watching me, convincing himself that I was all right, Mickey turned off the lamp and spooned himself against me, his hand coming to rest on my stomach. The baby was active, but considering what I'd just put her through, she seemed relatively calm. I wove my fingers into Mickey's and felt her kick against our palms. I stared at the full moon framed in our window and listened to the in and out of my untrustworthy respirations. I pulled Mickey's arm tighter around me.

"I'm right here," he whispered into my hair with a calm voice that

I barely recogniz
on Mickey's face,

He squeezed
before he said, "I

I traced his ja
finish line, Mic. I

"Me, too," sai
moonlight.

"I should have
a terrible mistake,
out on something—
much more to unde
The man I met on t
remembering. "Talk
newspaper in a year, ... know the things other people know."

"Me, too, baby." He kissed me the
Mickey," I whispered.
"Lu, no. We can't."
"Yes, we can."
"I don't know," he said
"Shhh," I said, gen
He kissed me
appetite for me
with him.

"Shhh."

"I can't. My whole life I've hung my hopes on a statement my dad made to me when I was just a little girl." I took a breath, grateful that Mickey was brave enough to open this door. "I've never doubted it," I insisted. "In my whole life, I've never doubted what he told me, Mic. But what does it all mean? Is death just a step into another life? Do I get to remember everyone I love?" My voice was suddenly small and high.

"I want to believe those things," he said. "Maybe then it wouldn't hurt so much."

"That's what I mean. We should have explored it, Mic. We should have found something solid to believe. It would have been so much easier." I thought again of what Thomas Worthington had said on the plane—with not a moment of hesitation. His belief in a hereafter filled with the people we love—*and in perfect health*—was second nature. He knew what he believed.

Mickey and I had been quiet for a long time when he lifted my chin and looked into my eyes. "It doesn't matter where you are, Lucy. Here, there, wherever. I'm just going to keep on loving you. I figure I'll always have that."

, softly. "Make love to me,

, his voice suddenly husky.

tly tugging on his bottom lip with my teeth.

en, a cautious kiss that still managed to betray his

, and I sighed into his mouth, willing to go anywhere

key and I have made all kinds of love over the years; contrary to lar belief, there are upsides of bipolarity. Sometimes it seems a parade of passionate men has found habitation in my husband, making me, I'm convinced, just about the most satisfied woman in the world. But when Mickey took me in his arms that night, I was to meet my favorite.

As though he was fearful of hurting me, Mickey made slow, melting, unbelievably tender love to me. I was a mess in my sore and unwieldy body and felt, at first, like a stranger beneath his hands. But the longer he touched me, the higher I rose above the pain and rebellion until I was lost in nothing but sensation. He stroked my scarred breast and swollen places so indulgently and with such unhurried grace, I don't think in all my years of making love with him I had ever responded so absolutely. It was the purest thing I'd ever known, and I didn't want it to end. Our bodies did the work, but it was our souls that conjoined.

We both wept through it and clung to it. When it was over, I think we both realized that it was probably the last time.

I finished out the weekend without another episode. Mickey babied me and hovered over me, barely letting me get out of bed. By Monday morning, I was feeling my usual run-down self, but I was breathing, so I was fine.

Or I thought I was fine.

It came out of nowhere. I was driving to school, and I started to cough. It felt like my chest was being torn down the middle. The sound was terrifying, like a strangled bark, wet and desperate. I couldn't breathe. As panic bubbled in me, I prayed I wouldn't pass out and cause an accident, and by the grace of God I made it into the school parking lot. Beads of perspiration had bloomed on my forehead and my face was starting to tingle. When I coughed into my hands, I coughed droplets of blood into them, and my heart started to pound. I willed myself to calm down. But I couldn't catch my breath. *The baby!* I couldn't breathe! I remember digging through my purse for my phone, but I don't remember dialing it. . . .

The beep of monitors seeped into my awareness, followed by the sound of familiar voices talking over me. I was in a hard bed that was not my own and someone with cold hands was taking my pulse. I was in the hospital. That realization should have filled me with anxiety, but it didn't. I wasn't coughing, and I wasn't starving for air. Someone was taking care of me. Having established that, I let myself be pulled down again into leaden sleep.

This happened a few times—same routine, same series of realizations, same conclusion—until I was finally close enough to the surface that I was conscious. It took everything I had to pry my eyes open, and even then I could barely manage more than a slit. Someone was holding my hand, rubbing it, but it didn't feel like Mickey. I forced a sound out of my throat, a little moan that might as well have been a scream for all the effort it required.

"Lucy? Honey?" It sounded like Priscilla. I felt long, cool fingers on my face. "Lucy, wake up. Open your eyes."

I turned my head and lifted my eyelids to the sound of her voice. Something was over my face, and when I tried to push it away, I found I couldn't lift my hand. I tried to move, but as I strained, I realized I was tied down.

"Lucy, you're okay." My sister was standing over me, her breath warm on my cheek.

"Baabee?" was all I could force out of my dry mouth.

"The baby's fine." Then I felt the weight of Priscilla's hand on my stomach.

Mickey was suddenly on the other side of me, kissing my face, coaxing me to open my eyes. "C'mon, babe, look at me."

I moaned and Mickey laughed, relief floating tangibly on the sound.

Later, that night, Charlotte explained that my lungs had filled with fluid, which had impeded my breathing. The technical term for this malady was malignant pleural effusion. That problem, in conjunction with a cough that took my breath away, had caused me to black out. While I was in the emergency room, a tube had been threaded into each of my lungs to drain the fluid.

"If you weren't pregnant," Charlotte told me, "Dr. Gladstone would have removed your left lung. Before this is over, you will probably need surgery, Lucy."

I had an oxygen mask clamped over my nose and mouth, but I could tell that Charlotte was still able to decipher my hardening expression. She took my hand. "I know how you feel. We all do. But you need to understand: at this point we're just trying to keep you alive, Lucy. We've kept you sedated for the past three days so you could be mechanically oxygenated and give your overworked system a little rest."

"What about the baby?"

"We've monitored the baby the entire time. She's fine. It's you I'm worried about."

For a moment as I looked into her eyes, fear washed over me. I needed more time. I squeezed her hand and Charlotte did not avert her gaze; steady, strong, and true. "Charlotte," I whispered. "Whatever you have to do to make sure this baby is born, you do it."

She nodded. "I will."

twenty-six

Last night I dreamed Lucy had died and no one told me. I came home from the club and she was just gone. I woke up from this nightmare in a cold panic, my heart racing, and had to remind myself why I was alone in my bed; Lucy was still in the hospital. I sat up and tried to settle myself before I called to check on her. The nurse assured me that Lucy was resting comfortably, and I breathed out my thanks on a shaky breath. When I couldn't go back to sleep, I walked down the hall and quietly opened the door to the nursery—or what would have become one. I didn't turn on the light, but I could see it all clearly by the glow of the moon. Walls not painted, wood floor not finished, an empty closet where little dresses were supposed to hang.

I looked around at what should have been: a little girl's haven, a place of dolls and books and soft things. I would have built her a two-story dollhouse that would sit in the corner. I would have filled it with carved furniture and papered each small room. I would have . . . I would have. A familiar ache spread through me as the bright image of my family—Lucy, me, and our baby girl—faded with my tears. It didn't belong to me. Not anymore.

＊　＊　＊

Within a couple of days, I was amazed at how good I felt. I wasn't even pretending. There was no need. Suddenly I could breathe without my chest hurting. I could actually feel my lungs expanding, and my cough had been reduced to a mere annoyance again. I asked Dr. Gladstone about it when he came in to discharge me. He shook his head, his expression grim. Peter Gladstone is tall, imposing, with a blond flattop. His face is chiseled in serious lines that make him look angry, even when he's not.

"Sorry to tell you it's temporary, Lucy. We've drained your lungs, but, unfortunately, they will fill again."

"How long will it take?"

"You might have a week or two, or just a couple of days. There's no way to predict, other than to say your condition is advancing. I did an ultrasound, and the left lung is far worse than the right. I'm not sure simply draining it will suffice next time."

I nodded.

"I'm going to have a respiratory therapist set you up with a tank and nasal cannula—a device that blows oxygen into your nose. You're going to need it frequently from now on."

"Okay," I said in a shaky voice.

"Stay in touch with me, Lucy." Dr. Gladstone looked hard at me and nodded. "I want to see you in my office the day after tomorrow."

"I'll be there."

He turned to leave just as a young girl in a white lab coat walked in dragging a green tank on wheels. Her name badge said DAPHNE and she had a Julia Roberts smile. "Hi," she said.

"Hello."

"The best doctors are so serious," she clucked, placing a small device on my finger. She introduced herself as the respiratory therapist, then informed me that she was checking my saturation level, whatever that was. "It was normal last night when we took you off the O_2. Let's see if you've maintained." After a moment, Daphne nodded, pleased. "Good."

She then pulled up a chair and started writing on a flow sheet. As she wrote, she instructed me on how to use the green oxygen tank; her advice was repeated, word for word, on the instruction sheet she handed me. Daphne wrote down her department's beeper number. "Feel free to call us—even in the middle of the night—if you run into any trouble."

I nodded.

"Do you have any questions?" she asked, finally making eye contact.

I cleared my throat. "Do you know about me? That I've had my lungs drained?"

"I know."

"How long does it usually last? I mean, in your experience, how long before . . ."

Daphne Boyd stood up and leaned over the railing of my bed. "Not long. Could be a few days or it could be a week. If I were you, I'd enjoy this small reprieve. It gets tough from here on out. You know your cancer is growing."

"Yes."

"Then don't waste any time." She smiled sadly.

"Thank you for being honest with me."

Daphne reached down and touched my wrist. "You call me if you need me."

"I will," I said, hoping that she would be assigned to help me when I had to come back. When Daphne turned to leave, I realized Lily had walked into the room. Her eyes shone with sad comprehension, but she still smiled as she stepped aside to let Daphne pass.

"Hey," I said.

"Hey. How're you feeling this morning?" Lily's tone was too polite, forced.

"Good. Really good. Dr. Gladstone said I could go home."

"No way!" Lily looked sincerely skeptical, and I had to admit that I'd never expected to be leaving so soon either. But I wasn't about to argue.

Lily pulled the chair close to my bed and sat down. "I heard some of that," she said, nodding toward the door. "Was she another doctor?"

"No. She was here teaching me how to use the oxygen."

"I heard her say your cancer is growing. What are they going to do about that?"

"I guess they're going to do what they can, Lil."

She looked at me, love and sadness pouring from her eyes, then she took my hand and kissed it. When she knew she wouldn't cry, she said, "So, when can you leave?"

"The nurse said I could take a shower. I was going to tell Mic to come in an hour."

"Or I could drive you. I'll call him. You get in the shower." Lily lowered my bedrail, and with surprising agility I hopped down.

I felt so much better that I laughed out loud. "Ask him if he wants to meet us for lunch."

"You're kidding, right?" my sister said.

"No. I'm starving."

That weekend, Ron and Lily invited Mickey and me over for spaghetti. Priscilla had driven in from Hartford—the third time this week—and she was invited, too. Mickey wanted to drive because it was a little chilly, but I insisted we put on sweaters and walk. It was a bit ambitious, but it was less than two blocks and I didn't know how long it would be before I wouldn't be able to walk to my sister's house ever again. So I pressed, and Mickey relented.

It was the fourth of November and winter had not yet arrived in Brinley. A few hay bales and cornstalks and shriveled-up jack-o'-lanterns still remained on porches from Halloween. I'd missed it all. I'd missed the leaf-rake and bonfire at the Dunleavys, and I'd missed the chili and hot cider. Mickey must have seen the turn in my expression because he stopped, alarmed, and asked me what was wrong.

"Oh, nothing," I groused. "I just missed the bonfire. That's all."

"I did, too."

"I'm sorry."

Mickey pulled my arm through his and patted my hand and I snuggled into him. He'd been so great since I came home from the hospital.

"How 'bout I build us our own bonfire?"

"That would be fabulous," I said, squeezing his arm.

The night was crisp with a lazy breeze that carried a chill from the river. Mickey put his arm around me and kissed my head and I looked up at him. "I love you, Michael Chandler."

"I love you right back, baby."

"And I love this place," I said, looking on either side of this street that could be a Thomas Kinkade painting. It was all the world I had ever needed—a place where kids could still play outside and moms sat visiting on the front porches keeping an eye out for them. It was a place where your lawn mysteriously got mowed or your walks got shoveled if you'd been sick or gone or just too busy. Mickey and I had been on both sides of that equation.

I was pretty worn out, and trying to hide it when we turned up the walk to Ron and Lily's house—a little Craftsman cottage with the windows glowing with warm, golden light. Before Mickey knocked on the door, he kissed me, then folded me up in his big arms. It felt wonderful to stand there, inside that love, and I was reluctant to give up the moment. But Priss must have heard us because she opened the door, laughing. "Where's your car?"

"The missus wanted to walk, and what the missus wants, the missus gets," Mickey said.

"You're crazy! It's cold out there," she said, pulling Mickey and me into the house.

My sister looked ravishing. She was beautifully turned out in winter-white pants and a black cashmere sweater that clung nicely to her curves. She cupped my face in her hands and gently pushed my hair behind my ears. "You look pretty good, Lu. How are you feeling?"

"Can't complain."

"She's doing great," Mickey put in, winking at me.

Priscilla placed a hand on his shoulder and pecked him on the cheek. "Looks like you're taking very good care of her, Michael."

Mickey and I exchanged a look of mutual perplexity and followed my sister into the dining room, where her good humor was quickly explained. Handsome Nathan Nash was there helping Ron start a fire.

"Mystery solved," Mickey muttered.

I gave his arm a warning pinch just as Ron clapped him on the shoulder and Nathan swallowed me in a bear hug. "Hey, good-lookin', I hear you've had quite a time of it."

I waved his comment away. "That was days ago. I'm doing much better now."

"You sure?" he asked, backing away from me to take in my pregnancy in all its fully evident glory. "Are you sure you should be out?"

"Absolutely. I feel good," I fibbed. "I really do." I thought Nathan looked a little self-conscious, and I didn't know if it was me or that his being here with my sister was making some kind of statement. "How are the kids?"

"Jess has been very worried about you. I guess she heard what happened at school."

"Yes, trust me to create a spectacle. I'm sorry about that." I wondered how exactly I was discovered after I blacked out.

I felt Ron's hand on my shoulder and turned to kiss his cheek. "I hope you're hungry. Lily has enough spaghetti in there to feed the neighborhood."

I laughed as I walked into the kitchen to see how I could help. I found my sister wilting over a steaming bowl of pasta. "What can I do?" I asked, looking around.

"Grab that garlic bread, will you?" Lily said, straining around to air-kiss my face.

In my opinion, she, like Priscilla, was overdressed in a teal sweater and matching skirt. "I didn't get the dress code for tonight," I complained.

"No, you didn't," Priscilla said, eyeing my denim dress and boots. She was cutting radishes, so I sidled up to the counter and swung my hip into hers. "Sooooo?"

She grinned. "What?"

"How long have you been seeing him?"

"A few weeks. It's nothing. We just talk, we're friends."

"I think that's the way it should be," Lily said, pouring marinara sauce into a bowl. "It's only been, what? Just a year since Celia—"

"I'm *aware* of that, Lilianne," Priscilla interrupted with a bite.

"Just checking," said Lily, unaffected. "I think we're ready as soon as you're done with the salad," she announced as she walked out of the kitchen with her enormous bowl of noodles.

"Little twit," Priscilla muttered. "Of course I know!"

"Well"—I shrugged—"at least you look fabulous."

"I do, don't I? And I didn't even really have to work at it."

I laughed, filling a basket with bread.

The men were already seated around a big mahogany table, and I stopped, recognizing it. "Lil, is this from the store?"

"Yes! I couldn't sell it."

Ron groaned, "We had three different buyers, and she wouldn't let me sell it."

Lily grinned sheepishly. "I just love it. It's a George the Third drop leaf, and way too big for this room, but I don't care."

Nathan Nash fingered the wood. "What's it worth?"

"About eighteen grand. So don't be spilling spaghetti sauce on it," Ron gibed.

Nathan was sincerely surprised, and his expression made me laugh out loud.

"It's not actually worth that much," Lily rushed to explain. "It's not in mint condition."

"Phew," he said, recovering from his sticker shock.

Lily set the pasta in the middle of the table and asked Ron to bring in the sauce. In a moment, Priscilla brought the salad, and we all sat down. I looked around with true appreciation for the spirit of this small gathering. My sisters were watching over me, but trying not to be obvious about it. We were all together with a table full of Italian food in front of us. It just didn't get better than this. Ron caught my eye and seemed to read my thoughts. He smiled at me and passed the salad.

It was a long, chatty dinner with lots of reminiscing. Such as the time Priscilla and Trent got locked in the high school after a basketball game and the township organized a search party. My sister turned eight shades of red when Mickey asked her what they were doing when they were found. Then there was the time that Lily and Ron found Mom's stash of Christmas presents and told Priss and me everything we were getting. Somehow Mom found out. She took it all back and we got shoes, pajamas, and underwear instead.

I laughed until I could hardly breathe when Ron told Mickey how he proposed to Lily.

"He broke into our house," Priscilla cut in. "I thought he was a burglar and I nearly shot him, or I would have if I could have found the BB gun."

Mickey chuckled. "I can't imagine you'd need a gun, Priss. You were always deadly enough on your own."

"I'll take that as a compliment, thank you very much," Priss piped.

"That's exactly how I intended it." Mickey grinned, then leaned over. "Okay, my turn. So, Nathan, what's the deal with you and Priscilla?"

A forkful of chocolate cake was suddenly suspended midway to Priscilla's mouth, and I watched color bleed down her face. My cake made it into my mouth without interruption, and Lily and I grinned at each other across the table.

Nathan didn't miss a beat. "How should I put this? I guess you could say that it's a pretty *good* deal." He turned his grin on my embarrassed sister and picked up his glass. "To Priss, my good friend. And my wife's good friend." Only then, and only for a second, was a bit of weight added to our lighthearted conversation.

But Priss just shrugged her shoulders. "I'll drink to that—or better yet, let's drink to Celia."

After that, we stacked the dishes in the sink and played Texas Hold 'em, betting with pennies. I kicked butt. Lily added extra incentive to win by imposing dishwashing duty on the loser, and when I effectively eliminated Mickey and Nathan with my brilliant bluffing, they were sent to the kitchen with heads hung low. But after the game was finished and they were still in there, I went to check on them.

I found my husband and Nathan quietly discussing something serious and knew immediately that they were talking about me. I stood just out of sight and heard Mickey say, "I just don't understand what happened, Nathan. I mean, I don't get why she's not sick, but then out of the blue, she has this attack that nearly kills her. What's that about?"

"I'm not an oncologist, Mic. I treat bones, not cancer," Nathan said. "But it seems like the tumors are probably growing and interfering with her lung capacity."

"And there's nothing they can do to slow it down?"

Nathan Nash sighed. "Oh, buddy, I don't know. Advanced lung cancer is pretty tricky. All they can really do is aggressive chemo and radiation, and Lucy's not going to do that at this stage of the game. After the baby . . ."

"But can she last that long, Nathan?"

I heard the desperation in Mickey's voice, but I also heard a rational man bravely asking a difficult question.

"I wish I knew, Mic. Have you talked to her doctors?"

Mickey sighed. "I have. I just don't like their answers."

"Oh, man, I'm so sorry."

"I just don't get why she can seem so normal. I mean, she's tired, but look at her."

"It's because she's not having chemotherapy. Chemo is hell. Without it, well, it's pretty unbelievable how long you can walk around with cancer. But then all of a sudden . . ."

"Yeah. All of a sudden," Mickey echoed.

On the way home, I asked Mickey what he and Nathan had been talking about in the kitchen. He snorted, "Priscilla."

"Oh, really?"

"He claims they're just good friends. And I hope that's true because I really like Nathan."

I shoved Mickey with my shoulder. "Be nice."

His arm came around me and he kissed my forehead. After a quiet moment he said, "How you holding up?"

"I feel pretty good, that was a great night. I'm so glad we did it." As Daphne had warned, this was a reprieve, and I did not plan to waste it. "Mic?"

"Yeah."

"What do you think about painting the nursery tomorrow?"

"Oh . . ."

"I just think we should take care of it. I'm feeling good, and besides, we're running out of time." Realizing what I said had sounded glib and fatalistic, which was not the way I meant it at all, I added, "The baby will be here before we know it."

"Yes, she will," Mickey agreed, not looking at me.

"Mickey?"

"We'll see, Lucy. I don't want to talk about the nursery right now."

"Okay," I said, not wanting to push it. He knew as well as I did how all our preparations had come to a sad and silent standstill in August when Charlotte had paid her fateful visit. That night, after she'd told us what Dr. Matthews had found, I'd closed the nursery door, and neither Mickey nor I had been in the room since. The paint cans sat in the middle of the floor having never been opened. The wood floor had been sanded, but not varnished. We walked past an unfinished room every day. How much longer could we really wait? She'd be here in seven weeks.

Mickey looked down at me with an unreadable expression, somber and a bit hardened. "There's something we need to talk about, Lu."

"Okay."

"I've been thinking about it for a while now, and we can't put it off any longer."

"What is it?"

"It's the baby, Lu."

There was not a day since we'd started this conversation back when Mickey was in the hospital that I hadn't imagined the end of it. I took a deep breath and stopped. Mickey stopped, too.

"What about her?"

"Lucy, you know there's a chance . . . There's a possibility that by the time the baby comes you won't . . ."

"I know," I said, barely able to hear my own voice.

Mickey shook his head and I heard him swallow. "Lucy, I've done everything I can think of to prepare myself for what's coming—what *might* be coming. But there's just no way. And I need you to listen to me for once, Lu. I *can't* do it. I cannot raise her by myself."

"I don't believe that for a minute, Mickey."

Tears filled his eyes, but he didn't lift his gaze from me. "You're not listening to me, Lucy. This is so hard."

"I'm sorry. Go ahead."

"Lucy, I don't mean just for a little while, or just until I get used to the idea. I'm not strong enough or good enough to *not* screw her up with my weirdness. We both know my limitations." He stared at me and neither of us breathed. "Lucy, I want to give the baby up."

I looked up at this hulk of a man who seemed suddenly a stranger, hardly comprehending his words. "What?"

He almost broke down then, and in the night shadows I could see the crushing weight he carried. "Please don't look at me like that, Lucy. It's not that I don't love her, and it's not that I don't want her." His eyes were full of pain and I stepped closer to him. "Lucy, you have to believe that I'd give anything to be a different man . . . for her." He breathed out a shaky breath. "Every morning I look in the mirror hoping I'll see someone curable and capable and strong. Hell, I'd even settle for someone who's just going through a terrible time, but will be okay someday. But that's not who I see. I see the same broken man I've always been."

Mickey took my hands. "A lifetime ago you told me you couldn't fix me, but you could love me broken. Do you remember?"

I nodded.

"I never imagined you could actually mean that, that you could take *me* and love all the pieces. What I ever did to deserve that kind of gift, I'll never know. But because of you, I've had a life I never dreamed I'd have. Sometimes—even now—when I'm driving home at night, I catch myself not believing I'm actually going home to you. *You,* Lucy. That I—Mickey Chandler—get to spend my life with you."

"Mickey." I lifted my hands up to his face and he kissed my palms.

"But I'm still broken, Lu," he whispered. "I'm still broken, and alone my brokenness can only hurt my daughter. I can't do that to her. I won't."

"Oh, Mickey." I thought back to my conversation with Gleason. *He won't know what he can do without you until he's without you,* he'd said. And as I stared up at my trembling husband, I realized how prophetic Gleason's words had been. I pulled Mickey close and his arms came around me. I couldn't imagine having to leave him. What was God thinking?

We walked the rest of the way in silence, and when we got home, Mickey was so restless that I made him take two Ambien. We talked until he finally fell asleep in my arms around two. But long after he was softly snoring, I was still staring at the ceiling, digesting his words. For hours now, my mind had wrestled with what to do. I was running out of time and ways to convince him that his limitations did not make him unworthy. But Mickey wasn't just afraid of the responsibility of raising our daughter, he was looking out for her the best way he knew how.

Tears filled my eyes again. If I couldn't leave him our baby, then what had I been doing all this for? The very thing he was pushing away was the only thing I had to leave him.

As I lay there in the dark with Mickey's soft breath playing over my cheek, I wondered again how I had gotten here: hopelessly in love with a damaged man, pregnant with his child, dying, and now facing the possibility of giving her up to someone else to rock to sleep at night.

It wasn't the answer. It couldn't be.

I did not choose Mickey Chandler to be my husband for things to turn out this way. I chose him because he was a warrior. Every day he fought to be his best self, despite his illness. He didn't always get there—and when he slipped, the consequences could be devastating—but he fought for that man every day. And because he did, the good days had far outweighed the bad. Yes, at times he was buried in his pathology. But the man at Mickey's core was a good man, an admirable man who would be a wonderful father.

He had so much to teach his daughter. And my family had so much to teach her. How could fate be so cruel as to not allow Lily to be her doting aunt, Ron to teach her quiet kindness, Priscilla to teach her diligence? No. They all had a role to play. I just had to rearrange them.

It took me some time to think it through, and it wasn't my first choice, but as I imagined it, I knew it could work. This could work. It was the only possible solution, and if I couldn't have what I wanted, this wasn't a bad plan B.

twenty-seven

I called my dad today. I hadn't talked to him in a while and we hadn't seen him since Christmas two years ago. I'm not really sure why I called, I was so much more comfortable with short notes, but he knew something was wrong from the sound of my voice. "What's happened, Son?"

"She's dying, Dad," I coughed out.

"Let me turn off the TV, Mic. Start from the beginning."

So I did. He knew most of it, because Lucy had been good about e-mails, but I didn't know she'd sent him a picture of the ultrasound. I'd have to tell him another time that I wouldn't be keeping the baby, but I just couldn't do it then, not when he seemed so excited about the prospect of a grandchild. What I really called for was to ask him how he did it—how he lived through the loss of my mother.

He didn't skip a beat. "You live maimed. Altered. But you live."

This response surprised me; he'd seemed so detached throughout my childhood.

"You'll think of her every day for the rest of your life. And it won't always hurt, but it will most of the time. I'm not sure what you're looking for, Mic. But when you love

a woman like she's the air you breathe—like you love
Lucy—like I loved your mother—it can take a lifetime
to rearrange yourself." He paused, but the stone in my
throat made a response impossible.

He swallowed. "You might not have known that
I loved your mom that much and I'm not surprised. I
wasn't very good at it. But it was always right there, Mic.
Right under the Jim Beam and broken heart. I'm not a
strong man and it took me a long time to reconcile loving
a woman who'd rather be dead than married to me. But
you didn't call to drudge up all that heartbreak. You'll
do it better than I did, Son, because you'll have better
memories to pull you up. It'll hurt like hell; I'm not going
to lie. But Lucy's one in a million, and she's given you lots
to hold on to. And of course you'll have your little girl to
help you through it."

I woke with a jolt as a dry, airy cough burst from my throat. Mickey
stirred and rolled over, but didn't wake up. I was instantly alert and
frightened. I knew what this was. I hadn't had a spasm since the day
I passed out, but I hadn't forgotten the feeling of one coming on. Not
wanting to wake Mickey, I got out of bed and padded down the stairs
to the bathroom by the laundry room. But as I leaned over the small
sink and stared into the mirror at my pale face, nothing came. I didn't
taste blood in my mouth, did I? And my breathing—was it any more
labored than usual? No, I was okay. I was okay.

I nearly convinced myself that I'd experienced a tickle in my
throat and nothing more, but then it was upon me in earnest. Without warning, I was hacking, deep and gravelly. I tried to stay calm, to
breathe without gulping, without panicking. I sat down on the toilet
and held a tissue to my mouth, trying to muffle the sound, and was
relieved when it came away mostly clean, with just a couple of specks
of blood. Hardly worth the worry.

In a moment it was over. As quickly as it had come, the attack subsided. I wet a washcloth and held it against my neck, breathed slowly and deliberately through my mouth. After a few minutes, I turned the light off and made my way to the moonlit kitchen. I filled a glass with water from the tap and sat down to look out the window. It was so still, so quiet. The only sound was the whooshing of my heartbeat in my ears. It had been six days since I came home from the hospital. Surely my reprieve wasn't up yet.

On Thursday morning, Mickey drove me to Dr. Gladstone's office for my second visit of the week. The nurse smiled and showed us into an exam room. It was a short routine. I breathed while Peter Gladstone listened to my lungs through his stethoscope. He made a *humph* sound and wrote something in my chart. Then he clipped a small device on my finger that would translate my oxygen saturation level onto his little handheld monitor. So far, he'd been pleased. Today, he frowned.

"You're dropping. You're down to eighty-seven, so I want you on the oxygen all the time. How are you sleeping?"

"Pretty well. A little restless."

"Not surprising. Any attacks?"

"Just a little one a couple of nights ago," I admitted, watching as Mickey's eyes widened in alarm.

"Any blood?"

"No."

"You're doing better than I expected, but I'm hearing some crackles today, so it's starting to happen. The fluid is building up again."

I nodded, avoiding Mickey's glare.

Dr. Gladstone shook his head and sighed. "I'd feel better if you were closer to delivering, Lucy. As it is, we have to keep you as oxygenated as we possibly can. Once the baby comes, we'll get aggressive."

I nodded. I always felt hopeful when Peter Gladstone spoke in terms of *after*. He looked stern as he attached a thin, clear tube to an outlet in the wall and fingered a small dial. At the end of the tubing was an adjustable noose, and in the center of the noose were two small prongs. He tucked the noose behind both my ears and gently arranged the prongs in my nostrils. "Let's see what you come up to in five minutes."

"Okay," I said as my nose filled with wind.

With that, he walked out of the room and Mickey followed him.

I sat there for a moment and looked around. Crackles? Whatever they were, apparently they did not bode well for me. I looked around and spotted a telephone on the wall, debating only for a moment before I picked it up and punched numbers until I had an outside line. I knew Harry was supposed to get back in town last night, and I knew Jan had probably told him I'd been trying to reach him. I dialed their number and Jan answered on the second ring. "Hi," I said.

"Hi, sweetheart."

"Hey, is Harry in his Brinley office today?"

"No, sweetie. He's in New Haven today and tomorrow, then he has a hearing in Hartford on Friday. His plane didn't get in until after eleven last night or he would have called. Can it wait?"

"I don't think so."

"Then call him in New Haven. He'll find the time."

"Thanks. Listen, Jan, I'm at the doctor's so I can't talk."

"Are you all right?"

"Yes, it's just my regular checkup. I'll call you later." I hung up, tempted to call New Haven, but I heard Dr. Gladstone just outside the door and decided not to risk it. In a moment, he and Mickey walked back into the room. Mickey looked upset, but his expression said he didn't want me to know it. The doctor placed the clip back on my finger and was pleased to show me a throbbing ninety-three on his little screen. "Okay, that's helping. I want you on oxygen as much as possible, Lucy. You can have it off for brief periods but not for long."

I nodded.

"Come back on Monday and we'll check your saturation again."

"Okay."

He scribbled something in my chart, then turned to Mickey and clapped his shoulder before walking out. Mickey obviously didn't want to talk about it, so we drove home in silence until he asked me why I hadn't told him about my attack.

"I'm sorry. It only happened once, and it went away after I had some water."

Mickey turned to me. "I want to know when it happens again."

"Okay."

After a minute of staring out of our respective windows, Mickey pulled my hand to his lips and I felt our tension dissipate.

When we got home, Mickey turned off the engine but didn't move to open the door. He turned to me and asked if I was tired.

"A little."

"Why don't you rest while I run some errands."

"Where are you going?"

"I need to run over to East Lyme to interview a manager, then I'm having my blood drawn. I'm supposed to see Gleason at one."

"Okay. I'll take a nap, and then I think I'll run downtown for some pajamas."

"Good. I'll call when I'm finished. I can pick up some dinner. Maybe rent a movie."

"Okay." I leaned over to give him a quick kiss and ended up giving him a long one. "I love you," I murmured. "I'll see you in a little while." I got out of the car and walked slowly to the porch, but when I turned around, Mickey was still looking at me. He lifted his hand as if to wave, but he didn't start the car. We stared at each other for a long moment before I opened the door and went in the house. After another long moment I finally heard the engine turn over.

I hated it. I hated the plodding, torturous pace our lives had taken on. I hated the pain in every look, the fear in every breath, the pretense. This was probably what my dad had meant when he said death was the easy part. The dying? Well, that was another story.

I was tired, that was true enough, but it was not the kind of tired that sleeping would ever cure. And while I still had the desire to milk meaning out of my remaining breaths, I was reluctant to waste them trying to sleep. I looked at the kitchen clock. New Haven was only a thirty-five-minute drive, and if Harry had time to see me, I could be home before Mickey finished his errands.

I wasn't feeling well when I left Harry's office, and on my way out of the building I broke out in a cold sweat. I worried I'd faint if I didn't sit down. I knew there was a coffee shop on the ground level so I turned around and went back inside to find it. When I was seated, I asked the waitress for a glass of water and told her I was expecting someone so she would leave me alone. But when she turned from me, I felt so vulnerable and frightened that I almost shouted for her to stay. I knew what was happening and braced myself for the sudden pain behind my ribs, but soon realized that this was different. This wasn't my breath getting caught. This was muscles ripping apart. It burned and spread heat through the very center of me until I doubled over the table. I held my breath and hung suspended in its grip.

I was a prisoner of this horrible ache until it finally went slack, like a fist slowly releasing its hold. As it subsided, I sipped my water and used the napkin to blot the cold sweat from my face. If I'd been driving, I would have crashed. This was such a stark contrast to how good I'd felt all morning. I felt duped and angry. And I knew what it meant. I dug through my purse for the Life Savers that usually soothed my burning throat. I breathed in slowly and blew out slower, and soon I was back to baseline. But I was anxious about driving, so I sat back and waited for some faith in my abilities to return.

Almost an hour later I was so grateful to pull into my driveway that I almost wept. At least there was no sign of Mickey, so I didn't have to put on a face for him. I went right upstairs to lie down, and the first thing to greet me was the green oxygen tank, propped up in the corner of the bedroom. It looked like a missile, old and chipped, something you'd load into a tank and fire at an enemy. I guess that fit.

I attached the tubing to the appropriate valve and pulled the little noose over my face and behind my ears. After fitting the tiny prongs into my nose, I turned the dial to the prescribed setting and eased myself down on the bed. I was so glad to be home. Propped up on two pillows and connected to this invisible life force, I willed myself toward sleep, but my heart was still racing. After a half hour of stupidly waiting for another attack, I dragged myself downstairs to find something to do, something else to think about.

In the kitchen, I carefully rehearsed the words I'd say to Mickey, then I made him a cake. By the time he walked in with fried chicken, I had the table set and the candles lit, and I was feeling much better. He gave me a weird little smile.

I kissed him and asked where he'd been all day. He just grinned.

"Are you going to tell me or is it a surprise?"

"Later," he said, still smiling.

"A surprise, huh?"

"You'll see."

I grinned as I busied myself arranging the chicken and potatoes on a platter. Then I poured the gravy into a bowl and filled our glasses with ice. I took my time because I was getting winded and didn't want to put the oxygen back on for this. When everything was on the table, I turned the kitchen light off and sat down. It felt good to sit.

Mickey stared at me for a long time through the candlelight. "You're beautiful, baby."

"I've seen myself and you are a bad liar." But I leaned over and kissed him anyway.

"I love you, Lu."

"Backatcha, Michael."

Mickey bit into his chicken. "So, did you rest this afternoon?"

"Actually, I went to see Harry."

"How is he?"

"He's good. I talked to him about an adoption."

Mickey looked at me.

"A three-way adoption."

"I don't know what that is."

I put down my fork. "I've been thinking about it since our talk the other night. And Harry said it wouldn't be impossible."

Mickey leaned over. "I'm listening."

"You and Ron and Lily will share custody of our daughter." I held my breath and watched Mickey in the candlelight. When he didn't say anything, I reached over and took his hand. "What do you think?"

"I don't want to talk about this, Lu."

"I know, babe, but we have to. It's all *just in case,* anyway," I soothed. When he still didn't say anything, I plowed ahead. "This way she'll be raised here in Brinley, which, of course, is what I want more than anything. She'll get to know her wonderful father, and you'll be as involved as you're strong enough to be. Lily and Ron will pick up the slack, and they'll be fabulous parents. You all will. Think about it, Mic. It's the best of all worlds. It's a win-win-win."

I watched a series of emotions filter through Mickey's eyes. At first I could tell he didn't like the idea. At one point he even said it made more sense to sever all ties with the baby, which was unimaginable to me. "I just think it would be easier that way, Lu."

I ran my finger over his hand, and the more I talked about Lily and Ron as primary guardians with him having as much involvement as he wanted, the more he seemed to settle into the idea. When I finished my spiel, I took a deep breath. "Soooo?"

Mickey shook his head and didn't say anything for a long moment. Then he stood up and kissed the top of my head. "I can't imagine watching them raise my daughter," he said. Then he walked out of the kitchen.

"What *can* you imagine?" I called out after him, but he was gone.

I blew out the candles and sat in the dark for a long time. I was cleaning up a little while later when Mickey came back downstairs. He had showered and his hair was wet and he smelled like shampoo.

He walked over and took the plate out of my hand and wrapped me in his arms. "I can only imagine how hard it was to go see Harry. It was hard just hearing about it."

"I know."

"I don't want to think about it anymore, Lu. Tonight, let's just pretend it's a nonissue. You're going to have our baby, and then you will do whatever the doctors tell you. . . ." He shrugged. "And your visit with Harry will turn out to have been all for nothing."

"Well, of course. Harry was just in case."

Mickey nodded. "I want to show you something." He walked me into the living room and I looked up at him grinning. He sat me down on the sofa, then pulled the ottoman over and lifted my feet onto it. Then he retrieved the oxygen tank I had abandoned before dinner and hooked me back up to my air supply. When he'd covered me with a quilt, he sat down next to me and handed me a present.

"What's this?"

"Happy birthday."

"You missed my birthday."

"Minor detail. Open it."

It was a book. A big red book with the words *Mickey Loves Lucy* printed in gold letters that blurred under my sudden tears. I looked at him. "What have you done?"

"Just a little compiling."

It was a thick book full of our history. I couldn't believe how young we looked when we first started out. There was a picture of us kissing on my twenty-first birthday at Colby's, which Lily had taken. She'd also snapped one on the day I graduated, when Mickey proposed and tied a string from my tassel around my finger. There was one of us in a mess as we gutted the main floor of this house, me wearing Mickey's tool belt and a hard hat. Another was of us all wet and spinning around on our wedding day, and another of Priscilla trying to save the canapés as it poured. There were several of us and Lily and Ron and Jan and Harry on the cruise we took just before I got cancer the first time. One of just the girls getting facials. One of just our fabulous men. And a beautiful shot of Mickey kissing me in the moonlight.

"Oh, that was a great trip." I looked over at Mickey, who was nodding, trying to hold back the tears. I remembered he hadn't had even a hiccup for over a year. Then I got cancer.

Mickey had taken just one picture of me during my first bout with the disease. I was laughing. I had lost most of my hair and Priscilla had bought me the most hideous wig. It was bad Farrah Fawcett hair, and I'd lost so much weight that I looked more like a twelve-year-old hooker than one of Charlie's original Angels. I looked ridiculous. Even Priss thought so.

There was a picture of Mickey's dad and me standing on the rubble that used to be his house before Katrina hit. We'd heard about the hurricane and took the first flight out. Mic's dad cried when we showed up on his broken stoop, but he'd refused to come back with us. He had a little restaurant near Bourbon Street, and he wasn't about to abandon it. I got another picture of him hugging Mickey the day we left, and if gratitude had a face, it was that old man's. Every picture was a memory. Our first Christmas when the tree tipped over. The next year when it was too big to get in the house. Lots of photos of us on the boat. One with Mickey up to his ears in leaves just before a bonfire. One of us in Cancún, our hair braided by a little kid for $5. This book was the best gift Mickey had ever given me.

"What a fabulous time we've had," I said, stroking the cover. And since we were being so optimistic, I added, "I want another one in eleven more years."

Mickey tousled my hair. "It's a deal."

I opened the book and started at the beginning. Again.

After that, the weekend only got better. On Saturday morning, I had just gotten out of the shower when Mickey brought the phone to me. "Jan wants to talk to you," he said, kissing the top of my head.

"Hey, Jan."

"How's my little mama-to-be?"

"Not too bad," I said, a little out of breath.

"Well, do you think you could come over here? I need to look at your nose."

I laughed.

"I know it's silly, but I'm just finishing the cover portrait for your fairy tale and I want to make sure I've got your nose right."

After I pulled my jeans on and dried my hair, I could have used a nap. Suddenly, it seemed, the most minor tasks were wearing me out. But I'd rest later. "Mic," I shouted. "I'll be right back; I'm just going over to Jan's for a minute."

"What about your oxygen, missy?"

"I'll be two minutes." And that's all I'd planned on until I walked in Jan's back door and found her home full of my neighbors. It was chaotic with female energy, and when I walked in, Jan hugged me and said, "Welcome to your baby shower, you sweet thing!"

My mouth fell open.

"It's about time you got here," Lily said, wrapping me up in her arms.

"What have you done?" I said, taking it all in. The tower of pastries was from Matilda Hines. A baby quilt was being tied in Jan's living room, and a pile of presents were on the coffee table. And pink everywhere. Balloons, streamers, even pink letters that said IT'S A GIRL. I wanted to cry. Diana Dunleavy did her best to smile through her sadness as she took my hand and led me to a chair. Muriel Piper pushed a pillow behind my back, then pecked my cheek. Charlotte chucked my chin. "How're you feeling, darlin'?"

"Stunned. Absolutely stunned."

In a moment Mickey walked in with my oxygen, and the ladies started hooting and teasing him. He just grinned and said it took some courage to walk into a house so full of hormones and perfume. He then pulled a wolfish face at Wanda Murphy. "But that's my favorite kind of house." He hooked me up, then kissed me. "Have fun."

Lainy Withers fixed him up with a plate of goodies and sent him on his way. Lily brought me some juice and a muffin, and Priss, who was taking pictures, handed her camera to Jan. "Will you get one of us?"

"Absolutely!"

Priss sat down on the arm of my chair, Lily got on her knees and leaned in, and we all smiled. I was the luckiest girl on the planet to have friends and sisters such as these. Lily kissed my cheek. "What can I get for you?"

"I've got it all, Lil. Did you do this?"

"We all did."

"Well, it's fabulous." I looked around and drank it all in, all the sweet chatter and clucking over me, all the wet-eyed concern and soft embraces. And the gifts! Never in my life had I seen such adorable things. I had no choice but to cry happy tears for my daughter. She got everything a baby girl could need and then some. Muriel had knitted her the smallest pink sweater with tiny seed pearls as an embellishment, and I nearly knocked Muriel over hugging her for it. Jan gave us a stack of storybooks, and when I hugged her, I didn't want to let go.

When there was just one gift left, Lily said, "This one is from me and Priss."

I tore away the wrapping and opened the box to find it filled with tissue paper. I peeled back the layers and started to cry again as I gently lifted out the most beautiful christening dress I'd ever seen. It was four feet long at least and lacy and delicate and completely exquisite. There was even a matching headband with a big silk daisy. I held the dress to me and imagined how it would feel to hold my baby daughter as she wore it. My sisters were crying, I was crying, Muriel was blowing her nose, Jan and Charlotte were both sniffing. I looked at this tender gathering of women, and at their generosity piled up at my feet. Would they ever know what they meant to me? "I love you all." I wept. "Thank you so, so much!" I didn't mean for it to sound like such a good-bye, but it did.

Priss walked over and kissed my head, then thankfully she burst the sad bubble I'd created. "We'd love to be worthy of all this emotion, Lu. But the truth is we were just in the mood for a party and you were a great excuse."

Finally laughter, tender laughter, but laughter all the same, and I laughed with the relief of it. Priscilla saved me; she saved everyone from looking too closely at what was really happening.

twenty-eight

*Gleason tells me that before a mountain falls, pebbles first drop
in warning. If that's true, then I received my initial warning
years ago when Lucy first told me of the cancer that plagued
her genes. Five short years after we were married, she was
diagnosed with the horrid precursor for what's happening now.
At least in theory. All I know for sure is that every worried
thought and fear is another stone, until now I am completely
in the shadow of the mountain that will soon crush me. Dr.
Gladstone offers optimism so slim it's a lie. It will happen,
he says unequivocally—he just doesn't know when. So I
balance myself against this agony and try to concentrate on
the moment. I am under doctor's orders not to look past the
immediate, to stay firmly within the small landscape of the
here and now. My job is to love my wife enough that she will
feel it for eternity. And above all else, I must stay strong. There
will be plenty of time to fall apart . . . after. For now, I hoard
each weary smile, each weakening touch, each sober kiss, and I
brand them on my heart.*

I turned off the engine and gazed up at the walkway that led to my
parents' graves. From the curb, the distance was daunting, and for a

moment I considered not going up at all. I didn't feel well. The difference between today and yesterday and the day before was light-years. I'd been coughing all night, and when I woke up this morning, I woke up a different person, undeniably sick. I spent the morning at Charlotte's with Mickey pacing in her waiting room while she checked me over and shook her head. But the baby was okay, and I held on to that.

I leaned my forehead against the steering wheel and summoned the strength to get out of the car. At least I was alone, with no audience I had to convince that I was fine. Mickey believed me when I said I felt better than I did because he needed to. Lily was the same way. But this charade I'd committed myself to had a price. I was exhausted, and I knew I couldn't keep it up much longer. I didn't even want to.

I hadn't been here in a while, so I'd brought a bucket and some clippers. I'd even thrown in some rags and Windex for good measure. When I got out of the car, I could feel the warmth of the November sun directly above me. It felt delicious despite the chilly breeze. I pulled my paraphernalia from the trunk and made my way up the gravel path, dragging my oxygen tank behind me. I was reminded, for the thousandth time, how I'd taken the simple act of breathing for granted. Never had I offered a moment's gratitude for the marvelous freedom of filling my chest with air and blowing it out at my leisure. I sure did now. Now I was ever conscious of the mechanics of taking oxygen into my lungs. Oh, how I craved a sigh, deep and mindless and rejuvenating. But I knew I'd pay dearly if I indulged.

The reprieve was officially over, and it didn't take much of anything to overwhelm my tattered respiratory system. When it happened, my breath would catch somewhere between inhaling and exhaling and refuse to move. Then I'd cough, which further robbed me of the ability to breathe. Last night I coughed so hard I prayed to die and didn't even feel bad about it. The episode was by far the worst yet, and it left me utterly depleted and fearful beyond words for my baby. I found that my life was reduced to avoiding these episodes. Every thought and movement revolved around maintaining smooth and continuous breathing. So, I was profoundly careful as I climbed the short distance to my parents' graves. I moved slowly and breathed my little rations and tried not to think about it.

By the time I got to the marble bench under the elm tree, my heart was thudding like I'd run a marathon. I had to sit and breathe slowly through my teeth to calm myself, but I regained control soon enough. I looked around. I was alone except for the dead that surrounded me, and I found it incredibly comforting to be in such company. I always had. Even when I was little, I'd had no apprehension about this place.

Once when I was small, and my father hadn't been dead too long, I came here after school to read to him—to practice my letters and sounds. The loss of our morning ritual was nearly as disruptive to my young life as losing him. So one day, I simply decided to get off the school bus two stops over and walk my little self to the cemetery. I spread my sweater on the grass in front of his headstone, sat down cross-legged, and started reading. I must have gotten lost in it because I wasn't even aware of the patrol car that had pulled up to the curb, or my mother and Deloy Rosenberg making their way up the path. I remember being quite perplexed by their reaction at finding me. Sitting there reading to my father didn't seem worthy of such tears and attention. After my mother died, I found myself visiting even more often.

Priscilla, of course, thought it was morbid that I spent so much time at the cemetery. She asked Charlotte to talk to me about it, and Charlotte met me here one afternoon to chat about my sister's concerns. It was early autumn, a day much like today, when the air was cool but the sun was warm.

It was the first time I learned Charlotte and I felt the same about the nearness of my parents. That afternoon she recited—by heart— John Donne's famous sonnet "Death Be Not Proud." I'd heard it before, but I'd never really understood it until that day. *One short sleep past, we wake eternally, and death shall be no more . . .* I hadn't thought of the poem for years, but this afternoon Donne's radical notions felt like a nod of reassurance.

I pulled myself from my reverie, knelt down, and began clearing away the brown grass that cluttered my parents' gravesite. I tried to use my clippers to tidy up the base of the headstones, but I was too weak to work them. On my knees, my pregnant belly hanging away from me, it was possible to take in a bit more air without triggering a reaction. So I simply leaned my head against the cool stone of my parents' marker and closed my eyes.

Since I was on my knees anyway, I found myself praying for the strength I'd need to get through the next few minutes. And though I don't usually engage in such casual conversation with God, I felt what had to be God responding to my little petition. The answer descended on me like a cloud of something soft, something I trusted to hold me for a moment. It was lovely, strange, and I thought surely this peace was an offering from my parents.

I think I would have stayed there on my knees, nuzzling the cool marble all day, except I heard a car door slam. I opened my eyes to see Ron walking quickly up the path. He was hurrying, and I realized it must have looked as if I'd fallen and couldn't get up.

"Lucy! What happened?"

"Nothing," I said, taking his outstretched hand. "I was just doing a little supplicating."

When we were face-to-face, he said, "You're not okay, are you, Lucille?"

"I've been better." I brushed the grass off my pants and took Ron's arm. "Sit with me, Ronald, and hold my hand. I have something important to talk to you about."

"Ronald, huh? Must be serious," he said as we walked over to the bench and sat down. I looked over at my handsome brother-in-law in his jeans and a blue turtleneck. Sitting this close to him, I could see the handful of gray threads in his light brown hair. "What can I do for you, Lucy?"

I gazed over at my parents' marker, freshly Windexed and gleaming in the sun. "I'm dying, Ron."

He didn't say anything, but I felt a little squeeze on my shoulder.

I took as deep a breath as I could muster. "I'm tired of pretending that I'm not."

"You don't have to pretend anything with me, Lucy."

"That's why I love you, Ron." I took his hand in both of mine. "Thank you for meeting me here. I need to ask you something."

"Anything," he said without hesitation.

"You know how much I love Lily," I finally managed.

Ron nodded.

"I don't think you do. You couldn't possibly. She's been everything to me, Ron. Everything."

Ron nodded, his agreement shining in his eyes.

"She's a perfect mom—the mom I'd want to be if all this wasn't happening."

"I know."

We were quiet for a minute as I tried to arrange my words. Then finally I gave up and just said what was on my mind. "Ron, you've watched my life unravel and put itself back together again. You've watched Mickey." He nodded. "You know this was never going to be easy for him."

"I can't imagine what he's going through."

"You and Lily must have thought about my baby."

"We think about all of you, all the time." Ron's voice was a whisper.

I squeezed his hand. "You have to know how important you were always going to be in her life. How important Lily was going to be."

"Where're you going with this, Lu?"

I looked at my sweet brother-in-law. "Ron, I'm out of time and Mickey doesn't think he can do it without me."

"Do what?"

"Raise our daughter."

"Oh."

"I have something huge to ask."

"Lucy—"

"No, listen. *We*—Mickey and I—want for you and Lil to adopt our baby. But it's a little complicated."

"Lucy, what are you talking about?"

"I'm talking about something very unique, Ron. A three-way adoption—between you and Lily, and Mickey."

"Wow."

"I know."

"Lucy, are you sure we need to talk about this now?"

"I'm out of time, Ron. And I wanted to talk to you first because I'm going to need your help talking to Lily." I sniffed. "I've had this conversation with her in my head a hundred times, and I never get past the part when I tell her I'm really dying." I ran my hands over my face. "I have no illusions, Ron, but I think Lily still might. She's not ready to hear that my time is just about up, and this has to be decided."

Ron squeezed my shoulder. "Shhh. We'll figure something out."

"We need to figure it out now, and you are the one person I can always count on to be real, so please, don't blow me off." I wiped my nose and reined in my jagged emotion.

"Okay. How's this for 'real'? Why would Mickey give up his child? Even to us?"

"Where do I even start?" I looked at my brother-in-law for a long time, the explanation for Mickey's antics on the tip of my tongue, but eventually I just shook my head. "He thinks he's too damaged to be her father." I wanted to explain further, but started to cough instead, and soon I was coughing so hard I prayed for that same comforter from a moment ago to step in and save me. Trying not to panic, I rifled through my bag for my water and let a small stream trickle down my scorched throat. Ron didn't say anything. He just kept his gentle hand on my back—steady, constant, and soothing.

I leaned over, willing myself to calm down as he rubbed my shoulder. He offered no platitudes, which I greatly appreciated, and in a moment I could breathe again.

"So?"

"I don't think I can do it, Lucy. I've had a baby taken from me, remember? It was hell."

"Of course I remember. But it's not the same. Mickey wants this. He loves his daughter and this is the best way he knows to show her."

"I just can't believe that, Lucy."

"Yes, you can. You know Mickey."

"I do, but still . . ."

"I wish it was different, Ron, but there's no magic here. Mickey is Mickey, and it doesn't matter that I have complete faith in his ability to love her; he has none in himself." I shook my head and fought new tears. "He tries so hard, Ron. You know he does. But in Mickey's mind, success is absolute control over his diagnosis, and he just can't always swing that. He can keep it in check for long stretches. But, even when he does everything right, he still sprouts wings. The sanest part of Mickey has convinced himself that he can't have an innocent little person dependent on him."

Ron didn't say anything, but I saw the pity in his eyes.

"Don't look like that. Please, not you. He's doing the best he can."

"I know he is," Ron said.

We were quiet for a moment, then I whispered, "I love him so much. I think I've loved him from the moment I saw him. That might sound funny because there's been so much *lunacy* over the years, but that's not what I remember. People look at me like I'm something special because Mickey's Mickey and I've put up with him all this time. The only thing special about me is that Mickey loves me." I shook my head and gazed out at the river. "But the fact is, Mickey's not like you and me, Ron. And I don't know what's going to happen to him after I'm gone."

"Lucy . . ."

I pushed the tears off my face. "This sacrifice he wants to make—this distance he wants from his daughter—that's Mic at his best and most rational. You get that, don't you?"

It took a long time for my brother-in-law to speak. "I get it. But no man should have to lose his wife *and* his child. What will that do to him?" Ron settled his gaze on my parents' headstones, and I watched his jaw tremble. "This just isn't right, Lucy."

"I know. But at least this way he'll get to know her. She'll get to know him. And she'll be safe and loved by all of you."

He turned back to face me.

"Ron, I want you and Lily to have my baby because I know you'll let Mickey in. I know you'll let him be part of her life."

"That goes without saying. We'll do whatever you want us to do, Lucy. But isn't this all just a little premature? How about Lil and I just take care of the baby while you're recovering? Let's just go that far since we don't know what's going to happen."

"That's a good idea," I said, indulging him. "But when what's going to happen actually does happen, will you adopt her?"

Tears and anguish filled his eyes.

"Will you do it?"

He nodded.

There was so much more to say, but I was too tired. Ron turned and gently pulled my face into his chest. "Ah, Lucy." He held me for a moment, and when I quieted, he lifted my chin. "You know we'll love her like she's ours. But I promise you, she'll always know who her parents are."

It was all my heart needed to hear. I knew my sister and Ron would make it work. No woman had ever wanted to be a mother more than Lily. Now I could give her this. She would love my baby for me. And she would take care of my Mickey. She'd let him love his child and never be threatened by it. But beyond that, Lily would protect her if she ever needed it. And she would make sure my daughter knew how much I loved her.

"Will you talk to Lily?" I whispered. "Will you tell her this is what I want?"

My dear brother-in-law cleared his throat, but I still heard the sob he tried to swallow as he nodded.

"Thank you, Ron. Thank you."

There was nothing else to say. I rubbed my belly and my baby responded by kicking me. She was healthy and strong, of that I had no doubt. I picked up Ron's hand and placed it on my stomach. She kicked again, and a tear rolled down Ron's cheek.

Later that evening, I was trying to stay awake as I waited up for Mickey. He had reluctantly gone over to Partners when his bartender called from the emergency room, where his little girl was getting stitches in her head. Mickey promised he'd be back as soon as he could. That was two hours ago and I was dozing to *Conan* when Lily knocked and let herself in. She'd been crying like the world would end. Her nose was bright red, her eyes swollen beyond what seemed possible. She walked over to where I was sitting, new tears brimming, and knelt down in front of me. Her pain was palpable, and I could see that she had finally accepted the immediacy of what was happening. I ran my hand over her short hair.

"Lucy," she whimpered. "Please don't die."

"Okay," I whimpered back.

Then neither of us spoke for a while. As I looked into her eyes, I could not imagine who I would have been if she had not been my sister, and I couldn't imagine who I was going to be without her. Lily had been the keeper of my secrets and the holder of my dreams since we were little girls. We were supposed to grow old together.

Lily shook her head, fighting more tears. "I don't think I can be in this place," she said, her lip trembling.

"What place, Lil?"

"The place where I can finally have a baby . . . but only if I lose my sister."

"I know. I'm sorry."

"Are you sure this is what you want?"

"I can't have what I want, Lil. So, it's up to you. You'll be a wonderful mother." I cupped her chin, catching her tears.

She leaned into my hand. "I don't know what I'll do without you. I've never known."

"I was just thinking the same thing."

"Lu, do you remember when you got stuck in that tree?"

"I got stuck in a tree?"

Lily nodded. "It was in the park. There were lots of people, but I can't remember the occasion, maybe the Shad Bake. I was seven, I think I was seven. You were little and there were lots of kids and we were all playing and I lost track of you. And when I realized it, I panicked. I looked for you everywhere, and when I couldn't find you, my heart started to hurt. Somehow I was able to eke it out to Dad, who got scared and started yelling for you. Then Mom yelled for you. Everyone was looking for you. Then for some reason I looked up. And there you were, up in the tree, just looking down at me, at all of us. I remember I started to cry with the relief of it," Lily rasped.

She shook her head. "You weren't gone and I could breathe again," she whispered. "Nobody could figure out how you got up there, and it was a miracle that you didn't fall and break something. When Dad got you down, he swatted your bum, of course, because you'd scared him and he didn't know where you'd gone. You just looked at him and said with all the wisdom of a three-year-old, 'I wasn't gone, you just couldn't see me.'"

I nodded, vaguely remembering this.

"I'll never forget that," Lily said. "You weren't gone, we just couldn't see you. That's the way I'm going to survive this, Lucy; you just won't be gone."

"I won't be gone," I echoed.

twenty-nine

*I now know the difference between sadness and depression.
Clinical depression has no source from which it springs—
it just is. Intractable sadness has nothing to do with
synapses, or brain chemistry, or essential salts, it's born of
something. It's the product of injustice and helplessness.
It can be anesthetized, I suppose, but it's there, unaltered,
when the medication wears off, like an intruder who has
broken into your house and is still there every morning
when you wake up.*

*Given the choice, I would rather be depressed. I've
come back from depression.*

Priscilla came to town for the meeting with Harry and informed me that
she was staying with us for a few days. That's what she said, anyway—
just a few days. It was too cold to stay on the boat, and rather than take
up residence in the guest room she always had access to at Lily's, she'd
chosen to hover over me. But I was too tired to mind. And besides, the
arrangement proved to be a good distraction for Mickey, who sorely
needed one.

Somehow, the current state of my health made it possible for
Priss and Mickey to rise above their low opinions of each other.

And it helped that Priscilla was just plain different these days. Softer. Some of it was naturally obligatory because I was sick. But some of it, I was sure, came from a deeper source. It seemed to me she was just sick and tired of carrying around all that wrath. I hoped I wouldn't reverse that when I told her why I'd asked her to come to Brinley tonight. I figured it was better to explain why we were meeting with Harry before he showed up in his official capacity, with papers for us all to sign. So I got up and brushed my teeth, but then I went back to bed. It had been a rough day, and at two thirty in the afternoon I still wasn't dressed. Priscilla was checking on me every few minutes, and when she came in for the third time, I finally managed to sit up and tell her I wanted to talk. Now she was sitting at the foot of the bed waiting for me to quit coughing. Needless to say, the delivery of my message became utilitarian at best. Not at all how I'd planned to tell her I was giving my baby to Lily.

"To Lily? You're giving your baby to Lily?"

"Yes."

Priss looked up at the ceiling. "I don't know what to say."

"Say you'll be a good aunt."

"I'd be a good mom, you know."

"I'm sure you would," I said, pleased that I had sounded like I meant it.

Her upturned face crumpled, and I could see she was truly hurt. "Did you even think of me?" When I didn't answer, she leveled her gaze on me.

I didn't know what to say. If I'd done as my sister had insisted, my baby wouldn't even be here. But I couldn't remind her of that when she had tears in her eyes. "It boiled down to Brinley," I said. "You know I love it here, and this is where I want her to grow up."

After a few heartbeats of tension, Priss's hurt dissolved in a slump of her shoulders. "Lily will be a great mom," she admitted grudgingly.

"She will. But it's more than that. I want Mickey to be very involved, and the two of you couldn't pull that off. Besides, I need you to rescue them from each other when they need it. And, you know, Priss, this way she will just have one aunt. Do you realize you are the only one who can officially spoil her? It's a very distinguished role you're walking into."

She nodded, preoccupied. "I guess that's all true." She stared hard at me. "But I want to ask you something."

"Okay."

"I want the truth, Lucy."

"I'm listening."

"If you'd known then how things were going to turn out, would you have had the abortion?"

"No," I said without hesitation. "Even if I'd had it, I'd still have ended up right where I am now, and with nothing to leave behind. I couldn't have done that to Mickey. And just because I don't get to know my daughter right now doesn't necessarily mean I'll never get to know her."

"What are you talking about?"

I started coughing and waved away her question. "I have no regrets," I managed to push out.

Priscilla poured me some water, and when I stopped hacking, she touched my cheek and said, "I knew you would say that. I just wanted to hear it, to make sure."

"Hear what?" Mickey said, walking into the bedroom.

"I think I'll go find us something to eat," Priscilla said, scooting off the bed.

"The Dunleavys just brought over a big pot of soup and some hot bread," Mickey said. "I came up to see if you were hungry."

I patted his hand. "I'll have some later."

Mickey kissed my forehead, and as he lingered there for a moment too long, I felt him start to tremble. Out of the corner of my eye, I saw Priscilla pull her hand to her mouth and leave the room. I wished I could do something to alleviate this landslide of raw emotion, but I was just too tired. Mickey slid down next to me and nuzzled his face into my neck.

"I love you, baby," I whispered, stroking his bristly chin.

I woke up a couple of hours later and Priscilla was sitting in the chair by the bed reading my baby book. She told me Mickey had gone to see Gleason, which surprised me since I knew he didn't have an appointment.

"Good," I said. "This has to be getting old, watching me . . . do what I'm doing."

"I brought you some apple juice," Priss said, holding the cup to my lips. It tasted delicious and I drank quite a bit before I fell back on the pillow. Then I asked my sister to run me a bath. I wanted to surprise Mickey with a fresh wife and clean sheets, which was about as much as I could manage today. I had almost three hours before Harry would be here.

Priss took great pains to set the perfect temperature, and the water felt glorious against my sad skin. When I laid my head back into the suds, my whole body felt like it was being cradled in a soapy palm. After I'd been in there a while, Priss knocked on the door and poked her head in. "Do I need to worry about you?"

"I think I'm doing fine."

"Is your oxygen on?"

"Yes."

"Do you need your back scrubbed?"

"Oh, that would be lovely," I moaned.

Priscilla soaped up a washcloth and positioned herself on the ledge of the tub. I leaned up and gave her my back and heard a tiny gasp that Priss tried to hide in a cough.

"Sorry, I should have warned you. It's not a pretty sight."

"Lucy, how can you be this thin?" Awe was in her voice. Then I heard her sniff and knew she was crying.

"Are you going to scrub my back or what?"

Priscilla ran the washcloth over my spine so gently I told her it didn't count. "Scrub! You're not going to hurt me."

"Are you sure?"

"I'm sure."

It felt delicious when she finally got serious. When she was done, Priss poured water over my back, then unpinned my hair and poured more over my head. I hadn't asked her to wash my hair, but I didn't argue. In fact I nearly melted as her long fingers gently scrubbed my scalp. Her sweetness, the indulgence of this kindness, made me weep, and I let my tears run freely down my wet face and didn't apologize.

After she wrapped a towel around my head I took her hand and kissed it. Priss was crying, too.

I leaned back into the water and pulled the suds over me. Even so, my belly protruded like a slippery island. Priss smiled sadly. She wasn't wearing any makeup and her hair was pulled back in a clip.

"It's going to be okay, Priscilla," I said softly.

Her eyes filled with tears again, but she didn't look away. "I should be telling you that. Don't you ever get tired of taking care of all of us, Lucy? Don't you ever get mad?"

"All the time, lately. I'm especially mad at the timing of this little dilemma."

"Only you would call *this* a little dilemma."

I shook my head. "I'm not ready, Priss."

"None of us are, sweetie."

After a moment of heavy silence, I said, "Mom wasn't ready either, and I think I understand how she felt. She wasn't *done*. She had important things she wanted to finish."

"Like what?"

"She wanted to finish raising me. Get Lily and Ron married. And she really wanted to make up with you."

"What?"

"Did you think it didn't matter to her?" I asked. "How things were between you? You know she loved you, Priscilla."

"I don't know how she could. I was so unbelievably horrible."

"Well, that's true," I said wickedly. "But even so."

Priss pulled herself up in a little girl's shrug. "I did something awful and Mom never forgave me for it."

"I'm sure you're wrong."

"I got pregnant." Her words hung in the air for a few heartbeats.

"I know."

"How did you know? Did she tell you?"

"No. I just figured it out when I got old enough. Did you have an abortion? Is that why you think Mom never forgave you?"

"No. I wanted the baby. Trent and I—it was Trent's—we were going to get married. We were seventeen, and we knew everything. But then I lost it. After that, everything fell apart. I was so angry. At everything and everyone. I know Mom died hating me."

"How can you be so smart and so dumb at the same time?"

Priss shook her head. "I was so screwed up, Lucy. But I know that's the reason I've never dared hold on to anything. There was no point. I'd just lose it."

"What are you talking about?"

"When I was a kid, I just never understood how God could take Grandma from me—from us. Then Dad. Then my baby. By the time Mom got sick, I already pretty much hated the idea of God." Priscilla covered her face with her hands and for a moment she didn't speak. "When I found that lump all those years ago at the same time Kenny Boatwright went back to his wife, I just gave up."

"Oh, honey."

A single tear dripped down my sister's cheek. "I've been so careful not to lose anything that I've got nothing." She sighed. "And here I am facing another loss, with absolutely no control."

"We never had control, Priscilla. Neither did Mom."

My sister looked through me. "You may not believe this, and in another mood I probably wouldn't admit it, but I always felt bad about being such a pain in the ass."

"You should."

"I do!"

"Mom knew that anyway. She was worried about you because she knew how tender you were. The tenderest of us all, she said."

"She did not."

"Yeah. She said you were the sensitive one, and Lily was the one with the sweetest disposition."

"What were you?"

"I don't remember, I think she thought I was strong."

Priss ran her hand under her nose and didn't say anything.

"She knew you, Priss. Probably better than you ever knew yourself. She used to say it was going to take someone very patient a very long time to dig to the center of you."

"She did not say that," Priss said softly and without conviction.

"Yes, she did. And she said when he found it, he'd be the luckiest man in the world."

My sister started to weep. "I don't believe Mom ever said that about me."

"Well, you should. She knew all the important things moms know. She even knew you and I would have this conversation someday."

"Right."

"She did! She was so sick—it was just a few days before she died—and she was telling me all the things she was going to miss. And she said, 'Someday Priss will want to talk about me, Lucy, and you tell her I never stopped loving her and I never believed she stopped loving me.'" I tried to glare at Priss for emphasis, but I couldn't pull it off. "So there you go."

Priscilla pulled her knees up to her chin and folded herself nearly in half. She looked like a little girl, vulnerable and hopeful. "She really said that?"

"Every word."

Priscilla stared at the floor, and for a long time we didn't speak. I thought of those last terrible days when my mother was in so much pain, but still holding on. She wasn't finished. I knew exactly how she felt. Even when Death had been ready for her, the ghostly presence in her room undeniable, my mother would think of something else to tell me; some nonsense that bubbled out of her pallid delirium like last-minute instructions. None of it rational—except the last thing.

I'd dozed off in Dad's chair holding her hand. I don't know how long I'd been asleep, but I woke up when I heard the train, and Mom was looking at me through her regular eyes—not the ones dulled by pain and medication. She seemed so different that I thought for a moment I might be dreaming. She looked the way she did before she ever got sick. Peace had erased all the deep lines in her face, and somehow I knew it was time. And she did, too.

She tugged on me, pulling me down close to her. "You're such a good girl, Lucy," she whispered. "Don't ever be afraid, my darling, because there is *nothing* to be afraid of." I didn't know what she meant, and before I could question her, she asked me to get her some ice. I remember my reluctance to leave the room because Death was there. *Her* familiar eyes letting me know that when I came back, my mother would be gone. And I knew that was how Mom wanted it. So I kissed her cheek and went downstairs and got the ice.

I started to cough and Priscilla was immediately at my side. "Let's get you out of that tub. You're probably freezing by now." Priss got me a towel and helped me stand up. She gasped again at my thin legs and arms, my disproportionate belly covered with blue veins.

I pulled the towel around me. "You'll probably have nightmares now."

"I probably will," she said, only half-kidding. She helped me into some fresh pajamas and I sat down in the big chair, Dad's chair. While I coughed into the towel, my sister dried my hair. I don't think in all my life I'd ever felt such tenderness from Priscilla. When she was done, she sat on the edge of the bed and took my hand. "Lucy, there is so much I should have said to Mom. I don't want to make that mistake with you." When her eyes filled with tears, I brought her hand to my lips. "I love you, Lucy."

"I know that, sweets. I've always known."

While I rubbed lotion over my dry skin, Priscilla changed my sheets. She took great care with the corners and even shook the down comforter before she laid it across the mattress. Then she folded it over and helped me back into bed. I vowed to rest just until Harry arrived.

I fell immediately into a semblance of sleep but was aware that somewhere behind the noise of my breathing and the hum of the oxygen, the doorbell had rung. I remember Lily kissing me and touching my face. She had the saddest eyes. "Lu," she rasped. "Are you sure this is what you want to do?"

"Yes. I want to give her *you*." A tiny sob broke out of my sister then, and I did my best to squeeze her hand, but I could not stay awake.

The next thing I remember was all of them standing in my bedroom—Ron and Lily, Harry, Priscilla, and Mickey, who'd knelt down next to the bed. He'd been crying again; I think they all had. Mickey stroked my cheek and ran my sad hair between his fingers. "Are you sure?" he whispered.

I knew what he was asking me and I looked from him to my sisters and then to Ron. "Just like we talked about, right?" Ron nodded. Lily—tears streaming down her face—nodded. I turned back to Mickey and lifted my hand to his shoulder. "Are *you* sure?"

"I am," he whispered.

He helped me sit up in bed, and when I was situated, Harry sat down beside me with the documents. "Here you go, kiddo," he said, opening the folder. He handed me the pen from his pocket. Then, using my belly as a table, I added my signature to the papers that made the adoption of my daughter official.

thirty

Lily has taken to stopping by first thing in the mornings to help Lucy get ready for the day, comb her hair, rub lotion into her hands, put her socks on. I could have done all that, but it seems profoundly important to Lily to be afforded this intimacy. Now I watched as Lily slowly, gently guided one of Lucy's thin arms, then the other, through the sleeves of a sweater. When she was done buttoning it, she bent to kiss my wife's forehead, and Lucy looked up at her and tried to smile. Neither said a word, but there was bottomless meaning in that moment.

I'd known there was something special between these sisters since Lily came into Colby's to set up Lucy's twenty-first birthday party. I remember she was thin and fair and easy to underestimate. She still is, but Lily has a depth born of painful things, and it manifests itself in true kindness and generosity. Years ago, as we planned the party, she had described Lucy in layers—all of which she admired. They varied from young and tenacious and confident, to patient and forgiving, to indomitable and freakishly unflappable. Lily had said "freakishly" and it made me smile recalling it. No doubt she would describe Lucy the same way today, even though today was a bad day.

Lucy had been sick all night, and her breathing was

wet and labored. Peter Gladstone had made room to see us so I'd come to the bedroom to hurry things along. But I felt like an intruder bursting in on the sacred; Lily had sat down and Lucy's head was on her shoulder. They were holding hands and staring at something in the distance, raw affection and devotion etched into their faces. The connection between them seemed without beginning or end, and for the first time I looked outside myself to Lily's heartbreak. It was hard to see and I had to walk away.

It snowed in Brinley on November 19. As if by sleight of hand, the season changed from a lazy, prolonged autumn, quiet and gushing with color, to a blanket of sludge that draped the world in cold, depressing dullness. Mickey and I were on our way to the hospital to see Peter Gladstone, and my spirits were as heavy as the day. For one thing, I could not get warm. Despite the car's forced heat blowing in my face, I was freezing. And I did not feel well this morning. Breathing was hard and my body was one big ache. Mickey tugged on my hand, rousing me out of my waking slumber.

"Hey. You okay?"

I didn't open my eyes when I nodded my lie. I just tried to quiet the wet, sucking sounds coming from me as I inhaled. Mickey squeezed my fingers, and I did my best to squeeze back, but I couldn't muster the strength. My lungs were once again filled with fluid, and today breathing felt like trying to suck air through a soaking-wet towel. I think I could even hear sloshing going on inside me, but that could have been my imagination.

I was so tired. There was no such thing as rest for me anymore; not when every single breath had to be calculated and earned. And I hurt. I hurt everywhere. Waves of pain rolled over me, threatening to consume me. I couldn't tell where it started or where it ended, just that it throbbed through my body all the way down the backs of my legs. And coloring it all, every muscle it took to draw breath seemed to rebel, as did each one it took to breathe out.

"I'm sure Dr. Gladstone will be able to do something to make you feel better, baby," Mickey offered with little conviction.

I nodded in polite agreement, loving him for the sentiment. But in truth, I was losing my grip. No, that wasn't even right. The real truth was, I was losing my desire to hold on. After meeting with Harry to sign the papers, it was as though I'd met a deadline and relaxed my hold. It was weird. When everyone walked out of my bedroom that night, it felt like, aside from actually having the baby, the last thing I'd had to accomplish could be crossed off the list except the very last thing. Everything else, all the pressing things that had once needed doing, had either been taken care of or had faded into unimportance. I simply didn't care because I knew it would all land safely in someone else's waiting hands.

I started to cough just as we pulled into the hospital parking lot, and damn if my exertions didn't make me pee. I cried as the warm wetness spread out under me. I was such a mess. When Mickey came around to help me out of the car, he must have thought better of it, because he quickly ran in for a wheelchair. It seemed to take an eternity for him to come back, and another one for us to get into the building and up to the office.

At the desk, I asked Dr. Gladstone's nurse if she had something I could change into because I'd had an accident. Her kind smile reached in and stroked a place in me too raw to be humiliated. She told Mickey to have a seat, then said to me, "You come with me, sweetie, and we'll take care of it." Her name was Sadie, and at that moment I thought she was the sweetest thing in all the world. She helped me to a tiny restroom where I leaned against the wall as she rummaged through a cabinet. "Here ya go. You just slip into a pair of these scrubs. They're so comfortable, I steal them every once in a while," she said to me conspiratorially. She helped me out of my coat. "You be all right in here by yourself?"

I nodded what I hoped was the truth, and she left me alone. I sat down on the toilet and did my best to nudge my shoes loose without bending over. When I got them off, I stood up and peeled down my maternity jeans and kicked them aside, the effort of it all making me sweat. I couldn't catch my breath and I felt the world growing small and thin around me. "Please . . . please," I begged the air. I sat down again on the toilet, willing myself to stay present as I turned my oxygen up as high as it would go. Stronger wind filled my nostrils, and I breathed as deeply as I dared. With everything I had, I forced myself to focus, closed my eyes, and breathed. Slow and easy.

All I had to do was get out of my underwear and into the scrubs. I could do this. I stood up and the image in the mirror frightened me. I was so pale and so drawn and so *not me*. My eyes filled with tears as I pushed my lifeless hair behind my ears. I was a shell, ugly and obscene. As I stood there lamenting my god-awful reflection, *she* slipped in behind me. As I stared into her eyes, I wondered if I had willed her there even as I mentally scolded her for showing up. "It's not time," I croaked.

Her kind eyes stared into mine and I couldn't look away. I wasn't even sure I wanted to. My heart knew it and my head knew it, and part of me was almost grateful. Except that I needed just a bit more time. "I'm not going yet," I informed her.

As tears stretched everything out of focus, I rubbed my eyes. I rubbed hard, and when I looked back in the mirror, she was gone. I dropped my underpants and kicked them over to where my jeans lay in a heap, but something surprising caught my eye.

At first I couldn't force what I was seeing to make sense. Red underwear?

I didn't have any red underwear.

I stared at the color as if it were alive, the meaning not registering. As I stared, unblinking, at what refused to be real, I felt something running down my legs. I couldn't see it because of my swollen belly, but I felt it pooling at my feet. I slowly stepped away and looked down. Blood. Blood tracing the outline of my foot. Red underwear! When realization finally hit my brain, my heart started to pound and I was aware that, with each throbbing pulsation, more warmth dripped out of me. Blood! Thirty-four weeks. Blood. And Death in the mirror? After all this, was she not here for *me*?

I wrapped my arms protectively around my middle and screamed with all my strength, straining for breath. But there wasn't enough. As I tried once more to make myself heard, I slid down the wall, my watery legs losing the ability to support me. I was retreating, falling deeply into myself, as surely as if I were falling down a well.

I experienced what happened next as a sort of bystander, trapped, but trying to stay out of the way of all the commotion. I was aware that Sadie, and then another nurse, crowded into the small bathroom. As they got me into the scrubs, I thought, *Good. You take care of that— the pile of sick woman. And I'll see to this—my suddenly compromised passenger.* Every cell, every impulse I possessed, was directed toward seeing to her survival. My brain commandeered all that was left of my lifesaving forces and aimed them at my tiny daughter.

Strangely, through the panic, I felt myself start to sink beneath the surface, but I pulled myself back. I looked for Death, but I couldn't find her. At the thought of her, I felt both betrayal and reassurance, but I refused to allot any of my precious reserves to bargaining with her. I would not let her take my daughter! It was as simple as that.

Suddenly, Mickey burst into the little room. He picked me up as if I were a rag doll and took command. "Where! Where am I taking her?" he boomed, immediately hyperventilating. He was running and kissing my head, and the whole time I bounced in his arms, I felt blood leaking out of me.

"Follow me," Sadie yelled. "I don't know where a gurney is. Should I take her to the ER?" she shouted at someone. "Or upstairs? Call upstairs and tell them we're coming," she shouted again.

This was obviously not what anyone expected, and everyone in charge was suddenly outside their zone of authority, but Mickey had me—he had us—crushed solidly against him, and I knew he would not drop me.

I must have dipped below the surface for some time because

I woke—well, not woke exactly, but became aware of myself once more. I was lying in a bright room. A room so bright I could see the brightness even from behind eyelids that, despite my best efforts, would not open. I heard a lot of people shouting alarming information such as *late decelerations. Metabolic crisis. Disseminated intravascular coagulation.* But the worst was *We have to get the baby out! Now!*

Someone was demanding to know where the hell the epidural tech was, and someone else shouted, "We're losing her, pressure is sixty-six over forty."

"Roll her onto her side!" a male voice shouted, and in a moment I felt something cold flow into my back. It didn't hurt, though. Strangely, nothing hurt.

Mickey was crushing my hand and refusing to leave, though the doctors had apparently asked him several times. I knew he would never leave me, but he probably never imagined how his continual chanting in my ear, "Hang on baby, hang on," was keeping me tethered to the planet. He couldn't possibly know that without him I'd be swallowed up in the chaos happening around me, and I'd disappear.

Suddenly, I felt a cool hand on my face and knew that Charlotte had arrived. She leaned down and said into my ear, "What do you think you're doing, missy?" I wanted to cry, but I couldn't open my eyes. She said to Mickey, "How's our girl? You taking good care of her?"

"Doing my damnedest, Doc," he said in a shaky voice.

"We're ready for you, Dr. Barbee," someone said from the other side of me.

"What are you going to do?" Mickey asked like a frightened child.

"We're going to deliver your daughter."

I felt Charlotte's strong, capable hand squeezing my arm and her low voice once more in my ear. "You stay with me, young lady," she said firmly. "You're not done yet."

I was then jostled onto my back, and though I tried to be helpful, I couldn't feel myself. When they had me in position, I waited for them to tell me to push, but no one said anything. Not even Charlotte.

Whenever she can, Charlotte delivers her own babies. And though I presumed her presence here meant she would deliver mine, she seemed to be but a part of the larger group attending to me. Another doctor seemed to be running the show—asking for instruments, calling out for levels, making sure Mickey was not going to faint—and he was making quick work of cutting me open.

I desperately wanted to see what was happening because it had grown so quiet. Even Mickey seemed to be holding his breath. There was some muttering but I couldn't capture the words until I heard, "She's a tiny one—three pounds if she's an ounce. C'mon, sweetheart, take a breath. Take a breath, dammit!" When she didn't, the room ignited with activity. I heard suction and a little gagging cough. Then a strange word—*Apgar*—followed by the response "Three at one minute," which for some reason infused the scene with more urgency.

"What's happening?" Mickey said softly, then he let go of my hand and repeated his question louder. No one answered him. "Charlotte?" Mickey cried, his voice bulging with hysteria. "What's wrong with the baby? What's happening? Why isn't she breathing?"

thirty-one

*She was only twenty-one when I met her, and she terrified me.
A hundred times at least I'd picked up the phone and hung it
up again. I dreamed of her. No one had ever talked to me the
way she did; no pity. Fully expecting that I would rise to the
occasion, even a bit confrontational.*

*If you want to take a chance on me, I'm right here,
she'd said. Me, take a chance on her! But she didn't mean
it. She couldn't. I had no intention of going to her roof
that night, but I drove there anyway. I must have sat in
my car for two hours outside her building, torn between
the extremes. I wanted her more than I had ever dared
want anything, but I was deathly afraid she would see
me—me! And take it all back. I drove most of the way
home before I knew I was throwing away the greatest
chance life could hand me. There are many voices in my
head, but one finally rose above the thrum to tell me I
was a fool if I did not let her love me. Still, when I got
there and saw her sitting on the edge of the roof, all I
could do was watch her. I was going to leave, but then
she got up and walked toward me. There was fear in her
face that mirrored my own. Bright hope. Trust, unearned,
in her eyes. Promise. How did she do that? How did she*

speak to my soul in the exact language it would under-stand?

Tonight as my wife lays dying I marvel over how close I'd come to walking away. How impoverished would be my life if I had not gone to the roof that night. Even as I lose her, I shudder more at the thought that I nearly never had her.

Coma. Unresponsive. Actively dying. These words floated on the air around me in the bold and tearful discussions taking place over me. I struggled to move, to speak, to understand. Mickey was stroking my fingers and I could smell his terror. Oh, if I could just squeeze his hand, kiss his cheek, I knew I could make him feel better. I struggled to wake up. With all my strength I tried to lift myself awake, to respond to Mickey's repeated plea: "Lucy, honey, open your eyes. Wake up. Please wake up."

I could hear myself breathing, noisy and wet, but strangely I could not feel the effort I knew it was taking me to draw breath. I tried again to speak, to push the words out of my throat. The baby. Why was no one talking about the baby? I was filled with sudden dread and again tried to harness all my paralyzed power and wake up. But I couldn't open my eyes.

I became aware of *her* at the same instant I realized they were talking about me. The apparition was there, but she was standing a bit off, so I couldn't see her clearly. But I felt her. I felt her eyes on me. "My baby?" I said, but not with words.

She didn't answer and the heaviness of my family's grief fell upon me.

"You can't take both of us. It would kill them," I said. "Is it time?" I asked, trying to make my thoughts louder.

"Soon," she answered.

I closed my thoughts to her, irritated at the helplessness she'd imposed upon me, and I lifted my awareness to the outside of my body. I concentrated on the hand holding mine. I was right there. I just had to push through the barrier that separated me from everyone else.

"Lu?" Mickey rasped. "Honey? Please open your eyes."

I heard Peter Gladstone walk in and address everyone in the room.

Everyone but me. He told my family about the form I had signed two weeks earlier; my living will. It stated that I had prohibited the use of artificial oxygenation except if needed to save the life of my unborn baby. At that time, Dr. Gladstone had explained what he predicted would be the final phase of my illness. He told me that though I could be kept alive by mechanical means; doing so would not impact the outcome of my cancer. He was adamant that by the time a ventilator would be required, the only purpose it would serve would be to prolong the suffering of those around me. I had pictured exactly this scene in my mind. Everyone I loved encircling me, brokenhearted. I had signed the paper without hesitation, quickly banishing the image of Mickey clinging to a *me* that would never wake up.

This grave news was delivered to my family not unkindly, but neither was it done with enough warmth. Peter Gladstone had always maintained a slightly judgmental demeanor, and today was no exception, and now I heard Mickey start to cry—big, gulping sobs. Priscilla got angry, announcing, "This is bullshit!" and I heard Lily say with emotion, "So this is it? There is nothing we can do for her? She can't breathe!"

"Lucy wanted no heroic efforts," the doctor said. "She wanted nothing done that would simply prolong the inevitable. It's all clearly explained in this document."

"How long, Dr. Gladstone? How long are we looking at here?" Ron asked, his quiet voice trembling.

"I wish I could say. Lucy has surprised me at every turn, and she might surprise me yet. But, I would say not long."

I looked into the eyes I had known since I was a child. The specter was lovely and familiar to me. I turned toward her, knowing that she alone could alleviate my fear. "Not long?"

"Soon," she said.

A while later the apparition nodded and reached out her hand to me. I felt something in me let go, but reined it in. "I can't leave without saying good-bye," I said in my fashion.

She nodded, and suddenly I felt myself surface; that's the only way I can describe it. I came up into wakefulness and was immediately aware of my pain, and the terrible sensation of suffocating. I opened my eyes and found the room dim except for the light next to my bed. Mickey's head was bent near our joined hands. "Mic?" I rasped.

He looked up at me and quickly got to his feet. His eyes were swollen with tears. "Hey," he whispered. He kissed me then and touched my face with his rough hand. There was such relief in his eyes, such unrealistic hope. He kissed me again. "We have a daughter, Lu. A beautiful daughter. You did it, baby."

I struggled to ask how she was, but couldn't push the words out. It didn't matter.

"She's a fighter, Lu. Just like her mom. She's not quite breathing on her own, but she's close. A real nice doctor is taking good care of her." Mickey came close and cupped my face in his hands. "She's beautiful, Lu. You did good."

"Mic . . ." I was so tired, and each breath took exquisite effort. "I love you," I creaked. "I love you so much."

"I love you, baby," he said, his voice catching.

As I looked at him, I knew I'd love him forever. With that realization, I suddenly understood what my mother had meant when she told me there was nothing to be afraid of. I struggled to breathe. "Mickey . . . don't be afraid."

"Hey. None of that kind of talk," he said, trying to sound like he was in charge.

I looked at him for a long moment. His thick, wonderful hair was now more than half silver and badly needed to be cut. I tried to reach up and run my hand over it, but I didn't have the strength. He caught my palm and kissed it.

"Do you hurt, Lu? What do you need, baby?"

What did I need? What was there left to need at this moment except more of what I could not have? I couldn't answer him. I just looked into his sad eyes, burned them into my brain so I would never forget. Then I asked my precious husband to get me some ice.

"Ice? Sure, baby. And I'll tell the nurse you're awake." He kissed my forehead, my parched mouth, loomed above me with raw need in his wet eyes. "I'll be right back." Then he walked out and I was alone.

With a single labored breath, I let myself go and reached for the hand that beckoned me. As I did, the beautiful, ghostly apparition became solid and dimensional, and I wept with recognition. "It's *you*."

"Yes, my darling. It's me."

thirty-two

I knew before I walked in with the ice that she was gone. My breath caught in my throat, in my heart, as I stared in at my beautiful wife, who for all the world looked like she was merely sleeping. I watched her, but could not walk into that room. Dimly lit. Warm. Two plants and unopened cards sitting on the bedside table, and a water pitcher, which, had I bothered to notice before, would probably be filled with ice. A special bed for the ill, elevated to partial sitting. And quiet. So god-awful quiet. It all looked so foreign to me.

I breathed and told myself Lucy was just sleeping, her dark hair spilling over the pillow. I repeated it until I believed it. She was just resting until I came back with her ice. I would sit down and she would open her eyes. I would lift spoonfuls into her dry mouth and she would smile as she began to feel better. The baby was here and she would be so happy about that. She'd made it. Now she could start on all the life-saving drugs she had refused until this very day when the baby had come. It was all right, I told myself. But another self shook his head in pity at the lies I was telling as I walked ever so slowly to the bed.

"Lu? Baby? Lucy?" I tried to keep from crying, I needed to be strong for her. I did not want her to catch me bawling. Not when she'd just gotten through the hardest day of her life. But the tears fell despite my reasoning. I took her hand and ran my thumb over her warm knuckles. No more strain was in her face, every muscle was relaxed, the crimp in her brow that had broadcast her pain had melted away. I begged her to breathe and watched her still chest ignore my prayer.

"Oh, Lord. Please, no." I fell into the chair, into the skin of the man who knew she was gone. Knew it and yet could not imagine it. "Lucy . . ."

I was not ready. Not today. Today I had watched her give birth to a daughter without recognizing the pain of it, or the joy of it, or the accomplishment of it. But I never imagined she would actually leave, that the life in her would truly evaporate.

I could not take my eyes off her, this woman who held my life in her smile, in her touch. I could not take my eyes off her. Not when Ron put his arm around me. Not when Lily and Priscilla and gradually everyone else crowded around to cry with me. I could not pull my eyes from her because if I did, I was sure she would be gone when I looked back.

When that finally did happen, I thought my heart would stop. Someone had called the Withers' Funeral Home, and Earl and Chad showed up in their official capacity to take my wife away. I could not let go of her hand. Chad had to untangle my fingers from hers, but he did it with such kindness. They worked in silence, wrapping my Lucy in a sheet, gently, carefully tucking it in around her feet. They lifted her onto their gurney, and Earl patted my wet face before he wheeled her out of the room. As he rounded the corner with my wife, I started to crumble from within. It was excruciating. I looked back at her empty bed and felt my knees buckle, but Harry caught me, and like a child I wrapped my arms around his neck and sobbed. Jan ran her hand through my hair and through her own tears said, "C'mon, sweetie. Let us take you home."

I remember them taking hold of me; each of them had an arm and I was a prop carried between the two of them. For a moment it was surreal, otherworldly, much like psychosis, though I was painfully sane and present. My wife was dead, and I could not make it real. Harry kept saying things like "You're stronger than you think you are, Mic. You can do this, we're right here with you." And Jan tried to keep control of her tears, but they were all clogged up in her throat as she muttered over and over, "Oh, that sweet girl, that sweet girl. She loved you so much, Mickey."

At the main lobby, I disengaged from them and thanked them for loving me. They were my parents in every sense of the word, but I needed to be away from them, from their sadness, because I didn't have room for any more than my own. "I'll be fine," I lied. "I'm going to drive up to Partners, tell Jared. And I need to call my dad." I answered their collective concern for me with a reassuring nod that could have won me an award for acting.

"You'll call us?" they said.

"I will," I promised. Then they went one way and I went the other. I did go to Partners. And Jared, my good friend, cried when I told him. "You take as long as you need," he said. "Whatever you need, man. When's the funeral?"

"I don't know. I'll find out and call you."

"We'll all be there, Mic. We'll close up in Lucy's honor."

I drove home after that, but as I approached my house, my chest tightened and I knew I couldn't walk in there alone. So I drove to the pier and stared out at the black Connecticut River. It was ten thirty in New Orleans, and there was a good chance my dad was in bed. I dialed his number, thinking with any luck he wouldn't answer. When his machine picked up, I said, "Hey, Dad, it's me. I have some bad news, and I'm sorry to leave it in a message." My voice broke and it was a minute before I could finish. "It happened . . . tonight, Dad. Lucy's gone and I . . . I have a daughter." I'd still have to tell him that she was mostly Ron and Lily's, but I didn't have the energy to go into it now. Instead, I asked him to call David if he got the chance because I didn't have my brother's number.

I don't know what time it was, or how long I'd sat in my car, before I pushed the door open to find the pier blanketed in deep, soft, powdery snow. I trudged through it to the slip where our sailboat was marooned for the season. It was up on blocks and I had to use a trash can to get up there. The deck was slippery where I tore the tarp and exposed it to the weather, and I had to crawl to the galley door. I was surprised I could find the combination of the padlock in my addled brain, but I did. I pulled the door open, then shut it behind me as I slid down the stairs like a drunk. For a long time, I sat in the dark on the last step, then I settled myself on the bed. I guess I slept, but if I did, it was rest in name only.

It could have been an hour or a day later when Ron found me, but when he did, the horror in his eyes made me wonder if I had grown another head. He apologized all over himself as he drove me to his house. He made me eat oatmeal, actually fed it to me, I think. Then he got me in the shower and dressed me in my dark suit, literally moving my arms and legs for me because they refused to function. Then he drove me to Lucy's viewing. I felt every eye on me when we walked in, and when I saw my wife lying in her casket, a man inside me screamed and wept and beat at the walls of my chest. But the walls were thick and the man couldn't break through—not his voice, not his tears.

I was staring at her, my beautiful Lucy, willing her to wake up and be with me, but Lucy just slept, and I just watched her. I could have watched her for the rest of my life, but Earl said he had to close the casket, and his words meant nothing to me, until he did it. Then the man inside escaped.

The only thing I know for sure about Lucy's funeral is that I made a lot of noise and had to miss it. Ron missed it as well, taking care of me. Gleason missed it, and Harry missed it. It was an awful day for a funeral anyway. Bitter winds blew off the river and blinding snow was swirling everywhere. It was as though the day was repelling the terrible occasion.

They admitted me to the hospital. They had no choice. I was crazy with grief, combative and noisy. I could have hurt someone lashing out the way I was at these, the most important men in my life. Thank God I didn't, but it took Gleason's twisting my arm to prevent it. He's strong for an old guy.

When I finally stabilized, I was in the psychiatric lockdown and had had a few shots of Haldol. I was groggy, but not groggy enough to keep it all from rushing back. Lucy was gone. I had no idea how long I'd languished in that cave of a room. I only knew that Lucy was dead, and the weight of that knowledge immobilized me. Gleason came by

but we didn't talk. I'd grown docile under the influence of my medica-
tion, so after he left, two burly psych techs walked me down the hall
to a regular room. Here I sleep, or at least I lie in this bed and face
the wall. Ron has come by several times, but I don't honestly know if
it's been several days or several times in one day. Time means noth-
ing here, and the darkness of the thick winter sky beyond my window
seems never to change.

I've only made one request to the nursing staff, and that is not to
allow anyone to visit me. Peony said she'd do it but would not include
my immediate family in the mandate. So Ron comes by, and Lily, and
strangely, Priscilla. Lily cries when she's here. Sometimes I pretend
I'm asleep just so she'll leave me alone. She says she wants to name the
baby but doesn't want to do it without my input. I'm ashamed to say
I couldn't care less.

Lily came earlier tonight and I kept my eyes shut when she begged
me again to come see the baby, but she wasn't fooled. Despite the tears
in her voice, she just kept yammering at me about names, about the
nice doctor taking care of the baby, about her still not breathing on
her own. But Lily's best efforts to distract my grief failed, mostly be-
cause she was swollen with her own. I could hear it in her voice. If I
opened my eyes, I would see it in her face. I wanted her to go away.
Finally, I felt her touch my shoulder.

"I know you can hear me, Mickey. I'm leaving you something to
look at. Jan made it for Lucy." Her voice broke then, and I felt my own
sob threatening, but I didn't move. "Lucy found this fairy tale my dad
wrote about us when we were little, and Jan added her amazing art,
and I thought you'd like to see it. I don't know how she did it, but it's
exactly how we looked when we were little. Anyway . . ." She kissed
me and watched me for a minute. Then she walked out.

It must have been late because it was quiet. Up the hall, I heard
Lily say good-bye to the nurse, then the magnetic door slammed shut.
I lay there and let the noiseless night swallow me, then I slept until
my bladder woke me. I pulled myself up, turned on the bedside lamp,
and squinted my way to the bathroom. Honest horror shone back at

me in the mirror. I looked awful. It was almost as if Lucy had been embedded in my features, and now that she had gone, she'd left them heavy and sagging and wholly ruined. I hardly knew myself. Back in my room I sat down and hung my head. I did not know how to survive this.

The something Lily left was a book, and it was sitting on the bed-side table. It looked like a child's story, colorful and oversized. I picked it up with a shaking hand. The cover was a vivid painting of three little princesses, two blondes flanking a little, brown-haired Lucy. Each wore a crown in her tangled curls, and each was easily identifiable as a Houston daughter. The sob I'd been able to swallow when Lily was here now burst out of me, and my heart hurt to see the unspoiled joy on their faces, the mischief Jan had captured in their wide, green eyes. I opened the book to find an inscription on the inside cover:

Sweet Lily,

Lucy found this story written by your dad and asked me to illus-trate it. She wanted to surprise you, and I worked hard to do this last favor for her, but I didn't quite make it before she died. Now I realize it was never for Lucy, but for you and Priss. A small comfort she could leave behind. A remarkable message from your father, who loved you all so much.

I turned the pages, and by the soft light at my bedside I lost myself in the world of a man who adored his daughters. The words blurred beneath my tears as this mere man dressed up like a king flawlessly described his children. I kept turning back to a page that depicted a sleeping Lucy sucking her thumb. The rendition of my wife and her guardian angel sister being watched over by their worried father nearly stopped my heart. I could feel how much this man, a man I'd never met, loved his daughters. How anxious he was for them. How he would give anything to protect them. I could not imagine being loved like that as a child. I turned to the last page, where an angel was holding a tear that had fallen from the king's eye. The sight of her on *the page was surprising; she was just a baby, conjured by a prayer. The king implored her to carry his love to the princesses:* Oh, angel, I would that you bless and keep my daughters. Fill them with my love and guard them in my absence. Can you do this for me? *In the warm, institutional silence of my hospital room, that angel's voice lifted from the page:* It will be my honor. *As she made her vow to the king, I could almost hear it. Her name was Abigail.*

Abigail: keeper of the love.

It was nearly four thirty in the morning when I walked down the hall to the community phone. When Lily answered, sounding groggy but alarmed, I simply said, "Abigail. I want to name her Abigail."

thirty-three

I was sitting at the foot of my bed staring out the window when Lily walked in.

"You're awake," she said softly, then she kind of gasped. "Mickey, you're so thin."

I pulled my robe around me to hide that I hadn't been eating. "Hi, Lil."

She pulled a chair over in front of me and sat down. "How you doin', sweetie?"

My eyes filled with tears and I reached over and took her hand. There were no words, so we sat there for a few quiet minutes united in our grief.

Finally she spoke. "Mickey, I don't know how to do this."

"Me neither, Lil."

"I'm worried about you. What can I do?"

"Lily, your heart is broken, same as mine."

"That's true, Mic. But I'm not hiding." Her voice broke then and I saw how hard she was fighting back tears. "We all lost Lucy," she rasped. "You can't stay here in this room forever. You have a daughter."

I shut my eyes.

"Mickey. Come with me to the nursery. You haven't even seen her."

"I can't." I let go of her hand and turned back to the window. Lily tried a little longer to talk me into going with her, but after a while, she gave up and walked out. I was hiding. I knew it, but I didn't know how to do anything else. Gleason had asked me earlier this morning to describe what I was feeling. I had no language besides heaviness—a leaden sorrow that made movement impossible. Lucy was gone, and I did not know how to move my feet without her.

I wanted to be dead, but I didn't even have the strength to pull that off. I closed my eyes and pushed it all away.

I woke to the insistent prodding of bony fingers and the overwhelming scent of Chanel No. 5—Priscilla. The gentle sister had failed to rouse me, so it was time to bring out the big guns. I rolled over and faced the wall, but still she poked. "I'm not leaving until you get up, Mickey." Her tone was flat, without life, heartbreakingly sad. I kept myself shut off from her for as long as I could, but Priscilla, too, was stubborn. Finally, I pushed myself upright and leaned against the wall. I must have had a scowl on my grizzled, unshaven face because Lucy's sister slapped me—slapped me hard across the cheek. "Don't you dare look at me like that."

I would have slapped her back, flattened her, if I could have lifted my arm. "Priscilla, go away."

"I'm not leaving. And I have nowhere else to be, so I have all day to give you hell."

I expected rage to wind itself through me, but even that took too much to muster. "What do you want?"

"I want you to get your shoes on and walk up to the nursery with me."

"No."

"Yes."

"Go to hell, Priscilla."

"Maybe later. Right now we're going up to see your daughter."

Priscilla sat down on the bed and leaned her face into mine so close we were almost kissing. "Now you listen to me! You don't get

346   Ka Hancock

to play the crazy card, Mickey. Not now. Not when the rest of us don't have that luxury!" Through clenched teeth she said, "I don't care about your mental health, or even your grief. We all lost Lucy. We all have to deal with it. Even you! Now get up!"

She pulled on my arm and I surprised myself by not fighting her. Instead, I sat up, dizzy with the ruin that was my life. I dropped my head into my hands. The raw and throbbing sensation of loss was sitting squarely on my chest, making it hard to breathe. Truth be told, I envied Priscilla's passion, her energy, her ability to channel everything into anger.

"Get up," she said again.

I looked up at her and we stared at each other for a long time—me drowning in pathos, and her glowering with indignation.

"I can't move, Priscilla."

"Pretend the building is on fire. Get up."

"A fire would be an answer to my prayers."

"Oh, cry me a river, Mickey."

She was goading me, and all I could do was sit there and look pathetic.

"Stop it. Stop it right now, Mickey. Quit being pitiful." Then quieter and with a warble in her voice, she said, "Give someone else a turn."

I saw it then, pain just like mine, deep and bottomless, only hers was hanging out and mine was trapped inside. Priscilla realized that I'd seen through her smoke screen and dropped her bitchy pretense with a heavy sigh. She slumped down next to me on the bed and stared at the wall. I reached for her hand.

"I'm so mean, and I'm so damn tired of being mean," she whimpered.

"You are mean."

Priscilla started to cry, quiet tears she did nothing to hide as she stared at the wall. I watched her for a minute, then I stared at the wall, too.

Priscilla did not leave for a long time, and though I would never tell her, I was glad she stayed as long as she did. It was gentle on my pain to be with someone who loved Lucy the way I did. Suddenly I was so hungry for company that even Priscilla was a blessing.

I sat on the edge of my bed for a long time after she'd gone, until the hospital sounds started to evaporate and the lights were dimmed. I sat there while the unit outside my door grew silent, all the patients having been medicated and sent to bed. Peony poked her head in to check on me. The white of her uniform was neon against the black licorice of her skin.

"How you doin', Michael?"

I didn't answer.

"I got your p.m. meds here, and a sleeping pill."

"Can I take them later?"

"I guess you could. I'll come back in an hour."

I nodded at her. Peony had not always been as amenable as she was right now. She was usually a barking drill sergeant who could tackle you with one hand tied behind her back. But she'd been completely disarmed by the death of my wife, and neither of us knew how to be with the other. She walked away, and again the night settled on me like a weight. I pulled myself up to standing with great effort, my body a sack of unwieldy cement. I stood there for a minute because I was a little dizzy, probably from my medication, but maybe because I had not eaten anything all day. To get the nurses off my back, I flushed the contents of my tray and hid the apples and oranges that came with every meal in my bottom drawer. I hadn't eaten for days.

In the bathroom, I steadied myself against the sink and took some deep breaths, then I brushed my teeth and combed my hair. In the mirror I looked beaten, my eyes sunk deep in their sockets. I needed a shave in the worst way, but I was not allowed my razor, and what was left of my dignity would not permit being babysat as I groomed. I splashed water over my face and felt a little better. Then I walked out of my room.

At the nurses' station, I surprised the oncoming shift, and Peony eyed me with concern as her report to the night charge-nurse hung in the air. "You okay, Michael?"

"I wonder if I could take a walk."

"It's late. Cafeteria's closed, except for vending machines."

"I know."

"Let's just take a look at Dr. Webb's note. I think you might be on unit restriction." Peony flipped through my chart and nodded confirmation at me. "Sorry, Michael, maybe tomorrow."

"Can I use this phone?" I said, picking it up and keying the numbers I knew by heart.

"It's late. If you wake him, it'll be your hide."

I ignored her as Gleason said hello. "Can I go for a walk if I promise not to kill myself?"

"We're civilized people, Mickey, we greet each other before we make a request."

"Hello, Gleason. Can I go for a walk?"

"Do I need to worry about where you're going?"

"No. I'm okay."

"You headed to the fifth floor?"

"Maybe."

"Call me when you get back. Tell me how it went. And let me talk to Peony."

"Thanks." I placed the phone in the nurse's ready hand.

Peony buzzed me out of the security door and I headed for the elevator. I meant it when I told Gleason I didn't know if I was going to the fifth floor. But that's where I headed. I don't know why I was so scared, but there it was like a vise around my chest. I got off the elevator but once out, I did not move. The hall was dim and the sign in front of me said NEWBORN ICU and pointed left. I turned left. The shades on the windows of the nursery were drawn, but I didn't turn back. It was quiet except for two women in scrubs discussing something at the nurses' station. They paid me no mind. I listened for a baby crying, but I didn't hear anything. I thought maybe Lily was behind that shade, sitting beside my daughter, but I didn't have the nerve to find out. I just stood there, my broken heart pounding.

I don't know how long I stood there before a doctor, or maybe a nurse, in green scrubs came out of the door marked NBICU. She looked at me as though she knew who I was and walked over to me. "Would you like to come in, Mr. Chandler?"

Her invitation caused a sudden lump to form in my throat and tears to fill my eyes, and all I could do was shake my head. I stepped away from her like a child refusing a gift just to be obstinate. She laced her hands together.

"I'm Dr. Sweeny. We met last week."

The name was familiar but the face sparked no recognition.

"I just finished spending some time with your daughter. You sure you don't want to come in and sit with her?"

"I don't think so," I muttered.

"Well, maybe later then. Is there anything you'd like to know?"

"How is she?"

"She's still struggling to breathe, and we're watching her very closely. That's the big issue with preemies. They're lazy, but she's a bit better than she was yesterday. Would you like me to pull the blind so you can see her?"

I stared blankly at her, but nodded my tacit appreciation.

"I'll be right back," she said, disappearing into the intensive care nursery. In a moment the shade was lifted and a bright and busy room shone through the glass. Ellen Sweeny walked to a bassinet and adjusted a minuscule IV bag. She then moved a monitor just slightly to improve my view. The tiny baby was lying in a clear container that reminded me of an acrylic coffin. I drew back and stared at my daughter. She had a lot of black hair from what I could see, and so many wires were attached to her chest that she looked like a discarded marionette. She was the littlest human being I'd ever seen. Scarily small—certainly too small to live—yet her heartbeat was captured on a screen looming above her bed. It was strong and steady, not at all like mine.

I'd seen her only once, and that was just before her mother died, when I was rushing back to Lucy's bedside. Then, this little creature looked like the teeny product of the two people who'd made her. Now, she looked like so much more. Like all that was left of all that mattered in the world. I didn't know what was happening to me as I stood there, unexpectedly grateful and overwhelmed. She was six days old. Her mother had been dead the entirety of her life. I'd had terrible dreams about loathing this infant and had for weeks feared that these were my true feelings. I'd screamed at Lucy for insisting the baby be spared when I only wanted her. I had begged her to have the abortion, and now I hung my head in shame and wept.

I was so lost in my despair that I did not see Ellen Sweeny come out of the nursery—wasn't aware of her presence until she touched me softly on the arm.

"How can I help you, Mr. Chandler?" she asked in the kindest voice.

For a moment I sobbed, big, heaving sobs that took some effort to compose. But when I got control of my emotions, I asked her if I could go in and meet my daughter.

After Dr. Sweeny had shown me where to gown up and wash my hands, she pulled a chair close to the warming bassinet where my baby lay. I peered down at her in sheer wonder. Who could imagine a body this small, with bones and fingernails and eyelashes this minute? She looked so fragile, as though to stroke her would tear away her skin. As if reading my thoughts, Dr. Sweeny told me I could, in fact, touch my baby. Actually, she encouraged me. "And while you're at it, give her a little talking-to." She smiled and said, "Don't be afraid of her. She knows who you are."

I looked up at this young woman, this insanely young doctor who'd been so kind to me. "She knows me?"

"Absolutely. It's remarkable, but it's true. Even with so many loved ones praying over them, cheering on their tiny accomplishments, they know their parents from the rest of the crowd. It's innate, I guess." Ellen Sweeny smiled as she walked away, leaving me alone with my daughter. The pink card taped to the head of her bed said, CHANDLER, GIRL. BORN AT 2:26 PM, 11/19, APPROXIMATELY 34 WEEKS. WEIGHT—3 POUNDS 9 OUNCES. A red mark was crossed through GIRL, and in its place was written ABIGAIL.

Abigail. Abby. I could not take my eyes off her, and it boggled my mind that six days ago she'd been inside my Lucy. Aside from her size, she was perfect. I leaned in to inspect the features of her face. A miniature of her mother's upturned nose, long eyelashes the same dark color as her hair. The tiniest mouth. Seemingly endless tears blurred the scene before me and I let them fall, unashamed. Lucy would have loved her so much. For as long as I'd known my wife, she had wanted to be a mom. For a while, in the beginning, a family had been the plan. But then Lucy got sick, and I kept getting sick, so we'd agreed that babies would not fit into our equation. But that never took away the want.

That want had only intensified from the moment she knew about this little one. Forget the plan, forget the reasons we were never going to be parents. God was giving us a baby, who were we to argue? Until later, of course, when God abandoned us. I nearly doubled over with the pain of it. But when I dried my eyes, again my baby took away my breath. I watched her sleep, her thin, little chest quivering as she breathed, or tried to. I wanted to touch her, but I was afraid. Twice my hand hovered over her, but I withdrew it, too anxious, too fearful. But then the unthinkable happened and she became very still. I watched in horror as her chest did not rise. At the same instant, the monitor screeched. Without thinking, I reached in and laid my hand on that fragile, little chest. She startled. Instantly a nurse and Dr. Sweeny were at her side, but the monitor had resumed its tracking.

"What did I tell you?" Ellen Sweeny said. "She's lazy. Breathing is hard and she doesn't know she can't just take a break." She smiled at me. "You're a natural."

"What?"

"That's just what we do," the nurse said, typing out a notation on the computer. "Just reach in and shake her a little, kick-start her motor."

I sighed, certain my thudding heart could be seen through my shirt. My hands were now clenched in my lap, as if they had done a bad thing. I couldn't quite believe that instinct—a father's instinct—had led me to respond in exactly the right way.

"You did good, Dad," the nurse said as she walked away.

Dr. Sweeny patted my shoulder. "We're right over there if you need us."

"Thanks," I said, looking back at my baby. I couldn't believe she had actually responded to my touch. My gaze floated between the monitor that kept track of her oxygen—not unlike the one that had been in her mother's room—and her perfect face. I stroked her so-soft cheek with the back of my finger and let it travel down the twig of her outstretched arm to a hand that was no bigger than the button on my suit coat.

I bent near her. "So, Abby, you need a talking-to, huh? You think you don't have to work, huh? Well, little one, you better breathe be-cause you're staying right here with me. No more straddling the space between me and mom." I heard these words roll out of my mouth in a voice I hardly recognized as my own, and I could not believe the feelings that were swimming through me. This was my daughter, and the only thing that kept her in this world was vigilant overseers who made sure she inhaled. The instant I absorbed that fact, she became utterly essential to me, precious beyond all imagining. If I ever feared I would reject this baby, I had been wrong. My nightmare of not being able to love her vanished in the time it took for my heart to beat one time. But a new sadness quickly filled its place. This premature baby, this born-too-early life, was completely dependent. Because I was ago-nizingly the most unreliable human being God ever created, Ron and

Lily would be her parents. The thought stabbed me. But this was the plan. The decision was made. I would not be Abby's father, I did not have the requisite capabilities. And Lucy knew it. I'd been telling her as much for weeks. But then why this terrible pain?

"Lucy," I whispered, "I need you. You can't leave me here alone."

From somewhere deep in my broken heart, I heard Lucy's voice, clear and familiar, strong and substantial. "You are not alone, my darling."

At that moment, I felt a tiny hand wrap itself around the tip of my finger, and my heart stopped. Three pounds of tenuous life clinging to the likes of me. I was a goner from that moment on, and nothing, not even the prospect of losing my wife, had ever frightened me more.

It's hard to explain what happened to me after that first night with my daughter. I walked away adoring her, but I knew I didn't deserve her. To imagine an attachment to Abigail was a fantasy. Nothing had changed. I would live in the house on Chestnut where she could visit but not live. Ron would be her father because he was better qualified to take care of her. These thoughts made me cave in on myself. For days, I refused to see anyone—anyone but the baby. But the night I had found her alone was a fluke—every time since, Lily had been with her, and I could not bring myself to go in. I love Lily, but I just could not bear to see her with my daughter. Acceptance would come with time, but for now I needed space. Gleason shook his head and said things like "You get what you settle for, Michael."

I told him I would do what I had done my whole life. I would try like hell to stay on my meds. I would not hide in denial when I was off base. I would try even harder for my daughter, but the truth was I had always tried hard for her mother because I wanted to be my best self for her. Lucy had been my safety net whenever I tripped, and under no circumstances could I ask that of my daughter. So Lily and Ron would be Abby's parents. That is what I could do for her. That is how much I loved her.

After days of inner turmoil, the rational part of me acquiesced and fell into a deeper despair. Lucy was gone; the baby was out of my reach. I went to bed and stayed there. I was as depressed as I had ever been. I wanted to die, but I would not kill myself because my daughter would know what I'd done, and that shamed me into clinging to life.

When medication failed to lift me, Gleason sent me to a support group sponsored by the hospital. He made my attendance a condition of being able to walk to the nursery. So, because the privilege of seeing my daughter was all that got me through the day, I dragged myself out of bed and went. I pulled up a chair in the circle of sad people all dealing with their own losses, hung my head, and refused to participate. But I couldn't help but hear someone smarter than me describe exactly what I was feeling. She had lost her two children in a boating accident, and you could hear her soul bleeding. She said the most profound thing: that her grief was bottomless and that every minute of every day she was falling deeper and deeper into her loss.

That was exactly how I felt. I lifted my head and watched her. She was maybe Lucy's age, but the grief had ravaged her. She wore her pain so deep it distorted the very shape of her muscles. Her haunted look was keenly familiar to me; I had seen it in the mirror. When the meeting concluded, I walked over to her and she greeted me like the kindred spirit I was. I had no words, and neither did she, but she held her arms out to me anyway and for a few minutes we wept each other's tears.

I took her analogy to Gleason the next day, having been unable to get it out of my mind. "There is nothing for me to land on," I said. "Just endless sadness. I hear Lucy's voice in my mind, and I fall. I remember a particular time that she touched me, or laughed at me, or pulled a face, and I'm falling further. It's true; it's bottomless."

Gleason shook his head, his eyes filled with compassion. "Mickey, my friend. It feels that way now because you're in pain. But life will go on around you, and without you even realizing it, a floor will have formed, a floor where your grief can finally land. It will get easier, I promise you. And just as Lucy planned, you have your daughter to see you through until that happens."

"I don't have my daughter, Gleason. Ron and Lily have my daughter."

"Because you don't want to be her father."

"Because I have no right to be her father! Not when they're healthy, stable, good, kind, wonderful people. They have adopted her. End of story. It's what Lucy wanted."

Gleason leaned back and tapped a pencil lightly on his chin. "Michael, you know Lucy only wanted that by default. You worked so hard to convince her of your inabilities that she had no choice. But that's not what she wanted. Lucy gave her life to that baby upstairs so she could leave her in your hands. She left you a daughter to give you a reason to get up and conquer the day. That's what children do for us."

"I don't know what she was thinking, but she was wrong," I groused.

"Was she, Michael?" Gleason's tone changed enough that I wondered what I'd missed. "What else was she wrong about?" he prodded.

"What?"

He stared hard at me. "I just can't think of another time that Lucy was actually wrong about something this big. Was she wrong to love you? Was she wrong to marry you? I shudder to think, my friend, of who you would be today if you had not met that girl. Lucy loved you by choice. She became your wife because she could not find a reason not to. She stayed with you because she couldn't imagine a finer man. This was the life she chose, and in my opinion, if you were good enough for that amazing woman, you're good enough for her daughter."

"But I'm a mess!" I rasped over the stone in my throat. "Look at me."

Gleason pulled his chair close to mine. "Yes, you're flawed, Mic, but so is every parent on the planet. You know your disorder inside out. You know exactly what it takes to stay even. You know all the signs of an episode, and what to do about them."

"So?"

Gleason sighed. "So settle down, Mickey. I don't particularly care where your daughter lives. But I do care that she knows you're her father, not some visitor who can only show up if all the stars are aligned."

thirty-four

I thought about what Gleason had said, but I didn't buy it. Still, Abby was my refuge. As heavy and unwieldy as my pain was, she was my anesthetic. I couldn't sit with her without thinking of her mother. But my baby daughter made it all manageable somehow, gave me respite for a few minutes. I relished the few times I found her unattended. I didn't like hiding from Lily, but I didn't like sharing Abby more. So I usually waited until after Lily had gone home. But then Lily started staying into the night, and I found I couldn't avoid her.

I had not told my sister-in-law about my conversation with Gleason. There was no point. Nothing had changed. The adoption was in place, and there was not a doubt in my mind that it was right. Lily had slipped into motherhood with surprising ease. She worried like a mom and crooned like a mom and hovered like a mom. It was hard to watch. Ron wasn't quite so in my face with his adoration of Abby, and I think it was because he saw something in me—an extra ache I'd been unsuccessful at hiding beneath my grief and depression. I'd catch him eyeing me as I watched Lily and wonder if I was being obvious.

It happened one night as I sat with them in the Newborn Step-Down—a sort of relaxed intensive care for babies no longer clinging to life, but who still needed close monitoring. When I got there, Abby was alone, but I'd barely sat down before Ron and Lily showed up. I could see Lily felt the same way I did—a little jealous of her private time with the baby. But her smile didn't let on that she was bothered by my presence, nor did the little sideways hug she gave me. As I watched her, I could see the purity of her love for Abby and I could not begrudge her; I wouldn't. I stood up. "It's time for my medication, so I'll be shoving off."

"You sure? You haven't been here that long."

"I'll come back later." I leaned over to brush my lips against Abby's soft forehead. Her eyes were open and I swear she was looking right at me—right into my wreckage. I hung there a beat longer, long enough that Lily got concerned.

"You okay, Mic?"

"Yeah. Just something Dr. Sweeny told me."

"What?"

"She just said that Abby knows who I am—that I'm her father—and it made me feel good." I turned then to find a look of pained surprise on Lily's face, and because I'm an idiot and didn't have a clue what to do to fix the situation, I just stared at her discomfort for a second and shrugged. "I'll catch you guys later."

"See you, buddy," Ron said with no indication that he'd caught any of Lily's reaction. Lily smiled a pretend smile that didn't linger as she dropped her gaze to Abby, who had fallen back asleep.

"Hey, Mic," Ron called as I turned to leave. "We've been talking and we have a proposition for you."

I paused.

"We want you to plan on coming home with us when you're discharged. I mean, it just makes sense, you know. Until you're ready to go home."

"Really?"

"Absolutely," Ron insisted. "It's the holidays. Let's just get through them, and then when you feel ready, we'll just help you ease into it."

I walked back over to shake his hand, which he ignored, opting instead for a big hug. His generosity humbled me, and Lily had tears in her eyes as she nodded her agreement.

"Really, Lil?"

"Definitely. We're your family. We want you with us."

"I don't know what to say. I may take you up on it," I said, knowing there was no question. Of course I would go. That's where my daughter would be.

Abby was in the hospital three weeks. I was there for twenty-nine days. Not a record by any means, but plenty long. As was the plan, I went home with Ron and Lily. However, what seemed like a good idea at the time turned out to be a mistake. Within a few days, I felt like an intruder in their home. They hadn't done a single thing to make me feel unwelcome, far from it. I just felt apart, somehow—as if my face were pressed up against the window of their new life, their new family. It was completely obvious how much they adored Abby, who was thriving under the glow of their dauntless attention. Lily was as kind to me as she had always been, Ron more so. And because of their grace, it was hard to define what was happening. But something was going on, something just beneath the surface of all our good manners.

I felt it especially with Lily. She wasn't exactly selfish with Abby, but it was almost as if I had to pry the baby out of her arms if I needed a fix. She was always hovering nearby, waiting for me to drop Abby on her head. But that was probably my fault, because at the hospital Lily never saw that I knew exactly what a football hold was, or how to wrap a tiny baby like a mummy so she thought she was still in the womb. I'd given Lily no choice but to assume that I didn't know what I was doing. And frankly, the first time Abby quieted for me, Lily seemed genuinely shocked and a little hurt.

One night when the baby was particularly fussy and had been all afternoon, Lily was at her wit's end but would not admit it. She'd had a deep crease between her eyes for hours, and she'd snapped at Ron when he tried to help, so at first I just kept my distance. But as Abby got more upset and Lily got more tense, I grew increasingly antsy to hold my daughter. You wouldn't think a tiny pair of lungs could push everyone over the edge, but they can, and they were. So, without thinking, I stood up from the kitchen table and lifted our crying baby out of Lily's arms, folding her against my chest. Then I walked up to the nursery, crooning in her ear.

As so often happened when I held her, the world shrunk to just me and my daughter. It may have been my voice or my heartbeat in her ear, but she calmed down almost instantly, and I held her a little closer and kissed her head. I sat down in the antique rocker Lily had Ron bring home from Ghosts and just rocked her until she fell asleep. In the dim light that illuminated the rosy walls of the nursery, I just drank her in, this little miniature of Lucy.

I don't know how long I sat there, but when I glanced up, Lily and Ron were standing in the doorway. An unreadable expression was on Lily's face, and I was suddenly self-conscious. Lily didn't say anything to me, she just tried to smile past the pain in her eyes. When she realized she couldn't hide her feelings, she gave up and walked away, leaving Ron to apologize for her.

"She's just tired," he said, walking into the room.

"I know."

"Boy, Mic. You've really got the touch. She's sound asleep."

"Yeah, well, that'll only last until I put her down."

Ron chuckled.

I stared at Abby for a few minutes, not sure what else to say.

"You know, Lily will be all right," Ron said, sounding incredibly tired.

I looked up at him. "If you say so. But I'm sorry, Ron."

"What for?"

"Everything. I need to go home so you guys can get on with your lives."

"You'll stay until you're ready, however long that takes."

I shook my head. "Ron, you know I'm never going to be ready to walk into that house by myself." I looked down at my baby. "So I think I'll head out this weekend. Saturday."

Ron kind of coughed out a laugh as if I were fooling around. But I wasn't.

"That's Christmas Eve," he said. "You can't do that."

"Yeah, I can. I won't lie, it will be hard, but I've got to do it."

"Why? Why does it need to be Christmas Eve?"

"Because Lucy loved Christmas Eve. Really loved it," I said as the memories flooded back. "I think that's the first time I met everyone. We were just starting to get serious, and she invited me to her Christmas Eve party. That's when I fell in love with her world. I thought it was so cool that her mom started that tradition, way back when they were all kids. Having the whole neighborhood over to fill up that little house. I think Lu loved it more than Christmas Day."

Ron nodded. "Yeah, it was always a big shindig."

"So I figure if I can go home then, walk through that door on that night, it will never be that hard again. But I gotta tell you"—I stared down at Abby—"I can hardly imagine leaving her. In my wildest dreams, Ron, I never thought I'd feel this way. I just didn't see it coming." The nothing weight of Abby's tiny body in my arms made my chest throb. "But Lucy did," I rasped. "She knew me so well."

Ron was quiet, and when I looked up at him, he was staring at me. "Mic, are you sure you're okay . . . with the way things are?"

Ron knew my answer; it was mirrored in the sad intelligence of his eyes. "Of course. It's the only way. You and Lil are wonderful. Abby will always be safe with you."

Ron's look was sad and insistent. "She would be safe with you, too, Mickey. You've never hurt anyone in your life. You've got to cut yourself a little slack."

I slid my finger beneath Abby's tiny hand until her fingers were resting in a loose grip. "Well, I would never hurt her on purpose, that's for sure."

"Mickey, I know what it feels like to lose a baby, to have one and then lose him. It's hell. It's hard to believe you'll ever survive."

I looked up at my quiet friend standing there in a T-shirt and flannel pants, ready for bed. He was completely vulnerable. "But you did survive? Right?"

"I guess that's what we did. But I don't know if it's really survival *if you still think about him, imagining what he would look like now, now that he's thirteen. Imagining when the phone rings that it might be him, all grown-up, asking if I'm Ronald Jerome Bates, and did I remember that for a while I used to have a baby boy." Ron shrugged and looked at the floor. "He's out there, Mic, and I always wonder if I've passed him on the sidewalk or stood in line next to him. It never goes away."*

I looked at Ron, amazed that he had walked around every day with this pain that he had never talked about.

"I'd just never wish that on anybody, Mic. Least of all you."

Later that night, I heard Lily crying. The walls are thin in their house, and though I could not decipher the words, the emotion was undeniable. I had not left the nursery. When Ron said good night, I told him I was right behind him, but I hadn't left, and now I felt as if I could not move. They weren't arguing. There was no shouting, just the soft weeping of a woman and a man doing his best to comfort her. Abby stretched in my arms and was soon whimpering. I shifted her to my shoulder and rubbed her back, which did nothing but make her mad. I lay her on the changing table and fished around for a diaper, but that wasn't it either. Annoyed whimpers soon turned to angry, red-faced howls. I was just about to head downstairs to mix the formula when Lily walked in with a bottle. Her eyes were red and puffy, but she smiled anyway. "It's like she's on a timer," she said. "You could set your watch by her."

"Sorry we woke you. I'm a little slow on the uptake."

"You didn't wake me, Mickey."

"Lil . . ." I reached for her with my free hand, but she backed away.

"Mickey, don't. It's fine. I'm fine."

"I'm sorry this is so hard, Lily."

She bit her lip. "Don't be sorry. It's just me getting used to everything."

We gazed down at Abby, that safe place where the two of us could hide our awkwardness. "Well," she said, "it looks like you have things under control here. I guess I'll go back to bed."

"Why don't you feed her, Lil? My back is a little stiff."

Lily smiled at me as tears again surfaced in her eyes. She looked at me for a moment, sizing up my offer, then leaned up to kiss my cheek. "Thanks, Mickey."

I placed Abby in her arms and watched as this time our fickle baby quieted for Lil. Lily shrugged. "Looks like she has us both wrapped around her finger."

"I was just thinking the same thing," I said, handing Lily back the bottle.

I did not sleep well that night, and the next day I called Gleason's office for an appointment. He didn't have an opening but he had a lunch hour, so I met him at the Crab Shack in Woodbury. When he saw me, he did what he always does: He gave me a hug. Nothing major, just the kind of thing a father would do for a son who was having a hard time. "Thanks for meeting me," I said.

"You know I can't refuse a free lunch. So, what's happening?"

I sat down and ran both hands through my hair. "I don't know what's happening. I'm in love with my baby and I can't stand being at Ron and Lily's and every day this situation that's supposed to be getting easier is getting harder."

"Take a breath, Mic."

I looked at him. "It was easier when I thought I couldn't love her."

"Your daughter? You can say it, Mickey." His eyes bored into mine.

"My daughter." But then, shaking my head, I took it back. "No. No. You're not going to do that to me. She belongs to Ron and Lily, and I'm buying you lunch so you'll tell me how to get my head back on that track."

"Well, then, let's at least start with honesty. You love her."

"Yes, I love her."

"And Lily and Ron will raise her because you love her."

"Yes. That's exactly why."

"It's very noble, Mickey. And where do you fit in?"

"I don't know yet."

"You're her father. You should know."

Over the next three days, I worked up the courage to leave. I meant what I'd told Ron—it was Christmas Eve or bust. But when I thought too hard about actually going home, it felt like a bust. I was terrified of being by myself. Being alone meant nothing was between me and the abyss.

That said, I had to get out of Lily's house, and soon, because I could feel my daughter becoming the ground beneath me. And Lily could see it happening.

It didn't seem to matter if I was changing Abby or fixing her bath or talking her down from one of her tantrums. Lily was always watching, and it left me feeling like I was trespassing.

The final straw came Friday night when Lily was feeding her. Abby forgot to breathe, and when she did, she sucked milk into the wrong place and started to choke. The sound was awful, more a croak than a cough, so ominous it stopped my heart. Lily panicked. I think she even screamed, and for me the whole terrible thing unfolded in slow motion. The bottle dropping from Lily's hand to bounce on the tile floor. Abby turning red. Then blue. Lily's completely ineffective "Oh, God, oh, God." Hands that seemed independent of me reaching for my daughter, tipping her upside down, slapping her back. The cough, the cry, her dinner dripping down my arm. The humiliation in Lily's eyes that morphed into anger.

Later, when I was on the phone with Dr. Sweeny discussing the possibility that Abby might have colic, that same look hardened Lily's expression. I was only wondering if trying a formula without iron might lessen our baby's fussiness—something I had read on the Internet—but it seemed I had once again done the unforgivable. So I left Lily to deal with our ornery baby and said I was going to Partners to talk to Jared.

Our township is nearly two miles long from the pier to Brinley Loop, and I was surprised at how good it felt to be outside. It had snowed all evening, and now the world seemed crisp and clean, and all mine, since my footprints were the first to mar the newly powdered landscape. As I made my way up Main Street, I realized how comforting it was to pass by neighbors I had known for as long as I'd been married to Lucy. I imagined all the conversations going on behind the familiar doors. For a dozen years these people had been my friends. I knew their stories, and they certainly knew mine. And many of them loved me anyway.

I thought back on that early-November night when Lu and I were walking back from Lily's spaghetti dinner. I had told my wife then that I did not want the baby, but I never told her I had actually decided to leave Brinley. I'd finally considered that Lucy might die, and if it happened, my plan was to walk away from here, from everything that reminded me of my wife, and lose myself in whatever it was going to take to hurry my destruction.

But then Abby came, and everything changed.

I looked around this quiet street flanked by homes filled with people I had grown to love. My daughter would grow up here in this great little town and be beloved because her mom was beloved. How had I ever thought I could walk away and not be part of that?

Lost in what-ifs, I had reached the Loop, and it looked as though Brubaker Inn was doing a sparse business, not surprising this close to Christmas. But if history was any indication, they were booked solid next week. I'd come to talk to Jared, but now that I was here, I didn't think I had much to say. I knew I could start back at Partners anytime. Hell, I could go in and start working right now if I wanted to. Instead I took the long way back to Ron and Lily's, down Chestnut and toward my house.

Of course it was dark and empty, but it was my house and it knew me. I might actually have been strong enough to walk in, but I just watched it, willing the lights to go on, willing Lucy to open the door.

But of course nothing like that happened. It was an empty house, unchanged from the morning Lucy woke up so sick and so sore she had me call the doctor. I had poured her some apple juice that she'd refused. It was still on the counter. The bed wasn't made, there was laundry in the dryer, and we were out of milk. How could everything stay exactly the same when the unimaginable had changed everything?

There was easily a foot of snow on the roof and on the drive. I hesitated only a moment before I walked around back to the garage door, which I never locked, and retrieved the shovel. It was a deceptively heavy snow—not airy powder the way it looked—and the exertion felt good. It was bitter cold except for the hot tears I could feel running down my face, but it felt good to be physical, to feel my heart beat and frigid air glide in and out of me. When I was finished with my driveway, I started in on Harry's, and I got about halfway through before he pulled in.

Jan was out of the car before Harry had even cut the engine. "Mickey, you sweet thing, what do you think you're doing?"

I shrugged against her embrace. "I was just out for a walk." I'm a grown man, but I gotta say, being loved by this mom of a woman felt just as it should have felt when I was a kid.

"All right, you're finished, here," she insisted. "Harry will finish up tomorrow. You come in now, you must be freezing. C'mon, we'll have some tea, or soup. Hot chocolate?"

Harry had lifted the shovel from my hand. "There's no use arguing, Mic. She's going to get some tea, or soup, or whatever else she's got down you, so you might as well come in." Harry gave my back a soft slap, and at that point what choice did I have?

Inside, I realized how cold I'd been. Jan took my coat and hung it by the fireplace, then draped a thick afghan over my shoulders. As I sat at Jan's kitchen table and let the two of them cluck over me, something in me just burst, and I started to bawl like nobody's business. Jan was all over me like a good mother. Harry was quieter. He just sat down and put his hand on mine. "It's okay, son, let it out."

I can't begin to describe what it was like to be in the heart of these people. Neither did I realize how raw I was. I just knew it felt unimaginably good to sob, to let everything I had kept reined in at Lily's flow out of me. There must have been quite a buildup of stored emotion because it took a while. When I was finally able to settle myself, I told them I had needed to do that for a long time. I had cried a lot of tears over these last months, but never before had I acknowledged how unprepared I was for a life without Lucy.

Jan and Harry held me together until I could do it for myself. After that, we had soup. It was ten after eleven and we had soup and some of Jan's homemade sourdough bread and honey butter and apple juice pressed from her own apples. Everything was delicious, and it had been so long since I had actually been hungry, had actually tasted anything. Later, Harry insisted on driving me home, but I told him I really wanted to walk.

"Then promise we'll see you on Christmas for brunch," Jan said.

"I promise. And don't be alarmed if you look outside and see my lights on over there. I'm coming home tomorrow."

"Oh, honey, are you ready?"

"I'm never going to be ready, Jan. But it's time."

"Christmas Eve? Are you sure?"

"Yeah. I'm sure. If I do it tomorrow, it can only get easier from there on out."

Jan leaned up and kissed my cheek. "You know we're right here."

I nodded.

"Well, at least take this." Harry pulled a ski cap over my head. "If you won't let me drive you, at least be warm."

"Thanks. Thanks for everything." I gazed past them at the gigantic Austrian pine that took up half of their living room. It was loaded with soft light, colors twinkling, bathing the room in that ambience that is uniquely Christmas. Despite everything that had happened, I felt a measure of comfort.

I walked back out into the cold. It was snowing again and the full moon lit the night with silver sparkle. I thought of my wife, and for the first time the pain of losing her didn't stab me as it usually did. That surprised me so I ventured further. I thought of our first Christmas together. Of the tree that was totally lopsided and the way it would not stand up straight, and how when I tried to balance it, the sucker fell over on me. Lucy had laughed so hard she lost her breath and could not help me out of my predicament: a big man trapped under a bigger tree. I thought of that night so long ago, every detail rich and dimensional. I thought of Lucy's heartless belly laugh so hard I could almost hear it.

It sounded like music.

thirty-five

I had dragged my feet all day, inventing things to keep me busy so I could put off going home for as long as possible. I did my laundry. I did Abby's laundry. I cleaned the bathroom I'd been using. I made my bed. And every chance I had, I held my daughter. Maybe it was because I was still here, or maybe it was that Christmas had snuck up on her, but Lily seemed unusually quiet today. Not cold or unkind, just subdued. While I rocked Abby, she'd been busy wrapping presents and trimming the tree, which had sat naked all week. Only once, when she was hanging the stockings, did I see her become emotional.

She'd hung hers and Ron's and then picked up a third stocking. I watched her run her hand down the front of it as she looked over at me. "I don't think I've shown you this," she said, holding it up for me to see. On the front of it was the scene of a baby sleeping underneath a Christmas tree. It looked like a painting but it was really made up of those tiny stitches that boggle the mind—needlepoint, or something like it. Even at this small distance I could see it was old, with lots of character like everything wonderful in Lily's house. She fingered the edge of it. "I think this was done by a new mom because she'd do it at her baby's side while she slept, or maybe a granny because she was alone and had the time. It was probably stitched next to a window when the light was good, or maybe a lantern, but either way, it was definitely done with lots of love." Lily shook her head. "Since it was made for a baby girl by someone who adored her, I thought it would be perfect for our Abby."

"How do you know it's a girl?"

Lily walked over to me. "Because you can see a bracelet around her little wrist."

I followed Lily's slender finger as she pointed this out to me. Sure enough, on the wrist, half-hidden beneath the tree, a tiny silver chain could be deciphered. I would never have noticed it, but Lil was right. "How old is it, do you think?"

"Oh, it's dated. See, it's very small and a little frayed, but it looks like 1872—maybe 1878. But it's been beautifully preserved, probably a precious family heirloom until it reached someone more interested in the four hundred and eighty-five dollars I bid for it on eBay."

"Wow. Hard to believe anyone would part with it."

Lily turned back to the tree. "One man's treasure is another man's car payment." Lily laid the stocking over the arm of the chair, and as she fished through a box of ornaments, I wondered why she hadn't hung it up with the others. But then I realized that was probably for my benefit. I appreciated the gesture.

When I glanced outside the big window in Lily's hearth room and saw the afternoon was fading, I realized I had officially stalled the day away. Abby was asleep in my arms and I pulled her to my lips and kissed her head. I lingered there a long time, breathing her in. When I let go of the moment and looked up, I found Lily was staring at me. Her eyes were moist with understanding as I'm sure mine were, but neither of us looked away. I held my entire world in my arms, and acknowledging this, I felt desperation creep into my expression, but I didn't know what to do about it.

Lily walked over to me and gently lifted Abby from my arms. "Let's leave her with Ron," she whispered. "We need to go see Lucy."

"Oh, Lil, I—"

"It's time, Mickey. For both of us."

We drove to the cemetery without saying a word to each other. No one was there when we pulled in, but there had obviously been many visitors this week. Boughs of holly, frozen poinsettias, even miniature Christmas trees, dotted the gravesites. Lily parked at the edge of the *little path that led up to where Lucy was buried and cut the engine. We sat for a few minutes, still not talking, and watched the snow start to fall. Finally Lily opened her door. "You take your time, Mickey," she said, getting out of the car. She lifted some small potted pines from the backseat and nudged the door shut with her hip. I waited only a moment, then I got out, too. It was cold and the wind blew right through my jacket as I followed Lily up the hill.*

I had not been here for a long time, and it shamed me to be walking here now, having missed Lucy's funeral. At the top of the hill we stopped in front of the marble bench and gazed at this small family of markers. Lucy's parents' was a slab of coral granite that somehow diminished them to just that stone. Lucy's grandmother's small, white marker was off to one side, and I was stunned to see that Lucy was next to her. I guess because I'd been incapacitated, Ron and Lily had taken care of business for me. For my wife they'd chosen dark granite, a rough-hewn stone that was mirror smooth only on the front. I crouched down in front of it, unable to control my emotion. It was beautiful. I ran my hand over the smooth part and traced her name with my fingers.

"Do you like it?" Lily said, kneeling beside me.

"I like it very much," I rasped.

"I think it's perfect. Kind of formidable. Like her."

I touched Lucy's name again. "I loved her so much, Lil."

"I know you did."

"I miss her."

"Me, too."

I thought of Lucy's sound declaration that God would never fill her heart with love for me and then take it away. I wanted to believe that. If love was really that essential, why would God let me have it only to take it back? And if he wouldn't, did that mean love—Lucy's love—could transcend everything I understood? What a thought. If it was true, I think I could survive anything.

Just after seven, Ron pulled into my neighborhood. Chestnut

Street was a riot of lights, every house drenched in twinkling color and holiday finery. My heart sank, knowing I was going home to emptiness and darkness and a glass of evaporated apple juice.

Lily seemed to read my thoughts. "You can change your mind, Mic."

"I'll be fine, Lil," I lied. I watched a look pass between her and Ron that I couldn't read. As my house came into view, I heard Lily giggle.

"Whoa. What's all this?" I said, stunned at the sight. My house was awash in white lights, and for a moment, I thought we were on the wrong street. But it was my house, covered in Christmas. Lucy had always loved just clean white lights, and we had a plethora that someone had dug out of our basement and hung. In the window, a Christmas tree shown with more white lights that defined its size and shape. A current of emotion surged through me. My house looked the way it had every Christmas since I'd moved in. I could almost imagine my wife sitting in our kitchen watching for me to arrive with the famous last-minute this or that that had become as traditional as the holiday itself.

"Oh, Lord." My voice was shaky and didn't quite sound like mine. I met Ron's eyes in the rearview mirror. He chuckled as he pulled into the driveway and put the car in park.

"Are you surprised?" Lily laughed. "Merry Christmas, Mickey."

"Oh, what have you guys done?"

"Just a little Christmas cheer."

I was so numbed that it took me a few tries to unbuckle Abby's car seat. Lily had to help me, and she tucked the blanket gently around Abby's head—just as I would have done—to ward off the frigid breeze blowing off the river.

I think Ron was worried about me because he grabbed hold of my arm as we headed up the walk. But I was okay. As Lily got the groceries she had loaded me up with out of the trunk, I rummaged for my key to the front door. But the door opened from within and there stood Harry wearing a ridiculous reindeer sweater—the same one he'd been wearing on Christmas Eve for as long as I'd known him. He pulled the door wider to reveal a room full of Christmas. Decorations, music, the unbelievable scent of roasted turkey, and beloved neighbors were all waiting for me in my living room.

I searched Harry's face for some indication that this was a dream, but he just smiled. I stared in at this gathering utterly amazed and suddenly humbled. Jan was the first to plant a kiss on my cheek and hug me. With my free hand I grabbed her like a man drowning, and when I emerged from her embrace, she touched her fingers to her mouth and tried to fight the tears.

Harry relieved me of the car seat so I could float along this remarkable wave of welcome. Charlotte Barbee tapped my chest and told me I was looking good. Diana Dunleavy took both my hands in hers and kissed them. Earl Withers palmed my shoulder. Every interaction shored up my ability to be here without Lucy. Above the din, I heard Abby, and I tried to backtrack to where she was because I knew that soon her cry would turn ugly as she insisted on being fed. I wanted to hold her, but Ron had quietly gotten a bottle together and sat down with her on the sofa, where he was quickly flanked by Muriel Piper and Elaine Withers. These women looked as though they had never seen a baby before, and I relaxed knowing Abby was well taken care of.

Once again I lost myself in sensation, hands touching my face, kind words, kisses on my cheek, soft slaps on my back. Words extracted from a dozen conversations—"He looks good . . . he'll be okay . . . he's lost weight, bless his heart . . . the baby looks just like Lucy, absolutely adorable." It was all a little overwhelming, but I was loath to forfeit even a portion of it.

From across the room I watched Lily help Jan put the finishing touches on the dining room table. I was amazed that, in spite of her frustration, Lily had helped pull off this surprise for me.

The doorbell rang just then, and when Harry answered it, there stood Priscilla and Nathan. They were kissing but they parted quickly, looking a bit embarrassed. Nathan indicated the eave, where a big bunch of mistletoe hung, and Harry laughed as he opened the door wider and took their coats. My sister-in-law spotted me immediately, and the room parted for her as she made her way toward me. She was a stunner in a short red dress and stiletto boots, but as she stopped in front of me, she gave me a look that belied her cool exterior.

"Mickey," she whispered, hugging me. "Merry Christmas, honey. You okay?"

"Getting there," I said in her ear.

The door again opened and I watched as Gleason Webb, bundled in an overstuffed parka, made his way into the room.

"Well, aren't you just the sweetest thing to haul all the way out here tonight?" Jan said, kissing him on the cheek.

"Well, I don't know about that. But I heard food was involved so I had to come." He chuckled and caught my eye, then began making his way toward me across the crowded room.

When he reached me, he said, "Doesn't get much better than this, Mic."

"I think you're right."

Near the kitchen, Harrison clanked a spoon against his glass and the room quieted. He cleared his throat and looked far more serious than a man wearing a reindeer sweater should. "I want to welcome everyone to Christmas Eve at the Chandlers'. But mostly I wanted to welcome Mickey back. It's been too long." His lip quivered as he looked hard at me. "It's good to have you home, son."

The room was still and seemed to hold a palpable breath as I imagined one thought filling every mind: poor Mickey. I stood there and did my best to not fall apart, but I had to look down at the floor before I could speak. When I looked up, I lifted my glass. "What would I do without my friends? Thank you. Thank you for all of this. And thank you on behalf of Lucy. You know she loved sharing this night with you."

As if on cue, Abby let out a burp that shattered the awkward silence and effectively dissolved the tension. I actually laughed. "That's my girl. Now are we going to eat or what? I'm starved."

After that, the party got back on track as everyone lined up to serve themselves. People sat down wherever they could, including the stairs and the floor. I looked around and marveled. If I lived another hundred years, I could never thank them enough.

Nor could I begin to repay the kindness wrapped in the crowning jewel of the evening, which was when Oscar Levine took hold of my hand and said, "A few of us put together a little Christmas present for you, Mic. Why don't you come on upstairs and take a look."

I followed Oscar up and faltered just a bit at the top of the stairs as I glanced into my bedroom. I would surely cry there. But it would be later, alone. Not now. Oblivious to this emotional stumble, Oscar led me to Priscilla's old bedroom and turned on the light. I heard a sound come out of me, a moan that was partly heartbreak and partly awe, but it pretty much conveyed my feeling. I was looking at a beautiful nursery. My friends had picked up where Lucy and I had left off and transformed this room into something from a storybook. It was painted the soft warm pink Lucy had picked out, and all the soft things, the curtains and pillows and blankets, were in pastel greens and yellows. Lucy would have loved it.

I walked in and sat down on the newly upholstered window seat and took in the room. It could be in a magazine, it was that pretty. Of course, Lucy's fingerprints were everywhere. It was just as she'd dreamed it, I was sure, but the final product was beyond anything I could have imagined. "Who did this?"

"We all did," Oscar answered. "Treig and I painted, Ron finished the floor, Earl and Chad redid the window seat."

"And the rocker is a gift from Lucy," Treig said, smiling sadly. "She bought it from me last summer. Thought it would fit you perfectly, and I have to agree."

I shook my head as an ache filled my chest.

"Jan, of course, painted the mural, and the gals did all the frilly stuff," Oscar said quickly in an attempt to distract me.

Jan's mural spanned one entire wall. In a forest of lush greenery a beam of sunlight shone down on three little, green-eyed girls hav-

ing a tea party on the stump of a tree. They looked remarkably similar to the princesses in the book Lily had left for me at the hospital. When I recognized my wife as a child, I gave in to tears that had been threatening me all night. Jan walked over and kissed my forehead. "I couldn't resist. I hope it's okay."

"It's phenomenal."

Jan's work had the same effect on Priscilla, who was holding tight to Lily's hand and crying. Her mouth was open but no words were coming out.

Ron walked in with Abby. "What do you think, Mic? Pretty nice, huh?"

"Way beyond," I said, taking my daughter. Abby was wide-awake and looking at the ceiling, calm and pleasant and completely unaware that all this was for her. I kissed her head. "This is your new room," I whispered in her hair. Or at least it was the room she would use when I tended her. The thought pinched my heart.

After all the oohs and aahs had been expressed, people began drifting back downstairs, where dessert had been laid out. Soon it was just Lily, Priscilla, and me. Seen in this light, Lucy's sisters looked young and vulnerable. Priscilla looked almost shell-shocked and was becoming more emotional by the second. Big tears were running down her cheeks, so I walked over and put my free arm around her shoulder. "Hey, you're going to ruin your face," I said, trying not to let on that it was too late. She cried harder, even snorted a couple of times, but she looked at me, unembarrassed, her makeup smeared and her nose running, and said, "I got it so wrong, Mickey. I'm such a fool. And I'm so, so sorry."

"About what?"

"Everything. You. Lucy. Especially this angel," she said, stealing Abby from me. "I don't know what I was thinking."

"Well"—I gulped—"you and me both," I said, suddenly aware, too, of what I had insisted my wife do. I watched as Priscilla nuzzled Abby into her neck; the look on her face was one of profound regret, and one I completely understood.

Priss walked Abby over to the wall and bent close to the tea party, taking in each little girl. Throughout all of this, Lily had kept her distance. She seemed enthralled, not so much by the room, or even Priscilla's breakdown, but by me. She'd been staring at me as if something important was on her mind.

"You okay, Lil?" I said.

She nodded almost imperceptibly and shifted her attention to the ruffles in the crib. "It's all so lovely, isn't it?" she said with a little shake in her voice.

"It's absolutely enchanting," Priscilla blubbered, distracting me from Lily. "Jan has completely captured the three of us. It's unbelievable."

I nodded and turned back to Lily, but she was gone.

An hour or so later, I'm sure it was more than obvious to my friends that they were welcome to stay as long as they wanted. All night. All winter. But I was gracious when each said his or her good-bye and each one offered to feed me the next day. I didn't decline or accept any invitation. I just thanked them for thinking of me and stacked up my options. Wanda Murphy placed both of her cold hands on my face and pulled me down to her eye level. "God love ya, Mickey, and God love that little girl," she said, and kissed me on the nose. Gleason's concern touched me to the core when he offered to keep his cell phone on throughout the holiday. I hugged him harder than I'd planned to.

"You'll be okay," he reassured me. "Eventually. For now, just know it's gonna take some time. And call if you need me."

"I will."

Ron had Abby bundled and belted in her car seat. She had on a tiny hat pulled almost to her eyes, which were wide-open and, I swear, looking right at me. I bent down to kiss her and willed myself not to break down. Everyone would be gone in five minutes. I could wait that long.

Ron placed a hand on my shoulder. "You all right, Mic?"

I stood and nodded, not speaking until I could trust myself. Finally I said, "I'm good. I'll see you tomorrow."

Lily had busied herself zipping Abby's assorted paraphernalia into the enormous bag she brought with her wherever she went. Besides Lily, Harry and Jan were the last ones in my house. Jan was giving me an inventory of all the food that was left when Lily squeezed past me. She would have slid out the door without a word if I hadn't grabbed her arm. "Lil?"

She turned. "Yeah?"

I opened my mouth. I guess I thought I had things to say, but none of them surfaced. Instead I tried for a smile and told her thanks for everything. She looked as if she might cry when she leaned up to kiss my cheek. "We'll see you in the morning, Mic."

"Okay."

"You know if this is too hard, you can still come back home with us."

"I'll be okay, Lil. But thanks."

I walked out with them and stood there as Ron buckled Abby in the backseat. He waved as they pulled out of my driveway.

Jan kissed my cheek. "I'll leave the back door unlocked, in case you need my couch," she said.

I watched Harry slip his arm through his wife's as the two of them trudged through my snowy front yard. I stood on the front porch for a few more minutes watching my friends drift away. Then I walked back inside.

thirty-six

I locked the door and stood stone still listening for an echo of the sound that had filled my home only minutes before. Nothing. I was alone. As I absorbed my solitude, I was surprised and a little pleased at my nonreaction. I wandered into my kitchen for some water. But it didn't look like my kitchen. Jan and her crew had left it spit-shined—not one tiny thing out of place. The table that had held all the food earlier was now covered with a tartan cloth and a basket of pinecones was sitting dead center that I did not recognize as ours. The chairs were tucked in uniformly, the counters spotless, the sink gleaming.

It bothered me. It was too straight. Too orderly. I took three spoons and a knife out of the drawer and tossed them on the counter. Then I took an apple out of the fridge and rolled it across the table. It stopped just short of the edge, but if it had fallen off, I would not have picked it up. I turned on the water and filled a glass, but I didn't drink it, I left it on the counter. On my way out I turned a chair a few inches to the left. I felt a little less anxious when I turned off the light. But not much.

It felt better in the living room; more relaxed. The afghan on the back of the couch was crooked and a pillow was on the floor. I left them. I had always liked this room. It was cozy, and most nights when I came home late, I would find Lucy curled up in the chair in the corner, reading, or sleeping with an open book on her chest. I tried to remember what book she was in the middle of when she . . . If I could find it, I would read it. I had to find it. Where was it?

I felt a little shiver just before I started to tremble, and I leaned against the wall to steady myself. Only jitters at first, but soon my heart was a racing hammer and my whole body was quaking. I slid down the wall until I felt the floor beneath me, then I buried my head in my knees. I knew what panic was and I wasn't sure this was it, but whatever it was, I hoped it would soon pass. It didn't. It took quite a while, and I guess that was okay. There was no one here to judge me, no one I had to protect from my drama. I kept telling myself as soothingly as I could manage, "I can do this. I know I can do this." *Just as Gleason had repeatedly told me, there was no way through it but through it, so there I sat, waves of sadness and fear and dreadful anxiety rolling over me.*

I don't know how long I sat there, but when I could finally stand, I breathed deep and wandered like a drunk back into my kitchen and drank the water I'd left on the counter. I also put the apple back in the fridge.

I found my duffel bag in the closet where Ron had put it and headed slowly up the stairs. It was so quiet, but it was the loud kind of quiet that comes from listening hard to unwelcome silence. It almost hurt my ears. I looked around and tried to conjure some of the noise that had filled this hall, this house. As I concentrated, the deafening silence blessedly became a mosaic of words and remembered conversations with my wife. Don't you dare leave without kissing me. Will you grab some milk on your way home, and some small black pantyhose? Please? I'll love you forever. Have you seen the checkbook? Have you taken your pills? Don't talk to me right now, I'm in a mad mood at you. I rented *Weekend at Bernie's* again. Not again! Yes, again, we're going for one hundred times and we're only at forty-one. I love you, Mic. I love you, Mickey. I love you, Michael. *I was calmed by the free-flowing recollections and decided that I would probably self-destruct the moment I could no longer hear her voice in my head. I also decided I could never again watch* Weekend at Bernie's *or* French Kiss *or* Waking Ned Devine. *Or maybe I would watch them one right after the other for the rest of my life.*

I pushed open the door to my bedroom and turned on the lamp. It was spotless in here as well. The vacuum tracks in the rug were sad evidence that someone had sucked up all the footprints. Lucy's footprints. I sighed and walked into the bathroom. No evidence of her was in here either, and I didn't know which was worse: finding traces of her everywhere or nowhere.

I emptied my bag onto the floor and fished around for my seven prescription bottles. When I found them, I lined them up on the back of the toilet in their usual place. The three I took in the morning separated slightly from the two I took at night, separated slightly from the ones I only took when I needed them. One of those was for anxiety, and I opened that bottle and dumped two orange pills in my hand. But I stared at the little Ativans so long they blurred in my palm. I put them back in the bottle. The sane guy inside me who had been on hiatus for a while was with me tonight. I heard him tell me clearly that if I started taking pills to feel better about Lucy, I'd never stop.

I took a shower instead, and under the scalding water I decided to not get out until I was done bawling. But after nearly a half hour, the water had turned cold. I ran my hands over my face. My head was pounding, and standing there dripping and shaking, I could see myself in the mirror and my heart hurt for the man I saw there. He looked ruined beyond repair.

I stepped out and wrapped a towel around my waist. I took a deep breath and blew it out slowly. I could shave, I needed to, but my hands were not yet that steady. I rubbed them over my face again and back through my hair and ground my fingers into my eyes, took another deep breath, and thought I had made some progress. A bit later, dressed in sweats, I stared down at my crisp and perfectly made bed. I was exhausted and my head hurt, but I knew I was simply not strong enough to crawl in there yet.

The clock radio on the dresser said 10:58. Was almost eleven too late to call and just check on Abby? Probably. I picked up my pillow and walked down the hall to Abby's room, and there, too, I hesitated, peering in at the dark, little space made for a baby who was not here. Instead of the overhead light, I turned on the lamp that was sitting on the bureau. It cast the softest glow—a whisper of light perfect to check on a sleeping baby without waking her. The room took my breath away all over again. I walked over to the enormous rocking chair Lucy had planned to surprise me with. It had been refinished to match the crib, and I ran my hand over it. Lucy. I sat down in the chair and let it gentle the throbbing places in me. She was right; it fit me perfectly. I looked around. Lucy would adore this room. I could imagine her reaction if Oscar had surprised her with it. She would have giggled and kissed everyone in sight. It was a little paradise. It was the perfect room for a baby girl who lived two streets over.

Eleven fifteen. Lily was probably feeding her.

I closed my eyes and leaned my head back, willing it to stop aching. I never got headaches unless my meds were off, and they were not off according to the labs I'd had drawn two days ago. I just had to get myself settled down and go to sleep. I thought I could actually sleep in here easier than I could in my own room, but in the end I figured I would stay downstairs on the couch by the fire, keep the tree lights on, and maybe watch some TV to distract me.

I was just grabbing a comforter from the hall closet when I thought I heard a knock on the door. At first, I dismissed it, thinking I was imagining noises in my empty house, but then I heard it again. I hurried down the stairs to see who was worried about me and opened the door. There stood Lily in her long coat and a red knit hat. My immediate reaction was alarm, and I had a hard time getting out "What's the matter, Lil? Is Abby . . ."

Lily shook her head. She was holding the car seat in one hand and juggling the big bag in the other.

"What are you doing, Lil?"

"Can I come in?"

"Of course you can. I'm sorry."

She moved past me, dropping the bag on the floor as she made her way to the couch. She set Abby down and reached in to loosen her buckles. I looked at her, the angst in me rising. "Lily?"

"Just give me a minute," she warbled. She didn't take Abby out of the seat, but she unwrapped her by one blanket. I stayed firmly planted across the room, afraid to ask Lily again what was going on, but good Lord, what was going on? Lily looked up at me and her eyes filled with tears. "Mickey, I . . ."

I moved to the couch. "Lily, what is it? What are you doing?"

She slipped the hat from her head and ran a hand over her short hair. "Sit down."

I sat, stealing a glance at my sleeping baby. "Lil, do you want to take your coat off?"

"No. I won't be here that long."

"Okay . . ."

Lily turned to face me and took both my hands in her freezing ones. "Mickey . . ."

She breathed deep. "Mickey."

"Lily, you're scaring me."

She shook her head and looked at the floor. "I know. I know." She took another deep breath. "Okay." She nodded. "Mickey, I have watched you for the last five weeks like you were a bug under a microscope. I've watched you, and at first there was no question in my mind that I was the best choice." She let go of my hands to push the tears off her face. "But then, dammit, you crawled back from wherever you went. Just like Lucy knew you would. And I thought, 'Well, so what, he's still way too fragile and unstable.' But that wasn't true either. I thought if I looked hard enough that I could find a reason—and I only needed one—that you should not have your daughter. If I could find it, then I could live happily ever after as her mom."

"Lily—"

"Shhh. I'm not finished. I tried hard to find some terrible proof that you're incompetent. I'm ashamed of myself, Mickey. And I'm so, so sorry." Lily shook her head, her eyes soft and wounded. "But I never found a reason that you shouldn't have her, Mic. Abby belongs with you. I know it in my heart. And no matter how much I want her—and I so want her—this is where she needs to be."

"Lily, I don't understand."

"Yes, you do. You're going to be a wonderful father."

"No. No!" I stood up. "What are you doing?"

Lily took my hand again and pulled me back down beside her. With sudden calm in her voice she said, "I love this baby with every breath, but she's not mine, and if I kept her, I would always know I had cheated you. And worse, that I had cheated my sister. This is what Lucy wanted. This is all she ever wanted."

My heart was pounding, and for a moment I could not find my voice. "Lily, no. You're wrong."

"I would love, love to be wrong, Mickey. But I'm not." Lily reached down in the side of the car seat and pulled out a piece of paper that had been torn in half. "This is for you," she said, tearing it in half again before she handed it to me.

It was the last page of our lengthy adoption agreement, the page that held all the necessary signatures. I looked at Lily. "You're serious."

She nodded, indicating the papers. "That was about ownership, but Abby was always yours. She belongs with you. Ron and I are less than two minutes away and we will always—always—have your back."

"But what if I get sick?"

Lily put her arms around me then and I thought my heart would pound its way out of my chest. "Mickey, I'm available twenty-four hours a day for the rest of my life, and between us, Abby will be just fine. We'll make this work."

"Lily . . ."

She stood up and walked to where she'd dropped the bag. "These are just some of her things. There are about a dozen diapers in here— I'll bring more tomorrow. And here are three bottles all ready for you, just add the water. And there's formula in here. I just fed her so she's good until about two thirty." Lily got quiet as she lifted something from the bag and pulled it to her chest. It was the ancient Christmas stocking she'd shown me earlier. She walked to the mantel and ran her fingers underneath it, feeling for the hooks her father had placed there when she was a little girl. When she'd found the one she wanted, Lily hung the stocking and stood back. "That's exactly where it belongs," she said quietly. Then she pulled an envelope from inside her coat. She kissed it and slid it into the stocking. "After you've read that about a hundred times, I'd like it back." Lily then walked over to where I was still sitting on the couch and pressed her lips to my forehead. Fresh tears were in her eyes, but not the anguish I had seen so many times lately. She bent down and lifted Abby from her seat and held her close for a moment. Then she kissed her tiny head and gently placed her in my arms. "Call me if you need me, Mic. But you won't need me."

"Lily . . ."

"You'll be fine," she said at the door. Then she was gone.

I was stunned, as if I'd been dreaming and woken up too fast; disoriented and uncertain. I looked around. The same silence greeted me, except I could hear my heart beating. The furniture was the same except for the baby luggage and an empty car seat, and an utterly limp baby girl in my arms. She stirred but did not cry.

This was wrong. This wasn't the plan.

Yet, I pulled her closer and laid my cheek against her soft head. My daughter. My Abby. I thought of the man I had just seen step out of the shower. Ruined, possibly beyond repair. But I was still standing, wasn't I? Tears filled my throat and I hung my head at the impossibility of what had been handed to me.

I stared down at the baby in my arms. Her head full of black hair, that flawless little body. Lucy's baby girl. Her gift to me. I remembered the letter Lily had put in Abby's stocking and walked over to the mantel. As I unfolded the pages, sudden tears filled my eyes and I had to sit down. The letter was in Lucy's handwriting.

Dearest Lilianne,

I love you. God was surely watching over me when he made

us sisters. You are my heart and I am yours, and I want you to remember that as you read this letter.

My body is a crumbling mess, but I'm still here and my mind's still working, like a chandelier swinging from the ceiling of a condemned building. My point is, my time is up but I am thinking clearly. Just last night Harry—sweet Harry—provided all the legalese to make you and Ron the parents of my daughter, and I am 99 percent sure that this is the way things were meant to be.

But, my darling sister, there is that one percent I so need you to understand. There is a slim chance—the slimmest of chances—that Mickey will change his mind. He does that sometimes. It is no secret that this would be my fondest wish, but it is not my decision. Mic is adamant that he's not capable of being a father. But that's just a wicked voice that whispers lies in his ear. I know, because this same voice once insisted that he was incapable of being my husband. Well, that voice was wrong then, and it's wrong again now.

Lily, I know Mickey's heart and it's a very good heart, and my daughter is blessed already that he is her father. More than that, she needs him. She needs him as much as he needs her, and all that need is what God grants us imperfect people. It is a daily chance to live for someone else and to best our yesterdays. You watch. Mickey will prove me right.

Lily, I know that swollen tender place in your soul where your son still lives. And I know what I am asking will hurt you all over again. But, my sweet sister, surely you know that you will always be the mother in my baby's life. You will be the soft kiss on her bruises; you will be the vault that will hold her secrets. The love I have for this little angel will shine in your eyes. I know this, you know this, and Mickey's role in her world will never diminish your place there. So the bottom line is, if Mickey rises to this occasion, I need you to let it happen, Lil.

Mickey is wonderful in ways you cannot begin to know. Yes, he is broken in places, but because of that, other places in him have built bridges to compensate. I promise you, Lily, Mickey will never hurt our baby, even though he probably thinks he will. If I know him, he's convinced himself of it. But he won't. He will, however, need enormous help because he will fall. He won't be able to do this without his world huddling close around him. He'll need you, Ron, Harry and Jan, Charlotte, and Priss. Make no mistake, it will take a village because Mickey will fall, that is the nature of his disorder. But he will always get up again because that is the nature of the man.

Lily, we are twins four years apart—we share one soul—so I know you are not surprised by any of this. You know what I want, and only you will know if it's possible, and I trust you like I have always trusted you.

I'm tired, Lily, so I will leave all this (unfairly, I know) in your tender hands. I love you, my precious sister. I love your Ron like the brother he has forever been to me, and I know the two of you will be fabulous parents if the 99 rules the day.

No matter what your title turns out to be—mom or aunt—Lily, please tell my daughter about me. Tell her that even as the rest of me failed and what little I could offer grew smaller every day, my love for her filled the universe. Tell her I will love her forever and not to be afraid. Not of life. Not of death. Tell her if I never got the chance to hold her or kiss her face, I know I will someday. Tell her, Lil, that she is my amazing little miracle. And tell her every day how much I loved her father.

Lily, I have adored Mickey since I laid eyes on him, but I chose him because I never knew another man who could swim through concrete. He is extraordinarily strong. Don't ever let him forget that. And when he drifts to that thick, dark, terrible place, remind him to start kicking and to not stop until he's reached the other side, where it's warm and safe and there is peace and light . . . and his daughter.

Michael Chandler was always my hero. And now you must let him be hers.

All my love, to all my loves,
Lucy

I read the letter so many times I could hear Lucy's voice lifting off the page. God, I loved her. God only knows what would have become of me if she had not turned twenty-one in my path. But Lucy found me and believed in me. She loved me. She loved me into a man she knew was strong enough to raise our daughter, even if I didn't yet know it myself.

Abby stretched in my arms. This littlest of angels was Lucy's priceless gift to me. Her faith in me was another. I looked down at my daughter, into her perfect face. She was staring at me through eyes that looked much like her mother's. "I love you, little one," I croaked. "And if love was enough, we'd have it made." I pulled her to my neck, knowing I had never spoken truer words.

epilogue

I left Damian's, where I'd met Gleason for lunch, and took the side-walk along Brinley Loop to Cemetery Road. I was feeling pretty good because my labs had all come back within normal limits. I was Stable Guy, and Gleason was happy about that. But he didn't really need my blood work to verify this. I'd been stable for more than a year, which pretty much coincided with the last time I'd tweaked—as Lucy would have said—my meds. I had also been seeing Gleason twice a week, once for therapy and once for dinner (or lunch), sometimes a basket-ball game and a burger. He was semiretired, but he'd told me more than once, he was retiring from psychiatry, not from me. I'd promised him that I wouldn't turn into a What About Bob? poster child, and I hadn't. But even with Gleason's unfailing support, it had taken some time to get here.

They say the first year after a major loss is the hardest. That's an understatement; loss is its own brand of insanity and there is no relief from it. There are no shortcuts and the only way through grief is through it. You just have to get up every day and wait to go to bed every night, then wake up and do it all again. Until one day you land. Gleason was right; a floor did eventually take shape beneath me. I stopped falling through the sadness and landed on it. That was a rough year. But I was able to stay out of the hospital except for four days in November when Abby turned one, and Lucy had been gone that long. Abby saved me, though. Or I guess it's more accurate to say being Abby's father saved me. Just as Lucy knew it would.

I turned into River's Peace—an apt name today with the gentle breeze, the quiet, the sea of blue sky. After that Christmas Eve when Lily brought me here, I didn't come back for almost two years. Not until Muriel Piper died. After her service, it took all I had and Ron's promise to wait at the curb, but I finally made it to Lucy's gravesite by myself. And it was like she was waiting for me. Where I'd expected the pain to overwhelm me, I found quiet comfort, a warmth that almost felt like her hand in mine again. Not quite, of course, but it did feel like she was nearby, and it felt good.

It's been easier now to drop by, and I come on special occasions, or whenever I can invent one. Such as today. Today's date on the three-year-old calendar in my kitchen is circled in pink and blue ink. It was when I met my daughter for the first time, the day of our ultrasound. It was the day Lucy and I bought the pink paint that will always be the color of the walls in Abby's room. When I come here remembering times like this, I tell myself that Lucy is remembering them as well.

I made my way up the hill, and when I stopped at my wife's grave, I kissed my fingertips and pressed them to her name. "Hey, baby," I said without crying.

I could tell by the white roses that Priscilla had been here this week. She always left white roses. Lily usually left daisies or sometimes daylilies. Abby left an assortment of tokens—a stuffed monkey, a key, a completely indecipherable drawing she swore was a mommy and a daddy and an Abby.

I leave broken glass.

I placed my latest offering on top of Lucy's headstone with the other pieces that had accumulated there. Pink, topaz, milky turquoise, and today a deep-red shard, probably from an old fishing float. Broken glass. It was symbolic of our marriage, but to me it was even more symbolic of our love. Lucy used to tell me she loved me so much she'd dance on broken glass with me forever if she could.

I was counting on it.

I was lost in the idea, so I didn't notice Lily pull up to the curb and park. I didn't notice until she had opened the rear door and freed her little passenger. Abby's giggle pulled me from my reverie. My daughter is a two-and-a-half-year-old miniature of her mother, except *she has my eyes. She has a mop top of dark curls that I'm lucky to get a comb through, and a perpetual smile, except when I make her eat peas.*

Today she was wearing a little white dress and pink flip-flops, which she struggled to keep on her feet as she navigated the gravel path. But when she got on level ground, she made a beeline for me and I scooped her up. I never get tired of the feel of her solid little body in my arms. Lily had painted her toes, and Abby was explaining the process, complete with a blowing demonstration that required some serious contortion on her part. I laughed as Lily made her way up the path with a pot of Shasta daisies.

She set them down. "Looks like Priss has been here."

"Looks that way." I smiled. Lily had had it rough, too. But we'd shared our grief and it seemed to help us to help each other.

I sat down on the marble bench and Abby wriggled off my lap and went to stand by her aunt. "Mama?"

Lily nodded. "Mama." She stooped to pull a daisy from her pot and slipped it behind Abby's ear. Then Lily came to sit by my side. "How're you doing?"

"I'm good, Lil."

We were quiet for a minute, both watching Abby hunkered down and tracing her mother's name with her finger. "So how was the commander in chief?" I said.

"Delightful as always."

"Are you still good with tonight?"

Lily nodded. "Just drop her off at Ghosts on your way. She can help me lock up."

"It'll be around six," I said, checking my watch. I sighed. "C'mon, Abs. Let's go to Mosely's."

"Treat?"

"If you're good."

Abby scampered past me to bestow a kiss on her aunt.

"Bye-bye, munchkin," Lily called after her. "I'll see you later."

"Are you coming, Lil?"

"Not just yet." She smiled. "I think I'll hang out with my sister for a while."

For a minute Lily and I just looked at each other. Losing Lucy had made us kindred spirits.

I nodded. "I think she would like that." Then I swung my daughter onto my shoulders and walked down the gravel path.

Dancing on Broken Glass

KA HANCOCK

Introduction

In her lyrical debut novel, Ka Hancock has written a story about the enduring power of love and the devastation of loss, a story about fighting for a happiness that's often shadowed by the cruelties of fate.

Lucy Houston and Mickey Chandler are far from an ideal match. With her destructive family history of cancer and Mickey's bipolar disorder, it would seem a blissful union is impossible for them. But despite the risks, despite unstable highs and the guaranteed lows, they cannot imagine living without each other.

Geared up for a life of romance and excitement, albeit with some serious pain mixed in, Lucy and Mickey promise to keep each other grounded. Being confident that they can make each other happy is one thing, but with so much stacked against them, they make the most difficult promise of all—not to have children. After nearly eleven years of marriage, they're very accustomed to their life with just the two of them. But when Lucy gets some unexpected news at a routine check-up everything changes. Everything.

An engrossing story that explores the depths of fear and grief and what it really means to love someone, *Dancing on Broken Glass* is an emotional journey for both the characters and the reader.

Discussion Questions

1. The story opens with Death, a character who continues to visit throughout the novel. Lucy's father tells her that there are three things she needs to know about death: "It's not the end. . . . And it doesn't hurt. And finally, if you're not afraid of death . . . you can watch for it and be ready." (p. 3) How does this wisdom affect Lucy throughout her life? How can you relate to it?

2. How does reading Mickey's perspective at the beginning of each chapter affect the story? What would the ending have been like if that were the first time you got to hear Mickey's voice?

3. Brinley Township is as much a character in this novel as any of the people. How important do you think the setting is to the story? How does this small town help shape the main characters?

4. How does each of the Houston sisters fulfill her role as oldest, middle, and youngest, respectively? In what ways do they go against those stereotypes?

5. Lucy and Mickey are each damaged in their own way and yet their ability to love each other is limitless. What positive characteristics do they each have that help them overcome the challenges to their relationship, and remain devoted to each other throughout the darkest hours? Do you think you could trust a love so risky?

6. At Celia Nash's memorial service, Jessica asks Lucy which she thinks is worse, to have lost someone suddenly or after a long illness (p. 68). Do you think one is worse than the other, or are they just equally terrible in different ways?

7. Lucy and Mickey both have people in their lives serving as surrogate parents. How do these characters fill the roles of mom and dad? Who would take on this position in your life?

8. There's a lot of hardship in these pages, and many of the characters can be called real fighters. What are they each fighting for? Against? Who's the biggest fighter?

9. How do the flashbacks to earlier moments in Lucy's life and her relationship with Mickey help move the story forward? What do you think the story would have been like if it had been told completely in chronological order?

10. Lucy has a very different relationship with Lily than she does with Priscilla. Discuss these sisterly bonds—how do each of Lucy's sisters take care of her? How do they relate to Mickey? How do these relationships change throughout the course of the book?

11. Gleason tells Lucy that every marriage is a dance, and there will be times with Mickey that are like dancing on broken glass (p. 113). Discuss this as a metaphor for their relationship. What kind of meaning does that imagery conjure up for you?

12. Because of their unfortunate medical histories, Mickey and Lucy had written into their contract that they agreed not to have kids. Do you agree with their initial decision? Is it fair to bring a child into the world when you might not be there for them? Or worse, when the child might inherit a life-altering illness?

13. There comes a time when Lucy knows in her bones that she's not going to survive the cancer this time around. Do you think she was really capable of knowing this? Do you think she should've fought for her own life harder, or do you agree with her decision?

14. At the end of the book, Mickey comes to learn that "there are no shortcuts and the only way through grief is through it" (p. 391). Lucy knew he would step up, and just as Gleason predicted, Mickey didn't know that he could do it on his own until he was forced to. Do you think things worked out the way that

they should have for Abby's sake? Are there people in our lives who know us better than we know ourselves, know what we're capable of when all we can see is impossibility?

Enhance Your Book Club

1. Lucy and Mickey made their own marriage contract consisting of a list of rules that would keep them from hurting each other and their relationship. Come up with your own list of non-negotiables for a healthy relationship.
2. Brinley is full of fabulous small-town traditions, from the big Labor Day softball tournament, to the neighborhood chili and hot cider bonfire, to the Houstons' Christmas Eve party. Talk about some of your local celebrations and traditions, and then try to create a new one together!
3. As a police chief, Lucy's father may have seemed an unlikely fairy tale writer, and yet he crafted a beautiful story to leave his three daughters. Try your hand at writing a fairy tale for someone special in your life.

A Conversation with Ka Hancock

Q: Having come from a background in nursing and mental health, what initially inspired you to write a book?

A: I've been writing pretty much my whole life, and have applied that old adage—*write what you know*—to some degree in everything I've written. *Dancing on Broken Glass* was originally an idea—actually a question—that woke me up one night. *What if a woman*

(Lucy) who became terminally ill in the middle of her unplanned pregnancy wanted to give that child to her sister (Lily) who was never able to have children of her own? The answer became the first version of *Dancing on Broken Glass*, which was a story that ultimately did not work. But, because I liked my premise, I went back and dug a little deeper, asked myself: Why wouldn't Lucy want her husband to have the baby? The answer had to be pretty compelling, and because I'm familiar with mental illness and know my way around a diagnosis of bipolar disorder, I applied it to Mickey. That was a pretty compelling reason; a stereotypical crazy person has no business raising a child, right? Problem solved. Not! The truth is, Mickey refused to be defined that way, and more importantly, I knew I would be cheating to create him that way. Mental illness affects about 20 percent of the population in the U.S. alone—or roughly 44 million people. The profoundly debilitated comprise but a small portion of this number. Many of the rest struggle with treatment compliance, but there are also many who work hard every day at managing their diagnosis. I admire them tremendously. That's where I found my inspiration for Mickey—and ultimately the story. Right there beneath the stereotype.

Q: What was the writing process like for you? How did the story come to you and evolve?

A: As I've mentioned, the kernel of the story woke me up one night. I wrote down everything I could remember, including the description of the town, the sisters, and Dr. Barbee. Mickey was an incidental character in my first draft since I'd set out to write a story about two sisters. I was not working at the time, so I spent most days cranking out pages. I polished up the "Mickeyless" version and sent it out into the world where it was returned to me with invaluable feedback: "Interesting premise, but . . ." fill in the blanks. However, one agent told me that if I ever did a major revision, she'd like to see it again. I took the story back to my writers' group and we tore it apart looking for where I'd gone wrong. In the process I had a "duh" moment. My good friend

Dorothy asked me why Mickey wasn't the one to take over the narrative after Lucy died—originally Lily had done this. I just looked at her. Why indeed! And with that the floodgates opened. It took me a year to give Mickey his voice, and then I sent my revision back to the same agent who'd thrown me the lifeline. This time Mollie Glick liked it, and she later became my agent. I think as soon as I plumbed the depths of Lucy's relationship with Mickey, the magic took over. I loved every minute of writing their story.

Q: What has been the most exciting part of having your book published?

A: It's a little surreal because yesterday I was Ka Hancock: wife, mom, day-shift worker bee, folder of laundry, mopper of floors, and of course, closet writer. Today I'm the very same person only published (and out of said closet). I think the most exciting part of this process has been the process itself: the evolution of an idea from thought, to words, to pages, to book, to recognition. That's been awesome. Oh, and when complete strangers tell me they like what I've written, I like that part, too!

Q: Is there one character in *Dancing on Broken Glass* that you relate to most? Do you have a favorite character?

A: The supporting cast always makes the movie for me, and it's the same with *Dancing on Broken Glass*. So I'd have to say Lily is the character I probably appreciate most. She's my unsung hero, and the story could not have been told without her. She was devoted to Lucy from childhood and remained so even after she died. Heartbroken over not having a child of her own, she showed tremendous grit when she looked truthfully at her sister's dying wish and brought it to pass. It would have been so easy for Lily to keep Abby, but Lucy's trust in her trumped everything else. And because Lucy trusted Lily, I think the reader trusts her as well. Because of Lily, we know that Abby will thrive despite Mickey's mental health challenges. She and Ron were the ideal backup plan.

Q: The grief that Lucy and Mickey endure is palpable. How have your own experiences helped you to understand and create such real emotions for your characters?

A: I'm not unique; like most, I've lost people important to me. But in my life, it's been almost harder to be the helpless bystander. It's agonizing to watch the unimaginable happen to someone you love—and to know that you're completely powerless. You grieve for the grieving as they grapple for answers and peace and beg for a reversal of fortune. That kind of emotion rubs your heart raw. It makes you squirm and you really can't escape it.

Q: Brinley is the perfect picture of small-town America. Did you grow up in a town like Brinley or do you live in one now? What was your inspiration for the setting?

A: I wish! I so love small towns, but no, I did not grow up in one. I would have to give credit for Brinley to *Gilmore Girls* and *Runaway Bride*. I melded Stars Hollow and Hale, Maryland, to create Brinley Township. But then I visited and fell in love with Essex, Connecticut, and Brinley became its fraternal twin, right down to the cemetery.

Q: From where did you derive Lucy's father's soothing words about death? Was this advice that someone once gave to you, or wisdom that you created on your own? Do you believe in it?

A: I grew up in a home and a faith where I was taught that there was a life before, there's a life now, and there will be a life after. So having fully accepted that premise, for me the secrets about death are not really secrets. I *do* believe that death is not the end. I *do* believe that slipping out of this world will be painless. I *want* desperately to believe that if I'm paying attention, I might be granted time enough to say good-bye—for now—and I love you and, maybe even, I'm sorry.

Q: How did you decide on the ending for the story? Did you always know how it was going to end?

A: I actually had Lily reading the fairy tale to Abby as my original ending, but my editor did not want to introduce another voice (Lily's), so she asked me to write the scene from Mickey's point of view. But he surprised me and took a completely different direction. I knew I wanted time to have passed, and I also wanted some healing to have occurred. But it was Mickey's idea to take the long way home and end up in the cemetery. Once there, at the foot of Lucy's grave, I think the story ended the only way it could. The accumulation of broken glass on Lucy's headstone serves as a reminder that their story is not over. Lucy's promise to dance with him through eternity was where Mickey found his peace. I think the end did just what it needed to do.

Q: **Lucy and Mickey have a real tearjerker of a story, and a lot can be learned from them and from all your characters. Is there one thing above all that you hope your readers will take away from this story?**
A: I think the overriding message would be that love is serious business. True, down-to-the-crap love is not for the shallow or faint of heart. People are messy. Marriage is messy. You have to bring your best self to the game despite your limitations. I think that's what I admire most about Lucy and Mickey.

Q: **What's up next for you? Are you working on anything new?**
A: Absolutely! I'm in first-draft territory with a story about three women. Rose Winston is a recent widow, newly liberated from a love-starved marriage. She's estranged from her only daughter, Patrice, because the girl defied her and married a mortician, Tanek Duzinski. When a tragic accident kills Tanek and leaves a pregnant Patrice gravely injured, she is not expected to live. Miraculously, she gives birth to a healthy baby girl. Fast-forward sixteen years—January has been raised by her paternal grandparents, Stasio and Diana Duzinski, in a mortuary called the Duzy House of Mourning—my working title. There are two aunts; Tess, who is the chief embalmer, and Cleo, who is said to be severely retarded.

It is through Rose's cruelty that January learns who Cleo actually is and what really happened the night of the accident. At its crux, this is January's journey into the life of her incredible mother, a woman trapped in a broken body who has loved her daughter from an agonizing distance.